THE WORKS OF
ALEXANDRE DUMAS

IN THIRTY VOLUMES

THE TWO DIANAS

VOLUME ONE

ILLUSTRATED WITH A FRONTISPIECE
IN PHOTOGRAVURE

British Library Cataloguing-in-Publication Data
A catalogue record for this book is available from the
British Library

Alexandre Dumas

Alexandre Dumas was born in Villers-Cotterêts, France in 1802. His parents were poor, but their heritage and good reputation – Alexandre's father had been a general in Napoleon's army – provided Alexandre with opportunities for good employment. In 1822, Dumas moved to Paris to work for future king Louis Philippe I in the Palais Royal. It was here that he began to write for magazines and the theatre.

In 1829 and 1830 respectively, Dumas produced the plays *Henry III and His Court* and *Christine,* both of which met with critical acclaim and financial success. As a result, he was able to commit himself full-time to writing. Despite the turbulent economic times which followed the Revolution of 1830, Dumas turned out to have something of an entrepreneurial streak, and did well for himself in this decade. He founded a production studio that turned out hundreds of stories under his creative direction, and began to produce serialised novels for newspapers which were widely read by the French public. It was over the next two decades, as a now famous and much loved author of romantic and adventuring sagas, that Dumas produced his best-known works – the D'Artagnan romances, including *The Three Musketeers,* in 1844, and *The Count of Monte Cristo,* in 1846.

Dumas made a lot of money from his writing, but

he was almost constantly penniless as a result of his extravagant lifestyle and love of women. In 1851 he fled his creditors to Belgium, and then Russia, and then Italy, not returning to Paris until 1864. Dumas died in Puys, France, in 1870, at the age of 68. He is now enshrined in the Panthéon of Paris alongside fellow authors Victor Hugo and Emile Zola. Since his death, his fiction has been translated into almost a hundred languages, and has formed the basis for more than 200 motion pictures.

CONTENTS

4 *CONTENTS*

THE TWO DIANAS

CHAPTER I

A COUNT'S SON AND A KING'S DAUGHTER

IT WAS on the 5th of May, 1551, that a young man, about eighteen years of age, and a woman about forty, issuing out of a house of humble appearance, traversed together the little village of Montgommery, which lies near Auge. The young man was of that beautiful Norman race, distinguished by their chestnut hair, blue eyes, white teeth, and rosy lips; he had that soft, fresh complexion, which occasionally takes something of power from the beauty of the Northern men, making it almost womanly. His figure, however, was both strong and flexible; he was elegantly dressed in a pourpoint of deep violet cloth, with embroideries of the same color; his boots of black leather, mounting above the knees, were such as were then worn by young pages; and a velvet cap, set a little on one side, and shaded by a white plume, covered a brow indicating at once firmness and sweet temper. His horse, whose bridle was over his arm, followed him. The woman seemed to belong to the lower class of society, or at least to the grade between that and the *bourgeoisie*; her dress was simple, but extremely neat. Often the young man offered her the support of his arm, which she always declined, as if an honor too exalted for one of her condition.

As they went through the village, every one, young and old, saluted the young man, who replied to them by a friendly nod. Each seemed to recognize a superior in him, who scarcely knew yet, himself, that he was so.

Leaving the village, they took a path which, leading to the top of the mountain, scarcely left room for two people to walk abreast, and the young man asked his companion to go first, as it was dangerous for her to walk behind, on account of his horse; she obeyed, and he followed her, silent, and evidently preoccupied. They were approaching a fine old castle, which had taken four centuries, and ten generations, to attain its present venerable appearance. Like all castles of that period, that of Montgommery had little regularity; it had descended from father to son, and each proprietor had, according to his own caprice, added something to the giant of stone. The square tower had been built under the Dukes of Normandy, and others, more florid in their construction, had been subsequently added. Toward the end of the reign of Louis XII. a long gallery, with painted windows, had completed the building; from this gallery, and from the top of the tower, the view extended for many leagues, over the rich plains of Normandy.

At last they arrived at the grand entrance. Strange to tell, for more than fifteen years this magnificent castle had been without a master; an old steward continued to collect the rents; servants who had grown old in this solitude remained in the castle, which they opened every day, as if each day the master was expected to return.

The steward received his two visitors, with friendship for the woman, and deference for the young man.

"Maître Elyot," said she, "let us come into the castle; I have something to say to M. Gabriel, and I wish to say it in the state room."

"Go in, Dame Aloyse," replied he, "and say where you wish what you have to say to monsieur; you know that, unfortunately, no one will come to disturb you."

They crossed the hall, where formerly twelve armed men had constantly watched. Seven of these had died, and had not been replaced. Five remained, doing the same duty as in the count's time. They entered the drawing-room; it was left just as the count had quitted it. Only, into this apartment, where formerly all the nobility of Normandy was to be seen, no one had entered for fifteen years but the servants. It was not without emotion that Gabriel gazed on this room, but the impression which he received from the sombre walls was not sufficiently powerful to distract his thoughts for a moment, for as soon as the door was closed he said, "Now, my dear Aloyse, my good nurse, although you really seem more moved than myself, you have no longer a pretext to avoid the history which you have promised me. Speak at once, I pray; have you not hesitated enough, and have I not waited like an obedient son? When I asked you what name I had a right to bear, what was my family, and who was my father, you replied to me, 'Gabriel, I will tell you all on the day that you attain your eighteenth year, the age of majority for those who have a right to wear a sword.' Now this 5th of May is the day, and I came, my good Aloyse, to summon you to keep your promise; but you replied to me, with a solemnity which almost frightened me, 'It is not within the humble walls of a poor squire's widow that I will disclose to you your birth; it is in the state room of the castle of Montgommery.' We have climbed the mountain, and are now in the chosen place—so speak."

"Sit down, Gabriel, for you permit me once more to give you this name?"

The young man took her hands with a movement full of affection. "Sit down," continued she, "not on this chair—nor that."

"Where, then, good nurse?"

"Under that dais," said Aloyse, in a solemn voice. The young man obeyed. "Now listen to me."

"But sit down first."

"You permit it?"

"Are you jesting?"

The good woman sat down on the steps of the dais, at the feet of the young man, and then began:

"Gabriel, you were hardly six years old when you lost

your father, and I, my husband. You were my nursling, for your mother died in giving you birth. From that day, I, the foster-sister of your mother, have loved you as my own child; the widow devoted her life to the orphan, and as she gave you her milk, she gave you her heart. You will render me this justice, will you not, Gabriel—that I have never ceased to watch over you?"

"Dear Aloyse," said the young man, "many real mothers would have done less than you have done, and none, I feel sure, could have done more."

"All, however," continued the nurse, "have been anxious to do their best for you. Dom Jamet de Croisin, the worthy chaplain of this castle, who died about three months ago, instructed you carefully, and no one, they say, can surpass you at reading, writing, or in the past history of France. Enguerrand Lorien, the intimate friend of my poor husband, and the old squire of the Counts of Vimoutiers, have instructed you with care in the science of arms, in the management of the lance and the sword, in horsemanship, and in all things pertaining to chivalry. At the fêtes and jousts, which were held at Alençon, on the occasion both of the coronation and the marriage of our gracious king, Henry the Second, you proved, even two years ago, how well you had profited by these lessons. I could but love you, and teach you to serve God; that I have always tried to do. The Holy Virgin has aided me, and now at eighteen you are a pious Christian, a learned gentleman, and an accomplished soldier. I trust that with God's help you will not be unworthy of your ancestors, Monseigneur Gabriel, Seigneur de Lorge, Count de Montgommery!"

Gabriel rose with a cry. "Count de Montgommery—I!" cried he. "Well, I hoped it, I almost suspected it. Do you know, Aloyse, that in my childish dreams I once said so to my little Diana. But what are you doing there, at my feet, Aloyse? Come into my arms, good nurse; can I no longer be your child, because I am the heir of the Montgommerys —a Montgommery!" repeated he, proudly, while he embraced his good nurse. "I bear, then, one of the oldest and most glorious names in France—yes, Dom Jamet has taught me, man by man, the history of my noble ancestors. Of my ancestors! Embrace me again, Aloyse! What will Diana say to all this? St. Godegrand, bishop of Suez, and St. Opportune, his sister, who lived under Charlemagne, were of our house; Roger de Montgommery commanded one of the armies of William the Conqueror; William de Montgommery went a crusade at his own expense. We have been allied more than once to the royal houses of Scotland and of France, and the first English and French noblemen will call me cousin"—but suddenly stopping, he said in a lower tone, "Alas! with all this, Aloyse, I am alone in the world; the great lord is a poor orphan; the descendant of so many royal ancestors has no father. My poor father! and my mother— dead, both of them dead. Oh! speak to me of them, that I may know what they were, now I know that I am their son. Begin with my father. How did he die?"

Aloyse was silent. Gabriel looked at her with astonishment. "I asked you, nurse," repeated he, "how my father died."

"Monsieur, God only knows. One day Count Jacques de Montgommery left his house in the Rue des Jardins de St. Paul, at Paris; he never returned to it. His friends and his cousins sought him in vain. King Francis himself ordered a search to be made, but it was without success. His enemies, if he perished—the victim of some treason—were very skilful, or very powerful. You have no father, and yet the tomb of Jacques de Montgommery is not among those of his ancestors, for he has never been found, dead or living."

"Ah! it was not his son who sought for him," cried Gabriel. "Oh, nurse, why have you kept silence so long? Did you hide the secret of my birth from me because I have my father to avenge, or to save?"

"No; but because I wished to save you yourself, mon· sieur. Do you know what were the last words of my hus-

band, of the brave Pierrot Travigny, who was devoted to
your house? 'Wife,' said he to me, some minutes before he
drew his last breath, 'as soon as you have closed my eyes
quit Paris immediately, with the child. Go to Montgommery—not to the castle, but to the house that monseigneur
was kind enough to give us—and there you must bring up
our master's heir, without mystery, but quietly. Our good
country people will respect, and not betray him. Hide his
origin from himself, above all; he would show himself, and
be ruined; let him know only that he is noble—that will
preserve his dignity; then when age shall have made him
prudent and grave, as his blood will make him brave and
loyal, when he shall be eighteen, tell him his name and his
race; he can then judge for himself what he should do.
But take care until then; formidable enemies and invincible
hatreds will pursue him, and those who have succeeded in
seizing the eagle would not spare the eaglet.'

"He spoke thus and died, monsieur; and I, faithful to
his orders, took you, a poor orphan, not six years old, who
had scarcely seen your father, and brought you here. The
disappearance of the count was known, and it was suspected
that powerful enemies would threaten whoever bore his
name. They saw and doubtless recognized you in the village; but, by a tacit agreement no one asked about you, or
wondered at my silence. Not long after, my only son, your
foster-brother, died; God seemed to wish that I should be
entirely devoted to you—may God's will be done! All pretended to believe that it was my son who had survived; but
still they treated you with a touching respect and obedience.
You already resembled your father, both in face and in disposition; the instinct of the lion revealed itself in you—one
could see that you were born chief and master. The children of the neighborhood had already begun to submit to
your guidance; in all their plays you were at the head. The
finest fruits, the tithe of the harvest, came unasked for to
my house; the finest horse in the pastures was always kept
for you. Dom Jamet, Enguerrand, and all the servants at

the castle gave you their services as a natural duty, and you accepted them as your right.

"You showed your race in everything," continued the nurse, "but these instincts and impulses betrayed you only to the faithful; you remained hidden and unknown to the malevolent, and you have arrived safely at the age at which Pierrot authorized me to trust to your prudence. But you, ordinarily so grave and prudent, you see your first words were for vengeance and exposure."

"Vengeance, yes; exposure, no. You think, then, Aloyse, that my poor father's enemies live still?"

"Monsieur, it is safest to presume so. If you go to court quite unknown, except by your name, which will draw all regards upon you—brave, but inexperienced, strong in good intentions and in the justness of your case, but without friends, allies, or personal reputation—what will happen? Those who hate you will know you, and you will not know them; they will strike you, and you will not know whence the blow comes. Not only your father will be unavenged, but you will be lost."

"That is precisely, Aloyse, why I regret not having had time to make myself friends and renown. Ah! if I had known two years ago! But never mind, it is but a delay, and I will make up for lost time. I will go to Paris, Aloyse, and without concealing that I am a Montgommery; but I will not say that I am the son of Count Jacques. There are plenty of titles and branches in our family, and it is sufficiently numerous for me to pass unrecognized. I will take the name of Viscount d'Exmès, Aloyse, and that will be neither concealing nor betraying my proper character. Thanks to Enguerrand, I know the family history well. To whom shall I address myself? To the Constable de Montmorency, that cruel repeater of paternosters? No; I believe you are right. To the Marshal de St. André? No, he is neither young nor enterprising enough. To Francis de Guise? Yes; he is the man. Montmédy, St. Dizier, Boulogne, have already proved what he can do. I will go to

him and win my spurs under his orders. Under the shade
of his name I will fight for my own."

"Monsieur will permit me to observe that the honest and
good Elyot has had time to put large sums aside for the heir
of his master; you can live like a prince, monsieur, and all
the young men, your tenants, whom you have exercised so
well in arms, will feel it both a duty and a pleasure to follow
you to battle. It is your right to call them round you; you
know that, monsieur."

"I will use it, Aloyse."

"Will monsieur receive now all his servants and depen-
dants, who burn with desire to congratulate him?"

"Not yet, good Aloyse: I must take a ride before anything."

"To Vimoutiers?" said Aloyse, smiling.

"Yes, perhaps. Do not I owe Enguerrand a visit and
my thanks?"

"And with the compliments of Enguerrand, monseigneur
will be very happy to receive those of a pretty little girl
called Diana."

"Why," replied Gabriel, laughing, "this pretty little girl
is my wife, and I have been her husband for the last three
years—that is to say, since she was nine years old."

Aloyse looked thoughtful. "Monsieur," said she, "if I
did not know that, in spite of your youth, you are grave and
thoughtful, I would not say what I am about to say; but
what might be play to others is a serious thing to you; remember, monsieur, we do not know whose daughter Diana
is. One day the wife of Enguerrand, who had himself gone
to Fontainebleau with the Count de Vimoutiers, his master,
found, on entering her house, a child in a cradle, and a
heavy purse of gold on the table. In the purse was a considerable sum of money, half of an engraved ring, and a
paper containing the single word, 'Diana.' Bertha had no
child, so she gladly accepted this charge; but she died soon,
and on Enguerrand devolved the care of the little girl. He
and I, each with a similar charge, have exchanged cares: I

have tried to make Diana good and pious; he has made you learned and adroit. Naturally you have known Diana, and naturally you have become attached to each other; but you are the Count de Montgommery, declared so by authentic documents, and known to many, and no one has yet come to claim Diana. Take care, monsieur. I know she is only a child now; she will grow, however, and will be very beautiful, but her birth may never be known; and in that case you are too great to marry her.''

"But, nurse, I am about to leave her.''

"True. Pardon the old Aloyse for her too great anxiety, and go to see, if you like, this charming child; but remember that you are impatiently waited for here.''

"I will soon return. Embrace me again, dear Aloyse; call me ever your child, and receive a thousand thanks, my good nurse.''

"A thousand blessings, my child and master!''

Master Martin Guerre awaited Gabriel at the gate, where they mounted their steeds and departed.

CHAPTER II

A BRIDE WHO PLAYS WITH HER DOLL

ALTHOUGH Gabriel, to make better progress, took bypaths well known to him, he nevertheless let his horse take its own pace. Numerous feelings, some sad and some joyful, filled his mind. When he thought only that he was Count de Montgommery, his eyes sparkled and he spurred on his horse; but soon the remembrance returned, "My father was killed, and has not been avenged"; and he allowed the bridle to fall from his hand. Then the thought that he was going to fight, to make a name for himself, raised his head proudly again—till again saddened by the thought that he must leave his little Diana, his old playmate. But he would return; he would have found the enemies of his father, and the parents of Diana.

When he arrived at the door, the joyful thoughts had decidedly gained the victory over the sad ones. Through the hedge which surrounded the garden, Gabriel could see among the trees the white dress of Diana. He cleared it with a bound, and was soon standing beside her, radiant and triumphant. But Diana was weeping.

"What is it, dear little wife?" said Gabriel. "Whence comes this bitter grief? Has Enguerrand been scolding you for tearing your dress, or neglecting your lessons; or has your bullfinch been stolen? Tell your faithful knight, Diana; he is here to console you."

"Alas! Gabriel, you can no longer be my knight, and that is why I weep."

Gabriel thought that Enguerrand had been telling the

little girl his rightful name and birth, and that it placed a barrier between them, so he said—

"And what, Diana, be it good or bad fortune, do you think could ever make me renounce the title which I am so proud to bear?"

But Diana did not appear to understand; and weeping more than ever, and hiding her face on Gabriel's breast, she sobbed out, "Gabriel! Gabriel! we must see each other no more."

"And who will prevent us?" cried he.

She raised her charming blond head, her blue eyes full of tears, and with a profound sigh. "Duty," she answered, with solemnity. Her pretty face had an expression at once so unhappy and so comic that Gabriel could not help laughing; but he drew her toward him, and kissed her.

"Oh!" cried she, "*mon Dieu!* I am forbidden to allow that."

"What in the world has Enguerrand been saying to her?" thought Gabriel; but he said, "Then you love me no longer, my darling?"

"I not love you!" cried she; "how can you think such a thing, Gabriel?—you, who have always been so good to me, who carried me when I was tired, who helped me with my lessons; you, who screened my faults, and shared my punishments, when you could not prevent them; you, who have always been with me, who made me beautiful bouquets, who brought me bird's-nests. Oh, Gabriel! I shall never forget you. I never thought we should be separated; but that does not prevent it, and we are to meet no more."

"But why? Is it because you let your dog Phylax into the poultry-yard?"

"Ah, no! For something far different."

"For what, then?"

She hung her head, and said, in a low voice, "Because I am the wife of another."

Gabriel laughed no more; his heart sank, and he said, in a troubled voice, "What do you mean, Diana?"

"I am now," replied she, "Madame la Duchesse de Castro, and my husband is called Horace Farnèse, Duc de
Castro;" and the little girl smiled through her tears at
the words, "Madame la Duchesse" and "husband." But
her grief returned on seeing Gabriel's; he stood before her,
pale and wild-looking.

"Is it a joke?" asked he.

"No, my poor Gabriel, it is a sad reality. Did you not
meet Enguerrand? He went to Montgommery half an hour
ago."

"I came over the hill," said Gabriel; "but finish."

"Oh, Gabriel! why did you stay away four days? It
brought us misfortune. The day before yesterday I was
uneasy; I had not seen you for two days, and I had made
Enguerrand promise that if you did not come the next day
he would take me to Montgommery. Well, the next morning I slept rather late, so I dressed in haste, told my beads,
and was about to go down, when I heard a great noise under
my window. I looked out, and saw before the door cavaliers magnificently dressed, followed by squires, and behind
them a gilded carriage. As I was looking, and wondering
what it meant, Antoine knocked at my door, and said that
Enguerrand wished me to come down immediately. I felt
very frightened, but descended. The room was full of these
gay gentlemen when I entered, and I was more frightened
than ever. One of the grandest came toward me immediately, and giving me his hand, led me up to another gentleman, and said, 'Monseigneur le Duc de Castro, I have the
honor of presenting to you your wife. Mademoiselle,' added
he, turning to me, 'this is M. Horace Farnèse, Duc de Castro, your husband.'

"The duke smiled; but I, frightened and in despair, ran
to Enguerrand, who was in one corner, and throwing myself
into his arms, I cried, 'Enguerrand, this is not my husband;
I will have no other husband than Gabriel; pray tell these
gentlemen so!' The one who had presented me to the duke
frowned. 'What means this nonsense?' said he. 'Noth-

ing, sir; only a childish fancy,' replied Enguerrand, looking very pale. Then he whispered to me, 'Diana, you must
obey your parents, who have sent to claim you.' 'Who are
my parents?' asked I, aloud; 'it is to them that I wish to
speak!' 'We come in their name, mademoiselle,' replied
the gentleman; 'I am their representative. If you do not
believe me, here is the order, signed by the king!' He presented to me a parchment, sealed with a red seal, and I saw
at the top of the page, 'We, by the grace of God,' and at the
bottom, 'Henri.'

"I was bewildered, thunderstruck, overwhelmed. Enguerrand abandoned me! The idea of my parents, the name
of the king! You were not there, Gabriel; if you had been,
I might have had courage to resist; but as it was, when the
gentleman said, in an imperious voice, 'Come, there has been
enough delay; Madame de Leviston, I confide to your care
Madame de Castro. We wait for her to go to the chapel'—
I permitted myself to be led, quite stupefied."

"Go on; that's easy to understand," said Gabriel.

"They took me to my room, and then, taking from a box
a white silk dress, Madame de Leviston and her women put
it on me; then a pearl necklace and earrings. I cried all
the time, but they only laughed at me. When I was dressed
they told me that I looked charming, and I think, Gabriel,
that it was true, but I cried all the same. At last I thought
I was dreaming a magnificent yet dreadful dream; I walked
without conscious effort, and went up and down like a ma-
chine. Meanwhile the horses were stamping at the portal,
and squires, pages, and servants stood about. We descended
the stairs, and again the gaze of the whole assemblage seemed
to go right through me. The gentleman with the disagreeable voice gave me his hand again, and conducted me to a
litter of gold and satin, where I was placed upon cushions
nearly as lovely as my dress.

"The Duc de Castro rode by my side, and we went to
the chapel at Vimoutiers. The priest was at the altar; they
said some words, which I did not understand, and put a ring

on my finger. Then we came out again. They called me 'Madame la Duchesse,' and I was married. Gabriel, do you hear that? I was married!"

Gabriel answered with a savage laugh.

"It was only when we came back," continued Diana, "that I recovered myself sufficiently to think of examining the husband that they had given to me. Ah, my poor Gabriel, he is not so handsome as you; he is not tall, and in all his rich clothes he did not look so elegant as you; and then he looked as haughty and impertinent as you do sweet and refined. Add to this that his hair and his beard were red, and you will see how I have been sacrificed. Soon he approached me, and taking my hand, said, with a cunning smile, "Madame la Duchesse, pardon me that I am forced to leave you so soon; but you know, perhaps, that we are at war with Spain, and my presence is immediately required there. I hope to have the pleasure of seeing you before very long at the court, whither you are going this week; I beg you to accept some presents which I leave for you. *Au revoir*, madame. Keep yourself gay and charming as suits your age; play and amuse yourself while I am fighting.' So saying, he kissed me on the forehead, and his long beard pricked me. Then all the ladies and gentlemen bowed to me and went away, leaving me alone with Enguerrand.

"He had not understood much more of this adventure than I had. They had made him read the parchment containing the king's orders for my marriage; all that he knew more than I did was that Madame de Leviston would soon come and fetch me and take me to court. That's my whole mournful tale, Gabriel. Ah, no, I forgot.

"When I went to my room, I found in a great box—what do you think?—a superb doll, with a complete trousseau of linen, and three dresses—white silk, red damask, and green brocade. Fancy, Gabriel, treating me like a child; it is shameful. However, the doll looks best in red, it has such a beautiful complexion; the little shoes are charming; but it is shameful, for I am no longer a child."

"Yes, you are a child," interrupted Gabriel, sadly; "but never mind, you cannot help being only twelve years old. I have been wrong, however, to waste a sentiment so ardent and profound as mine, for I feel by my grief how much I love you. But if you had been strong, if you had found in yourself sufficient energy to resist an unjust order, we might have been happy, as you have recovered your parents, and they appear to be of good birth.

"I, also, Diana, came to tell you a secret which has been revealed to me to-day, but now it is useless—it is too late; your weakness has ruined all. All my life I feel that I shall remember you, Diana; and our young loves will occupy a large share in my heart. But you, Diana, in the lustre of the court, will soon forget all that you cared for here."

"Never!" cried she; "and, Gabriel, now that you are here, I feel brave. Shall I refuse to go when they come for me? Shall I insist on remaining with you?"

"Thanks, dear Diana; but henceforth, before God and man, you belong to another; we must go each our own way —you to the court and gayety, and I to camps and battles. God grant that we may meet again some day."

"Oh, Gabriel, I must see you again! I shall love you always!" cried the poor Diana, throwing herself weeping into his arms; but at that moment Enguerrand appeared, followed by Madame de Leviston.

"Here she is, madame," said he, pointing out Diana. "Ah, it is you, Gabriel; I was going to Montgommery to seek you, when I met Madame de Leviston, and was obliged to return."

"Yes, madame," said the lady to Diana, "the king is impatient to see you. We shall, if you please, set out in an hour; your preparations will not take long, I presume?"

Diana looked at Gabriel.

"Courage!" said he.

"I am glad to tell you," said Madame de Leviston, "that this good Enguerrand can join us to-morrow at Alençon, and accompany us to Paris if you desire it."

"Oh!" cried Diana, "I know no other father but him;" and she gave her hand to Enguerrand, who covered it with kisses, while she looked through her tears at Gabriel, who stood by, looking sad, but firm and resigned.

"Come," said Madame de Leviston, "remember that we must be at Caen before night."

Diana, then, suffocated with sobs, ran to her room, and in about an hour returned ready for her journey. She asked leave to go once more round the garden. Enguerrand and Gabriel followed her. She picked two roses, and putting one in her dress, gave the other to Gabriel, and he felt that, at the same time, she slid a paper into his hand, which he hastily hid in his doublet. After Diana had bid adieu to all the paths and groves and flowers, she was obliged to accept the idea of departure. On reaching the carriage which was to bear her thence, she gave her hand to each of the servants, and to the good people from the village, who all knew and loved her. Poor child, she could not speak a word; she only gave them each a kind nod. Then she embraced Enguerrand, and, last of all, Gabriel, without being at all embarrassed by the presence of Madame de Leviston. In his embrace she found her voice, and, when Gabriel murmured "Adieu! Adieu!" she replied, "*Au revoir!*" When she was in the carriage Gabriel heard her say, through her sobs, "Are you sure that they have put in my big doll?"

When they were gone Gabriel opened his paper, and found in it a lock of her beautiful blond hair. A month afterward he arrived at Paris, and had himself announced at the Hotel Guise as the Viscount d'Exmès.

CHAPTER III

THE CAMP

"YES, gentlemen," said the Duke de Guise, as he entered his tent, to the attending noblemen, "to-day, the 24th of April, 1557, after having entered Neapolitan territory, and taken Campli, we lay siege to Civitella. On the 1st of May we shall be masters of it, and shall go on to besiege Aquila. Then we shall soon be at Capua; and on the 1st of June, gentlemen, I hope to show you Naples, if it please God."

"And the pope, my dear brother?" interrupted the Duke d'Aumale. "His Holiness, who had promised us the support of his troops, leaves us here reduced to our own resources; and it seems to me that our army is not strong enough to venture so far into the enemy's country."

"Paul the Fourth," said Francis, "has too much interest in our success to leave us without assistance. What a clear, beautiful night it is, gentlemen! Biron, do you know if the partisans, whose rising in the Abruzzi the Carraffas promised us, are making a move?"

"No, monseigneur, they are quiet; I have certain and recent news."

"Our guns will awaken them," said the duke. "M. d'Elbœuf, have you heard anything of the provisions which we ought to have received at Ascoli?"

"Yes, but at Rome, monseigneur; and alas—"

"A delay, a simple delay," interrupted the duke; "and after all, we are not so very badly off. The taking of Campli has set us up a little; and I would wager that if I entered any of your tents in half an hour I should find a good supper served up, and perhaps at table with you some pretty widow or orphan from Campli, whom you have undertaken to console. Nothing better, gentlemen; besides, it is the duty of the victor, and it makes victory sweet, eh? Well, I will keep you no longer. To-morrow, at daybreak, we will concert the means of taking Civitella. Till then, good-night, and a good appetite!"

The duke smilingly escorted his generals to the door of his tent; but when the curtain which formed the door had fallen behind the last of them, and Francis de Guise was left alone, his manly features at once assumed a careworn expression, and seating himself at a table, and leaning his head on his hands, he said, beneath his breath, with much anxiety, "Can it be that I should have done better to renounce all personal ambition, to content myself with being simply Henry the Second's general, and to limit my achievements to the recovery of Milan and the liberation of Sienna? Here am I in this kingdom of Naples, of which, in my dreams, I have heard myself called the king; but I am without allies, and shall soon be without provisions; and all my officers, my brother at their head, with not an energetic, capable mind among them, I can see plainly are beginning already to be disheartened, and to lose their courage." Shortly after, hearing steps behind him, he turned round with an angry expression at the intruder, which, however, instantly vanished when he saw who it was; and holding out his hand he said, "Dear Gabriel, *you* will not hesitate to advance because bread is scarce, and the enemy numerous— you, who went the last out of Metz, and entered the first into Valenza and Campli? But do you come to announce any news?"

"Yes, monseigneur, a courier from France, bearing, I think, letters from your illustrious brother, Monseigneur le Cardinal de Lorraine."

"Will you fetch them for me, yourself?"

Gabriel went out, and soon returned, bearing a packet

sealed with the arms of Lorraine. Six years had but little changed our friend Gabriel; he looked more manly, it is true, but he preserved unaltered the same pure and grave expression, the same frank and honest look, and, let us add, the same heart, full of youth and of illusions. The Duke de Guise was thirty-seven, and although of a great and generous nature, he had, in the battle of life, lost many a youthful feeling and enthusiasm; but he still comprehended and loved the chivalric and devoted character of Gabriel. An irresistible sympathy drew him toward the young man.

"Listen, Viscount d'Exmès; my secretary, Hervé de Thelen, whom you knew, died under the walls of Valenza; my brother D'Aumale is only a soldier, gallant, but without ability; I need a right arm, Gabriel, a confidential friend and assistant. Now, since you came to me at my hotel at Paris, some five or six years since, I should say, I have become convinced that you have a mind above the ordinary, and better still, a faithful heart. I know nothing of you but your name—and there never lived a Montgommery who was not brave—but you came to me without a word of recommendation from any one, and, notwithstanding, I was attracted by you at once. I took you with me to the defence of Metz; and if that defence is to furnish one of the fairest pages of my life's story, if after sixty-five days of assault we succeeded in driving from before the walls of Metz an army of a hundred thousand men, and a general who was called Charles the Fifth, I must remember that your gallantry, conspicuous at every turn, and your keen mind, always on the watch, had no inconsiderable share in that glorious result. The following year you were still with me when I won the battle of Renty; and if that ass, Montmorency, well christened the— But rather than insult my foe, it would better beseem me to praise my friend and brave companion —Gabriel, Viscount d'Exmès, worthy relative of the worthy Montgommerys. I must say to you, Gabriel, that on every occasion, and more than ever since we came into Italy, I have found your assistance, your advice, and your affection of advantage to me, and have absolutely but one fault to find with you, and that is, being too reserved and discreet with your general. Yes, I am sure that there is, somewhere or other in your life, a sentiment or a thought that you are concealing from me, Gabriel. But what of that? Some day you will confide it to me, and the important thing is to know that there is something for you to do. *Pardieu!* I also have something to do—I, Gabriel; and if you say the word, we will join our fortunes, and you will help me, and I you. When I have an important and difficult undertaking to intrust to another, I will call upon you; when a powerful patron becomes essential to the furtherance of your plans, I will be on hand. Is it a bargain?"

"Oh, monseigneur," Gabriel replied, "I am yours, body and soul! What I desired first of all was to be able to trust in myself and induce others to trust in me. Now I have succeeded in acquiring a little self-confidence, and you condescend to have some regard for me; so I have succeeded in my ambition up to the present time. But that a different ambition may hereafter summon me to fresh exertions, I do not deny; and when that time comes, monseigneur—since you have been kind enough to allow me to take such a step —I will surely have recourse to you, just as you may count upon me in life or in death."

"Well said, *per Bacco!* as these drunken dogs of cardinals say. And do you be quite easy in your mind, Gabriel, for Francis de Lorraine, Duke de Guise, will spare no warmth to serve you in love or in hatred; for one or the other of these passions is at work in us, is it not, my master?"

"Both, perhaps, monseigneur."

"Ah! so? And when your heart is so full how can you resist letting it overflow into the heart of a friend?"

"Alas, monseigneur, because I scarcely know whom I love, and have no idea at all whom I hate!"

"Indeed! Just suppose, then, Gabriel, since your enemies are to be mine henceforth—just suppose that that old rake Montmorency should happen to be among them!"

"It may very well be so, monseigneur; and if my suspicions have any foundation— But we must not bother about my affairs at this crisis; it is with you and your far-reaching plans that we have to do. How can I be of service to you, monseigneur?"

"In the first place, read me this letter from my brother, the Cardinal de Lorraine, Gabriel."

But Gabriel, after throwing a glance over it, returned it to him, saying, "Pardon, monseigneur, but this letter is written in some strange character which I cannot read."

"Oh, it is a confidential letter, then," said the duke; and taking from a box a paper containing the simple key to the cipher, and handing it to Gabriel, he said, "Now read."

Gabriel still hesitated; but the duke, pressing his hand warmly, said again, "Read, my friend."

Gabriel read, " 'Monsieur, my very honored and illustrious brother (when shall I be able to call you, in one word, *sire?*).' " Gabriel stopped again.

The duke smiled. "You are astonished, Gabriel, I but trust that you do not suspect me; the Duke de Guise is no Constable de Bourbon. May God preserve to our king his crown and his life. But is there in the world no other crown except that of France? As chance has put you in our confidence, I will hide nothing from you; you shall enter into all my designs and my dreams." The duke rose and walked up and down the tent as he spoke.

"Our house, Gabriel," continued he, "may, I think, aspire to any greatness; our sister is Queen of Scotland—our niece, Mary Stuart, is about to wed the dauphin. Our grand-nephew, the Duke de Lorraine, is the chosen son-in-law of the king. Then we have claims, through the second house of Anjou, upon Florence and Naples; let us content ourselves with Naples for the present. Would not this crown be better on the head of a Frenchman than of a Spaniard? We are allied to the Duke of Ferrara, and united with the Carraffas; Paul the Fourth is old—my brother the cardinal will succeed him; the throne of Naples is tottering, and I

mount it, and that is why I have come South! The dream
is splendid, but I begin to fear that it is only a dream. Gabriel, I had not twelve thousand men with me when I crossed
the Alps, but the Duke of Ferrara had promised me seven
thousand, which he now keeps at home. Paul the Fourth
and the Carraffas had boasted that they could raise in Naples a powerful faction, and they engaged to furnish soldiers, money, and provisions; they have not sent a man, a
wagon, or a crown; but in spite of all, I will persevere. I
will not quit this promised land till the last extremity, and
if I am forced to retreat, I shall return." The duke stamped
on the ground, as if to take possession of it. His eyes shone;
he was a noble sight.

"Monseigneur," said Gabriel, "how proud I am to bear
even so small a part in your glorious ambitions."

"And now," continued the duke, "having twice given
you the key to my brother's letter, I think you can read and
understand it. Go on, then, I listen."

" 'Sire'—that was where I stopped," said Gabriel. " 'I
have to announce to you two pieces of bad news, and one
good. The good news is, that the marriage of our niece,
Mary Stuart, is decidedly fixed for the 20th of next month,
and will be solemnized in Paris on that day. One of the
others, of evil tenor, comes from England. Philip the Second, of Spain, is there, and is exciting his wife, Mary Tudor,
who obeys him so lovingly, to declare war against France.
No one doubts of his success, though his wishes are opposed
to those of the English people. They speak already of an
army on the frontiers of the Low Countries, of which the
Duke Philibert Emanuel, of Savoy, will have the command.
Then, my dear brother, in the scarcity of men here, the king
will certainly recall you from Italy, and our plans there will
be, at least, adjourned; but remember, Francis, that it is
better to defer them than to lose them altogether; so no
rashness.' "

"Yes," interrupted the duke, striking the table violently
with his fist, "my brother is but too much in the right;

Mary, the prude, will certainly obey her husband, and I certainly will not disobey the king, openly, when he recalls his soldiers; so there is a new obstacle to this cursed enterprise —for it is cursed, in spite of the benediction of the pope. Is it not, Gabriel? Tell me truly, do you not think it desperate?"

"I would not wish, monseigneur, to be among those who you say discourage you, but if you appeal to my frankness—"

"I understand you, Gabriel; I am forced to agree with you. It is not on this occasion that we shall do great things together; but it is only delayed for a time, to strike a blow at Philip the Second, I swear. Continue, Gabriel; we have still more bad news to hear, if I remember rightly."

Gabriel went on: " 'The other unlucky affair of which I have to tell you is of a more private, but not less disagreeable nature. Since your departure the Constable de Montmorency is not less jealous and bitter against you than before, and never ceases to grumble at the goodness of the king to our house. The approaching marriage of our niece with the dauphin naturally does not at all please him, and doubtless it disturbs the equilibrium which the king has endeavored to preserve between the houses of Guise and Montmorency. The old constable loudly demands an equivalent, and has at last found one, which is the marriage of his son, Francis, with—' " Gabriel did not finish; his voice failed him, and a deadly pallor covered his face.

"What is the matter, Gabriel?" cried the duke.

"Nothing, monseigneur—a sudden giddiness. I will proceed; where was I?—'the marriage of his son, Francis, with Madame de Castro, legitimatized daughter of the king and Diana de Poitiers. You remember that she, a widow at thirteen, her husband having been killed at the siege of Hesdin, has been for five years at the convent of the Filles-Dieu, in Paris. The king, at the solicitation of the constable, has just recalled her to the court; and let me tell you, brother, that she is a pearl of beauty, and you know that I am a good

judge. Her grace has won all hearts, and above all, her
father's; he had before given her the Duchy of Châtellerault,
and now has added that of Angoulême. She has scarcely
been here a fortnight, but her ascendency over him is immense.

"'Indeed, her mother, Madame de Valentinois, who, for
some unknown reason, does not openly acknowledge her,
seems almost jealous of the new power. It would be good
for the constable, for you know, between ourselves, that
Diana de Poitiers can refuse nothing to the old rascal. This
cursed marriage is therefore but too likely to come off.'"

"You seem faint again, Gabriel," interrupted the duke;
"go and rest while I finish this letter, which interests me
deeply, for it would be a dangerous advantage for the constable. I thought that his booby of a son was affianced; let
me read."

"I am really quite well, and quite able to finish;" and
he went on: "'There is only one chance for us; Francis de
Montmorency is secretly married to Mademoiselle de Fiennes,
and a divorce will be necessary, which Francis is going to
Rome to solicit from the pope. Let it be your business,
therefore, my dear brother, to be beforehand with him, and
endeavor, through your own influence and that of the Carraffas, to make his Holiness reject this request, which will
be, I warn you, supported by a letter from the king. Defend your position as well as you did St. Dizier and Metz;
and I, on my side, will exert myself to the utmost, for, on
my faith, it is necessary. I pray God, brother, to give
you a long and happy life. Your brother, G. Cardinal de
Lorraine. From Paris, 12th April, 1557.'"

"Come, nothing is yet lost," said the duke, when Gabriel
had finished, "and the pope, who refuses me soldiers, may
at least make me a present of a bull."

"Thus," replied Gabriel, trembling, "you hope that
his Holiness will not grant this divorce from Jeanne de
Fiennes?"

"Yes, I hope so; but how you are moved, my friend!

Dear Gabriel, you enter into our interests with warmth. But now let us speak of yourself; and as, in this unlucky expedition, you will hardly have an opportunity of adding to the eminent services that I owe you, let me begin to pay my debt. What can I do for you? Can I not be useful to you, in any way? Come, speak frankly."

"Oh! monseigneur is too good, and I do not see—"

"Five years," interrupted the duke, "you have fought heroically for me, and have never accepted a farthing from me. You must want money, *diable!* Every one always wants money. It would be neither a gift nor a loan, but a debt; so, no scruples, and although we are not too well off—"

"I know that, monseigneur; and I have so little need of money that I wished to offer you some thousands of crowns which might serve the army, and which really are very use·less to me."

"And which I will receive willingly, for they will come very *à propos*, I must admit. And so one can do absolutely nothing for you, oh young man without a wish! But stay," he added, in a lower tone, "that rascal, Thibault, my body·servant, you know, at the sack of Campli, day before yester·day, put aside for me the young wife of the *procureur* of the town, the beauty of the neighborhood, judging from what I hear, always excepting the governor's wife, on whom no one can lay his hand. But as for me, upon my word, I have too many other cares in my head, and my hair is getting grizzly. Come, Gabriel, what would you say to my prize? *Sang-Dieu!* but you are built just right to make amends for the loss of a *procureur!* What do you say to it?"

"I say, monseigneur, with regard to the governor's wife, of whom you speak, and upon whom no hand has been laid, that it was I who fell in with her in the confusion, and car·ried her away—not to abuse my rights, as you might think, · but to shield a noble and beautiful woman from the violence of a licentious soldiery. But I have since discovered that the fair creature would have no objection to adopting the cause of the victors, and would be very glad to shout, like the soldier of Gaul: 'Væ victis!' But since I am now, alas! less inclined than ever to echo her sentiments, I can, if you desire, monseigneur, have her brought to one who can appreciate better than I, and more worthily, her charms and her rank.''

"Oh, oh!" cried the duke, laughing heartily; "such extraordinary morality almost savors of the Huguenot, Gabriel. Can it be that you have a secret leaning toward those of the religion? Ah, take heed, my friend! I am, by conviction, and by policy, which is worse, an ardent Catholic, and I will have you burned without pity. But come, joking apart, why the deuce are you so strait-laced?"

"Because I am in love, perhaps," said Gabriel.

"Oh, yes, I remember, a hate and a love. Well, then, can't I show my good-will to you by putting you in a way to meet your foes or your love? Do you want titles, perhaps?"

"Thanks, no, monseigneur; what I covet is personal glory, and not vague honors. Thus, since you think that there is little more to be done here, it would be a great gratification to me to be sent to Paris, to carry to the king, for the marriage of your niece, the flags that you have taken in Lombardy and in the Abruzzi; and it would crown my wishes if a letter, from you to his Majesty, deigned to attest that some of them were taken by me, and not altogether without danger."

"Well, that is easy, and yet more, it is just; I should regret this parting, but that it probably will not be for long; for if war breaks out in Flanders, as appears very probable, I presume I shall see you there?"

"I shall be only too happy to follow you there, monseigneur."

"Well, then, when will you set out?"

"The sooner the better, I think, monseigneur, if the marriage is to take place on the 20th of May."

"True; then go to-morrow. And now retire to rest, and I will write the letter to the king, and also an answer to my brother, to tell him that I hope to succeed with the pope.''

"And, perhaps, monseigneur, my presence in Paris may contribute to the success of your wishes, on the point you have at heart."

"Always mysterious, Viscount d'Exmès; but I am accustomed to it from you. Adieu! I wish you a good-night."

"I will come to-morrow morning for my letters, monseigneur. I will leave my men with you, they may be useful; I only ask permission to take with me my squire, Martin Guerre; he is devoted to me, and is a brave soldier, who is afraid of nothing but his wife and his shadow."

"How so?" asked the duke, laughing.

"Monseigneur, he escaped from home to get away from his wife, and entered my service at Metz; but the devil or his wife, to punish him, took the form of another Martin Guerre, and he saw, fighting at his side, a striking likeness of himself. Dame! that frightens him, but, away from it, he mocks at balls, and is a host in himself; he has saved my life twice."

"Take, then, with you this valiant coward, and come to me early to-morrow, my friend; my letters will be ready."

Gabriel slept little; and, after receiving the last instructions and adieus of the duke, set off at six in the morning, on the 25th of April, accompanied by Martin Guerre and two others, for Rome, and from thence to Paris.

CHAPTER IV

DIANA DE POITIERS

IT IS the 20th of May in Paris, at the Louvre; and in the apartment of the grand Seneschal, Madame de Brézé, Duchess de Valentinois, commonly called Diana of Poitiers, nine o'clock in the morning had just struck, and Diana, dressed entirely in white, in a coquettish *négligé*, reclined on a velvet sofa. The king, Henry the Second, magnificently dressed, sat by her side.

The room was resplendent with all the luxury with which that epoch of art that we call the Renaissance could decorate a royal apartment. In the paintings which hung on the walls, Diana, the huntress, goddess of the woods and forests, was the heroine; and gilded and colored medallions and panels bore everywhere the arms of Francis the First and Henry the Second.

In similar manner memories of father and son were intertwined in the heart of the fair Diana. Emblems were no less historical and full of meaning, and in many places was to be seen the crescent of Phœbe-Diana, between the Salamander of the conqueror of Marignan, and Bellerophon overthrowing the Chimæra—a device adopted by Henry the Second after the taking of Boulogne from the English. This fickle crescent appeared in a thousand different forms and combinations, doing great credit to the decorators. In one place the royal crown was placed above it, and in another four H's, four *fleurs de lis*, and four crowns together; often again it was threefold, and sometimes shaped like a star. No less varied were the mottoes, most of them in Latin.

"Diana regnum venatrix" (Diana, huntress of kings): a piece of impertinence, or of flattery? "Donec totum impleat orbem" may be translated in two ways—"The crescent will become a full moon," or "The glory of the king will fill the whole world." "Cum plena est, fit æmula solis," can be freely translated, "Royalty and beauty are sisters." Then the beautiful arabesques which inclosed mottoes and devices, and the magnificent furnishings on which they were reproduced—all these, if we should attempt to describe them, would not only put the magnificence of our day to the blush, but would lose too much in the description.

Let us now turn our eyes to the king. History tells us that he was tall and active, and a man of great strength; he combated, by regular diet and exercise, a tendency to *embonpoint*, and surpassed the swiftest in the chase, the strongest at the tourney. He had a dark complexion, with black hair, and a full and black beard. This day, as usual, he wore the colors of his Diana—green satin, slashed with white and glittering with gold embroideries; a hat with a white plume, sparkling with pearls and diamonds, a double gold chain, supporting a medallion of the Order of St. Michael, a sword engraved by Benvenuto, a white collar in Venice point-lace, and a mantle of velvet, starred with gold. The costume was splendid, and the wearer elegant.

We have stated briefly that Diana was clad in a simple white morning-gown of peculiarly thin and transparent stuff. It would be no easy matter to paint her divine loveliness; and it would be hard indeed to say whether the cushion of ebon black, on which her head reposed, or the dress, startling in its purity, by which her figure was enveloped, best served to set off the snows and lilies of her complexion. And doubtless it was a combination of delicate outlines perfect enough to drive Jean Goujon himself to distraction. There is no more perfect piece of antique statuary; and this study was alive indeed—if common report may be believed, very much alive. It is as well to attempt no description of the graceful motion with which these lovely limbs were instinct; it can no more be reproduced than a ray of sunlight. As to her age, she had none. In this point, as in so many others, she was like immortals; for by her side the youngest and freshest seemed but old and wrinkled. The Protestants talked about philters and potions, to which they averred she had recourse to enable her to retain her youth; to which the Catholics replied that these magic potions consisted merely in taking a cold bath every day, and washing her face in iced water even in the winter time. This prescription of hers has been preserved; but if it be true that Jean Goujon's "Diane au Cerf" was carved from this royal model, the prescription no longer has the same effect.

Thus worthy was she of the affection of the two monarchs whom one after the other her loveliness had dazzled; for it has been most conclusively proved that before Diana became Henry's mistress she had already been that of Francis.

"It is said," writes Le Laboureur, "that King Francis, who was the first lover of Diana de Poitiers, having expressed to her one day, after the death of the dauphin Francis, some dissatisfaction at the lack of animation exhibited by Prince Henry, she told him that what he needed was merely a love affair, and that she would make him fall in love with her."

What woman wills, God wills; and so Diana remained, or became, for twenty years the tenderly and only beloved of Henry.

But now that we have taken a glance at the king and his favorite, is it not time to listen to what they are saying?

Henry, holding in his hand a parchment, was in the act of reading aloud the following verses, not without certain interruptions and gestures which it is impossible to chronicle here, being as they were a part of the setting of the piece.

> Douce et belle bouchelette,
> Plus fraîche, et plus vermeillette
> Que le bouton églantine,
> Au matin!

Plus suave et mieux fleurante
Que l'immortelle amarante,
Et plus mignarde cent fois
Que n'est la douce rosée
Dont la terre est arrosée
Goutte à goutte au plus doux mois!
Baise-moi, ma douce amie,
Baise-moi, chère vie,
Baise-moi, mignonnement,
   Serrement,
Jusques à tant que je die:
Las! je n'en puis plus, ma mie;
Las! mon Dieu, je n'en puis plus.
Lors ta bouchette retire,
Afin que mort, je soupire,
Puis, me donne le surplus.
Ainsi ma douce guerrière,
Mon cœur, mon tout, ma lumière,
Vivons ensemble, vivons,
   Et suivons
Les doux soutiens de jeunesse,
Aussi bien une vieillesse
Nous menace sur le port,
Qui, toute courbe et tremblante,
Nous attraine, chancelante,
La maladie et la mort![1]

"And what, then, may be the name of this polished versifier, who tells us what we are doing so exactly?" asked Henry, when he had finished reading.

"He is called Remy Belleau, sire, and, it seems to me,

---

[1] Sweet and pretty little mouth,
Fresher and redder than bud of eglantine
  At morn!
More sweet and fragrant than the undying amaranth
More delicious, a hundred times,
Than the honeyed dew that moistens the earth
Drop by drop, in the sweetest month!
Kiss me, sweet friend,
Kiss me, dear life,
Kiss me, lovingly,
   Passionately,
Until my mouth is forced to gasp:
Alas! I can no more, my life!
Alas! my God, I can no more! etc.

bids fair to rival Ronsard. Well," continued the duchess,
"do you value this poem at five hundred crowns, as I do?"

"He shall have them, this *protege* of yours, my beautiful
Diana."

"But this must not make us forget our earlier ones, sire.
Have you signed the pension that I promised in your name
to Ronsard, the prince of poets? You have, I have no
doubt. Very well, then, I have but one more favor to ask
at your hands, and that is the vacant abbey of Recouls for
your librarian, Mellin de Saint-Gelais, our French Ovid."

"He shall have his abbey, have no fear, my fair Mæce-
nas," replied the king.

"Ah, how happy you are, sire, to possess the power of
dispensing so many offices and benefices at your pleasure.
If I only had your power but for one short hour!"

"Have you not it always, ungrateful one?"

"Have I really, sire? But it has been two full minutes
since you have given me a kiss! That's right, dearest. So
you say that your power is always mine? Tempt me not,
sire! I warn you that I shall take advantage of it to pay
the enormous bill which Philibert Delorme has sent me on
the completion of my Château d'Anet. It will be one of
the glories of your reign, but a very dear one, I fear. One
more kiss, my Henry."

"And in return for this kiss, Diana, take for your castle the sum realized by the sale of the governorship of
Picardy."

"Do you think I sell my kisses, sire? I give them
to you. The governorship of Picardy is worth, I should
think, two hundred thousand pounds, is it not? And then
there is the pearl necklace which has been offered me, and
which I wish to wear to-day at the wedding of your son
Francis. A hundred thousand to Philibert, and a hundred
thousand for the necklace; this Picardy matter will do very
well indeed."

"I should think so, especially as you estimate it at quite
double its real worth, Diana."

"What! it is worth only one hundred thousand pounds? Very well, then, I shall be obliged to let the necklace go."

"Nonsense!" replied the king, laughing; "I have no doubt there are three or four vacant companies somewhere which will pay for the necklace, Diana."

"Oh, sire, you are the most generous of monarchs, as you are the dearest of lovers."

"Ah, do you really love me as I do you, Diana?"

"He really has the hardihood to ask such a question?"

"But you see, darling, I love you more and more every day, because you grow more beautiful. Ah, what a lovely smile you have, sweetheart, and what an expression! Let me kneel here at your feet; put your beautiful hands on my shoulders. Oh, Diana, how lovely you are, and how passionately I love you! I could remain here simply gazing at you for hours, nay, for years; I could forget France, I could forget the whole world."

"But certainly not the formal celebration of Monseigneur the Dauphin's marriage?" exclaimed Diana, with a smile; "and yet it is to be solemnized not two hours from now. And although you are all ready, sire, I am not at all, you see. So leave me, my dear lord, for it is time for me to summon my women; ten o'clock will strike in a moment."

"Ten o'clock!" said Henry; "and on my life, I have an appointment for that hour."

"A rendezvous, sire?—with a lady?"

"Yes."

"And pretty, doubtless?"

"Yes, Diana, very pretty."

"Then it is not the queen."

"Well, Catherine de Médicis has her own kind of cold beauty; however, it is not with her. Can you not guess with whom?"

"No, really, sire."

"It is another Diana—our daughter, our dear daughter!"

"You repeat that too loudly, and too often, sire," replied

Diana. "You forget that we agreed that Madame de Castro should pass for the daughter of another."

"But you love her all the same, do you not, Diana?"

"I love her because you do."

"Oh, yes! very much. She is so charming and so good; besides, she recalls to me my youthful days, when I loved you—not better than I do now, but madly, even to crime."

The king remained for a few minutes plunged in thought, and then said, "That Montgommery—you did not love him, did you, Diana?"

"What a question!" replied she, with a smile of disdain. "After twenty years, again this jealousy?"

"Yes, I shall be always jealous of you, Diana. But if you did not love him, he loved you."

"What mattered that, sire, while my heart was all yours? Besides, he has been dead so long!"

"Yes, dead," replied the king, in a hollow voice.

"Do not let us sadden a *fête* day with these souvenirs. Have you seen Francis and Mary this morning? They are very happy and joyful; but scarcely more so than the Guises, whom this marriage delights."

"Yes, and it equally enrages the constable, my old Montmorency. He will be more enraged soon, however, for I fear that our Diana will not have his son."

"But, sire, you have promised for her."

"Yes, but it appears that Diana is averse to it."

"A child of eighteen! What reason can she have?"

"That is what she is about to confide to me."

"Go to her, then, sire, while I adorn myself to please you."

"After the ceremony I shall see you again; but before I go, tell me once more that you love me."

"Yes, sire, as I always have, and always shall love you!"

"Adieu, then, my loved and loving Diana."

Immediately on the departure of the king a panel, which was concealed by the tapestry, opened on the opposite side of the room, and the Constable de Montmorency entered.

"*Mon Dieu!*" said he, rudely, "you have talked enough to-day, I hope."

"My friend," replied Diana, "you saw that long ago I tried to dismiss him."

"If you imagine that your discourse was edifying or amusing to me— But what is this new whim of refusing the hand of your daughter to my son, after it has been solemnly promised? I tell you that this marriage must take place. Do you hear, Diana? You must arrange it. It is the only way to prevent those cursed Guises becoming too powerful; therefore, in spite of the king, or the pope, I will have it."

"But, my friend—"

"Ah!" cried the constable, "when I tell you that I will have it, *Pater noster!*"

"Then it shall be so," replied Diana, frightened.

CHAPTER V

THE APARTMENTS OF THE ROYAL CHILDREN

ON RETURNING to his own apartments the king did not find his daughter; but the officer in attendance told him that Madame Diana, after waiting for him some time, had gone to the apartments of the king's children, leaving word that she should be apprised as soon as his Majesty had returned.

"Good," said Henry; "I will join her there. Leave me, for I wish to go alone."

Passing through a large hall, and then a long corridor, he softly opened a door at the further end and stood looking from behind a half-drawn curtain. The noise of his steps was drowned by the shouts of laughter and the cries of the children, so that he was able, himself unseen, to be the witness of a most delightful picture.

Standing by the window, Mary Stuart, the beautiful young bride, had gathered about her Diana de Castro, and the Princesses Elizabeth and Marguerite, all three of whom were eager to help her, and all talking at the same time. One smoothed out a fold in her dress, another rearranged a lock of hair that had half fallen from its fastening —in fact, they were giving the finishing touches to her lovely toilet in a woman's own way. At the further end of the room the brothers, Charles, Henry, and Francis, were laughing and shouting, and pushing with all their strength against a door which the dauphin Francis, the young bride-groom, was in vain essaying to open, while the little mischief-makers were doing their best to prevent him from seeing his wife till the very last moment.

Jacques Amyot, the tutor of the princes, was engaged in a serious conversation in a corner with Madame de Coni and Lady Lennox, the governesses of the princesses.

There in that one apartment, which could be covered by a glance, was assembled a great part of the history of the immediate future, its misfortunes, its passions, and its glory. There was the dauphin, who afterward became Francis the Second; Elizabeth, who was to marry Philip the Second, and become Queen of Spain; Charles, afterward the hated King Charles the Ninth; Henry, afterward Henry the Third; Marguerite, who married Henry the Fourth, and became Queen of Navarre; Francis, who became successively Duke of Alençon, of Anjou, and of Brabant; and finally, Mary Stuart, who was twice a queen, and at last a martyr.

The illustrious translator of Plutarch watched, with a look at once sad and interested, the sports of these royal children who represented the future destinies of France.

"No, no, Francis, you shall not get in," cried the rough Charles Maximilien, who in after days gave the fatal word for the terrible slaughter of Saint Bartholomew. And with the help of his brother, he succeeded in pushing the bolt through, and thus effectually barring out poor Francis, who in any event was too weak to have forced his way in, even against these children, and who now could only stamp and exclaim in his vexation from the other side of the door.

"Dear Francis, how they do torment him!" said Mary Stuart to her sisters-in-law.

"Don't move, Madame la Dauphine; at least, not until I have fixed this pin," laughed little Marguerite. "What a great invention pins are, and what a great man he who thought of them last year should really become!"

"And now that the pin is fixed," said gentle Elizabeth, "I am going to open the door for Francis, in spite of these young rascals, for it makes me sad to see him so unhappy."

"Oh, yes, that is all very well, Elizabeth," said Mary Stuart, with a sigh; "but you are thinking of your courtly Spaniard, Don Carlos, the Spanish king's son, who amused us all so at St. Germain."

"Just see Elizabeth blush," cried little Marguerite, clapping her hands mischievously. "But he is really a very fine and gallant lover, this Castilian of hers."

"Come, come," cried Diana de Castro, who was the oldest of the girls, in a motherly voice, "it isn't right for sisters to badger each other so, Marguerite."

Nothing could have been lovelier than the sight of these four beautiful girls, each so different from her sisters, yet so perfect in herself; they were beautiful buds just blossoming. There was Diana, all purity and sweetness; Elizabeth, affectionate, yet serious; Mary Stuart, full of grace and languor; and Marguerite, a mischievous madcap. King Henry, fascinated and moved, could not take his eyes off the charming picture.

At last, however, he decided to enter. "The king!" they all exclaimed with one voice; and they all rushed to meet their monarch and father. Only Mary Stuart held back a little from the rest, and went quietly to the door and drew the bolt which kept Francis a prisoner. The dauphin lost no time in entering, and the family was complete.

"Good-morning, my dears," said the king. "I am indeed overjoyed to find you all so well and happy. So they were barring you out, Francis, my poor boy? But then you will have time enough from now on to enjoy your sweetheart. Do you love each other truly, my children?"

"Oh, yes, sire, indeed I do love Mary," replied the dauphin, as he imprinted a burning kiss on the hand of her who was soon to become his wife.

"Monseigneur," remarked Lady Lennox, rather sharply, "it is not right to kiss a lady's hand like that in public, especially in the presence of his Majesty. What will he think of Princess Mary and her governess?"

"But this hand is mine, isn't it?" said the dauphin.

"Not yet, monseigneur," replied the governess; "and I shall do my duty to the very last moment."

"Have no fear," said Mary in a low voice, to her young *fiance*, who was almost in the sulks; "when she isn't looking, you may have it again."

The king laughed under his beard.

"My lady, you are strict indeed; but after all you are quite right," he added, controlling himself. "I trust you are not dissatisfied with your pupils. You must pay due attention to the word of your learned teacher, young gentlemen, for he is the intimate friend of the greatest heroes of antiquity. How long is it, Messire Amyot, since you have heard from Pierre Danot, our old master, and from Henry Etienne, our fellow-pupil?"

"Both the old man and the young are in good health, sire, and will be as happy as proud to hear that your Majesty has deigned to remember them."

"Well, children," said the king, "I wanted to see you before the marriage, and am very glad to have had this opportunity. And now, Diana, my dear, I am at your service, so follow me."

Diana made a deep courtesy and accompanied the king from the room.

CHAPTER VI

DIANA DE CASTRO

DIANA DE CASTRO, whom we saw as a child, was now nearly eighteen; her beauty had kept all its promise, and her features were at once regular and charming. She was but thirteen when the Duke de Castro, whom she had never seen again, was killed at the siege of Hesdin. The king then sent her to the convent of the Filles-Dieu, at Paris, and she soon became so attached to the nuns that she had requested permission to remain there.

It was impossible not to heed such a devout request; and the king had not, therefore, taken Diana away from the convent until about a month before this, when the Constable de Montmorency, jealous of the influence acquired in the government by the Guises, had obtained for his son the hand of the daughter of the king and his favorite.

In the course of the month which she had passed at court Diana had not failed from the first to attract universal love and admiration. "For," says Brantôme, in his book on famous women, "she was very kind, and did not offend anybody; and yet her spirit was high and noble, and she was very obliging and discreet, and most virtuous." But this virtue of hers, which shone forth so beautifully amid the general wickedness of the time, was entirely free from any touch of austerity. One day a gentleman made the remark, in her hearing, that a daughter of France should be strong and brave, and that Diana's modesty tasted somewhat of the convent; whereupon she began to take riding lessons, and in a few days there was no more fearless or daring rider than she. After this she usually accompanied the king to the chase; and Henry yielded more and more to the charming sovereignty that she was beginning to acquire over him. Diana was privileged to enter her father's apartments whenever she chose, always sure of a welcome. Her lovely grace and modest little ways, and the odor of sweet maidenliness and innocence which she seemed to exhale—even her smile, in which the least bit of sadness lingered—all combined to make her the most exquisite and fascinating personage of that whole court, which could boast of so many dazzling beauties.

"Well," said Henry to her, on entering, "I am ready to listen to you, *ma mignonne.*"

"Sire, you are so good!"

"I love you, my child, and I wish to please you as far as I may, without risking those grave interests which a king must consider, before all affection. And stay, to prove this to you, the good Sister Monique, who took so much care of you at the convent, has just been, by your recommendation, appointed abbess of the convent of Origny, at St. Quentin."

"Oh! I thank you, sire."

"Here are, also, the letters-patent which confer on you the title of Duchess d'Angoulême. But I see you sometimes sorrowful and thoughtful, and I wish to know how to cheer you; are you not happy, my child?"

"Ah! sire," replied Diana, "how could I not be so, surrounded by your affection and your benefits? I only ask that the present should continue."

"Diana, you know that I recalled you from the convent to marry you to Francis de Montmorency; it would be an alliance worthy of you, and would, moreover, have been useful to my interests, yet you seem averse to it. You owe me, at least, the reasons for this dislike, which grieves me, Diana."

"I will not hide them from you, my father. In the first place, they tell me that Francis de Montmorency is already privately married to one of the ladies of the court."

"It is true; but this marriage, contracted clandestinely, without my consent or that of the constable, is worthless; and if the pope pronounce a divorce, you surely need not be more scrupulous than his Holiness. So if that be the reason—"

"No, I have another, my father."

"Come, then, tell me; why do you object to an alliance which would honor the richest and noblest heiress in France?"

"Well, my father, because—because I love some one else!" cried Diana, throwing herself, confused, and tearful, into his arms.

"You love, Diana! And whom?"

"Gabriel, sire."

"Gabriel what?" asked the king, laughing.

"I do not know."

"What, Diana? Pray explain yourself."

"Sire, I will tell you all. He was my childhood's love—I saw him every day. He was so gentle, so brave, so handsome, so clever, and so tender; he used to call me his little wife. Ah! sire, do not laugh; it was a serious and holy affection—the first which was engraven on my heart; others have been added to it, but none can efface that. I permitted myself to be married to the Duke de Castro, but I knew not what I did—I only obeyed like a little girl. Since then I have bitterly regretted my treason toward Gabriel.

"Poor Gabriel," continued Diana; "when he left me he did not cry, but what profound grief in his look! All returned to my mind during the solitary years that I passed at the convent, so that I have lived twice over the years passed with Gabriel; and, returning here, sire, to your court, among the accomplished gentlemen who surround you, I have not seen one who can rival Gabriel; and it is certainly not Francis, the submissive son of the haughty constable, who can make me forget the gentle, yet proud companion of my infancy. Thus, now that I am of an age to understand, as long as you allow me, my father, I will remain faithful to Gabriel.''

''Have you, then, seen him again, since you left Vimoutires, Diana ?''

''Alas! no.''

''But you have heard of him ?''

''No; I only heard from Enguerrand that he left the country soon after my departure, and told Aloyse, his nurse, not to be unquiet about him—that he would return to her famous.''

''And have not his family heard of him ?''

''Sire, he had no family. I never saw any one with him but Aloyse, when I went to visit him at Montgommery.''

''At Montgommery!'' cried the king, turning pale. ''I trust he is not a Montgommery. Tell me that he is not!''

''Oh! no, sire; if he were he would have lived in the castle, and he lived in the cottage of Aloyse. But what have these Counts de Montgommery done to you, to move you so, sire? Are they your enemies? They speak of them all through the country with veneration.''

''Ah! truly,'' replied the king, with a disdainful laugh; ''but they have done nothing to me. What could a Montgommery do to a Valois? But this Gabriel—had he, then, no other name ?''

''None that I know of, sire; he was an orphan, and I never heard his father spoken of.''

''And you have no other reason to object to this alliance than your old affection for this young man ?''

''That is enough.''

''Well, Diana, I would not attempt to combat it, if he were here, and I could know him; although I fear that his origin—''

''Have I not also a bar in my escutcheon ?''

''But, at least, you have an escutcheon, and one that noble houses desire to quarter with their own. Your Gabriel, on the contrary— But that is not now the question.

You have not seen him for six years; he has probably forgotten you; he loves some one else, perhaps.''

"Sire, you do not know Gabriel; he has a faithful heart.''

"Well, Diana, perhaps infidelity to you is scarcely likely;
but you think he went to fight—probably he has fallen. I
afflict you, my child, and your beautiful eyes fill with tears.
Well, I am not much accustomed to believe in great attach-
ments, but I respect yours.   Still, *ma mignonne*, for a childish love, whose object has disappeared, for a remembrance,
a shadow, see into what embarrassment your refusal will
throw me.   The constable, if I withdraw my word, will
grow angry, and perhaps leave me; and then, it is no longer
I who reign, but the Guises.   See, Diana: the duke has
under his hand the whole military force in France; the cardinal, all the finances; a third brother, all my ships at Marseilles; a fourth commands in Scotland; and a fifth is going
to replace Brissac in Piedmont.   I speak gently to you,
Diana, and explain my circumstances; I beg, when I might
command, but I much prefer to let you judge for yourself;
I prefer that you should yield to the father, and not to the
king.   You are good and affectionate.   This marriage would
save me; it would give to the Montmorencys the power
which it withdrew from the Guises, and would restore the
balance once more.

"Well, you do not reply; will you be deaf to the prayer
of your father, who does not constrain you, but only asks
you to render him the first service which you have ever
had it in your power to grant, and which will, moreover,
contribute to your own honor and happiness?   Well, my
daughter, will you consent?''

"Sire,'' replied she, "you are a thousand times more
powerful when your voice implores than when it commands.
I am ready to sacrifice myself to your interests on one condition.''

"What is it, spoiled child?''

"This marriage shall not take place for three months,
and meanwhile I will send to Aloyse for news of Gabriel, so

that if he be dead I shall learn it, and if he be alive I can, at least, claim back from him my promise.''

"Granted, willingly!" exclaimed Henry joyfully, "and I will aid you in the search; and in three months you will marry Francis, whether your young lover be living or dead.''

"And now," said Diana, sadly, "I do not know whether I ought to wish most for his death or his life.''

The king was about to make a remark not very paternal in character, and of rather doubtful consoling power; but one look at the honest expression of Diana's lovely face, and the words died upon his lips. He betrayed his thought only by a smile.

"For good or evil," he said to himself, "she will doubtless obey the customs of the court.''

And then he added aloud:

"The time has arrived, Diana, to go to the church; allow me, madame, to escort you to the grand gallery; and afterward I shall see you again at the jousting, and at the games in the afternoon. And if you are not too much provoked with me, on account of my tyrannical conduct, perhaps you will condescend to applaud my strokes with the lance, and my passades, my beautiful umpire.''

CHAPTER VII

HOW THE CONSTABLE DE MONTMORENCY SAID HIS PATER NOSTER

ON THE afternoon of the same day, while the tournament at Tournelles was in progress, the Constable de Montmorency was at the Louvre, in the cabinet of Diana of Poitiers, examining one of his secret agents. The spy was of middle height, and dark in complexion, with black hair and eyes; and he resembled, in a most striking manner, Martin Guerre, the faithful squire of Gabriel; they looked like twin brothers.

"What have you done with the courier, Arnold?" asked the constable.

"Monseigneur, it was necessary to put him out of the way. But it was in the night, in the forest of Fontainebleau; they will lay the murder to robbers. I am very prudent."

"Nevertheless, it is a serious thing, and I blame you for being so prompt with your knife."

"I am always ready to do anything in the service of monseigneur."

"Yes; but once for all, Arnold, remember, that if you let yourself be taken, I shall let you be hanged."

"Be easy, monseigneur; I am a man of precautions."

"Now let me see the letter."

"Here it is, monseigneur."

"Open it, then, without breaking the seal. *Diable!* do you suppose that I can read?"

Arnold du Thill, taking from his pocket a sharp pair

of scissors, cut carefully round the seal, and opened the letter; he first pointed to the signature. "Monseigneur sees that I do not deceive him. The letter, addressed to the Cardinal de Guise, is from Cardinal Carraffa, as the miserable courier had the folly to tell me."

"Read it, then, at once."

Arnold read: " 'Monseigneur and dear ally, only three important words. First, according to your request, the pope will linger over the affair of the divorce, and will dally with Francis de Montmorency, who arrived here yesterday, only to refuse him at last.' "

"*Pater noster!*" murmured the constable; "may the devil take all these red hats!"

" 'Secondly,' " continued Arnold, " 'M. de Guise, your illustrious brother, after having taken Campli, holds Civitella in check; but to decide us to send him the men and supplies he asks for, we must be assured that you will not recall him for the war in Flanders, as report goes you will do. If we have a certainty that he is to remain, his Holiness will aid him efficaciously. Thirdly, I announce to you, monseigneur, the approaching arrival in Paris of an envoy from your brother, the Viscount d'Exmès, bringing to the king the colors taken in Italy. He will doubtless arrive nearly as soon as my letter; and his presence, and the glorious spoils which he will lay at the feet of the king, will assuredly be of service to your cause.' "

"*Fiat voluntas tua,*" cried the constable, furiously. "We will give a worthy reception to this cursed ambassador. Arnold, is that devil of a letter finished?"

"Yes, monseigneur, except the compliments and the signature."

"Well, you will have plenty to do."

"I ask no better, monseigneur, with a little money to help me."

"Knave, here are a hundred ducats; with you, one must always have money ready."

"I spend so much in the service of monseigneur."

"Your vices cost more than my service."

"Oh, monseigneur deceives himself about me. My dream would be to live calm, happy, and rich, in some country place, surrounded by my wife and my children, like a good father of a family."

"Quite virtuous and pastoral. Well, amend your ways; lay aside some money; marry if you can; realize your plans of happiness; who prevents you? But meanwhile reclose the letter, and take it to the cardinal; you will disguise yourself—you understand—and say that you were charged by your dying companion—"

"Monseigneur may trust to me. All shall be more probable than truth itself."

"Who comes here?" cried the constable.

"Pardon me, monseigneur," said a servant, entering; "but here is a gentleman arrived from Italy, who asks to see the king, on the part of the Duc de Guise, and I thought I had better tell you; he is called the Viscount d'Exmès."

"You have done well, Guillaume. Show him in here; and you, Arnold, place yourself behind that tapestry, and do not lose the occasion of seeing this man; it is principally for that that I receive him."

"I believe, monseigneur, that I have seen him already in my travels, but it is good to make sure."

The spy glided behind the tapestry, and Gabriel was introduced. "To whom," said he, bowing, "have I the honor of speaking?"

"I am the Constable de Montmorency. Monsieur, what do you desire?"

"I beg your pardon; it is to the king that I wish to speak."

"His Majesty is not in the Louvre, and in his absence—"

"I will go to his Majesty, or wait for him," interrupted Gabriel.

"His Majesty is at the *fêtes* of Tournelles, and will not

return before the evening. Are you ignorant that to-day they celebrate the marriage of the dauphin?''

''No, monseigneur; I heard it as I came along. Can I see the Cardinal de Lorraine? It was for him I asked, and I know not why they brought me to you.''

''M. de Lorraine,'' said the constable, ''being a man of peace, loves the mockery of war. I, who am a man of war, love only real combats; that is why I am at the Louvre, while he is at the Tournelles.''

''I will go to him there.''

''You come from Italy?''

''Yes, monseigneur.''

''From the Duc de Guise, perhaps? What is he doing?''

''Permit me, monseigneur, to lay my account before his Majesty in the first instance, and to leave you for that purpose.''

''*Pater noster!*'' cried the constable; ''he shall pay for these insolent airs. Hola, Arnold! Well, where is the fellow? Gone also—save and confound him.''

While the constable vented his ill-humor in oaths and *Pater nosters*, according to custom, Gabriel, in traversing a gallery to quit the Louvre, found, to his astonishment, standing near the door, his squire, Martin Guerre, whom he had ordered to wait in the court. ''Oh, it is you, Martin!'' said he. ''Well, go with the flags carefully rolled up, and wait for me at the corner of the Rue St. Catherine; the cardinal may wish me to present them to the king at the *fêtes*.''

''Yes, monsieur;'' and he ran quickly downstairs. Thus Gabriel, on coming into the court, was much surprised to find him still standing there, looking white and scared.

''Well, Martin, what is the matter?''

''Ah, monsieur, I have just seen him; he passed close by me just now, and spoke to me.''

''Who?''

''Who! Satan, I think. The phantom—the other Martin Guerre.''

"Again this folly, Martin! you are dreaming."

"No, no! he spoke to me, I tell you. He stopped be-fore me, and petrified me with his glance, saying, with his infernal laugh, 'Well, we are still in the service of Vis-count d'Exmès' (remark the 'we,' monsieur), 'and we are bringing back the flags won by M. de Guise.' How could he know that, monsieur? Then he heard the sound of your steps, and saying, 'We shall meet again, Martin Guerre,' he disappeared through the door, or rather through the wall."

"You are mad! he could hardly have had time to speak since you left me in the gallery."

"I! monseigneur; I have not stirred from the place where you left me."

"To whom, then, did I speak just now?"

"Assuredly to the other—to my double, my spectre."

"My poor Martin, you are ill; we have marched too long in the sun."

"Yes, you think that I am delirious, I know, but I do not know a word of the orders that you say you gave to me."

"You have forgotten them, Martin; well, I will repeat them. I told you to go with the flags, and wait for me at the corner of the Rue St. Catherine. Do you remem-ber now?"

"Pardon, monsieur; I cannot remember what I never knew."

"Well, you know it now; go quickly."

CHAPTER VIII

THE TILT-YARD

THE tilt-yard had been prepared across the Rue St. Antoine, and formed a square, surrounded on each side by scaffolds covered with spectators, while at one end sat the king and queen. At the opposite end was the entrance for the combatants. About three o'clock in the afternoon, when the religious ceremony, and the re-past which followed it, were over, the king and queen took their places amid *vivats* and exclamations of joy from all sides.

Then the king ordered that the tilting at the ring should commence. This game was, in those days, complicated and difficult; the post on which the ring was hung was placed about two-thirds from the entrance of the course, which it was necessary to traverse at full gallop, and in passing to bear away the ring on the point of the lance. The lance was not to touch the body, but to be held horizontally, with the elbow above the head. The prize was a diamond ring, given by the queen.

Henry, on his white horse, caparisoned with velvet and gold, was one of the most elegant and skilful cavaliers that it was possible to imagine; he held and managed his lance with admirable grace and certainty. However, M. de Vieilleville rivalled him, and even seemed about to obtain the prize; he had two rings more than the king, and there remained but three to be taken. But M. de Vieilleville, a perfect courtier, missed them all, and the king had the prize. On receiving it, he cast a glance toward Diana of

Poitiers; but it was the queen's gift, and he felt bound to offer it to the newly made bride.

Other games succeeded, and the king won a magnificent bracelet; he went and seated himself near Diana, and publicly placed it on her arm. The queen grew pale with rage; but, according to her usual custom, pretended to see nothing, and began to talk to her ladies. Several gentlemen then asked to be permitted to break a lance in honor of the ladies, which was readily granted.

Henry, taking a gold chain from his neck, offered it for a prize, adding, "Do your best, gentlemen, for I shall endeavor to regain it; at six o'clock the combats will finish, and the victor, whoever he be, will be crowned."

Several gentlemen held the ground alternately, but at last the Marshal d'Amville took his place, and kept it against five successive lances. The king could refrain no longer. "Oh," said he, "M. d'Amville, I will see if you are fixed there forever." He armed, and at the first course M. d'Amville was unhorsed. After him came M. Aussun; but when he, in his turn, was beaten, no other presented himself.

"How is this, gentlemen?" cried the king; "will no one tilt against me? No one fears, I trust; there is no king here, but the victor; no privileges, but those of skill; therefore come forward boldly, gentlemen."

Still no one came. All feared equally to be victor or vanquished, and the king was growing angry and impatient, when at last a new assailant passed the barrier. Henry, without looking to see who it was, advanced; the two lances broke, but the king tottered on his saddle—by which he was obliged to support himself, while the other remained motionless. At this moment six o'clock struck, and the king was vanquished. He descended joyfully from his saddle, and taking the victor by the hand, led him himself up to the queen. To his surprise he saw a face which was perfectly unknown to him; he was a handsome young man, and the queen smiled as she put the chain round his neck. He, after bowing, rose, and going straight up to Madame de Castro, offered her the chain, while "Gabriel!" and "Diana!" burst from their lips, but so low, that no one heard them, and it passed for a courtesy to the beautiful daughter of the king.

The king also took it as such, and thanked him for it, adding, "I, sir, who am well acquainted with my nobility, do not remember having seen you before; but I wish much to know the name of a cavalier who gave me just now so rude a shock."

"Sire, it is the first time that I have had the honor of being in your Majesty's presence. I have been, until now, with the army, and have just arrived from Italy; I am the Viscount d'Exmès." Then making a sign to two men, who stood near, they advanced, and laid the flags at the feet of the king. "Sire," continued Gabriel, "here are the flags won in Italy by your army, and sent to you by Monseigneur le Duc de Guise. His eminence, the Cardinal de Lorraine, assures me that your Majesty will excuse their presentation at what is, perhaps, an inopportune time. I have also the honor, sire, to place in your hands these letters from the duke."

The king took the letters, and reading them, said, "Thanks, M. d'Exmès; these letters recommend you to us—and what do I see?—that you took four of these flags with your own hand, and our cousin of Guise calls you one of his bravest captains! What can I do for you, M. d'Exmès?"

"Sire, you overwhelm me; I trust myself to your Majesty's goodness."

"You are a captain; would it please you to enter our guards? I was embarrassed for a successor to M. d'Avallon, and I see that you would be a worthy one."

"Your Majesty—"

"You accept; that is settled. We are now going to return to the Louvre, when you can give me more details of the war "

Gabriel bowed. The king gave the order for departure, and the crowd dispersed, with cries of " *Vive le Roi!*"

Diana drew near Gabriel for an instant and said, in a low voice, "To-morrow, at the queen's circle." Then she vanished, leaving to her old friend a heart full of sweet hope.

CHAPTER IX

THE PRISON

THE queen's circle usually assembled in the evening. Gabriel was informed that his new appointment, as captain of the guard, not only authorized, but required him to attend them. His only regret then was that he had twenty-four hours to wait for it. His first occupation was to go with Martin Guerre to seek for a lodging; he took one, rather splendid for a young captain, but consistent with his means, and went to bed, happy and content. He had done much alone, and with no support but his sword, and no recommendation but his courage; he had attained an eminent rank, and no little glory, and could now go boldly forward in pursuit of her whom he loved, and of those whom he ought to hate.

The one, he had found; the other, Aloyse should help him to trace—he would send for her.

The next day he was obliged to present himself to M. de Boissy, Grand Equerry of France, in order to furnish him with proofs of his nobility. M. de Boissy, who was a man of honor, had been the friend of Count de Montgommery; he was aware of Gabriel's motives in concealing his true title, and promised him to keep his secret. After that Gabriel was presented to his company by Marshal d'Amville.

Gabriel's duty on the following day was to visit the prisons in Paris—a duty which would fall to him once a month. He began with the Bastile, and finished with the

Châtelet. The governor gave him the list of the prisoners, pointing out any who were dead, released, or transferred, and he had to visit all who remained.

He thought he had finished his task, when the governor turned to another page, on which was written, "No. 21. Secret prisoner. If during the visit of the governor, or the captain of the guard, he attempts to speak, transfer him into a lower and worse dungeon."

"Who is this important prisoner?" asked Gabriel of M. de Salvoison, the governor of the Châtelet.

"No one knows," replied he. "I received him from my predecessor, as he from his. You see that the date of his entrance is left blank; it must have been in the reign of Francis the First. They tell me that he has twice tried to speak; but at the first word, the governor is bound under the most terrible penalties to shut the door of his prison, and then to have him moved into a worse dungeon.

"This has been done, and there now only remains one lower, which would be certain death. Doubtless they wished to bring him to that, but he keeps silence; he is always chained, and to prevent any possibility of an escape, a jailer enters his cell every five minutes."

"But if he spoke to this jailer?"

"Oh, he is deaf and dumb; he was born in the Chatelet, and has never been out of it."

Gabriel shuddered. This man, so completely separated from life, yet who still lived and thought, inspired him with profound pity—almost with horror. "What idea, or what remorse; what fear of hell, or faith in heaven," thought he, "could prevent this miserable being from dashing his head against the walls of his cell? Was it vengeance, or hope, which chained him to life?"

His heart beat fast as he descended to the cell; they traversed several black and damp staircases, several horrible vaults, and then stopping before an iron door, the governor said, "It is here," and opened it with his key. Then Gabriel saw a frightful picture—such as one might see in a fearful nightmare. Everywhere stone, black, mossy, and damp; for this wretched place was lower than the bed of the Seine, and in the high tides the water half filled it. Horrible reptiles crawled over the walls, and there was no sound save the regular dropping of water from the roof.

Here lived two human beings, one guarding the other; both mute, and seeming scarce alive. The jailer, three parts an idiot, but a giant in strength, stood against the wall, looking with a vacant eye at the prisoner, who was lying in a corner on his bed of straw—his hands and feet secured by a chain, which was fastened to the wall. He was an old man, with white hair and beard.

When they entered, he seemed to sleep, and did not move; you might have taken him for a corpse, or a statue. But all at once he sat upright, opened his eyes, and looked at Gabriel; he was forbidden to speak, but his terrible look spoke for him. The governor visited every corner of the cell, while Gabriel remained stationary, looking as if fascinated by those flaming eyes, while the sincerest pity filled his breast. The prisoner appeared also to contemplate his visitor with anything but indifference. Indeed, once he opened his mouth, as if about to speak, but the governor, turning round, recalled to him his threatened fate, and with a bitter smile he reclosed his eyes, and fell back into his stony immobility.

"Oh! let us go!" cried Gabriel; "this is dreadful. I must have fresh air and see the sunlight again."

He did not seem to fully recover life and calmness until he found himself once more in the crowded tumult of the streets, and even then the gloomy vision he had seen remained in his mind and pursued him all day long, as he wandered hither and thither through the city.

Something or other seemed to whisper to him that the fate of this miserable captive was connected with his own, and that a great crisis in his life was imminent. Wearied at last by this mysterious presentiment, he directed his steps

toward evening to the lists of the Tournelles. The tourna-
ments of the day, in which Gabriel had taken no part, were
just coming to an end. He saw Diana, and she him, and
this exchange of glances at once chased away his gloomy
thoughts—even as the sun's rays disperse the clouds. He
forgot the wretched prisoner in the Bastile, and busied himself entirely with thoughts of the beautiful girl he was to
see again in the evening.

CHAPTER X

AN ELEGY DURING A COMEDY

ACCORDING to a custom of Francis the First's reign, three times at least during the week the king and all the lords and ladies of the court met in the evening in the apartment of the queen. There they planned or talked over the events of the day in all liberty, sometimes with all license; and amid the general conversation many a private one found a place. "And finding there," says Brantôme, "a troop of human goddesses, each lord and gentleman conversed with her whom he loved best." Often, again, there was dancing or acting.

It was at one of these reunions that Gabriel presented himself, with his joy not unmingled with anxiety. Full of happiness at meeting Diana again, and at the tender glances which she cast on him, he had at first forgotten the cardinal's letter; but it now returned to his memory, filling him with distracting doubts. Would Diana consent to this marriage? Could she love this Francis de Montmorency?

Gabriel therefore decided to question Martin Guerre on the subject, for he had already made a number of acquaintances, and, like most squires, was likely to be more familiar in such matters than his master; for it is a matter of common observation in the science of acoustics that reports of all kinds sound much louder below than above, and that echoes are hardly ever heard except in valleys. His decision was the more fortunate just at this time, because Martin Guerre had also just made up his mind to interrogate his master, whose preoccupation he had noticed, but who certainly had no reason to conceal either his acts or his thoughts from one who had served him faithfully for five years, and who had even saved his life.

Martin Guerre informed him that general report said that she did not love him. This faithful squire, to do honor to his master at court, had ordered for himself a complete suit of brown cloth with yellow trimmings, which he paid for, and put on immediately; therefore the tailor was much astonished to see him return half an hour after in different clothes. This he explained by saying that, as the evening was cold, he had judged it expedient to put on something warmer; but that he was so much pleased with his new suit that he wished for another precisely similar.

The tailor in vain represented to him that he would appear to be always wearing the same; he persisted in his idea, and compelled the tailor to promise that he would not make the slightest difference in the suits, only for the second order he asked for a little credit.

Gabriel perceived Diana the instant he entered the room; she was seated near the queen dauphin, as Mary Stuart was generally called. To accost her at once might have appeared presumptuous in a new-comer, and would doubtless have been rather imprudent, so he resigned himself to wait for a favorable opportunity.

In the meantime he began conversation with a young courtier, pale of feature and of delicate appearance, who chanced to be standing near him. After some small talk on matters as unimportant as the young man himself seemed to be, the latter asked of Gabriel—

"Monsieur, with whom have I the honor of conversing?"

To which Gabriel replied, "I am Viscount d'Exmès. But may I venture to ask the same question of you, monsieur?"

The young man looked at him in astonishment, as he replied, "I am Francis de Montmorency."

As far as Gabriel was concerned, he would have left him in less haste if he had said, "I am the Devil."

Francis, the workings of whose mind were rather sluggish, was quite dumfounded; but as he was not overfond of using his brains, he soon gave up the riddle, and looked elsewhere for less unceremonious hearers, while Gabriel made his way toward Diana de Castro. His progress was, however, arrested by the king, who announced that, as a surprise to the ladies, a stage had been prepared, and that the evening was to be finished by a five-act play. This news was received with acclamation, and the gentlemen led the ladies to their places. Gabriel was too late to take Diana, so he stood a little way behind her. The queen soon noticed, and sent for him.

"M. d'Exmès," said she, "why were you not at the tourney to-day?"

"Madame, the duties which his Majesty has confided to me prevented my having the honor."

"So much the worse," replied Catherine, with a charming smile, "for you are certainly one of our best cavaliers. You made the king reel yesterday, which is what few can do; and I should like to see new proofs of your prowess." Gabriel bowed.

"Do you know the piece they are playing?" continued the queen.

"Only in the Latin, madame; for I hear that it is an adaptation of a piece of Terence."

"Oh, I see that you are as learned as you are valiant. Now go and seat yourself behind me, among my ladies."

Gabriel gladly obeyed, and as Diana was at the end of the line next to the passage, he seated himself beside her. The piece was a comedy, and was received with much laughter and noisy enthusiasm, so that the lovers found an opportunity to converse unheard.

"Gabriel!" and "Diana!" were the first words that passed.

"Are you then to marry Francis de Montmorency?" asked Gabriel.

"You seem high in the good graces of the queen," was Diana's reply.

"She called me."

"It is the king who desires this marriage."

"But you consent, Diana?"

"But you listen to the queen, Gabriel."

"Oh!" cried Gabriel, "do you really interest yourself in what another might make me feel? Diana, I am horribly jealous of you, for I love you madly."

"M. d'Exmès," cried the poor girl, trying to be severe, "I am called Madame de Castro."

"But you are a widow? You are free?"

"Free! alas!"

"Oh, Diana, you sigh. Confess that the childish feeling which sweetened our first years has left some trace in your heart. Do not fear to be heard, they are all laughing around us. Diana, smile on me, and tell me that you love me, as I love you."

"But you must tell me how that is," said the little hypocrite.

"Listen to me, Diana; for the six years that I was away from you, I have thought of you constantly. On arriving at Paris, a month after you, I learned that you were the daughter of the king and of Madame de Valentinois; but it was not this that made me fear to approach you; it was your title of Madame de Castro. Still I thought, 'Acquire renown—approach yourself nearer to her station—some day she will hear you praised, and will admire you.' I went to the Duc de Guise, who seemed the most likely to lead me to the glory that I coveted. I was with him at Metz, and while there I heard of the capture of Hesdin by the imperial troops, and the death of your husband, who had not even seen you again since your marriage.

"How I fought, you must ask M. de Guise. I was at Abbeville, at Dinant, at Chateau-Cambrésis—I was everywhere where there was danger. I heard you had retired to a convent, and I accompanied the duke to Italy. At

Civitella, by a letter from his Eminence of Lorraine to his brother, I learned your intended marriage. Then I asked permission to return to France, to bring to the king the captured banners; but my motive was to see you, Diana—to ascertain if your heart was in this new marriage, and to ask you, as I have done, do you love me?"

"Gabriel," said Diana, softly, "I will reply to you. When I arrived, a child twelve years old, at this court, after a short period of astonishment and curiosity I was nearly killed with ennui; the gilded chains of this existence weighed upon me, and I bitterly regretted the loss of the woods and fields of Vimoutiers and Montgommery. Each night I cried myself to sleep. Nevertheless, the king, my father, was very kind to me, and I tried to reply to his affection by my love. But where was my liberty? Where was Aloyse? Where were you, Gabriel? I did not see the king every day, and Madame de Valentinois was cold and constrained with me, and seemed almost to avoid me, and I required love, Gabriel; therefore I suffered much that first year."

"Poor, dear Diana," said Gabriel.

"Thus," continued Diana, "while you fought, I languished. It is the general fate; the man acts and the woman waits, and it is much harder to wait than to act. At the end of that time the death of the Duc de Castro left me a widow, and the king sent me to pass my time of mourning in the Convent des Filles-Dieu. The pious and calm existence of the cloister suited me much better than the perpetual intrigues and turmoil of the court, therefore I asked and obtained permission to remain there. In the convent, at all events, they loved me, and the good Sister Monique reminded me of Aloyse. Then I was free to dream —of whom, and what, you guess, do you not?"

Gabriel replied with a passionate glance. Happily the play was an interesting one.

"Five years of peace and hope passed," continued Diana; "I had but one misfortune—that of losing Enguerrand. At

length, however, the king recalled me, and informed me
that I was destined to become the wife of Francis de Montmorency. I have resisted, Gabriel; I was no longer the
child who knew not what she was doing. But then my
father begged me, and showed me how much this marriage
was for the good of the kingdom. You had forgotten me
—it was the king that said so, Gabriel. And then, where
were you? In short, he begged so much, that yesterday—
only yesterday—I promised all he wished, only stipulating
for three months' delay, and that I should find out what
had become of you."

"You have promised?" cried Gabriel, turning pale.

"Yes; but then I had not seen you, and I did not know
that on that very day you would unexpectedly appear to
renew in me all my old feelings—you, handsome, prouder
than ever, yet still the same. Ah! I felt at once that my
promise to the king was worthless, and this marriage impossible—that my life belonged to you, and that if you loved
me still, I loved you forever."

"Ah! you are an angel, Diana."

"But, Gabriel, since fate has brought us together again,
let us consider the obstacles that we have to contend
against. The king is ambitious for his daughter, and the
Castros and Montmorencys will make him difficult to satisfy, alas!"

"Be easy on that point, Diana. The house to which I
belong is as noble as theirs, and it will not be the first time
that it has been allied to the royal family of France."

"Oh, Gabriel, I am so glad to hear that; I am very
ignorant, and do not know the name of Exmès. So long
as you are not a Montgommery—"

"And why not a Montgommery?" cried Gabriel.

"Oh, the Montgommerys have done some wrong to the
king, it appears, for he hates them."

"Really?" said Gabriel, with a sinking heart; "but is
it the Montgommerys who have injured the king, or the
king who has injured them?"

"My father is too good to have been unjust. "

"Good to you, Diana, but to his enemies ?"

"Terrible, perhaps. But never mind; what are the Montgommerys to us ?"

"If I were one, Diana ?"

"Oh! do not say so."

"But if I were ?"

"If it were so—if I found myself thus placed between my father and you, I would throw myself at the feet of the injured party, whoever he might be, and I would weep, and beg that my father should pardon you, or you my father, for my sake."

"And your voice is so powerful, Diana, that all would yield to it, unless, indeed, blood has been shed, for then only blood can wash away blood."

"Oh! you frighten me. But you are only trying me, are you not ?"

"Yes, Diana, that is all."

"And there is no hatred between my father and you ?"

"I trust not, Diana; I should suffer too much if I made you suffer."

"Then, Gabriel, I hope to obtain my father's promise that he will abandon this marriage, which would kill me. A powerful king, as he is, must surely be able to satisfy these Montmorencys."

"No. Diana, all his treasures and all the honors he could bestow cannot compensate for you."

"So you think, Gabriel; but, happily, Francis de Montmorency does not think so, and he would prefer a marshal's baton to your poor Diana. But, *mon Dieu!* the piece seems to be finished."

"Impossible! already. But you are right, here comes the epilogue."

"Happily, we have said what we wished to say."

"I have not said the thousandth part!"

"Nor I either. But, Gabriel, do not go and talk again to the queen."

"No, not if you do not wish it. But, alas! here is an end to the epilogue. Adieu, for a time, Diana; give me a last word to cheer me."

"*Au revoir*, my little husband," replied she, with a charming smile.

Gabriel disappeared quickly, so as to keep his promise of not speaking to the queen.

Passing into the vestibule, he met Martin Guerre awaiting him, resplendent in his new costume.

"Well, monseigneur, did you see Madame d'Angoulême?" he asked of his master, when they were in the street.

"Yes, I saw her," replied Gabriel.

"And does Madame d'Angoulême still care for the Viscount d'Exmès?" continued the squire, seeing that his master was in good humor.

"Rascal!" exclaimed Gabriel; "who gave you that information? Where did you find out that Madame de Castro cared for me, or, that I loved Madame de Castro alone? Be kind enough to hold your tongue, you rascal!"

"Ah," murmured Master Martin, "I must be right, or monseigneur would not have spoken so sharply to me; and monseigneur must really be in love, or he would have noticed my new costume."

"What did you say about a new costume? Oh, I see; you surely didn't have that doublet a short time ago, did you?"

"No, monseigneur; I purchased it this very evening, to do honor to my master and his mistress, and I paid for it, too—for I learned economy from my wife, Bertrande, just as she taught me temperance, purity, and all the virtues. So much I will say for her; and if I had only been able to give her a little of the milk of human kindness, we should indeed have been a happy couple."

"Well done, you rogue; and since you have gone to this expense on my account, I will see that you are repaid."

"Oh, monseigneur is indeed generous. But if he wishes me to keep his secret, he should give me this proof of his confidence in telling me whether his love is reciprocated. After all, one is never so generous as when the heart is full. Besides, monseigneur knows his servant, and that he is trustworthy, as silent and faithful as the sword he bears in monseigneur's service."

"Very good, Master Martin; but enough for the present."

"I leave monseigneur to his dreams."

And indeed Gabriel was dreaming to such an extent that, on arriving at his apartments, he felt a longing to confide his thoughts to a sympathetic ear, and so he wrote that same night to Aloyse, as follows:

MY GOOD ALOYSE—Diana loves me; but this is not what I ought to tell you first. Come to me, Aloyse: after six years of absence I desire to embrace you again. I am now captain of the King's Guards, one of the most coveted military appointments; and the name which I have made for myself will aid to re-establish the glory of the one which I received from my ancestors. I want you here to partake of my joy, for Diana loves me—my Diana—my old playmate, who has not forgotten her good Aloyse, although she calls the king "father." Yes, the daughter of the king and Madame de Valentinois, the widow of the Duc de Castro, loves still with all her heart her old friends. She has just told me so, and her sweet voice still vibrates in my ear.

CHAPTER XI

PEACE OR WAR

ON THE 7th of June the king held a council, and the Viscount d'Exmès, as captain of the guard, stood near the door with a drawn sword in his hand. All the interest of the council consisted, as usual, in the working of the ambitions of the houses of Guise and Montmorency, which were represented, on this occasion, by the Cardinal de Lorraine and the constable himself.

"Sire," said the cardinal, "the danger is pressing, the enemy is at our doors; a formidable army is organizing in Flanders, and at any moment Philip the Second may invade our territory, and his wife, Mary of England, declare war against us. Sire, you want a young, active, and enterprising general, who shall act boldly, and whose name alone shall be a terror to the Spaniards."

"Like your brother, of course," sneered the constable.

"Yes, like my brother," replied the cardinal, boldly; "like the conqueror at Metz and at Valenza. Yes, sire, you must recall the Duc de Guise, who, from want of means in Italy, has been forced to raise the siege of Civitella, and who will be invaluable to you here."

"Sire," said the constable, "recall the army, if you please, since this invasion of Italy has ended, as I predicted, in ridicule. But you do not want a general; all is still peaceful, and you can keep it so. It is not a general that you require, but a minister, who is not blinded by his passion for war, but who will consider the true interests of France."

"Like yourself, of course," cried the cardinal.

"Yes, like myself," replied Anne de Montmorency, proudly; "and I counsel the king not to think of a war which depends entirely on his own pleasure (for Philip the Second trembles before France, and his wife is silent), but to think of the peaceful interests of the kingdom, to which those who contribute are worth one hundred times more than any general."

"And deserve one hundred times more of the king, I suppose?"

"His Eminence perfectly expresses my thoughts, and I am going even now to ask his Majesty for a proof that my peaceful services have pleased him!"

"What is it?" asked the king, with a sigh.

"Sire, I beg your majesty to declare publicly the honor that you intend to do my house, in granting to my son the hand of Madame d'Angoulême."

Gabriel grew pale, and shuddered, but recovered himself a little on hearing the cardinal reply, "The bull of the pope, dissolving the marriage of Francis de Montmorency with Mademoiselle de Fiennes, has not yet arrived, and may not arrive at all."

"We will do without it, then," said the constable; "an edict can dissolve a clandestine marriage, and I beg his Majesty to grant me one, to prove to myself, and to those who attack me, his approbation of my views."

"Doubtless I can make such an edict," said the king, whose weakness of character was not proof against such firm language.

The constable looked triumphant; but at this moment a trumpet was heard, playing a foreign air. All looked at one another with astonishment. Then an usher entered, and announced that Sir Edward Fleming, a herald from England, solicited the honor of being admitted into the presence of his Majesty.

"Let him enter," said the king, surprised, but calm; while the dauphin and the princes drew nearer to the throne.

The herald entered, and bowing to the king, commenced,
"Mary, Queen of England, France, and Ireland, to Henry,
King of France. For having given encouragement to the
English Protestants, enemies of our religion and of our
State, and for having received them in France, and pre-
served them from the just pursuit instituted against them,
We, Mary of England, France, and Ireland, denounce war
by land and by sea against Henry of France; in token of
which, I, Edward Fleming, herald, throw down my
glove."

At a gesture from the king, the Viscount d'Exmès
picked up the glove; then Henry said, simply and coldly,
to the herald, "I thank you, you may retire."

The herald bowed, and obeyed. The sound of the English trumpets was heard once more, then all was quiet.

At last the king broke the silence by saying, "My
cousin of Montmorency, it seems to me that you were
rather hasty in promising us peace, and the good intentions of Queen Mary. This protection of the Protestants
is a mere pretext; however, a King of France does not fear
war, and if Flanders lets us alone for a little time— Well!
what is it now, Florimel?"

"Sire," said the usher, "a courier from the Governor of
Picardy has arrived with special despatches."

"Go and see what they are, M. le Cardinal, I beg of
you," said Henry.

The cardinal soon returned with the despatches, which
he laid before the king. "Ah, gentlemen," cried he, after
glancing over them, "here is more news. The armies of
Philip the Second are uniting at Givet, and M. Gaspard de
Coligny sends us word that the Duke of Savoy is at their
head—a worthy enemy. Your nephew, M. de Montmorency, thinks that the Spanish troops are about to attack
Mézières and Rocroy; he demands instant reinforcements
to enable him to garrison these places, and make head
against our enemies. You were not happy in your predictions to-day. Mary of England was quiet, you said, Philip

afraid of us, and the frontiers quiet. M. de Lorraine, write to your brother to return at once; as to family affairs, we must adjourn them, and we can well wait for the dispensation from the pope, to celebrate the marriage of Madame d'Angoulême. The sitting is over for the present, gentlemen, but we will meet again to-night. Adieu! until then, and may God protect France."

"God save the king!" cried with one voice the members of the council. They then dispersed.

CHAPTER XII

A TWOFOLD ROGUE

THE constable returned home in a very bad humor; he was met there by his squire, Arnold du Thill, who had come to speak to him.

"I am not in the humor to speak to you just now, Arnold," said the constable.

"Oh! I know, monsieur; you are annoyed at the turn that matters have taken about the marriage, but you know that the king's humor may change to-morrow. There is, however, a far more formidable obstacle in Madame d'Angoulême herself."

"Ah! what do you know about her?"

"How does monseigneur think that I have spent my time this last fortnight?"

"Well, it is true that I have heard nothing of you lately—you, of whom there was some complaint every evening."

"Yes; but it is now Martin Guerre to whom this is transferred. It is he who was picked up drunk by the watch; and it is he who was accused of attempting to carry off the wife of M. Gorju, the ironmonger."

"Yes," said the constable, laughing; "and his master defends him, and says that he has been always the quietest and best-behaved of squires."

"He believes himself possessed of the devil."

"But what of Madame d'Angoulême?"

"Why, monseigneur, I have but to put on a certain

brown and yellow suit, and the Viscount d'Exmès speaks to me in the most confidential manner; and who do you think the viscount is?"

"*Parbleu!* a frantic partisan of the Guises."

"More than that—the favored lover of Madame d'Angoulême."

"What the devil do you mean? What do you know about it?"

"I am in the viscount's confidence, as I told you before; I am the one who usually carries his notes to his mistress, and brings back the replies. I am good friends with the duchess's maid, who is astonished only at having so changeable an admirer—impertinent as a page one day, and the next as retiring as a nun. Madame de Castro and M. d'Exmès meet three times a week at the queen's levees, but write to each other every day. But you may believe me, their love is an absolutely upright one. Indeed, I should love to help them, except that I value my own interests more. They love each other like cherubs, as indeed they have from childhood, I understand. Occasionally I have taken the liberty of opening their letters, and they have really touched me. Madame Diana is jealous; and of whom do you suppose? Of the queen! But she is quite wrong, poor child; it is indeed quite possible that the queen may think about M. d'Exmès."

"Arnold," exclaimed the constable, "what a slanderer you are!"

"But your smile is quite as slanderous as my words," returned the rogue. "I was going on to say that while it was quite possible for the queen to be thinking about the viscount, it is certainly sure that the viscount is not in love with the queen. The affection of Gabriel and Diana is of Arcadian simplicity and purity; it touches me like a sweet pastoral of old Rome or of the age of chivalry; and yet God knows it does not keep me from betraying them for the sum of fifty pistoles, the poor little turtledoves. But acknowledge, monseigneur, that I was right when I said that I had really earned these same fifty pistoles."

"Quite true," returned the constable; "but once more, I demand to know how you come to be so well informed."

"Ah, excuse me, monseigneur; that is my secret, which you may endeavor to make out if you like, but which I shall certainly not disclose. Besides, my method and means of information are of no importance to you (for, after all, I alone am responsible for them), providing that you only attain your object. Now, your object is to find out about all proceedings and plans which may do you injury; and it really seems to me as if the news that I have brought you to-day were not unimportant, and indeed that it may be of great assistance to you."

"Without doubt, you rascal; but you must not stop playing the spy on this cursed D'Exmès."

"By no means, monseigneur; believe me, I am fully as devoted to you as I am to wrong-doing. You will give me your pistoles, and I will give you my information, and we shall both be satisfied. Ah, is there not some one there in the gallery? A woman! The devil! I must bid you good-by, monseigneur."

"Who may it be?" asked the constable, who was somewhat near-sighted.

"Good heavens! it is Madame de Castro herself, who, without doubt, is going to join the king; it is of importance that she should not see us together, sire, although, indeed, she would hardly know me in this costume. She seems to be coming this way, and so I must go."

And he escaped in the opposite direction.

The constable hesitated a moment; then, deciding to make sure of the accuracy of the spy's report, he coolly advanced to meet Madame d'Angouleme.

"Were you going to the king's cabinet, madame?" asked he.

"I was, M. le Connétable."

"I have much fear that you will hardly find his Majesty

ready to converse with you," remarked Montmorency, somewhat alarmed; "he has just received very serious news."

"Which may make this the most opportune moment for me, monsieur."

"And a very bad one for me, madame, if I am not mistaken, for you certainly hate us bitterly."

"Ah, monsieur, I am sure I hate nobody in the whole world."

"Is your heart then kept by nothing save love?" asked De Montmorency, in so significant a tone that Diana turned red and dropped her eyes. "And I suppose it is on account of this love that you oppose the king's wishes, and therefore my son's hopes?"

Diana kept silent in her embarrassment.

"Arnold has spoken the truth," thought the constable; "without doubt she does love this messenger of M. de Guise's triumph."

At last Diana said, "Monsieur, my duty bids me obey the king, but still allows me to entreat my father."

"And so," said the constable, "you persist in going to the king."

"Without doubt."

"Very well, madame; in that case I shall go and see Madame de Valentinois."

"As you please, monsieur," she replied.

They exchanged bows, and left the gallery by opposite doors; and as Diana entered the cabinet of the king, the old constable passed the threshold of the favorite's apartments.

CHAPTER XIII

THE HEIGHT OF HAPPINESS

"MARTIN," said Gabriel, the same day to his squire, "take this letter, and bring back an answer as soon as possible."

"Yes, monsieur; but I have a favor to beg; pray send some one to take care of me."

"Why, what new folly is this? Of what are you afraid?"

"Of myself, monsieur," cried Martin, piteously. "It seems that I have all at once become a drunkard and a gambler; and now, monsieur, they declare that last night I attempted to carry off the wife of M. Gorju, the ironmonger."

"Come, Martin, you are dreaming; but stay, did you do this?"

"Dreaming, monsieur! here is the report; and, in reading it, I am overwhelmed with shame. I used to think that the devil amused himself by taking my form in which to play these nocturnal pranks, but you say that that is impossible; so I begin to think that I am sometimes possessed of an evil spirit."

"No, my poor Martin," said Gabriel, laughing; "only you give way to drinking sometimes, and then it seems you see double."

"But, monsieur, I only drink water."

"And yet, Martin, you were found drunk."

"Monsieur, that night I went to bed early, after saying

my prayers, and I awoke in it the next morning; and it was only later that I learned what I had been doing all night."

"Well, Martin, I cannot give you any companion, for you alone know our secret."

"Then, monsieur, I will do my best; but I cannot answer for myself."

"Oh, nonsense! go, and remember that on this note depends my happiness or despair."

Martin replied with a sigh, and went out. Two hours after he returned with the answer. Gabriel took it, and read: "Let us thank God, Gabriel, the king has yielded, and we shall be happy. You already know of the arrival of the herald from England, who came to declare war in the name of Queen Mary, and the news of the great movement which is preparing in Flanders. These events, menacing, perhaps, for France, are favorable for our love, since they augment the power of the Duc de Guise, and diminish that of Montmorency. Still, however, the king hesitated; but I prayed, Gabriel—I said that I had found you again, that you were noble and valiant, and I named you. The king, without promising anything, said he would reflect, and that after all, the interests of the State becoming less pressing, it would be cruel for him to sacrifice my happiness; that he could give to Francis de Montmorency a compensation with which he ought to be satisfied. He has promised nothing, but he will do all. Oh! you will love him, Gabriel, as I do; this good father will realize all our dreams. I have so much to say to you, and written words are so cold! Come to me this evening at six o'clock; during the council Jacinthe will bring you to me, and we shall have a whole hour to talk over our happy future. However, I foresee that this campaign will call you away, and, alas! you must go to serve my father and deserve me, Gabriel—me, who love you so much—for I do love you. Why should I try to hide it? Come, then, and let me see if you are as happy as your Diana."

"Oh, yes, indescribably happy," cried Gabriel; "what can now be wanting to my happiness?"

"Doubtless not the presence of your old nurse," said Aloyse, who had entered while he was reading.

"Aloyse!" cried Gabriel, running toward her, and embracing her. "Oh, yes, good nurse, I wanted you. How are you? You are not changed; neither am I—in heart, at least; but why have you been so long in coming?"

"The late rains, monsieur, have flooded the roads, but your letters made me brave all obstacles—"

"Oh, you are right, Aloyse, because I want some one to rejoice with me. Do you see this letter? it is from Diana—from your other child—and she announces to me that all the obstacles to our marriage are removed, and that she loves me. Am I not at the summit of happiness?"

"And yet, monsieur, if it were necessary to renounce Diana?" said Aloyse, in a grave, sad tone.

"Impossible, Aloyse! besides, I tell you that all difficulties have been overcome."

"One may conquer the difficulties which proceed from man, but not those from God," replied the nurse. "You know that I love you, and would give my life to spare you pain. Well, if I said to you, without asking the reason, 'Monsieur, renounce Diana, cease to see her, stifle your love by every means in your power; a terrible secret, into which I implore you not to inquire, lies between you'—if I said this to you, supplicating you on my knees, what would you say?"

"Aloyse, if it were my life you asked for, you should have it, but my love is beyond my power; but you terrify me, nurse. Do not keep me in this horrible suspense, but whatever you have, and ought, to say to me, say at once, I entreat."

"You wish it, monsieur? Must I reveal to you the secret which I had sworn to keep from you? Yet God himself seems now to order me to disclose it. But, monsieur, are you not deceived in the nature of your affection for Diana?''

''No, Aloyse, certainly not; and her beauty—''

''Oh, it must be so; for, according to all probability, Diana is your sister.''

''Diana, my sister!'' cried Gabriel, springing up. ''How can the daughter of the king and of Madame de Valentinois be my sister?''

''Monsieur, Diana was born in May, 1539. Your father disappeared in the January of the same year; and do you know of what he was suspected, and of what they accused him? Of being the favored lover of Diana of Poitiers, and the rival of the dauphin, now King of France. Now compare the dates, monsieur.''

''Heavens and earth!'' cried Gabriel; ''but let me see,'' said he, trying to collect his thoughts. ''My father was accused—who knows that it was true? Diana was born five months after the death of my father, but what proves that she is not the daughter of the king? He loves her as his child.''

''The king may be deceived, or I may be wrong. I do not say that Diana is your sister; I only say that it is probable. My terrible duty was to tell you this, Gabriel. Say, was it not? You would not have renounced her unless I had done so; but now your conscience must judge your love.''

''Oh, but this doubt is a thousand times worse than misfortune itself. *Mon Dieu!* who will teach me the truth?''

''The secret was known to only two people in the world —your father, and Madame de Valentinois; and she will never confess that she has deceived the king, and that Diana is not his child.''

''And at least, then, if I do not love my sister, I love the daughter of my father's murderer; for it was the dauphin, was it not, Aloyse?''

''No one knows that but God.''

"Everywhere confusion, doubt, and terror," cried Gabriel. "Oh, I shall go mad!—but stay, I will go to Madame de Valentinois; I will swear to her that her secret shall be safe; I will go to the queen, who may know something; I will go to Diana, and interrogate the feelings of my heart."

"Poor child!" said Aloyse.

"And I will not lose a minute," continued he, rising. "Perhaps, before I return, I may have lifted the veil."

"Can I do nothing for you?"

"Pray for me, Aloyse," said Gabriel, gloomily, as he left the room.

CHAPTER XIV

DIANA OF POITIERS

THE constable was still with Diana of Poitiers, and was speaking to her in a tone as rude and imperious as hers to him was gentle and mild.

"Eh, *mordieu!* she is your daughter," cried he, "and you have the same right over her as the king. Exact this marriage."

"But, my friend, you know that we have always been cold to each other, and see each other but seldom. She has gained, besides, so strong an influence over the king that I scarcely know now whether she or I be the more powerful. Leave alone this marriage, which presents so many difficulties, and replace it by one still more brilliant. We will obtain from the king the hand of the little Princess Marguerite for your son."

"My son sleeps in a bed, and not in a cradle," replied he; "and a little girl who can hardly speak cannot aid the fortunes of my house. It is just because your daughter has so much influence with the king that I desire the match, and I will have it in spite of every one."

"Well, I will do my best for you, if you will but be more gentle with me."

And the beautiful duchess touched the old constable's grizzled beard lightly with her red lips.

For of such nature was this peculiar affection, inexplicable, except on the theory of common depravity, which the adored favorite of a handsome young king felt for an old man who used her but roughly. The constable's brutality served as a foil for the caresses of Henry, and she took more pleasure in being ill-treated by the one, than in being made love to by the other. Strange caprice of woman's heart! Anne de Montmorency was neither brilliant nor particularly clever; and he was said to be covetous and even stingy. His name was hated on account of the severity of the punishments which he had inflicted upon the rebellious population of Bordeaux. Brave man, without doubt; but that quality is a common one in France, and up to this time he had almost invariably been unfortunate in the results of his battles. At Ravenna and Marignan, where he had held a subordinate command, he did not particularly distinguish himself; at Bicoque, where he commanded the Swiss Guards, he had allowed his regiment to be nearly cut to pieces; later, at Pavia, he was taken prisoner. Saint Laurent had made a miserable ending of a military career which had never been celebrated. He certainly would never have risen above second place in the council of the king, any more than in the army, had he not enjoyed the favor of Henry the Second, which was, no doubt, inspired by Diana de Poitiers. In spite of all this, Diana loved and petted him, and obeyed him in nearly everything, thus being the handsome young king's favorite and the laughable old man's slave.

At that moment some one knocked at the door, and announced that the Viscount d'Exmès begged for an audience of the duchess.

"The lover!" cried the constable. "Does he come to ask for the hand of your daughter, I wonder?"

"Shall I admit him?" asked the duchess, docilely.

"Certainly, in a few minutes; but first listen to me. If he comes to you, it is probably because he is in some difficulty; therefore refuse him everything he asks. If he wishes you to say yes, say no; be disdainful and implacable. Do you understand? and will you do it?"

"In every way, my dear constable."

"Good! In that case I think the young fellow's threads will get pretty well tangled up. Poor fool, to walk like this right into the jaws of the—" he was going to say, "she-wolf," but interrupted himself in time—"into the jaws of the wolves. I leave him to you, Diana; see that you take good care of this good-looking claimant. We meet again this evening."

He kissed Diana's forehead and went out, while Gabriel entered by another door.

He saluted Diana in the most respectful manner, but she replied with merely a nod. In spite of this, however, Gabriel, girding himself up for this unequal contest of burning passion against icy vanity, began serenely thus—

"Madame, the step which I have dared to take is a bold one, without doubt, and you may consider it even a mad one; but often in one's lifetime facts come to light of such serious importance as to lift us above ordinary convention-alities and scruples. I am at this moment standing, ma-dame, before one of these terrible crises in my destiny. I, who am now speaking to you, come hither to put my life in your hands; and if you let it fall, it will be forever destroyed."

Madame de Valentinois did not give the least sign of encouragement, but bending forward, and resting her elbow upon her knee, she looked at Gabriel with an expression mingled with tedium.

"Madame," continued he, trying to shake off the influ-ence of this affected silence, "you know, or do not know, perhaps, that I love Madame de Castro. I love her, ma-dame, with a profound, ardent, and irresistible love."

Diana gave a nonchalant smile.

"I speak of this love which fills my soul," continued Gabriel, "to show that I understand every effect of love and passion. Love to me is sacred, as it is all-powerful. Were the husband of Madame de Castro still alive, I should love her equally; I should not even try to overcome it—it

is only a fictitious love that can be conquered. Thus, madame, you yourself, chosen and loved by the greatest king
in the world, may not on that account have been sheltered
from the influence of sincere passion, and may not have
been able to resist it. A king is enamored, and no wonder,
of your admirable beauty; you are touched by this love,
but your heart cannot always respond to it. A gentleman,
handsome, brave, and devoted, sees you, loves you, and
this more obscure, but not less real passion, enters your
heart, when the king's fails to do so. It is not a title that
gains a heart. What could prevent you from having one
day in your generous good faith preferred the subject to
the monarch? It is not I, at least, who could make it a
crime in Diana of Poitiers, that being loved by Henry the
Second, she loved the Comte de Montgommery."

Diana started up, astonished; so few people knew that
secret.

"Have you proofs of this alleged love?" asked she,
uneasily.

"Only a moral certainty, madame, but that I have."

"Ah!" said she, recovering her insolent assurance,
"well, I do not mind confessing that I did love the Comte
de Montgommery. What then?"

"And I doubt not that you still love his memory; for,
if he has disappeared from this world, it was for you. It
is, then, in his name I come to you, and ask you a question
which will appear very bold, no doubt; but your answer,
if you will be good enough to give it, will fill me with
gratitude, for on this answer depends my life. If you do
not refuse me, I shall be devoted to you, body and soul;
and a devoted heart and arm are useful, even to the highest, madame."

"Finish, monsieur, and let us come to this terrible
question."

Gabriel knelt before her, and went on. "Madame, it
was in the year 1538 that you loved Jacques de Montgommery, was it not?"

"It is possible."

"It was in January, 1539, that he disappeared, and in May, 1539, that Madame de Castro was born."

"Well, what then?"

"Well, madame, this is the secret, which I come to implore of you on my knees—the secret on which my fate depends, and which I swear shall die in my bosom if you confide it to me. Madame, was the Count de Montgommery the father of Madame de Castro?"

"Ha! ha!" laughed Diana, disdainfully, "the question is bold, indeed, and you were right to preface it with so many preambles; however, you interest me, as an enigma, for what can it matter to you, whether she be the daughter of the king, or of the count? The king passes for her father; that should content you if you are ambitious."

"I have a very strong reason, madame, but I beg you not to ask for it."

"Oh, you want my secrets, and you keep your own. A good bargain, truly."

Gabriel took the ivory crucifix that hung over the *prie Dieu* behind him: "On your eternal salvation, madame, swear not to reveal the secret which I am about to confide to you, and not to use it against me."

"Such an oath!" cried Diana.

"Yes, madame, for if you swear that, I know you will keep it."

"And if I refuse to swear?"

"I must be silent, madame, and you will have refused me my life."

"Do you know, monsieur, that you pique my woman's curiosity strongly? If I swear, it is from pure curiosity, I warn you."

"I also, madame, wish to know; only I wait for my answer as a man waits for his sentence of death. Will you swear, madame?"

"Say the words, and I will repeat them;" and after him she repeated, "On my eternal salvation I swear never to reveal to any one the secret you are about to confide to me, and to act as though I were ignorant of it."

"Madame," said Gabriel, "I thank you for this first condescension. You will understand all when I tell you that I am the son of Jacques de Montgommery."

"His son?"

"Yes; so that, if she be his daughter, she whom I love with a mad passion is my sister."

"Ah," thought Diana, "this saves the constable."

"Now, madame, will you do me the favor of swearing on this crucifix that Madame de Castro is the daughter of the king? You do not reply, madame."

"Because I cannot pronounce this oath, monsieur."

"Ah, *mon Dieu! mon Dieu!*" cried Gabriel, "then she is my sister."

"No, monsieur, I will never confess that she is the daughter of any one but the king."

"Oh, truly, madame, how good you are! But pardon me, your interest in me may induce you to speak thus. Swear, madame, and your child will bless you."

"I will not swear, monsieur; why should I?"

"But, madame, you swore just now, to satisfy simple curiosity; and when it concerns a man's whole destiny— indeed two destinies—you hesitate."

"Well, monsieur, I will not swear," said Diana, coldly and resolutely.

"And if, nevertheless, I marry Madame de Castro, and she be my sister, will not the crime be upon your head?"

"No, as I have not sworn."

"Horrible!" cried Gabriel; "but think, then, madame, that I can proclaim everywhere that you loved the Comte de Montgommery, and that you had deceived the king."

"You have no proofs," replied she, with her cruel smile. "I should deny it, monsieur, and who would believe you? But, pardon me," continued she, rising, "I am obliged to leave you, monsieur; you have really interested me much, and your history is a singular one." So saying, she rang the bell.

"It is infamous!" cried Gabriel. "Oh! why are you a woman? But take care, nevertheless, madame, you will not play with my heart and life with impunity; God will punish you and avenge me."

"You think so," replied she, with her mocking laugh. At this moment the page whom she had summoned lifted the tapestry. She bowed ironically to Gabriel, and left the room. Gabriel retired, mad with rage and grief.

CHAPTER XV

CATHERINE DE MÉDICIS

BUT Gabriel was steady, of heart and full of resolution. After his first consternation had abated, he made an effort to shake off his melancholy, and lifting high his head once more, he went to request an audience with the queen.

Without doubt Catherine de Médicis was not a complete stranger to the mysterious tragedy in which the names of her royal husband and the Count de Montgommery were coupled; indeed, who can know whether she herself had not played a part in it. At that time she had hardly passed the age of twenty. Is it reasonable to suppose that the jealousy of a beautiful but deserted young wife would have allowed her to keep her eyes shut to the acts of her rival? Gabriel hoped that her memory would throw light upon the obscurity of the path along which he was groping his way, and which he so devoutly hoped, both as lover and as son, and for the sake of his happiness or of his revenge, to have illuminated.

Catherine received the viscount with that ostentatious kindness which she had never failed to show him.

"It is you, then, my comely king of the tournament?" said she. "To what happy chance am I indebted for this visit? You do not often honor us, M. d'Exmès; indeed, if I am not mistaken, this is the first time you have sought an audience of us in our apartments. But do not forget that you are now and always will be welcome here."

"Madame," replied Gabriel, "I have no words to thank you sufficiently for your kindness; I assure you that my devotion—"

"Speak not of your devotion," interrupted the queen; "but let us return to the subject which brings you hither. Is there any way in which I can serve you?"

"Indeed, madame, I think there is."

"All the better, viscount," replied Catherine, smiling most charmingly; "and if what you ask me is not beyond my power, I promise it beforehand. This may seem a good deal to grant, perhaps, but I know that the Viscount d'Exmès is not capable of abusing the confidence of his queen."

"God forbid, madame! Such is far from my intention."

"Proceed then, and let me know," said the queen, with a sigh.

"I venture to ask of you, madame, but a little information, nothing more; but this little is to me everything. You will then pardon me for calling to mind memories which may not be pleasant to your Majesty; they relate to an event which happened in 1539."

"Ah, me, I was very young then—hardly more than a child," said the queen.

"But already beautiful and most surely worthy of devotion," answered Gabriel.

"There were those who said so," mused the queen, pleased at the direction in which the conversation was proceeding.

"But, in spite of this," resumed Gabriel, "there was another woman who ventured to interfere upon the rights which were yours from God, and by your own birth and beauty; and not content with alluring from your side, by enchantment, no doubt, the eyes and the heart of a husband too young to weigh carefully his acts, this woman played the traitor to him who had betrayed you, and was the mistress of the Count de Montgommery. Doubtless, however, madame, in your just contempt you have forgotten all this.''

"No,'' replied the queen; "and this incident, with all its ramifications of intrigue, is still clear to my recollection. Yes, she loved the Count de Montgommery; and afterward, finding that her passion was discovered, she pretended that it was a mere ruse to put to the proof the dauphin's love for her; and when poor Montgommery disappeared, per- haps by her own machinations, instead of weeping for him she appeared the next evening at a ball gay with laughter. Ah, indeed, I shall not easily forget the means with which this woman destroyed my new-found power; for at that time it made me unhappy, and my days and nights were passed in tears; but my pride soon came to my assistance. I have never failed in my duty. I have compelled by the dignity of my conduct unfailing respect for myself as wife, mother, and as queen. I have given the king of France seven children; but I love my husband now only with a kind of affectionate serenity as a friend and as the father of my children, and 1 no longer acknowledge any right of his tenderer than this. I have devoted my existence long enough to the good of my people. May I not then indulge my own self a little? Have I not paid a sufficient price for my happiness? If some young and burning passion should be offered to me, would it be wrong in me not to put it away, Gabriel?''

Catherine's expression was at one with her words; but Gabriel's thoughts were far away. As soon as the queen ceased speaking of his sire, he had ceased to give atten- tion, and was lost in thought—a revery which Catherine interpreted as favorable to her wishes. At last Gabriel spoke.

"One thing more, and the most serious,'' said he. "You are kindness itself to me; I was sure that I should receive satisfaction if I came to you. You speak of devotion, ma- dame; you may rest assured of mine to you. But proceed, I beg you, in the name of Heaven, as you are acquainted

with this tragic event in the life of the Count de Montgommery; can you tell me whether there was ever any doubt
that Madame de Castro, who was born some months after
the disappearance of the count, was really the king's
daughter? Did not calumny allow the suspicion to be
disseminated that M. de Montgommery was the father of
Diana?''

Catherine de Médicis regarded Gabriel for some moments in silence, as if to discover the feeling which had
inspired his words. Thinking that she had found it, she
smiled.

"It has not escaped me," she said, "that you have been
attracted by Madame de Castro; in fact, that you have been
paying your court to her. Your motive is now open to
me; only, before you go further, you wish to assure yourself that you are not upon a false scent, and that it is really
a king's daughter before whom you are kneeling, is it not
so? You do not wish, after becoming the husband of the
legitimatized daughter of Henry the Second, to wake up
some fine day to the fact that your wife is the illegitimate
child of the Count de Montgommery. In one word, M.
d'Exmès, you are ambitious. Nay, protest not, for it only
raises you higher in my esteem, and moreover it may help
you rather than hurt you, so far as I am concerned. Now,
tell me you are ambitious; is it not so?''

"Madame," replied Gabriel, embarrassed, "it may seem
like that—"

"Excellent! you see I have divined your secret, young
man," exclaimed the queen. "Very well, then, will you
take the advice of a friend in your own interest? I counsel you to give up your ambition in regard to Diana; think
no more of this doll-faced hussy. To tell you the truth, I
really cannot tell whose daughter she is—whether of the
king, or of the count. The last supposition is as likely to
be true as the first. But even if she is the child of the
king, she is not the woman or the support that you need.
Madame d'Angouleme is a weak and easily turned nature;

she is full of life and grace, if you like, but she has no energy or courage. I admit that she has won the heart of the king, but she is not clever enough to take advantage of that. What is necessary for you, to realize the noble ambitions which fill your soul, is this strong and coura geous spirit which will help you even as it loves you, which will cleave to you even as you do to it, and which will fill both your heart and your life. Such a spirit, viscount, you have chanced upon even unawares.''

Gabriel gazed at her in utter astonishment, but Catherine continued in the warmth of her eloquence:

"Listen to me; we queens are, on account of the loyalty of our station, removed from the strict observance of the proprieties to which others are the slaves; and if we wish to indulge ourselves in the affection of one of our subjects, we ourselves must take the first steps to extend the hand of invitation. Gabriel, you are handsome, brave, and proud. Ever since first I saw you I have felt toward you a strange sentiment; and I trust that I do not err, when I say that your words, your looks, yes, and even the seeking of this audience to-day—all combine to strengthen in me the belief that I am not dealing with one capable of ingratitude.''

"Madame!" exclaimed Gabriel, whose astonishment changed to alarm.

"Ah, I see that you are touched, and even somewhat surprised," continued Catherine, with her most fascinating smile; "but I trust that you do not judge me harshly on account of my openness. I repeat that the queen excuses the woman. In spite of your ambition, M. d'Exmès, you are bashful; and if I had been kept back by principles which rule the common herd, I might have had to give up forever a devotion which is most dear to me. I therefore chose to be the first to speak. Very well, then, am I so very terrible to look upon?''

"Ah, yes!" exclaimed Gabriel, pale and trembling; but the queen quite misunderstood his exclamation.

"Ah, well," said she, playfully, pretending to control

herself, "I have not yet dazzled you to the extent of making you blind to your own interests, as you have shown by the questions you have asked me regarding Madame d'Angouleme. Be assured, however, that I do not desire to injure you, but rather to elevate you. Up till the present time, Gabriel, I have contented myself with remaining in the second rank; but, believe me, I shall soon take my rightful place in the first. Diana de Poitiers is no longer young enough to rule by the virtue of her purity or her spirit. On the day that this creature's prestige begins to wane, my rule will begin; and, believe me, Gabriel, when I say that I shall know well how to reign. I am assured of this by the instincts of sovereignty, which I feel within me, and besides it is in the blood of the Médicis. Some day the king will discover that he has no better counsellor than his wife, and when that moment arrives, Gabriel, to what elevation may not that man aspire who, when I was yet obscure, linked his fortune with mine; who loved in me not the queen, but the woman? Will not the sovereign mistress of the whole kingdom be in a position to reward worthily him who devoted himself to her—will not this man be her second being, her right arm—the true king with only the shadow of the other monarch behind him? Will he not hold in his power all the magnificence and all the influence of France? A beautiful dream, do you not find it so, Gabriel? Well, then, will you be that man?" and boldly she held out her hand to him.

Gabriel fell upon his knees and kissed the lovely white hand; but he was too open and honest to allow himself to be blinded by the tricks of a simulated affection; he was too courageous and too frank to hesitate for a moment between danger and deception, and raising his handsome head, he said—

"Madame, the humble gentleman who kneels at your feet asks you to look upon him as your most devoted servant and your most obedient subject; but—"

"But," said Catherine, with a smile, "these are not

the formal terms which I ask of you, my handsome cavalier."

"But, nevertheless, madame," continued Gabriel, "to you I cannot use words of more tender and affectionate import; for, and I ask you to pardon me, the one whom I tenderly loved, before my eyes ever had the happiness to rest upon my queen, is Diana de Castro; and no passion, not even that of a queen, can ever enter into this heart already occupied with the image of another."

"Ah!" cried Catherine, turning pale, and pressing her lips together.

Gabriel, with eyes cast down, waited calmly and courageously for the storm of wrath and indignation to break over him. Wrath and indignation are not usually long in coming, and in a few moments Catherine began.

"Do you know, Viscount d'Exmès," said she, in a voice trembling with anger, "do you know that I consider your words bold, to say the least? Who spoke of love to you, monsieur, and how do you happen upon the idea that I was playing the temptress with you? Your own qualities must occupy a most excellent place in your opinion, that you should dare to think of such things, and to give such a meaning to my kindness of heart, the only mistake of which was its bestowal upon an unworthy ingrate. Monsieur, you have insulted both a woman and a queen."

"Oh, your Majesty," replied Gabriel, "I beg you to believe that a veneration even religious—"

"Enough," interrupted Catherine; "I understand now not only that you have insulted me, but that you came here for that very purpose. Why, then, are you here? what purpose did you harbor? What is your love for Madame de Castro, or any of your affairs to me? Information you would have of me—ridiculous pretext! You dared to make the queen of France the confidante of your love affairs. It is impudent, I say; and worse than that, it is an outrage!"

"No, madame," replied Gabriel, raising himself proudly

to his full height, "it is no outrage to choose to wound rather than to deceive."

"Silence, monsieur! you hold your peace and retire; and fortunate you may consider yourself if I do not discover to the king your outrageous audacity. Never come again before my eyes, and look upon Catherine de Médicis henceforth as your implacable enemy. We shall meet again, be sure of that, M. d'Exmès. Now, leave me!"

Saluting the queen respectfully, Gabriel retired without a word.

"One more enemy," reflected he, when alone again; "but that would make little difference if I had only discovered something in regard to my father and Diana. To be hated by both the king's wife and the king's favorite! who knows but what fate may soon turn the king himself against me? But now to Diana, for the time has come; and Heaven grant that I may not leave her who loves me more desolate and despairing than I am now on leaving those who hate me!"

CHAPTER XVI

LOVER OR BROTHER

WHEN Jacinthe introduced Gabriel into the room which Madame de Castro occupied at the Louvre, she ran joyfully to meet him. "Here you are at last!" she cried; "I have waited for you so impatiently, for I want you to share my happiness. I have been talking and laughing all alone, but now we can be happy together; but what is the matter, Gabriel? You look cold and grave, and almost sad; is it thus that you show your love to me, and your gratitude to my father?"

"To your father—yes; let us speak of your father, Diana. As to this gravity that so astonishes you, it is my habit so to receive the good gifts of fortune, for I always fear them. I have been so little accustomed to them, and they often precede misfortune."

"I did not know that you were either so unlucky or so philosophical, Gabriel," replied the young girl, half amused and half piqued. "But, as you say, let us speak of the king; has he not been good and kind?"

"Yes, Diana; he loves you well, does he not?"

"With an infinite goodness and tenderness."

"Doubtless," murmured Gabriel to himself, "he believes her to be his daughter." Then aloud he said, "There is one thing that astonishes me, and that is, that he should leave you for twelve years without knowing or seeing you. Have you ever spoken to him of it, Diana?"

"Oh, yes; but it was not his doing."

"Whose, then?"

"Why, Madame de Valentinois, my mother."

"And why did she do that, Diana? Did not your birth give her a greater right to the love of the king? What had she to fear? Her husband was dead, and her father also."

"Indeed, Gabriel, I cannot explain the pride which keeps her from recognizing me as her child. She did her best to keep the king from acknowledging me, and refused to the last to be named in the act of legitimation. She seems to have a kind of aversion to me."

"An aversion which may be remorse," thought Gabriel, "if she knows that she has betrayed the king."

"But what are you thinking of, Gabriel, and why do you ask me these questions?"

"For no reason—a doubt of my unquiet spirit. But you love the king—you find in him a real father?"

"Oh, certainly; I felt drawn toward him at once. I love him—not as the king, not as my benefactor, but as my father."

"These instincts cannot deceive," thought Gabriel, joyfully, and he said, "It makes me very happy, Diana, to see you love your father so much."

"But now, Gabriel, let us speak of ourselves if you please."

"Yes, yes," cried Gabriel, "let us think of this attachment, which binds us for life to each other; let us look into each other's hearts. Tell me, Diana, what do you feel for me? Do you not love me less than your father?"

"Jealous!" cried she. "You know that I love you differently, and it is easy to explain it. When the king is here I am happy but calm, and my heart beats no quicker than usual; but when I see you a singular agitation seizes me. I say to my father, before every one, all the caressing things I can think of; but to you, Gabriel, I feel as though I should not have the courage to do so even when I am your wife. In a word, when my father is near all my pleasure is peaceful; and while you are present it is troubled—almost painful."

"Oh, hush!" cried Gabriel, "you love me, and that frightens me, and at the same time reassures me. God would not have permitted this love if it were not right."

"What do you mean, Gabriel? Why does the avowal which I have now the right to make trouble you?´ What danger can there be?"

"None, dear Diana, none. Do not mind what I say; it is joy that makes me act thus strangely. Too much happiness bewilders me. But you did not always love me as you do now; when we used to walk together in the woods at Vimoutiers you only felt the affection of a sister for me."

"I was a child then, Gabriel. I had not then dreamed of you during six years of solitude, and I had not lived for two months in the shadow of a court where ·the corruption of language and manners has made me cherish still more our holy and pure passion."

"Is it true, Diana?"

"But you, Gabriel, in your turn, open your heart, as I have mine. If my words have pleased you, let me also hear how you love me."

"I cannot tell you that," cried Gabriel. "Do not ask me to interrogate myself, it is too frightful!"

"Oh, Gabriel!" cried Diana, in terror, "it is your words that are frightful! What! can you not even tell me that you love me?"

"If I love you, Diana! You ask me if I love you? Yes, I love you like a madman—like a criminal, perhaps."

"Like a criminal! What crime can there be in our love? Are we not both free? Does not my father consent? What can be the matter with you, Gabriel; are you ill? Whence come these fears to you, who are generally so firm and strong? I am never afraid when near you; 1 trust you as I would my father. See, I do not fear you," and she approached nearer to him and laid her hand on his shoulder.

Gabriel repulsed her with terror. "No, no; go!" he cried; "leave me!"

"Oh, *mon Dieu!*" cried she, drawing back, "he repulses me—he does not love me!"

"I love you too much."

"If you loved me, would my caresses horrify you?"

"Do they horrify me? Is it indeed my instinct that makes me repulse you?" cried he. "Oh, come here, Diana, that I may learn what I really feel! Come, and let me embrace you once again!" He drew her toward him, and pressed a long kiss on her forehead. "Oh," he cried, "it is not the voice of blood which speaks in me, but that of love alone; I feel it. What happiness!"

"What do you mean, Gabriel? But you say that you love me, and that is all I care to know."

"Oh, yes, I love you. I adore you, passionately, madly; and to feel your heart beat thus against mine is heaven—or hell," he cried, suddenly disengaging himself. "Oh! leave me, for I am cursed!"

Then he rushed from the room, leaving Diana mute with terror and despair. He descended the stairs mechanically; but all he had gone through had been too much for him, and in the gallery of the Louvre he lost consciousness and sank fainting on the floor. When he returned to life he felt a hand on his forehead, and, opening his eyes, he saw the dauphiness, Mary Stuart, bending over him.

"It is you, M. d'Exmès," said she. "How you frightened me! I thought you were dead. How pale you are! what is the matter? Shall I call for assistance?"

"No, madame," replied he, trying to rise, "your voice has recalled me to life."

"Let me assist you," she said; "you had fainted. Are you really better?"

"Yes, madame; and I owe you a thousand thanks for your kindness. Oh, I remember, now—I remember all. Oh, *mon Dieu!*"

"Is it some great grief which has overwhelmed you?"

said Mary Stuart. "Oh, yes; it must be so, for you grow paler than ever. I will call some one to take you home."

"I thank you, madame," said Gabriel, trying to rally himself, "but I feel strong enough now. While I live I will remember your kindness; you seem like a consoling angel to me."

"Oh, what I did was very natural. I would have done as much for any one whom I saw suffering, and surely I should do it for you, whom I know to be a devoted friend of my Uncle Guise. I deserve no thanks."

"That little was much to me in my state. Adieu, madame."

"Adieu, then, M. d'Exmès, and take care of yourself." Then she held out her hand to Gabriel, which he kissed respectfully.

When he arrived at his rooms he found Aloyse waiting anxiously for him.

"Well?" said she.

Gabriel tried to overcome a second feeling of faintness which came over him, and replied, in a hollow voice, "I know nothing; both that woman and my own heart were silent. I know nothing, but that I burn and yet shiver."

"Courage, monsieur!"

"Courage? Thank God, I think I am dying," and he fell again into a state of unconsciousness, from which he did not so soon recover.

CHAPTER XVII

THE HOROSCOPE

"THE patient will live, Dame Aloyse; but the illness has been serious, and his recovery will be slow. So much bleeding has weakened him greatly, but he will live, you may be assured. I thank God that the weakness of the body has diminished the strength of the shock that his heart has received. That is a wound that we cannot cure, and his might have been mortal."

The person who spoke these words was a tall man with piercing eyes, who appeared about fifty years of age; he was called Nostradamus.

"But, *mon Dieu !*" said Aloyse; "it is now the 2d of July, and he has lain here since the 7th of June, and during all this time he has never said a word, and never once recognized me. He seems like one already dead; if you touch him, he does not seem to know it."

"So much the better, I repeat; I do not wish him to return till the latest possible moment to the remembrance of his troubles. If he remains in this state for another month, as I hope he will, he will be saved."

"Saved!" said Aloyse, raising her eyes toward heaven, as if in thanksgiving.

"He is saved already if there be no relapse, and so you may tell that pretty waiting-maid who comes here twice a day to ask after him; for in all this there is a passion for some great lady, is there not? It is to be hoped that he will recover the health of both body and mind at once; I can answer for the one, but not for the other. Still the constant visits of the servant would seem to pronounce it not a desperate case."

"Oh, yes, it is!" cried Aloyse.

"Come, come, Dame Aloyse; those who are rich, brave, young and handsome, like the Viscount d'Exmès, are not long repulsed by the ladies of a court like ours."

"But suppose that it is not so, and that when my master recovers his reason, the first thought that occurs to him is that the lady whom he loves is irrevocably lost to him; what will happen?"

"It would indeed be very serious—so powerful a grief in so weak a brain. So far as one can judge from the character of the features and from the expression of the eyes, your master, Aloyse, is no shallow-hearted man; and here his powerful and energetic will exposes him to an added danger: he will attempt to achieve the impossible, and when his will is broken his life will be destroyed."

"Ah, *mon Dieu!* my child will die!"

"There would be a great chance of a return of the inflammation of the brain; but surely you can hold out some hope? The most distant chance might save him."

"Then he shall be saved!" cried Aloyse; "I would perjure myself to save him."

A week passed, and Gabriel seemed to notice the people around him, and then to aid them in what they did for him. At the end of another week he could speak, although incoherently, yet his words often seemed to refer to his past life. Then he recognized Aloyse and Martin Guerre; he asked for what he wanted, and spoke gently and reasonably.

One morning he said suddenly, "Aloyse, what of the war?"

"What war, monsieur?"

"The war with England and Spain."

"Monsieur, the accounts are bad; they say that the Spaniards, with twelve thousand English, have entered Picardy."

"So much the better," said Gabriel.

Aloyse attributed this answer to the remains of delirium. But the next day he said, "I did not ask you yesterday whether the Duke de Guise had returned."

"He is *en route*, monsieur."

"What day of the month is it?"

"The 4th of August."

"Then on the 7th I shall have been confined to this room for two months."

"Oh!" cried Aloyse, trembling, "then monsieur remembers?"

"Everything, Aloyse; but it appears that I am forgotten, since no one comes to ask after me."

"Monsieur is mistaken," said Aloyse, watching anxiously the effect of her words; "a servant called Jacinthe came twice a day to ask after you; but for the last fortnight, since you have been better, she has not come."

"She comes no more? Do you know why?"

"Yes, monsieur; her mistress has obtained permission from the king to retire into a convent until the end of the war."

"Really," said Gabriel, with a sweet and melancholy smile, while a tear, the first he had shed, rolled over his cheek—"dear Diana."

"Oh!" cried Aloyse, "monsieur has pronounced her name calmly and without injuring himself. He is saved— he will live."

"I am saved, Aloyse, but I shall not live."

"How so, monsieur?" said Aloyse, trembling.

"The body has bravely resisted, Aloyse, but the soul is mortally wounded, and cannot recover. Happily France is at war—my place is there; I shall go as soon as I am able, and will take care never to return."

"You will get yourself killed, monsieur?—and why?"

"Why? Because Madame de Valentinois will not speak; because Diana is perhaps my sister, and I love her: because the king has perhaps murdered my father, although I do not know that for certain; and therefore as I can neither marry her whom I love nor avenge my father, there is nothing left here for me to do."

"No, monsieur, you are wrong. You have a terrible duty still to perform; but I will only speak to you of this on the day when M. Nostradamus shall assure me that you are strong enough to bear it."

This day arrived in the following week. Gabriel was well enough to go about as usual.

"Do you persist in your determination, monsieur?" said Aloyse.

"Certainly."

"But if I give you a hope of discovering this secret?"

"You told me it was known but to two people—Madame de Valentinois, and my father, who is dead."

"But if he were not dead?"

"My father lives! Do you know it, Aloyse?"

"No, but I suppose it."

"But how to find him? Speak, what clew is there? In Heaven's name, Aloyse, speak quickly!"

"Monsieur, it is a fearful tale, and I swore to my husband at your father's request never to repeat it to you; for the moment you have heard it you will at once rush into the midst of frightful dangers, and will enter the lists against enemies a hundred times more powerful than yourself. But the greatest danger is rather to be chosen than certain death. You had decided to die; and I, who know your character, know that you would not depart from this determination, and I therefore prefer to see you combat with the doubtful chances of the fearful conflict which your father wished to spare you. At the very least, your death will not be so assured nor so near accomplished. I shall therefore relate to you everything, monsieur, and I pray God to pardon me for breaking my oath."

"Yes, yes, dear Aloyse. My father lives, perhaps! Oh, speak quickly!"

Just at this moment there was a light knock at the door, and Nostradamus entered.

"Ah, Monsieur d'Exmès," he said, "how bright and cheerful you are! That is excellent! A month ago you were not thus. You seem to be almost ready to go afield."

"Ah, yes," replied Gabriel, with brightening eye and a meaning look at Aloyse, "I shall soon go afield, in-deed."

"In that case," said Nostradamus, "I see that there is no further business here for a physician."

"No, save to accept my gratitude, master, and that which I may not call the value of your ministration, for there are circumstances which make some lives of little value;" and Gabriel, shaking the physician's hand, gave him a purse of gold.

"I thank you, Viscount d'Exmès," said Nostradamus. "You will allow me, however, also to make you a present, which I trust will not prove valueless to you."

"And what may that be, master?"

"You are doubtless aware, monsieur, that the illnesses of men do not take up all my time. I have ventured to look further and higher. I have essayed to unravel their destiny—a work full of difficulty and uncertainty; but in spite of this I have at times, it seems to me, caught glimpses of the truth. I am sure that the Most High has designated twice over before his birth the stupendous plan of every man's destiny—in the stars of heaven, his native and eventual home, to which he so often raises his eyes on high, and in the lines of his hand, an obscure book of magic which he never lays aside, but which he cannot even begin to read without the most indefatigable study. Through many a day and night, monsieur, I have worked at these two sciences as bottomless as the cask of Danaïdes—namely, chiromancy and astrology. Future ages have appeared be-fore me, and thousands of years from now the people of that time will often be astonished at the fulfilment of my prophecies. But it is not always that the sun of truth shines clearly; for although my eyes often see, they are again, and, alas! often covered with a film. In spite of this, however, I am sure that now and then I am gifted with a clairvoyance which almost appalls me; and it was in one of these hours that I read about five-and-twenty years ago the horoscope of a cavalier of King Francis's court, written clearly in the stars which presided over his birth and in the lines of his hand. This wonderful, curious, and dangerous destiny impressed me strangely. Fancy my surprise, then, when in the lines of your hand and in the stars which watched over your birth, it seemed to me that I again read a destiny like that one of which I speak. It was impossible, however, to compare the two carefully, as the lapse of so many years had confused my memory. Furthermore, monsieur, during your fever last month you called out a name which I heard but once, but which riveted my attention. It was that of the Count de Montgommery."

"The Count de Montgommery!" exclaimed Gabriel, alarmed.

"Again I say, monsieur, that I heard the name only; and yet the rest is of small importance, for that was the name of the nobleman whose horoscope had appeared to me as clear as the noonday sun. I hastened to my house, and rummaged among my old papers until I found the horoscope of the Count de Montgommery. It is extremely strange, monsieur, more so than anything which has occurred during my thirty years of practice. There is, I am sure, some strange connection, some mysterious affinity between this man and yourself; and it must be that the divinity, who with few exceptions never ordains for two individuals the same destiny, has ordained for both of you the same fate. I cannot be mistaken, for the lines of the hand and the combination of stars are the very same. It is long ago since I have heard anything of the Count de Montgommery, but I understand that one of my predictions in regard to him was afterward fulfilled, in that he had the misfortune to wound the king, Francis the First, in the face."

"Has the rest of his horoscope been fulfilled?"

"This I cannot answer. I am only sure that the same misfortune and the same violent death with which he was threatened are at this moment threatening you."

"Can this be?" said Gabriel.

"Here, sir, is the horoscope which I wrote off years ago for the Count de Montgommery, and in which if I were to-day to write yours I would not make one change;" and Nostradamus handed to Gabriel the small roll of parchment.

"Thank you, master, thank you," exclaimed Gabriel; "this is indeed an invaluable gift, and you cannot know how precious it is to me."

"One thing more, Monsieur d'Exmès," said Nostradamus, "one last word for your protection, though indeed the divinity is supreme, and it is hard to turn aside God's plans. The birth of Henry the Second foretold that he would die in single combat.'"

"But where is the connection?" asked Gabriel.

"This you will understand, monsieur, when you have read this roll. In the meantime I must take my leave of you, in the hope that the misfortune which menaces your life may at least leave your heart innocent;" and saluting Gabriel, who in escorting him to the door shook his hand heartily, he took his leave.

When he was once more alone with Aloyse, Gabriel unrolled the parchment; and making sure that he should not be interrupted or spied upon, he read aloud as follows:

"En joûte, en amour, cettuy touchera
　　Le front du roy,
Et cornes on bien trou sanglant mettra
　　Au front du roy.
Mais le veuille ou non, toujours blessera
　　Le front du roy.
Enfin, l'aimera, puis, las! le tuera
　　Dame du roy."

"Be it so!" exclaimed Gabriel, his eyes flashing with a look of triumph; "and now, my dear Aloyse, relate to me how my father the Count de Montgommery was thrown into a living tomb by King Henry the Second."

"By King Henry the Second!" cried Aloyse, "and how do you know this, monsieur?"

"I divine it," replied Gabriel; "but at least you can tell me of the crime, since my revenge is indicated to me by God himself."

CHAPTER XVIII

THE COQUETTE

WE WILL complete from the chronicles of the time the mournful history of the Count de Montgommery, which Aloyse was only able to give in part to his son.

Jacques de Montgommery was, like all his race, brave and hardy, and fought valiantly under Francis the First, who raised him to the highest rank in the army and the first place at court. Among the most brilliant exploits of his youth was the one to which Nostradamus, in his conversation with Gabriel, made mention. In 1521 the Count de Montgommery was hardly twenty-one years old and but a captain. The winter was severe, and the young cavaliers, with King Francis at their head, were enjoying themselves in a snowball contest—a sport which was at that time very popular and by no means devoid of danger. There were two parties, · one of which defended a building which was assaulted by the other with snowballs. It was during such a game that Count d'Enghien was killed, and on the occasion of which we speak King Francis was very near being killed by Montgommery.

After the battle the contestants gathered about the fire to warm themselves, and the embers having burned low, the young fellows attempted carelessly to rekindle it. Montgommery was one of the first, and ran up with a blazing ember in a pair of tongs; but on the way he ran into King Francis, who, before he could protect himself, received a sharp blow in the face from a glowing coal. A very severe but not dangerous burn was the result, and the ugly scar which it left became, curiously enough, the cause of the fashion of wearing the beard long and cropping the hair short, which was brought into vogue at that time by King Francis. The king bore the Count de Montgommery no ill-will for his carelessness, as he made it good by one brilliant exploit after another.

In 1530 Montgommery married Claudine de la Boissière, a simple marriage of convenience; but she died three years afterward, leaving Gabriel an infant. Soon after, Jacques fell deeply in love with Diana de Poitiers. For three months he hovered near her, without daring to address her; but his looks were more than sufficient for her to understand his feelings, and she determined to make use of this passion when the occasion should arise. This was not long in coming. Francis the First began to neglect the beautiful Diana, and to turn to Madame d'Etampes.

When the neglect became flagrant, Diana spoke for the first time in her life to the Count de Montgommery—it was at a fete given by the king to his new favorite.

"M. de Montgommery," said Diana, calling him.

He approached with some confusion.

"How sad you are," continued she.

"Miserably so, madame."

"And why?"

"I wish to die, madame."

"Whence comes this terrible melancholy, monsieur?"

"I do not know."

"I know, M. de Montgommery—you love me."

Jacques turned pale, and trembled; then arming himself with resolution, said almost rudely, "Yes, madame, I love you; so much the worse for me."

"So much the better," returned she, laughing.

"What do you say, madame? Take care, my passion is no child's play, but is sincere and deep, although hopeless."

"And why hopeless?"

"Because, madame—pardon my frankness—the king loves you."

"It is true," replied she, with a sigh.

"You see, then, madame, that I must conquer my un-worthy passion."

"Unworthy of you?"

"Oh, no, madame, and if one day—"

"Enough, monsieur," said she, with a well-acted dignity, "let us change the conversation." And she went away, leaving the poor count oppressed with contending emotions —joy and grief, hate and love.

The next day Diana said to the king, laughing, "Do you know, sire, that M. de Montgommery is in love with me?"

"Oh," replied he, "the Montgommerys are of old fam-ily, and nearly as noble as myself—as brave, and doubtless as gallant."

"Is that all that you have to reply, sire?"

"What am I to say, ma mie? Must I absolutely hate Montgommery for having, like myself, good taste and good eyes?"

Diana, wounded, said no more, but she determined to make another effort; so when she again saw the count she said—

"What, M. de Montgommery; sadder than ever?"

"Yes, madame, for I fear that I offended you."

"Not offended, monsieur, only afflicted."

"Oh, madame, I who would give my life to spare you a tear—"

"Did you not hint that I was not worthy of the love of a gentleman?"

"Oh, madame, that could not be my meaning, for I love you deeply. I only intended to say that you could not love me since you loved the king, and he you."

"The king does not love me, nor I the king."

"Heavens! then you may love me?"

"I might, but I could never tell you so."

"And why, madame?"

"To save my father's life I consented to accept the protection of the king, but I could never do so for the Count de Montgommery."

She accompanied this speech with a look so loving that the count cried—

"Oh, madame, if you love me as I love you—"

"Well?"

"My world is you; for three months I have lived but in your sight. I love you with all the ardor of a first passion; your wonderful beauty intoxicates me. If you love me, be the Countess de Montgommery—be my wife."

"Thanks, count," cried Diana, triumphantly, "I will remember your noble and generous words; meanwhile, remember that my colors are green and white."

The following day Francis the First remarked to Diana that her new adorer began to wear her colors publicly.

"Is it not his right, sire? Can I do less for the man who offers me his name?"

"Is it possible?"

"Yes, indeed, sire," said Diana, who thought to reawaken love through jealousy.

But after a moment the king said, "If that be so, as the place of grand marshal has remained vacant since the death of your first husband, I will bestow it on M. de Montgommery as a wedding present."

The ambitious Diana, with rage in her heart, said the same day to the count, "My valiant count, my noble Montgommery, I love you from my very heart!"

CHAPTER XIX

HENRY II. AS DAUPHIN

THE marriage of Diana with Montgommery was arranged to take place at the end of three months from that time. The three months passed, and the count was as much in love as ever, although rumor said that Diana had been liberal in her favors to him. Still, on one pretext or another she postponed the marriage.

The reason of this was that not long after her engagement she had remarked that the young dauphin had begun to notice her. Thereupon a new ambition awoke in her heart. The title of Countess de Montgommery might cover a defeat, but to be loved by the dauphin would be a triumph. Madame d'Etampes, who sneered at her age, was only loved by the father; but if she were loved by the son, to her would belong the bright future. Henry would be king—and she, always beautiful, almost a queen.

It was Henry's character which made her still more certain of her success. At that time he was only nineteen years old, but he had already seen more than one campaign. For the last four years he had been the husband of Catherine de Médicis, but all the same he remained an uncouth, slow-witted boy. At the court balls and in the presence of ladies he was awkward, as he was bold and skilful in horsemanship or on the field of battle or in the tournament—everywhere, in fact, where skill and courage were required. Intellectually dull and slow-witted, he was easy game for any one who tried to get ahead of him. The Constable Montmorency, who was no particular friend of the king, spent his time upon the dauphin, who was soon filled with the tastes and views of the older man. Indeed, the constable did whatever he liked with him, and at last succeeded in implanting in the dull and elastic mind the powerful roots of his influence, so that he obtained such control over Henry that his ascendency seemed in no danger, save, perchance, from the influence of some woman. Before long, however, he was overcome with horror to find his pupil on the point of falling in love. He saw the dauphin neglect the friends which he had given him, and become, instead of shy and awkward, melancholy and given to dreams. Looking about him, Montmorency decided that only Diana de Poitiers could have done this; and the rough soldier really preferred that his rival should be Diana rather than any other, for in his practical way he put a more real value upon the royal mistress than did the high-thinking Montgommery. He therefore made his plans in accordance with the character which he attributed to her, and putting his mind once more at ease he allowed his pupil to sigh and dream as much as he liked.

It was the beauty and spirit of Diana which fired Henry's sluggish blood. She was lively, tantalizing, and roguish; her finely molded head moved gracefully hither and thither, her eyes were full of promise, and her whole person possessed a kind of magnetic attraction (magical, they called it then) which easily captured poor Henry's heart. He seemed in her presence to live a new life, and he gave himself up with abandon to her fascinating and dangerous charms.

All this was clear to Diana; but she still hesitated to risk her future, through fear of the past in Francis the First, and of the present in the Count de Montgommery.

One day, however, when the king, who was ever courteous toward the sex, even to those whom he had ceased to care for, was engaged in conversation with Diana de Poitiers near a window, his eyes fell upon the dauphin, who was watching them with a jealous expression.

The king called him. "Aha, my son, what are you about there? Come here," he said.

But Henry, turning pale with chagrin, after hesitating a moment between obedience and fear, suddenly turned round and went away as if he had not heard his father's voice.

"Well, what an awkward dog that is, to be sure!" exclaimed the king. "Can you understand such shyness, Madame Diana? Have even you, goddess of the chase, ever seen a stricken deer more terrified? Ah, it is a wretched weakness!"

"If it be your Majesty's pleasure, I will make it my task to amend monseigneur's ways," observed Diana, with a smile.

"A more charming teacher or a more fascinating apprenticeship would certainly be difficult to imagine," said the king, gallantly.

"Let us consider his education completed, then, sire," replied Diana. "From this time on, it is in my hands."

And forthwith she followed the fugitive.

That day the Count de Montgommery was on duty outside of the Louvre. Diana found the dauphin, and began conversation by saying—

"I fear I alarm you, monseigneur, do I not?"

It is not necessary to relate here how she brought it to a conclusion; how she carefully failed to see his awkwardness or to hear his mistakes; what attention she gave him; how upon leaving him it seemed to him that he should become more easy in the presence of women; and how in reality he did soon so become with her; how, in a word, she soon became his mistress in every sense of the word—laying her commands upon him, teaching him, and indulging him, all at the same time. It was the same old comedy played over again, but it will always be played, and never can rightly be described.

And Montgommery? Well, Montgommery was too much in love with Diana to suspect any treachery; and, in fact, his love was so blind that it was hard for him to see anything except her charms. Outside of himself, everybody at court was talking about this latest love-affair of Madame de Poitiers, but the noble count remained in a state of touching ignorance, which Diana took care should not be troubled. So fragile, however, was the structure of intrigue and ambition that she was erecting that she feared to expose it to the slightest shock; she therefore remained the friend of the dauphin, but still hesitated to break with the count.

CHAPTER XX

THE USE OF FRIENDS

WE WILL now let Aloyse finish the story in her own words.

"My husband," she said, "had not been deaf to all these reports, but he had not yet made up his mind to speak to his master about them. But one evening—it was the 7th of January, 1539—we were in the room with the count. He usually went every evening to see Madame de Poitiers, but this evening she had sent him word that she was indisposed. Suddenly M. de Langeais, M. de Boutières, and the Count de Sancerre—three gentlemen of the court—were announced. Each was wrapped in a cloak, and they all entered laughing.

"'You are welcome, gentlemen,' said the count; 'but what good chance brings you here?'

"'A triple bet,' replied De Boutières, 'and your presence here makes me gain mine.'

"'Mine,' said De Langeais, 'was already gained.'

"'What was your bet, gentlemen?'

"'Why,' answered M. de Boutières, 'Langeais has made a bet that the dauphin would not be at the Louvre to-night. We have just come from the Louvre, and he was not there. I bet that you would be at home to-night, and you see that I have won.'

"'And you have won also, Sancerre, for in fact all three bets are won, and we should have won or lost together. Sancerre, M. de Montgommery, bet one hundred pistoles that Madame de Poitiers would be ill to-night.'

"Your father, Gabriel, turned frightfully pale. 'You have gained, M. de Sancerre,' said he, 'for Madame de Poitiers has just let me know that she cannot receive me this evening, being indisposed.' Then they all three laughed again, but your father said gravely, 'Now, gentlemen, will you be pleased to explain this enigma?'

" 'With great pleasure; but it is no great secret, only you, whom it concerns, are as usual the last to know of it.'

" 'Speak, then.'

" 'My dear count, we are about to speak, for it gives us pain to see a brave gentleman so deceived; but it is on condition that you will take it philosophically, for it is not worth your anger.'

" 'I wait,' said the count, coldly.

" 'My dear count, you doubtless know the mythology— you know the history of Endymion. When he loved Diana-Phœbe he was about twenty, and his beard was not grown; and Endymion is not at the Louvre this evening, because the Lady Luna is at home.'

" 'Your proofs?' said the count.

" 'You do not live very far from the Lady Luna, go and seek them yourself.'

" 'You are right,' said the count, rising.

" 'Ah, count,' said M. de Sancerre, 'do not be imprudent; it is not good to beard the young lion.'

" 'Be easy,' said the count, as he opened the door for them to go out. Then turning to Perrot, he said, 'My cloak and sword.'

"Perrot brought them. 'Did you know this?' asked the count.

" 'Yes, monsieur.'

" 'And why did you not tell me?'

" 'Monsieur,' stammered my husband.

" 'I understand—you did not call yourselves my friends.' He was very pale, but he spoke quietly. 'How long have these reports been current?'

" 'I believe for several weeks.'

" 'Aloyse,' said the count, 'bring Gabriel to me, I want to kiss him.'

"You were asleep, M. Gabriel, but I wrapped you up and brought you to your father. He kissed you, and a tear fell on your cheek; then he said, 'Take care of my boy, Aloyse.' These were the last words I ever heard him speak.

" 'I will go with you, monsieur,' said my husband.

" 'No, Perrot, I wish to be alone.'

" 'But, monsieur—'

" 'I wish it.'

"Perrot said nothing, but when the count was gone he also took his cloak and sword. I did not try to stop him, for it was his duty to follow his master—even to death. He embraced me, and I wept bitterly as he left me. You, monsieur, meanwhile slept peacefully—that sleep from which you woke an orphan."

CHAPTER XXI

JEALOUSY SOMETIMES ABOLISHED TITLES, EVEN BEFORE THE REVOLUTION

"THE Hôtel de Brézé, in which Madame de Poitiers lived, was close to ours. Perrot followed his master at a little distance, and saw him stop at the door and knock. The servants tried to prevent his entrance, saying that their mistress was ill in her room; but the count persisted, and Perrot glided in also, unperceived by him. At the top of the staircase two of Madame de Poitiers' women met the count, and asked him what he wanted at such an hour; ten o'clock had just struck. The count replied firmly that he wished to see Madame de Poitiers; he spoke very loud, so that she could hear him, for her room was near. One of her women went in to her, and returned, saying that Madame de Poitiers was in bed, but that she would come and speak to M. de Montgommery, and begged him to wait for her in the oratory.

"Either the dauphin was not then present, or he was showing himself very cautious for a royal prince. Monsieur de Montgommery readily followed the two women, and they conducted him into the oratory.

"On this, Perrot, who had been hiding in the darkness of the stairway, went up on to the story above and concealed himself behind a high curtain in a corridor which separated the bedroom of Madame de Poitiers from the oratory where Montgommery was waiting for her. At the two ends of this corridor were two doors not at this time in use —one leading into the oratory, and the other into the bed-

room. To his great satisfaction, Perrot found that by hiding behind the hangings of either one of these doors, which
for the sake of looks had not been taken away though no
longer in use, and by listening carefully, he could hear
almost every word that was said in either room. Do not
think, monsieur, that my good husband was influenced by
mere curiosity; but the last words of the count when he
went from us, and a certain inward feeling, told him that
somehow or other his master was running some risk, and
that they were setting a snare for him, perhaps at that very
moment. He therefore resolved to remain near by in order
to aid him should assistance be needed.

"However, as will appear by my narrative, nothing that
he heard and afterward told me shed any light whatever
upon the obscure question which occupies us to-day.

"In a few minutes Madame de Poitiers entered hastily.
'What means this nocturnal invasion, monsieur,' said she,
'after the request which I made to you not to come to me
this evening?'

" 'I will reply truly to you, madame. They tell me
that I have a rival, and that this rival is the dauphin,
and that he is with you this evening.'

" 'And you believed it, since you came to see?' said
Diana, haughtily.

" 'I suffered, Diana, and I come to you to cure me.'

" 'Well, now that you have seen me, and know that it
is false, in Heaven's name leave me, Jacques, for I want
repose.'

" 'No, Diana; for if he be not here now, there is still
time for him to come, and I wish to convict these wretches
altogether of falsehood.'

" 'Then you will remain?'

" 'I will, madame. If you are ill, go and sleep, and I
will watch.'

" 'But by what right do you do this, monsieur? Am
I not still free?'

" 'No, madame, you are not free to render a gentleman whose hand you have accepted the laughing-stock of the court.'

" 'I do not accept your pretensions, monsieur. You have no more right to remain here than others have to laugh. You are not my husband yet—'

" 'Oh, Diana,' cried the count, passionately, 'what do I care for their laughter? *Mon Dieu!* that is not the question; it is not my honor which cries out the loudest, it is my love. If I had been offended by the mockery of these fools, I could have drawn my sword; but my heart was wounded, and I came here. I love you, and I am jealous; you have said and proved to me that you love me, and I will kill whoever shall attack that love, which is my right, if it were the dauphin or the king himself. As sure as I live I will have revenge.'

" 'And for what, and why?' asked, suddenly, an imperious voice behind him.

"Perrot trembled, for through the half-lighted corridor he had seen the dauphin advance.

" 'Ah,' cried Madame de Poitiers, sinking on a chair, 'this is what I feared!'

"M. de Montgommery turned round and uttered a cry; then Perrot heard him say, in a calm voice, 'Monseigneur —one word, I entreat. Tell me that you are not here because you love Madame de Poitiers, and because she loves you.'

" 'M. de Montgommery,' replied the dauphin, stifling his passion, 'will you give me the same assurance?'

" 'I am the accepted lover of Madame de Poitiers, and you know it,' replied M. de Montgommery, omitting, already, the title of the dauphin.

" 'A forgotten promise,' cried Henry, 'and if my rights are more recent than yours, they are not the less certain, and I will maintain them.'

" 'Oh, he speaks of his rights,' cried the count, mad with rage and jealousy. 'You dare to say that this lady is yours?'

" 'I say at least that she is not yours, and that I am here with her consent—which is, I think, more than you can say. Therefore, monsieur, I wait impatiently for you to retire.'

" 'If you are so impatient, let us retire together.'

" 'A challenge!' cried M. de Montmorency, advancing. 'You dare, monsieur—to the dauphin of France!'

" 'There is no dauphin here. There is only a man who pretends to the love of the woman that I love.'

"Then Madame de Poitiers cried, 'He insults the prince! He will kill the prince! Help!' and probably embarrassed by her situation, she ran into her own room, calling, on her way, for the escort of Monsieur le Dauphin.

" 'Oh,' cried the count, 'it is then with the swords of his servants that the dauphin fights.'

" 'No, monsieur,' replied Henry, 'mine will suffice to chastise this insolence,' and he put his hand to his sword.

"M. de Montmorency interfered, however, saying, 'Pardon, monseigneur, but he who might be king to-morrow has no right to risk his life thus. You are not a man, but a king; and a dauphin of France must only fight for France.'

" 'But then,' said the count, 'a dauphin of France must not tear from me all that I care for in life—that which is more to me than my honor, than my country, than my child in the cradle; for this woman has made me forget all these. Monseigneur, pardon my violence, and tell me that I have been mistaken. You would not surely come to see a woman you loved, accompanied by M. de Montmorency and a guard. I should have thought of that.'

" 'I followed the prince this evening, with an escort, as we were warned that an ambush would be laid for him.'

"Ah, doubtless the same kind friends who warned me, instigated, no doubt, by Madame d'Etampes, who wished publicly to scandalize Madame de Poitiers. Certainly, to have a guard waiting outside was to make the affair public enough. Ah, Henry de Valois, then you proclaim her publicly for yours! There is no more doubt nor hope; you have stolen her from me, and with her my happiness. But, Henry de Valois, because you are a king's son, that is no reason why you should cease to be a gentleman; and if you refuse me satisfaction, you are a coward.'

" 'Villain!' cried the dauphin, drawing his sword; but M. de Montmorency threw himself once more before him, and cried, 'Monseigneur, in my presence you shall never cross your sword with a subject.'

" 'With a gentleman more noble than yourself,' cried the count; 'the Montgommerys have been sufficiently often allied to the House of France to make it no disgrace for the dauphin to fight with one of them. Oh, monseigneur, if you loved this woman as I love her, or hated me as I do you—but, no; you are but a timid child, happy to hide behind your tutor.'

" 'Let me fight, Montmorency!' cried the dauphin, furiously.

" 'No, *pâques Dieu!* I will not let you fight with this madman. Help, here!' cried he, opening the door.

"Then Madame de Poitiers came out, and cried also, 'Help! will you let your master be murdered?'

"The escort ran up, and M. de Montmorency cried, 'Bind this madman'; the prince added, 'Do not kill him.'

"The count was seized and disarmed by the six men who had entered, and Perrot saw that his assistance was now unavailing, and that it was better to keep himself free to act as occasion served. The count, when bound, still cried, 'Did I not say that it was your soldiers' swords that you would oppose to mine?'

" 'You hear! M. de Montmorency,' cried the prince, trembling with rage.

" 'Let him be gagged,' said Montmorency. 'I will send word what to do with him. Till then keep him carefully,' and, drawing the dauphin with him, they went into the room where Madame de Poitiers was waiting. Perrot followed, and listened at the door.''

CHAPTER XXII

WHERE A WOMAN PROVES THAT A MAN IS NOT
LOVED BY HER

"WHEN the prince entered the apartments of Madame de Poitiers, his wounded self-love was the first thing to speak. 'It is at your house, and through you,' cried he, 'that I have received my first insult.'

" 'Alas! yes, at my house, but do not say through me. Have I not suffered as much, or more than you? Am I not innocent of all this? I do not love this man; I have never loved him. I love but you, monseigneur, and my life is devoted entirely to you. Formerly, certainly, I may have given this man some vague hopes, but nothing positive—no engagement; and when you came I forgot all else. Since that time, I swear to you, there has not been a thought of my mind, nor a pulsation of my heart, that has not been for you. This Montgommery lies; he acts in concert with my enemies, and has no rights over her who belongs solely to you. Not only I do not love him, but now I hate him. See—I do not even ask you if he be alive or dead.'

" 'Is this all true?' asked the dauphin, still hardly convinced.

" 'We will put it to the proof,' said M. de Montmorency. 'M. de Montgommery lives, but he is bound and incapable of resistance. He has grievously offended the prince, but it is not a crime for which we can judge him publicly. On the other hand, for M. le Dauphin to meet him in single combat is still more impossible. What, then, is your advice, madame? What shall we do with this man?'

"There was a moment's silence; Madame de Poitiers possibly had a struggle with herself before she spoke, but at last she said, 'M. de Montgommery has been guilty of high treason. What is the punishment for that?'

" 'Death,' replied M. de Montmorency.

" 'Then let him die,' said she, coldly.

"All shuddered, and M. de Montmorency said, 'Indeed, madame, you do not love this man.'

" 'But,' said the dauphin, 'I do not wish him to die.'

" 'That is also my opinion, monseigneur,' said Montmorency, 'although probably not for the same reasons. What you utter from generosity, I recommend through prudence. M. de Montgommery has powerful friends, and it is known to several that he was to meet us here to-night. If he be loudly demanded to-morrow, we do not wish to have a corpse to show. We must say that M. de Montgommery has fled, or that he is wounded; but we must always be able to say that he lives. If we manage thus, they will talk of him for a few days, but before a month has passed he will be forgotten; friends soon forget. He must not die, but he must disappear.'

" 'So be it,' said the dauphin. 'He has friends in England, let him go there.'

" 'Not so, monseigneur; exile is not enough. Do you wish him to tell in England how he has insulted you?'

" 'Oh, do not recall that.'

" 'But I must recall it to prevent you from committing an imprudence. The governor of the Chatelet is my friend, and devoted to his Majesty, and will be deaf and dumb as the prison walls; let M. de Montgommery be taken there this night. A good cell will keep him safe; and if there be an outcry, the register of the Chatelet will show that he, accused of high treason, awaits in prison the judgment on his crime. Then, if the prison prove unhealthy, and he die before the trial, that will not be our blame.'

" 'Oh, M. de Montmorency!' cried the dauphin—

" 'Be easy, monseigneur; we shall not have to proceed to such extremities. The inquiries will die away of themselves, his friends will forget him, and he may live in the prison though dead to the world.'

" 'But has he not a son?'

" 'Yes, a child, whom they will tell that his father's fate is uncertain, and who if he grow up will have his own interests to attend to, and will not seek to explore a history fifteen or twenty years old.'

" 'That is a very good plan,' said Madame de Poitiers, 'and I approve of it.'

" 'But I disapprove,' cried the dauphin.

" 'Monseigneur, leave all that to me. I take all the responsibility on myself—'

" 'It is a crime.'

" 'Well, let us not be precipitate. Let us assure ourselves of the person of the count, and we can afterward decide how it is best to dispose of him.'

" 'So be it,' said the dauphin, whose feeble will gladly accepted this compromise.

" 'Let us, then, return to the Louvre. To-morrow I will send him back to you,' he continued, addressing Diana, 'for I see that you really love him.'

" 'Is monseigneur the dauphin also convinced?' said she.

" 'Yes, you love me, Diana—terribly, indeed; and I need to believe it. I should feel too much grief in losing you; your love is necessary to my existence.'

" 'Oh, you make me happy,' cried Diana, with a passionate accent, kissing the hand which the prince held out to her.

" '*Au revoir*, Diana.'

" '*Au revoir*, Henry.'

"While the dauphin went down, M. de Montmorency

opened the door of the oratory and said to the men who guarded the count, 'I will send some one to you immediately who will tell you what to do with your prisoner. Till then, watch him well; you answer for him with your lives.'

" 'I will watch,' said Madame de Poitiers from her room.

CHAPTER XXIII

A USELESS DEVOTION

"PERROT saw that his master was lost, beyond redemption, if he allowed M. de Montmorency's messenger time to return. He had remarked, however, that no intimation had been given to those who guarded the count by which they should recognize the messenger; so after waiting a short time he went up and knocked at the door.

" 'Who is there?' asked a voice from the inside.

" 'From M. de Montmorency,' he answered. They opened the door, and Perrot entered boldly. 'I am,' said he, 'the squire of M. de Manffol; we were returning from the Louvre when we met M. de Montmorency, accompanied by a tall young man wrapped in a cloak. After some minutes' conversation, M. de Montmorency gave me some instructions, which I am here to fulfil. But you must first let me speak in private to the prisoner; so remove the gag.'

"The man hesitated, and said, 'Have you no written order?'

" 'How could they write in the street at two in the morning? Besides, M. de Montmorency said that he had told you to expect me.'

" 'That is true.'

" 'Then let me speak to him. Withdraw out of hearing for a few minutes.'

"He was obeyed. 'My brave Perrot,' said the count, 'how do you come to be here?'

" 'I will tell you, monsieur, at another time; but now

the moments are precious.' He then rapidly explained to the count his intended fate, and that he was there to frustrate the designs of his enemies.

" 'But what can we do? We are but two against eight.'

" 'Let me act, and you are saved.'

" 'Alas! I care little. Diana betrays me, and loves me no longer.'

" 'Think of your child, monsieur.'

" 'You are right, Perrot, I have not thought sufficiently of him. For his sake, then, I should and I will take advantage of this last chance of safety which you offer me, my good friend. But, listen to me. If this chance should not avail me—if this venture, rash almost to the point of madness, which you are about to undertake, fails—I do not wish to leave to my orphan the result of my unhappy death; I do not wish that he after my disappearance shall languish during his lifetime under the terrible hatred which has accomplished my ruin. Swear, then, that if the doors of the prison or the tomb open and shut again upon me, but you survive me, that Gabriel shall never know the circumstances of his father's disappearance; for if he should ever find out this terrible secret, he would surely make some effort either to avenge or to rescue me, and such an effort could only end in his own destruction. I shall have enough to make good with his sainted mother without adding to its weight. I wish my son to live happy, and free from anxiety concerning his father's life. Swear this, Perrot; and consider yourself bound by the obligation of this oath unless the three actors in the drama which you have described to me die before I do, and the dauphin, who will no doubt be king by that time, Madame Diana, and Monsieur de Montmorency carry their terrible hatred with them to the tomb, and thus can no longer be a menace to the happiness of my child. Should this improbability occur, let him endeavor, if he cares to do so, to discover my whereabout. But until then let him imagine as little as anybody else—yes, less than anybody else—what an end his father came to. Will you promise me this, Perrot? Will you swear it? For it is upon this condition only that I resign myself to your heroic and, I very much fear, useless devotion.'

" 'I swear, monsieur,' said Perrot; 'and now let me act.' Then, recalling the guard, he said, 'I am satisfied with my examination of the prisoner; untie him, and let him go.'

" 'Let him go! M. de Montmorency ordered us to guard him safely on the peril of our lives.'

" 'Do you refuse to obey me, who come in his name?'

" 'I hesitate to do that, certainly.'

" 'So be it, then; but you must answer to M. de Montmorency for your disobedience. I wash my hands of it.'

" 'Are you certain that it was M. de Montmorency, and that those were his orders?'

" 'Fool! how should I have known that you were guarding a prisoner if he had not told me?'

" 'Well, then, I suppose we must unbind him;' and they had commenced doing so, when Madame de Poitiers, hearing the sound of voices, appeared at the door, and seeing what they were about, cried out—

" 'How dare you unbind the prisoner?'

" 'We are obeying the orders of M. de Montmorency, madame.'

" 'Impossible! Who brought you this order?'

"They pointed to Perrot, who had been trying to keep out of sight; but a ray of light betrayed him.

" 'That man!' cried she; 'he is the squire of the prisoner. See what you were about to do!'

" 'It is false,' said Perrot; 'I am the squire of M. de Manffol, and I am sent by M. de Montmorency.'

" 'Who says that he comes from M. de Montmorency?' said an officer, who entered the room at that moment. 'I am sent by him, and here is his ring to show it. What! you have dared to unbind the prisoner? Let him be rebound and gagged immediately.'

" 'As you like, sir,' replied the captain of the guards;

'but the orders which this man gave us seemed perfectly plain and authoritative.'

" 'Poor Perrot!' was all the count could say. He did not allow himself to utter one word of reproach to Madame de Poitiers, although he had plenty of time to do so before they placed the handkerchief between his teeth. It is not improbable, also, that he wished to avoid compromising his devoted servant further; but Perrot, unluckily, did not prove so discreet as he, and cried out to Madame Diana in indignation—

" 'Good, madame! you go far indeed in the path of infamy! Three times Saint Peter denied his Lord, but even Judas only really betrayed him once; and here within an hour you have betrayed your lover three times. Of course, Judas was but a man, while you are a woman and a duchess.'

" 'Seize that man!' cried Madame Diana, furious with rage.

" 'Seize him!' echoed the officer.

" 'Aha, but you have not taken me yet!' cried Perrot.

"And goaded to desperation, he sprung to Monsieur de Montgommery's side with one leap, and began to cut the ropes with his poniard, crying out—

" 'Look alive, monsieur! Let us sell our lives as dearly as possible!'

"But before he had freed more than the left arm of his master, ten swords closed in on him. He was surrounded in a moment and attacked upon all sides at once; a powerful blow stretched him at his master's feet, and he fell unconscious like a dead man.''

CHAPTER XXIV

HOW THE TRACE OF BLOOD IS NEVER EFFACED

"PERROT knew no more. When he returned to consciousness his first sensation was of intense cold, and, opening his eyes, he found himself on the damp ground. It was still night, but there was sufficient light to show him that he was in the Cemetery of the Innocents. A dead body lay beside him. They had doubtless thought him dead, and thrown him there.

"He tried to rise, but the pain of his wound was intense. However, by a great effort, he contrived to walk a few paces. Just then the obscurity was removed by the light of a lantern; and Perrot saw two vicious-looking men coming toward him with spades and mattocks.

"'They said we should find them there at the foot of the image,' said the first.

"'Here they are,' said the other, stumbling upon the soldier. 'But, no, where's the other?'

"'We have got to find them both.'

"Hither and thither they turned their lantern, but Perrot had lost no time in dragging himself off behind a tombstone, where he was invisible to their eyes.

"'The devil must have been off with one of them,' remarked the first gravedigger, who seemed to be something of a wag.

"'For God's sake, don't talk like that,' exclaimed the other, with a shudder, 'at such an hour and in such a place!' And he crossed himself, trembling with terror.

"'Well, anyhow, there's no one here,' said the first.

'Oh, well, what's the odds? Bah! we will bury this fellow, and then say that the other man got away; or perhaps they didn't count right after all.'

"They then set to work to dig a grave; and Perrot, who had been dragging himself off little by little, was relieved to hear the jovial gravedigger say to his friend—

"'I have been thinking that if we say we only found one corpse and only dug one grave, we shall only get five pistoles instead of ten. Wouldn't it be better for our finances to say nothing about the strange disappearance of the second body?'

"'Yes, faith, it would!' replied his religious friend. 'We will simply say that we have done our work; and then we shall certainly have told no lie.'

"In the meantime, Perrot, fainting with weakness, had dragged himself as far as the street of Aubry-le-Boucher, and calling to a market-gardener who was driving by in his cart, he asked him whither he was going.

"'To Montreuil,' said the man.

"'In that case, perhaps you will be kind enough to take me along as far as the street of St. Antoine, where I live.'

"'Of course; get in,' said the gardener.

"After this fashion Perrot was able to make the best part of his journey to his home without much suffering; and yet there were many times during the journey when he thought he was on the point of death. But at last the cart stopped at his destination.

"'Well, here you are, my friend,' said the gardener.

"'A thousand thanks, my good fellow!' said Perrot. And with great difficulty he descended from the cart, but was obliged for a moment to rest himself against a wall.

"'My friend has been drinking a little too much, it seems,' said the peasant to himself as he cracked his whip.

"And off he went, singing the new song that had just been written by Master François Rabelais, the jovial pastor of Meudon.

"In about an hour Perrot arrived at the Street of Gardens. Fortunately the nights are long in January. He did not meet a person, and got home about six o'clock.

"In spite of the cold, monsieur, my anxious fears bound me to the window, and at the first call of my husband I rushed to the door to admit him.

" 'Silence! on your life!' said he to me; 'utter no cry, but help me to my room.' He got upstairs with my assistance; but when I began to undress him his blood covered my hands, and I saw his wounds large and gaping.

" 'Hush!' said he again; 'do not cry out.'

" 'But at least let me go for a surgeon,' said I, sobbing.

" 'It is useless,' said he; 'I know that my wounds are mortal. I should not have lived so long had I not been upheld by a feeling stronger than pain. God, who sooner or later punishes murderers, has doubtless prolonged my life so far to serve his future designs; but soon fever will come on, and then no doctor can do anything for me.'

"I begged him at least to spare himself and take a little repose.

" 'No,' replied he; 'I must speak while I can.' Then he told me all that I have just related to you, but not without frequent and long interruptions from weakness and pain. Toward the middle of the day the pain seemed to leave him; then he made me repeat the oath that he had taken not to reveal to you this history as long as there was danger for you in it. This oath, monsieur, I have just broken; but it was to save your life, and I trust that I shall be pardoned.

" 'When I am dead,' continued Perrot, 'shut up this house, dismiss the servants, and go to Montgommery with Gabriel, but do not live at the castle; bring him up quietly in our own house, so that his enemies may forget him; the chaplain and the steward will aid you in your task. Let the young count himself be ignorant of his rank until he be eighteen.' Then he told me that M. de Montmorency supposed him to be dead, and therefore he desired me to keep

his presence there and his death both secret; to tell no one
of his being there, and in the dead of night, when all were
asleep, to carry his body down to the caves of the lords of
Brissac, to whom the hôtel formerly belonged, that in this
way M. de Montmorency would believe the secret dead with
him, whereas, if he knew me to be privy to it, he would not
hesitate to destroy me as well.

"I promised all he asked. Toward evening fever came
on, then he said to me, 'Aloyse, give me some water.' I,
in my ignorance, had offered him some repeatedly, but he
always refused. I got him some then, but before drinking
it he said, 'One last kiss, and remember all I have said.' I
covered his face with my kisses and tears; then he asked
for the crucifix, and placing it to his lips murmured, 'My
God, have mercy on me!' and fell back dead.

"I went as usual to see you put to bed, and although I
wept incessantly no one was astonished, for all were in consternation at the disappearance of the count and Perrot.
About two in the morning, after having washed the blood
from my husband's corpse I wrapped it in a sheet, and descended with my dear burden, still heavier to my heart
than to my arms, and it was not without great difficulty
and many stoppages that I reached the cave. I found an
empty tomb, in which I placed the body. The fall of the
heavy lid as I reclosed it struck such terror to my heart that
I turned and fled, and never stopped until I arrived in my
own room. I had still to burn the sheets and the clothes,
which might have betrayed us, but by daylight my task
was completed.

"A long illness followed so much exertion and emotion
on my part; but as soon as I was able to travel I went to
Montgommery with you as I had promised. What M. de
Montmorency had foreseen happened. For a time every
one talked of the mysterious disappearance of the Count de
Montgommery, but new subjects and interests succeeded,
and it was forgotten."

"Well," cried Gabriel, "all this tells me nothing as to

who Diana is. But if my father lives I will find him. It is now both the son and the lover who is seeking. But have you never learned anything which could indicate the prison in which my father was confined?"

"Nothing, monsieur, but that M. de Montmorency said that the governor of the Chatelet was a devoted friend of his."

"The Chatelet!" cried Gabriel, bursting into tears; the remembrance of the miserable old man whom he had seen there in that horrid cell flashed suddenly across his mind.

CHAPTER XXV

THE HEROIC RANSOM

ON THE following day, Gabriel took his way with a firm step and a calm aspect to the Louvre, to ask for an audience of the king. After deep consideration he had decided that defiance toward a crowned enemy would be worse than useless, and he had resolved to make his request humbly and respectfully.

As he entered he met the Cardinal de Lorraine, who addressed him in a friendly way and asked him whither he was going. On Gabriel's replying, "To the king," he replied that he was also going to see his Majesty, and would conduct him, "although," he added, "the king has very much to occupy him. I suppose, M. d'Exmès, you have heard the sad news?"

"No, indeed, I know nothing."

"Really! well, M. de Montmorency, that skilful general, encountered the Spanish troops yesterday on the plains of Gibercourt; and although he had an equal number of men, admirable cavalry, and the élite of the French chivalry, he has sustained a dreadful defeat. He himself is wounded and taken prisoner, ànd with him numbers of other nobles."

"Great heavens!" cried Gabriel, struck in spite of his private griefs by this public misfortune, "are the days of Poitiers and Agincourt returning? But St. Quentin?"

"It still held out at the departure of the courier, and the constable's nephew, M. de Coligny, has sworn to be buried under the ruins rather than surrender; but it is feared that he cannot maintain himself much longer."

"But what would become of France?"

"May God keep her! But here we are."

They entered and found the king alone with Madame de Poitiers.

"Ah, M. de Lorraine," said he, "what a frightful catastrophe! Who could have dreamed of it? Your brother is on his way home, is he not?"

"Yes, sire; he is at Lyons."

"Praised be God!" cried the king. "Well, then, Monsieur de Lorraine, it is to the care of your illustrious brother that I confide the welfare of the kingdom. I confer upon both of you full power and authority to bring about this glorious result. Be monarchs as much as I am, and even more than I am. I have just written a letter with my own hand to the Duke de Guise, asking him to hasten his return. Here it is. I wish that your Eminence would have the kindness to write also, and make plain to your brother the terrible position in which we are, and the necessity for prompt action if France is to be saved. Tell Monsieur de Guise that I place myself entirely in his hands. Write, sir, write at once, I beg of you! You can do it here on the spot, for there in that closet you will find all the materials that you need; and a courier, booted and spurred, awaits below ready to spring into the saddle. Hurry, cardinal, I beg of you hurry! A half-hour more or less may be the saving or the ruin of the country."

"I obey, your Majesty; and be sure that my brother will be equally ready, and will do all that man can do. But if he fail, let your Majesty remember how desperate the affairs are that are placed in his hands."

"Say in danger if you like," replied the king, "but not desperate. But, tell me, does my good city of St. Quentin still hold out, with its brave defender, Monsieur de Coligny?"

"Yes, or at least it was not yet taken two days ago," replied the cardinal. "But it is not to be concealed that the fortifications were in a wretched state, and the starving inhabitants had already begun to talk of surrender; and if the Spaniard should take St. Quentin to-day, he will take Paris in a week. But be of good cheer, sire! I will write to my brother, and it is unnecessary to say that whatever a man can do will be done by the Duke de Guise.''

And the cardinal, making obeisance to the king and Diana de Poitiers, went into the cabinet to write the letter which the king desired.

Gabriel had remained standing one side, engrossed in thought and unnoticed. Contemplation of the desperate extremity to which his beloved country was reduced filled his generous young heart with alarm. He forgot that it was Montmorency, his worst enemy, who had been defeated, wounded, and taken prisoner. For the moment it was only the leader of the French army that he saw in him. In a word, his country's danger was as much in his mind as his father's sufferings. So sympathetic was the heart of this noble young man, and so easily stirred, that he pitied all who were unfortunate; as soon as the cardinal left the room, the king sunk back upon his couch with despairing gesture, rested his head in his hands, crying out—

"Oh, St. Quentin! on thee now depends the fate of France! St. Quentin, my noble city! If thou canst hold out but for one short week, Guise will have returned, and the defence of thy faithful bulwarks will be renewed! But if thou be taken, the enemy will march upon Paris, and both will be lost. Oh, St. Quentin! I will grant thee a new privilege for every hour that thou resistest, and a diamond for each of thy crumbling stones, if thou canst hold out but eight days longer!''

"Sire, it shall hold out for more than eight days!'' exclaimed Gabriel. He had taken a heroic resolve.

"M. d'Exmès! how came you here?''

"I came with the Cardinal de Lorraine, sire.''

"Oh, that is different. But what do you mean by saying that it shall resist?''

"Sire, if a man were to defend this city, and his energetic will were to inspire the garrison to resist while one stone remained on another, and were he thus to save France, would you promise to grant him one request?''

"Certainly," cried Henry; "what a king could do for him I would."

"It is a bargain, sire; for it is simply a pardon that I ask for, and neither titles nor gold."

"But where is the man who can do this?"

"Before you, sire. I am a simple captain of your Guards, but I feel in my arm a superhuman energy, for I have to save at once my country and my father."

"Your father, M. d'Exmès!"

"I am not M. d'Exmès, sire; I am Gabriel de Montgommery, son of Jacques de Montgommery whom your Majesty will remember."

The king turned deadly pale, as did also Madame de Poitiers. "Montgommery's son!" he murmured.

"Yes, sire," continued Gabriel, "I am the Viscount de Montgommery, who in exchange for preserving St. Quentin to you for eight days asks only the liberty of his father."

"Your father, monsieur, has disappeared, and is probably dead. What do I know of him?"

"But I know, sire. My father has been eighteen years in the Chatelet waiting for death, or for mercy. My father still lives; I am certain of it. As for his crime, I know nothing of that."

"Nothing?" asked the king, with a dark frown.

"Nothing, sire; but it must surely have been a terrible crime to have deserved an imprisonment of such duration. But since it was not deserving of death, it cannot have been unpardonable. Listen to me, sire. In the space of eighteen years, justice has had time enough to sleep and mercy to awake. The passions of man, either bad or good, cannot live so long as that. My father, who was in his prime when he went to prison, will issue from it old and broken down. However guilty he may have been, has his expiation not been complete? And even if injustice has perhaps been done him, is he not too weak to remember that? Liberate, oh sire, a miserable prisoner, who will from now on be of no consequence in the world! Do not forget, oh Christian king, the words of the Christian creed, and for give the sins of another that your own may be forgiven!''

The king and Madame de Poitiers exchanged a look of terror, and as if to interrogate each other.

''Observe, sire,'' continued Gabriel, ''that I do not come to say that he was condemned secretly, and without being heard, and that I do not call on all the nobility of France to aid me in procuring redress. I respect the privileges of the Crown and the secrets of the past; and I only ask per-mission to preserve St. Quentin for you. Surely, sire, that is worth an old man's liberty; and I feel that I can do it, for my cause is pure and holy, my will is strong, and I feel that God is with me. If you require it I will even under-take to wrest a city from the enemy.''

Madame de Poitiers gave an incredulous smile.

''I understand your smile, madame. You think that I shall fall before I accomplish my task. *Mon Dieu!* it is possible. My presentiments may deceive me. But if the enemy enter before the eight days I will die on the breach. I can do no more. I shall die on the field, and my father in his cell; the debt will be cancelled, and the creditor be forgotten.''

''That is true,'' whispered Diana to the king.

''But, monsieur, if you fall, leaving your task unaccom-plished, how do I know that some one else will not start up, armed with this secret, and make the same request?''

''I swear to you, sire, that were I dead all would die with me, and you would never be again importuned on the subject.''

Henry, always undecided, turned toward Diana for advice.

''Sire,'' said she, ''if you ask for my advice, agree to what M. d'Exmès asks, and pass your royal word to grant his request if he keeps his promise.''

"Allow me first to ask you, monsieur, how you became possessed of this secret."

"Sire," said Gabriel, solemnly, "an old squire of my father's—Perrot Travigny—who was killed in the events which led to the disappearance of the count, rose from his grave to tell me."

At this answer, the king turned paler than before, and even Madame de Poitiers shuddered. The belief in apparitions and spectres was at that time universal, and their uneasy consciences soon took alarm.

"Enough, monsieur," said the king, "I grant all you ask. You may now retire."

"Then I may set out, relying on your Majesty's promise?"

"Yes, I give you my word as king and gentleman."

Gabriel, with joy in his heart, bowed and retired.

"At last he is gone," said Henry, with a sigh of relief.

"Well, sire," said Diana, "you did right to promise him, and to send him to St. Quentin; he is sure to fall there."

At this moment the Cardinal de Lorraine returned with the letter for his brother, and the king could not reply.

Gabriel, when he left the king, directed his steps toward Madame de Castro's old apartments, hoping to find some one there who could give him some information regarding her. Jacinthe had gone with her mistress, but Denise, the second maid, had remained, and as soon as she saw Gabriel, she cried—

"Oh, M. d'Exmès, do you bring me news of my mistress? We are so anxious about her."

"And why so, Denise?"

"Oh, monsieur, do you not know where she is? She is in the convent of the Benedictines at St. Quentin, now besieged, and perhaps taken by the Spaniards!"

"Surely," thought Gabriel, "the finger of God is in this. He ever animates my feelings as a son by means of

those of a lover.   Thanks, Denise; here is something for
your good news."

He went down quickly to the court of the Louvre,
where Martin Guerre waited for him.   "We are going to
St. Quentin, Martin," said he.   "We are going where they
fight, and must set off at once."

"Oh, so much the better; I may have become a drinker
and a gambler, but surely not a coward!"

CHAPTER XXVI

JEAN PEUQUOY THE WEAVER

THE military chiefs and principal citizens of St. Quentin were assembled in the town-hall. The city still held out, but the despair of the inhabitants was at its height, and they began to say, "That as it was impossible to save the city, as it was only a question of a day or two more or less, it was better to abridge their sufferings."

Gaspard de Coligny, the brave admiral, thought differently. He knew that each day might be the saving of the kingdom; but he could do little against the general discouragement and discontent. This meeting was his last effort to try and inspirit further resistance. He began by an appeal to their patriotism, but this was received with a mournful silence. Then he turned to Captain Oger, one of his bravest officers, and asked for his opinion, trusting that he would support him.

"If you do me the honor to ask for my opinion, monsieur," replied he, "I must say, with regret, but with perfect conviction, that St. Quentin can resist no longer. If we could hold out for a week, for four or even two days, I should say that these two days would give time to the army to rally, and might save the country; and we will hold out to the last stone and the last man. But I am convinced ·that the ·next assault must be successful. Is it not then preferable to save what we can of the city by a capitulation, while there is yet time?"

"Yes, yes!" cried many voices.

"You speak, Lauxford," said M. de Coligny to the officer commanding the engineers. "Tell us honestly, can the fortifications hold out longer or not?"

"I will tell you," replied Lauxford, the leader of the engineers, "or rather I will let the simple facts speak for themselves; they will tell you the truth clearer than I, and without flattery. On this account, I must ask you to go over with me in your mind the weak points of our fortifications. Sir Admiral, there are at present four openings for the enemy; and I must confess that it is a matter of surprise to me that he has not already taken advantage of it. First, there is a breach in the wall near the Boulevard St. Martin big enough for twenty men to enter abreast. We have already lost more than two hundred men at that point —living walls, who cannot however make up for the lack of those of stone. At the gate of St. Jean the only great tower still stands, and the strongest of the ramparts is already crumbling. At this point there is a countermine, all sealed and ready; but I fear that if we fire it we shall destroy the great tower, which alone holds the enemy in check, and the ruins of which would serve them as ladders. At the village of Remicourt the Spanish have cut trenches through the outer wall of the moat; and they have established themselves there behind a mantlet, and are continually battering at the walls. Finally, on the side of the Faubourg d'Isle you are aware that the enemy is already in possession not only of the moats but of the boulevard and the abbey. It would be folly to try to seek to dislodge them from that point; while, on the contrary, they themselves are step by step nearing the top of the parapet—only five or six feet thick at that point—and have already begun to fire upon our men who are working in the Boulevard de la Reine, and make it so hot for them that they will soon have to cease work. The rest of the fortifications will perhaps stand; but there are the four fatal wounds, and they will soon bleed the city to death, monseigneur. You have commanded the truth of me, and I have told it with all its sad details, leaving to your foresight and experience what shall be done about it.''

Here the crowd began to mutter, and although no one dared to give expression to his thoughts, every one was thinking—

"The best thing we can do is to surrender, and not risk the terrible event of an assault.''

The admiral very bravely answered, "Wait, gentlemen, one word more! As you have said, Monsieur Lauxford, if our walls are weak, we have at least our gallant soldiers, living walls, to take their place. With these, and with the brave help of the citizens, can we not hold out at least for a few days longer? What would be an act of cowardice to-day will then be one of glory. I agree that the fortifications are too weak, but we still have sufficient troops, have we not, Monsieur de Rambouillet?''

"Sir Admiral,'' replied the officer addressed, "if we were talking yonder in the market-place, in the midst of the people who are waiting to hear the result of this meeting, I might say yes; for it would then be our duty to inspire hope and valor in every heart. But here, in this calm council, before those whose valor needs no proof or stimulus, I have no hesitation in saying that we have not men enough for this terrible and dangerous business. Everybody who can carry arms has been provided with them, and the rest are employed on the defensive works, even the children and the old men doing their full share; and I think you will find the women, too, assisting in the good work by nursing the sick and wounded. In one word, not a single arm is idle; and yet we need more. There is not a place on the walls where we have one man too many, but there are many where we have not enough. Do what we will, it is not possible so to arrange our forces that less than fifty more men are not absolutely necessary at the gate of St. Jean, and fifty more at the Boulevard St. Martin. The catastrophe of St. Laurent has cut us off from reinforcements that we had reason to expect; and unless you hope for help from Paris, it is well for you to consider whether, in such a terrible extremity, you have the right to risk the lives of the men still left us, who perhaps at some more auspicious time might help to save the country."

The murmurs became louder than ever on the strength of this opinion, when suddenly a voice of thunder cried, "Silence!"

All were immediately silent, for they recognized the voice of Jean Peuquoy, the head of the corporation of weavers, and a much respected citizen.

Jean Peuquoy was a fine specimen of the sturdy citizen of that time, who loved his city as a mother as well as a child, both praised and grumbled at her, gave up his life to her, and if necessary would die for her. There was no world outside of France for this honest weaver, and no city in all France but St. Quentin. No one knew as much as he about the history and traditions of the town, its customs old and new, and its legends. There was not a part of the city, nor a street, nor even a house, the present and past of which were not plain to Jean Peuquoy. He might have been called the municipality personified. His shop was in Grand Place, and his frame-house in the street of St. Martin was like another town-hall. This old mansion was distinguished by a very strange coat-of-arms—a shuttle crowned between a stag's horns. One of the weaver's ancestors (for Jean Peuquoy had ancestors as well as any gentleman)—a weaver like himself, but a famous archer as well—had put out the eyes of this stag with two arrows at more than a hundred paces distant. The superb antlers may still be seen at St. Quentin in the Rue St. Martin. Everybody for leagues about knew the horns and the weaver. Thus Jean Peuquoy was the city itself, and every dweller in St. Quentin seemed to listen to the voice of his country in that of the honest weaver. On this account, no one moved when his voice, rising above the muttering and grumbling, called out, "Silence!"

"Listen to me, my dear friends and fellow-citizens,"

said he. "M. de Coligny will, I hope, do us the justice to acknowledge that from the first we have done our best to assist him. We have given our provisions, our goods, and our money, and we have not been backward in fighting ourselves. We trusted that our king would think of his brave Quentinois, and send us aid. He did so; he sent M. de Montmorency, and we thanked God and the king. But the fatal battle of St. Laurent destroyed our hopes; the constable was taken, and his army forced to retreat. It is now five days since that battle, and the enemy have made the most of their time; their cannon has scarcely ceased to sound—indeed, you may hear it now. We have listened vainly for some sound from the other side, announcing to us further assistance; but none comes. Our resources are exhausted; but the king has the whole monarchy to save. If he thinks of us, it is only to ask if we shall live long enough to save the rest of France. But there is no chance of help, nor is there any salvation for us; our walls and our soldiers fall around us; we are lost!"

"Yes, yes! we must yield!" they all cried with one voice.

"Not so," replied Jean Peuquoy—"we must die. These officers say that we cannot resist, but M. de Coligny says that we ought to resist. Let us resist. You know, citizens, whether I love our good city or not—how devoted I am to her; but the general has, in his wisdom, weighed the fortunes of St. Quentin against those of all France, and he has pronounced it right that she should die like a sentinel at his post. He who murmurs is a coward, and he who disobeys is a traitor! If the walls fall, we must make new ones with our bodies. Let us gain two days, even an hour, at the price of our lives and our goods, for M. de Coligny declares that it may save France. The responsibility is on him; our duty is to die, when he tells us that we die for France."

All were silent.

"You do not reply. You will give your lives to the

king, and will leave your wives widows and your children orphans; but you cannot yourselves pronounce their doom. At least you can cry, ' *Vive la France!* ' "

A few faint cries responded, but sadly and mournfully.

Gaspard de Coligny then rose in much agitation. "Listen!" said he. "I cannot accept this fearful responsibility; and, since you are all against me, I also think your sacrifice would be useless—"

"What! are you also going to speak of surrender, M. de Coligny?" interrupted a voice.

CHAPTER XXVII

GABRIEL AT HIS WORK

"WHO dares to interrupt me thus?" cried M. de Coligny. "A peasant!"

"I," said a man, advancing, clothed like a peasant of the neighborhood. "Not a peasant, but the Viscount d'Exmès, captain of the king's guards, who comes here in his Majesty's name."

"In the king's name!" cried many voices.

"Yes, in the name of the king, who does not abandon his brave Quentinois, but thinks of them ever. I arrived in this disguise three hours ago, and in this time I have examined your defences and heard your deliberations. But what I have seen does not correspond with what I have heard. Whence comes this sudden discouragement, fit only for women and children, and which has caused a universal panic? Raise your heads, and revive your courage! and if you cannot conquer, let your defeat be more glorious than a victory! I come from your ramparts, and I say that you can hold out another fortnight, but the king asks only a week to save France.

"Let me come to your aid," he continued. "You, M. de Lauxford, say that you have four breaches open to the enemy. Well, that on the side of the Faubourg d'Isle is the worst. The Spaniards are masters of the abbey, and keep up so brisk a fire that our workmen dare not show themselves. Allow me to suggest a simple and very excellent method which I saw adopted at Civitella. We will make a rampart with old boats filled with earth—the balls lose themselves in the earth, and our workmen can proceed in perfect safety.

"At the hamlet of Remicourt the enemy are undermin·ing the wall, it is true; but it is there, monsieur, that we must countermine, and not at the Porte St. Jean, where it is not only useless but dangerous. You should move your men from the west to the south. You will say that the Porte St. Jean and the Boulevard St. Martin will be left defenceless. But fifty men at each point will suffice to pro·tect them. You may say again that you cannot spare these one hundred men. Well, I bring them to you."

A murmur of surprise and joy ran round the circle.

"Yes," continued Gabriel, "I met, not far from here, the Baron de Vaulpergues with three hundred lances, and he has promised to come to your assistance. I undertook to come here, braving all danger, through the enemy's camp, to reconnoitre the places where he may most safely enter with his men. I have come and arranged my plan. I shall return to Vaulpergues; we shall divide his company into three parts. I myself will take the command of one, and we will each direct our steps, under cover of the night, to a different point. We shall be very unlucky if we do not manage to introduce at least one hundred men into the place."

Universal acclamations hailed his spirited address, which reanimated all hearts.

"Oh," cried Jean Peuquoy, "now we can fight and conquer."

"Fight! yes," said Gabriel; "conquer, I do not dare to hope. I do not wish to make your position better than it is; I only wish to show you that the king does not abandon you, and that you may make your resistance useful and your defeat glorious. It is probable that the sixty thou·sand men who attack you will take the place at last, but do not think that your brave resistance will make your posi·tion worse in the end. Philibert Emmanuel is a brave sol·dier, who loves courage and will not punish it; and if you hold out for ten or twelve days, you will have saved France. Your children's children will be proud of you. The enemy may destroy your walls, but they cannot destroy the memory of your courage. Cry then with me, ' *Vive la France!* ' "

" *Vive la France! Vive le Roi!*" cried a hundred voices with enthusiasm.

"And now," continued Gabriel, "to the ramparts, and reanimate by your example those who await you there; tomorrow another one hundred men shall join you."

"To the ramparts!" they echoed as they rushed off to communicate their new-born hopes and enthusiasms to the rest of the inhabitants.

Gaspard de Coligny, the worthy and generous chief, had listened in astonishment and admiration. He now advanced toward Gabriel, and cried, "Thanks, monsieur! you have saved St. Quentin and me from shame, and the king and France from destruction."

"Alas! I have done nothing yet, monsieur. I must now return to Vaulpergues, and God only knows whether I shall go out in safety as I came in, and succeed in introducing my three hundred men."

CHAPTER XXVIII

WHERE MARTIN GUERRE IS UNFORTUNATE

GABRIEL and the admiral talked together for more than an hour, and arranged the best method of introducing the troops; and they parted with mutual esteem and admiration.

Martin Guerre, disguised like his master, as a peasant, waited for him at the foot of the city-hall staircase.

"Ah, here you are at last, monsieur!" cried the worthy servant. "I am overjoyed to see you again; for I have heard nothing else for over an hour but the name of the Viscount d'Exmès, accompanied with exclamations of extravagant wonder and praise! You have set the whole town by the ears. What spell have you brought with you, monsieur, to stir up such a revolution in the hearts of the inhabitants?"

"Nothing more, Martin, than the words of a resolute man. But enough of talking, we must now begin to act."

"Let us, then, monsieur, by all means—actions beseem me better than words. I suppose we are about to take a walk out into the fields under the noses of our enemies' post. Well, sir, I am ready."

"Softly, Martin," replied Gabriel; "don't be in so great a hurry, for we must wait until dark before we go, according to my agreement with the admiral. We have therefore more than three hours' leisure. And then I have something more to look after," he added, in an embarrassed voice. "Yes, a very important matter—in fact, I have to seek some information."

"Aha, I see," replied Martin Guerre, "something about the condition of the garrison or the weak spots in the walls? What indefatigable zeal!"

"No, you are not quite right this time," said Gabriel, with a smile. "I know all that I care to about the fortifications and the troops; this time it is a more personal matter which occupies me."

"Speak, monsieur; and if I can be of any service to you—"

"Ah, Martin, I know that you are a faithful and devoted servant, and I have no secrets from you except those which are not my own. If you cannot think whom I am looking for so anxiously and tenderly in this city, your memory must have become weak."

"Ah, monsieur, now I know! It is—she is a Benedictine, I believe?"

"Yes. What can have become of her? She undoubtedly changed her name when she entered the convent."

"Perhaps; but I must say the name of Diana sounded somewhat heathenish, on account of Madame de Poitiers, I suppose. Sister Diana! that wouldn't do at all!"

"But what is to be done, Martin? At first we must at least make some general inquiries in regard to the Benedictine convent."

"Quite right, monsieur. And then we will go from the general to the particular. Well, sir, I am always at your commands."

"We must work separately, Martin; and then, instead of one chance, we shall have two. Be very circumspect and careful, and above all things keep away from strong drink! We shall need all our wits about us."

"Oh, monsieur is aware that since leaving Paris I have not departed from my old soberness, and drink nothing but good pure water. I have only seen double once."

"I am very glad to hear that," said Gabriel. "Very well, then, meet me here in two hours."

"I shall be here, monsieur."

They separated, and met again two hours later as agreed upon. Gabriel was triumphant, but Martin Guerre depressed. The latter had found out nothing more than that the Benedictines were engaged with the other women of the town in nursing and caring for the wounded; that they scattered themselves about among the ambulances, and as a rule did not return to the convent until evening. Both soldiers and citizens were extravagant in their admiration and veneration for them.

By good luck, Gabriel had found out something better. The first person he met had told him all that Martin Guerre had learned, and also that the superior of the convent was Mother Monique, the friend of Diana de Castro. Then he asked where he could find her. "In the post where there is the most danger," was the reply. He found her indeed at the Faubourg d'Isle, and she received him as the savior of the city.

"You will not be surprised, madame," said he, "that, coming from the king, I ask for news of his daughter, Madame de Castro. She is well, I trust?"

"Yes, M. le Vicomte; but I insisted upon her remaining in the convent to take some rest to-day, for none of us has equalled her in courage and devotedness. She was always ready, and to be found everywhere exercising her kindly charities. She is truly a worthy daughter of France. It has been her wish that her rank should not be known here, and she calls herself by the name of our order, Sister Benedicta; but our patients, who do not know Latin, call her Sister Bénie."

"Can I see her to-morrow if I return?" asked Gabriel.

"You will return, my brother; and wherever you hear the loudest cries and groans, there you will find Sister Bénie."

Gabriel went away with a heart filled with fresh hope and courage.

CHAPTER XXIX

MARTIN GUERRE BUNGLES

FAVORED by the night, Gabriel and Martin Guerre passed noiselessly through the breach, and escaped into the open country; but they were not yet out of danger. Detachments of the enemy scoured the country night and day, and any rencontre with them might be fatal. They came presently to a place where there were two roads. Gabriel stopped and seemed to think. Martin Guerre stopped too, but did not take the trouble to think—a task which he usually left to his master. Martin Guerre was a loyal and courageous squire, but he had no wish to be anything more than the hand; Gabriel was the head.

"Martin," said Gabriel, "here are two roads, which each lead to the wood of Angimont, where the Baron de Vaulpergues waits for us. If we remain together, we may both be taken; but separate, we double our chances of success. You take this road; it is the longest, but M. de Coligny thinks it the safest. Still, you must pass the encampment of the Walloons, where M. de Montmorency is a prisoner. If you meet any troops, pass yourself off for a peasant of Angimont, returning after having delivered provisions to the Spaniards at St. Quentin. Imitate as well as you can the patois of Picardy—that is not difficult with strangers. Err rather on the side of impudence than that of hesitation. If you hesitate, you are lost."

"Oh, be easy, monsieur, I shall manage well."

"I," said Gabriel, "will go this way; for being the direct road to Paris, it is the most dangerous. I may never arrive, but do not let them wait for me more than half an hour. You know what is to be done: the troops are to be divided into three detachments, and each is to advance by a different road. We cannot hope to succeed with all, but the loss of one may save the others. Adieu, my brave Martin. We may never meet again; give me your hand, and may God protect you!"

"Oh, monsieur, I pray most for you; I am not good for much. Take care of yourself, monsieur."

So the master and squire separated. At first all went well with Martin; but as he approached the camp, the sentinels were numerous. All at once he found himself between two troops of men—one of horse, and the other of foot soldiers—and a loud "*Qui vive?*" showed him that he had been observed. "Now," thought he, "the time has come to show the impudence that my master recommended to me;" so he began to sing in a loud voice.

"Who goes there?" cried a voice.

"A peasant of Angimont," answered Martin, imitating the patois, and he recommenced his song.

"Stop that infernal song, and halt!" cried the same voice.

Martin knew that resistance was useless, so he stopped. "By St. Quentin," said he, "why do you wish to stop a poor peasant, already detained too late, and who wants to get home to his wife and his little ones?"

"How do we know that you are not a spy? You must go with us to the camp."

"To the camp? Well, so much the better, for I will speak to the chief. Ah, you arrest an unlucky peasant, who has been carrying provisions to your comrades before St. Quentin. I'll be hanged if ever I do so again; all your army may starve first. But I will complain to the general; I have done no harm, and shall be rewarded, and you will be punished."

"Comrade," said another, "I think he speaks the truth."

"I would let him go immediately but that I cannot help thinking that I recognize him, even by this imperfect light. We shall see clearly at the camp."

So Martin was placed between two soldiers and taken with them.

The moment the light of the torches fell on his face, the man who had spoken before cried out, "*Par le diable!* I was right. It is really that wretch. Comrades, do you not recognize him?"

"Oh, yes! yes!" cried one after another.

"You recognize me?" cried poor Martin, who began to be seriously alarmed. "I am Martin Cornouiller, of Angimont; now let me go."

"Let you go, wretch! villain!"

"For whom do you take me, then?"

"It is Arnold du Thill," cried a dozen voices, with frightful unanimity.

"Arnold du Thill! who is that?" said Martin.

"Oh, deny yourself," said the first speaker; "of course you are not the coward who promised me a ransom, and whom I treated so well, and who last night fled, carrying away all my money and my dear little Gudule? Wretch! what have you done with Gudule?"

"What have I done with her?" cried poor Martin. "Oh, I give myself up, if my aliases are beginning again. I can say no more; do what you like with me; at all events I am glad to know that I am called Arnold du Thill."

Whereupon poor Martin Guerre confessed anything that they liked, allowed them to heap upon him insults and reproaches, and offered up his all to God as a penance for these new offences with which they charged him. As he was unable to say what had become of Gudule, they bound him with chains, and subjected him to every kind of ill-treatment without destroying in any way his saintly patience. He only regretted that he had not been able to carry out his commission to the Baron de Vaulpergues; but who could have thought that so many new crimes would be thrown in his face and destroy his beautiful plan for showing his cleverness and presence of mind?

"My one consoling thought," he reflected, in the wet

corner where they had flung him in his chains, "is that perchance Arnold du Thill may get into St. Quentin with a body of Vaulpergues' company. But ah, no! that is a most delusive hope; and as far as I know of the rascal, I am inclined to think that he is already on the way to Paris with Gudule. Ah, alas! if I had a little better knowledge of my sins, my penance might be more complete."

CHAPTER XXX

RUSES DE GUERRE

WHEN Gabriel, after many escapes, entered the wood where the Baron de Vaulpergues waited for him, the first person he saw was, as he thought, Martin Guerre.

"So it is you, Martin?" he said.

"Myself, monsieur."

"How long since did you arrive?"

"About an hour ago."

"Really! but it seems to me that you have changed your dress since we parted."

"Yes, monsieur; I changed with a peasant, thinking his dress more likely to escape detection than my own."

"Good! and did you have no dangerous adventures?"

"None, monsieur."

"On the contrary," said the Baron de Vaulpergues, "he came here accompanied by a very pretty girl, apparently a Flemish *vivandière*. She was crying, the poor little thing; but he sent her away, remorselessly."

"Oh, Martin, Martin! here is the old man reappearing!"

"Say rather, the young one," replied he. "But pardon, monsieur; you have something more serious to occupy yourself with than my concerns."

"Well," said the baron, "my advice is, not to start for half an hour. It is not yet twelve o'clock, and I do not wish to arrive at St. Quentin before three o'clock in the morning. It is the best time for a surprise."

"Just so, monsieur; that is M. de Coligny's advice. We

arc to arrive at three in the morning if we reach St. Quentin at all."

"Oh, we shall get there, monsieur," said Arnold. "I profited by going through the camp of the Walloons, and undertake to guide you through it with perfect safety."

"That is wonderful, Martin—in so short a time to observe so much."

We must now explain the adventures of Arnold du Thill.

After having escaped—thanks to Gudule—from the enemy's camp, they had wandered in the woods for some time, fearing to fall again into their hands. Toward night he came upon a party ot Frenchmen, and joined them. Then he dismissed poor Gudule, who returned, weeping, to the camp. As for Arnold, they all saluted him as Martin Guerre and asked after his master. By listening to all that was said and saying as little as possible, he picked up sufficient of what was going on not to betray himself, and by the time that the Viscount d'Exmès arrived was quite *au fait* as to the state of affairs. He only feared to see Gabriel arrive with his squire, and was considering what he should do, when, to his great delight, he saw him approach alone. Then he abandoned himself to chance, and guessing that Martin had fallen into the hands of the Spaniards, he audaciously took his place.

In the meantime the conference between Gabriel and Vaulpergues was finished. When the three battalions were ready to start, Arnold claimed the right to accompany Gabriel on the route which led by the Walloon camp. This was the road which the real Martin Guerre was to have taken; and if it should happen that they should meet him, Arnold wished to be present, so that he might either cause him to disappear or disappear himself, as occasion might be.

But they went by the camp without seeing Martin; and the thought of this trifling danger was soon forgotten in the more serious peril which awaited Arnold and Gabriel, together with the little company of adventurers, before the walls of St. Quentin.

Within the town itself the anxiety was no less strong, as may well be imagined; for the safety or destruction of everything depended almost alone on the desperate *coup de main* which Gabriel was about to undertake. At about two o'clock in the morning the admiral himself visited the different points agreed upon between himself and Gabriel, gave his last instructions to the picked men who had been posted as sentinels at these points, and then mounted to the belfry tower, whence he could overlook the whole town and its environs. Once there, he listened, hardly daring to disturb the utter silence by his own breathing, and continued to gaze out into the night. It was in vain that he endeavored to throw off his nervousness, and he therefore determined to place himself at the spot where the fate of the city was likely to be decided. He then descended from the tower, mounted his horse, and, attended by several officers, rode to the Boulevard of the Queen and to one of the postern gates where Vaulpergues was expected, and waited there in an angle of the fortifications. Just as three o'clock struck, he heard the cry of an owl.

"God be thanked! here they are," said he, and the signal was responded to.

For some minutes after there was a dead silence. Then suddenly came the sound of firearms, and a general discharge followed. The first detachment had been discovered.

"A hundred brave men killed," cried Coligny; and without saying more he ran to the Boulevard St. Martin, where one of the other detachments was expected. The same cry was heard, replied to, and followed by the same alarm and general skirmishing.

"Two hundred martyrs," cried Coligny, and he hastened to the third point. But here nothing was heard.

All seemed lost to the admiral. The camp of the enemy was aroused. Without doubt every Spanish soldier was now awake. The commander of the third party probably thought it too desperate a case to march straight into such imminent danger, and had probably withdrawn without striking a blow. Thus the gambler had thrown thrice and lost. The admiral kept repeating to himself that in all probability the last detachment had been surprised together with the second, and that the noise and confusion of the two bloody fights had been heard together.

A tear, hot with rage and despair, rolled down the bronzed cheek of the admiral. In a short time the citizens, again discouraged by this last misfortune, would demand in indignant tones that the place be given up; and even if they should not make such a demand, Gaspard de Coligny no longer dared to hope, that, with troops so tired out and demoralized as were his, the first assault of the Spaniards would not break down the gates of St. Quentin and thus of France. Without doubt this assault would not be long in coming; and the admiral awaited the signal for it with the break of day and even before that, while these thirty thousand men, puffed up with pride over their slaughter of three hundred, were still intoxicated with their exploit.

As if to give the finishing stroke to Coligny's hope, the governor of the town, Du Breuil, whispered the word *alerte* in his ear in a low tone; and as he turned toward him, he pointed out in the dark and noiseless moat a body of men who appeared to be marching directly out of the very darkness toward the postern where they stood.

"Are they friends or enemies?" Du Breuil whispered.

Coligny looked earnestly at them; then, as they approached nearer, he gave the concerted signal. It was immediately replied to; and the admiral, transported with joy, threw open the gate, and one hundred cavaliers, wrapped in black cloaks, entered with a noiseless step, which, as they drew near, Coligny could account for by seeing that the feet of the horses were covered with rags. This expedient, of which only Gabriel had thought, had saved him and his men.

One hundred men were not much, perhaps, but they would suffice to keep the enemy for a time from two of the breaches. The news soon circulated, and a general rejoicing was manifested.

Gabriel said gravely, "No rejoicing! Think of the two hundred who have fallen!"

"Yes," replied Coligny, "we think of and deplore them; but you, M. d'Exmès, how can I thank you, for you have saved St. Quentin twice?"

Gabriel pressed his hand, and said, "M. de Coligny, you shall tell me that in a few days."

CHAPTER XXXI

ARNOLD'S MEMORY

GABRIEL, exhausted by fatigue, slept until a late hour on the following day. It was the admiral himself who awoke him, to beg him to be present at the council about to be held.

"One word only to my squire, and I am at your orders," he replied.

He then called for Martin, and on Arnold entering, he said: "My good Martin, go to the convent of the Benedictines, ask for the superior, and beg her to tell the sister Bénie that the Viscount d'Exmès, an envoy from the king, will call to see her in an hour, and to request her to wait for him."

"Yes, monsieur," replied Arnold, and he set off at once. He asked for *La mère* Monique, as directed, and when she came, he said, "Ah, *ma mère*, I am so glad to have found you; my poor master would have been so sad if I could not have fulfilled my commission to you, and to Madame de Castro."

"Who is your master?"

"My master is the Viscount d'Exmès. You know him, I believe?"

"Certainly, I know our valiant deliverer; we have prayed much for him. But I hoped to have the honor of seeing him here."

"He is coming; but M. de Coligny detains him, and in his impatience he has sent me with a message to Madame de Castro. Do not look astonished, madame; I am an old servant, and my master has no secrets from me."

"Well," said Mère Monique, "Sister Bénie expects him impatiently, for she longs to hear news of her father, from whom he comes."

"Yes," said Arnold, with an affectedly foolish laugh, "who sent him to St. Quentin, but not to Madame de Castro, I warrant."

"What do you mean?"

"Oh, madame, I am so glad that you assist **my** dear master and Madame de Castro in their love."

"Their love!"

"Of course Madame de Castro has told you all about it. Oh, you deny it from modesty. But I think your conduct sublime and most courageous. The king would certainly be in a towering passion if he knew that they had met."

"*Mon Dieu!*" cried the superior, clasping her hands in terror, "a king and a father deceived, and my name mixed up with amorous intrigues!"

"And see! here comes my master himself, to see his adored Diana."

As Gabriel advanced, and before he had time to speak, the superior, with an air of great dignity, said—

"Not a word, M. le Vicomte! I know now by what right and with what intentions you wish to approach Madame de Castro. Do not hope that I shall lend my aid to projects which I much fear are unworthy of a gentleman. I will do my best to prevent Sister Bénie from meeting you. She is free, I know, and has pronounced no vows; but as long as she remains in this asylum I shall protect, not her love, but her honor." Then, bowing coldly, she withdrew.

"What does this mean?" cried Gabriel, in amazement.

"I do not know, monsieur; the superior received me very badly, and said that she knew all your designs, but that she would oppose them, and act according to the wishes of the king. And she added that Madame de Castro loved you no longer, if she had ever done so."

"Diana loves me no longer!" cried Gabriel, turning pale. "But, alas! perhaps it is for the best. However, I will see her once more, and prove to her that I am neither culpable nor indifferent. You must help me, Martin, to procure the interview."

"Monsieur knows," replied Arnold, humbly, "that I am devoted to his will, and am ready to do my best to assist him." And he followed Gabriel, laughing inwardly at what he had done. On his return, he added to a list of charges which he had against the Constable de Montmorency these items:

"For having conducted skilfully the reinforcements which M. d'Exmès was bringing to the nephew of M. de Montmorency—100 crowns.

"For having, after entering into the service of the Viscount d'Exmès under the name of Martin Guerre, denounced him to the superior of the convent of the Benedictines as the lover of Madame de Castro, and thus prevented their meeting according to the wishes of M. de Montmorency—200 crowns."

The next day Gabriel sent him again to the convent, and we may judge how he performed his mission. Gabriel would have gone himself, but at ten in the morning the enemy made a fierce assault, and he was obliged to be present at the defence. He performed prodigies of valor, and conducted himself as though he had a hundred lives to lose.

CHAPTER XXXII

THEOLOGY

A S GABRIEL was coming back in a state of utter prostration, accompanied by Coligny, two men who passed near him were talking of Sister Bénie. Leaving the admiral, he went after the men, and asked them with eagerness if they knew aught of her whose name they had spoken.

"Oh, monsieur captain, no, no more than you yourself," replied one, who was no other than Jean Peuquoy. "The fact of the matter is that I was just saying to my friend here that I was afraid something had happened to her; no one has seen the brave and beautiful girl the whole day, and I was just remarking that after such a sharp fight as we have had there's many a poor wounded chap who is much in need of her sympathetic nursing and her lovely smile. But we shall soon find out whether she is ill or not; for to-morrow it will be her turn to do night duty, and this she has never yet missed. Furthermore, there are not so many nuns that they are able to get along without every one doing her share. To-morrow evening, then, if not sooner, we shall find her; and I thank God, for one poor sick man's sake at least, for she knows how to comfort and soothe the wounded and sick like Notre Dame herself."

"I thank you, my friend, I thank you!" said Gabriel, taking Jean Peuquoy's hand with gratitude, and leaving the worthy man surprised as well as honored.

Admiral de Coligny had overheard the words of Jean Peuquoy, and had noticed the joy of Gabriel. When they proceeded together, he did not mention the subject at first;

but when they were once more in the house and by themselves in the office of the admiral, he said to Gabriel with
his friendly smile—

"You seem to take great interest, I see, my friend, in
this Sister Bénie."

"Precisely the same as that which our good friend Jean
Peuquoy takes," replied Gabriel, with a smile—"undoubtedly the same interest that you yourself take, admiral; for
you too must have seen, as I have, how much our wounded
need her, and what a soothing effect her words and her presence have upon them, and indeed upon us all."

"Why do you endeavor to conceal something from me,
my friend?" said the admiral. "You must have very little
confidence in me to deceive me thus."

"What, admiral," replied Gabriel, more embarrassed
than ever, "who has been telling you—"

"That Sister Bénie is Madame Diana de Castro, with
whom you are so deeply in love?"

"You are aware of this?" cried Gabriel, in great amazement.

"Why should I not be aware of it?" replied the admiral. "You must remember that the Constable Montmorency is my uncle, and I ask you if there is anything going
on at court that he does not know about? Is it not true
that Madame de Poitiers has the king's ear, and that Montmorency has the heart of Diana de Poitiers? Inasmuch as
very important family interests are without doubt involved
in this affair, I was naturally informed of the whole matter,
so that I should be on my guard, and help in every way the
schemes of my uncle. I had not been more than a day in
command of St. Quentin, which I intend to defend or to die
in defending, when I received a despatch from the constable. It was not, as I at first fancied, information in regard to the movements of the enemy and the constable's
operations. Not at all! The messenger had run the risk
of his life a thousand times merely in order to let me know
that Madame Diana de Castro, the daughter of the king,

was at present in the convent of the Benedictines at St. Quentin under an assumed name, and that I was to watch closely her every movement. Yesterday, again, a Flemish messenger in the pay of my uncle asked for me at the south gate. It was natural that I should believe he came to en-courage me to hold out as long as I could in order to add to the fame of the Montmorencys, which had been somewhat besmirched at St. Laurent; and that the king would with-out doubt send an addition to the reinforcements which you yourself brought hither; and that at all events I should rather die in the trenches than give up St. Quentin. But all these suppositions were wrong; the messenger did not come to bring any such encouragement to me. He only had instructions to tell me that the Viscount d'Exmès, who had arrived at St. Quentin the night before on the mere pre-tence of duty, was the lover of Madame de Castro, who however is engaged to be married to my cousin Francis de Montmorency, and that an eventual meeting of the lovers was calculated to be detrimental to the plans of my uncle the constable; but that fortunately I was in command of St. Quentin, and that I should do everything in my power to keep Madame Diana and Gabriel d'Exmès apart, and above all prevent any lengthened conversation between them, and in this manner to assure the future elevation of my family."

The tone in which the admiral said all this was bitter and sad; but Gabriel was rather concerned with the blow which seemed to be aimed at his happiness.

"It was you, then, admiral," he said to Coligny, with his heart full of anger—"it was you, then, who denounced me to the superior of the Benedictines, and who, in order to fulfil the wishes of your uncle, intend robbing me one by one of all my chances of seeing my beloved Diana again!"

"Silence, young man!" exclaimed the admiral, with an expression of lofty hauteur. "I forgive you, however," he added in a more kindly tone; "for you are blinded by your feelings, and have not yet had time to know Gaspard Coligny."

These words were said in a tone of such nobility and good-will that Gabriel's suspicions vanished immediately, and he was even very much ashamed that he had allowed them to enter his heart.

"Pardon me, sir!" he said, giving his hand to Coligny. "It was wrong for me to suspect that you would allow yourself to have anything to do with such ignoble intrigues. A thousand pardons, admiral!"

"It is not worth mentioning, Gabriel," replied Coligny; "and I know that your impulses, though youthful, are pure. No, such intrigues as these are below me; in fact, I utterly despise them and their authors, and so far from wishing to further them they arouse in me but a blush. If these men who seek to aggrandize themselves by even dishonest and scandalous means; who, in their haste to gratify their ambitious greed, care not for the desolation and unhappiness of others; who would even destroy their native land to achieve their aims—if these men be my kinsmen, all I can say is that it must be a punishment which God has inflicted upon me for my pride, and with which he recalls me to lowliness. I regard it as an encouragement to me to chasten myself and be just to my neighbor in order to redeem the sins of my relatives."

"Indeed, sir," said Gabriel, "I am sure that the kindness and virtue of the apostles themselves live in your heart; and I again ask your pardon for having for a moment spoken to you as I would to one of these exquisite gentlemen whose faithlessness I have learned too well to hate and despise."

"Alas!" replied Coligny, "we should perhaps rather pity them—these poor slaves of ambition, these miserable, blind Papists. However, I forget that I am talking to one who differs from me in religious matters. Never mind that, Gabriel; you are worthy of being a Huguenot, and you will become one sooner or later. Yes, the Lord, in whose sight all means are holy that lead unto the right, will bring you to this truth through this very love of yours; and the unequal conflict which your passion is engaged in with the corruptions of the court will end in bringing you into our ranks. Then I shall be most happy in the thought that it was I who first spoke to you on this subject.''

''I was aware, admiral,'' replied Gabriel, ''that you were a Huguenot, and I must confess that very fact has raised them in my estimation. At the same time, you will understand that I am weak in faith as I am feeble in heart; and it does not seem possible to me to profess any other religion than that of my Diana.''

''Ah, well,'' said Gaspard, who just at this time was particularly enthusiastic in regard to his creed, ''if Madame de Castro belongs to the religion of right and truth she will belong to our religion, and so will you some time, Gabriel. You will become so, I repeat, because this corrupt court against which you are rashly contending will vanquish you, and revenge will arise in your heart. Do you for a moment suppose that Montmorency, who desires the hand of the king's daughter for his son, will ever consent to let this rich prize fall to you?''

''I may not contend for it with him,'' replied Gabriel. ''And if only the king will keep his oath to me—''

''His oath!'' exclaimed the admiral. ''Speak not of oaths in connection with a man who, after requesting the parliament to discuss the question of liberty of conscience freely before him, immediately had Dubourg and Dufaur led to the stake, because, relying upon the royal faith, they dared to plead the cause of the reform!''

''Oh, do not talk like that, admiral!'' exclaimed Gabriel. ''Do not tell me that King Henry will not keep faith with me! for then not only my belief would rise to rebellion, but my sword, too; it would not be a Huguenot that I should become, but perhaps a murderer.''

''There will be no danger of that if you become a Huguenot,'' replied Gaspard. ''Martyrs we may be, but assassins never. At the same time, your revenge, though it need not necessarily be a bloody one, can be just as terrible,

Gabriel. You will be of assistance to us with your youthful ambition and your devoted zeal in a work of reformation which is sure to be more hateful to the king than a blow of the sword. Remember, my friend, that it is our desire and our resolve to take from him certain privileges which in our eyes are iniquitous; do not forget that we wish to reform not only the religion, but the government. You have been able to judge, Gabriel, whether I love and serve France. Well, then, I belong to the party of reform in order to add to the real glory of my country. Oh, Gabriel, Gabriel! if you had only read the convincing arguments of our great apostle Luther but once through, it would not be long before you would feel a new soul in your body and a new life open before you.''

"All my life," replied Gabriel, "is nothing but my love for Diana; and my soul exists only in the divine work which God has given me to do, and which with his help I shall finish.''

"There is nothing in what you say," said Coligny, "which is inconsistent with your living the life of a Christian. You are young, and still somewhat blinded, my friend; but I foresee but too clearly, and my heart bleeds when I say this to you, that your eyes will one day be opened by misfortune. Your generosity and purity of heart will not be able to protect you from harm in that corrupt and scandalous court, even as lofty trees draw the lightning from the skies. Then you will remember what I say to you to-day. You will peruse our books—this one, for instance,'' and the admiral took up a book which lay on the table. "You will be able to understand these noble words, frank and severe but full of justice, which have been written for us by one no older than yourself—a councillor in the parliament of Bordeaux, Etienne Boétie. And then you will exclaim, Gabriel, in the words of this virtuous work, 'Voluntary Servitude': 'What a wrong, nay, what a crime it is to see an infinite number of human beings not obeying, but following most servilely—not being governed but being tyrannized over by the will of one man, and not even by a Hercules or a Samson, but by one little creature, often the most effeminate and insignificant in the whole country!' "

"Indeed," said Gabriel, "those are not only audacious but dangerous words, and, I have no doubt, stimulating to the thought. You are right, too, admiral; it is not impossible that some day indignation and rage will drive me into your ranks, and that oppression will lead me to take up the cause of the unhappy. But until that time shall come, you see I have too much to do to think of these new ideas to which you have called my attention; nor is there any time left to me for the reading of books."

In spite of Gabriel's words, Admiral Coligny ceased not to commend zealously the doctrines and ideas which were then working in his mind like young wine, so that the conversation was carried on for a long time between passionate youth and earnest maturity, between impetuosity and grand dignity.

Then, too, the admiral was not very wrong in his forebodings; for misfortune was soon to fertilize the seeds which this talk had sown in the ardent soul of Gabriel.

CHAPTER XXXIII

SISTER BÉNIE

IT WAS a serene and splendid evening in August, and the blue and calm sky was studded with stars, the moon having not yet risen. This sweet tranquillity contrasted singularly with the noise and turmoil of the day. The Spaniards had made two assaults, which had both been repulsed, but not without a heavy loss to the little garrison, which it could ill bear. The enemy, on the contrary, had powerful resources, and fresh troops to replace those who fell.

Gabriel, who had deemed that these frequent attacks were made for the purpose of exhausting the garrison preparatory to a great nocturnal assault, had been anxiously on the watch; but ten o'clock having struck, without any movement on the part of the enemy, he began to feel more at ease. Four days more, and he should have fulfilled his promise to the king.

He now directed his steps to the hospital for the wounded, for he had heard that it was the night for Sister Bénie to take her turn to watch there. On account of the heat of the night all the doors were left open, and Gabriel could, from the entrance, look down the great hall where the patients were lying. The spectacle was heartrending. There were here and there rough couches hastily put up, and covered with blood; but this luxury was only for the officers, and the greater part of the wounded men lay groaning upon mattresses, cloaks, and even straw placed on the floor.

The surgeons, with all their activity, could not attend to

all, and Gabriel turned pale with horror at the frightful picture; but suddenly he smiled, for he saw in the midst of the scene Diana—or rather Sister Bénie—pass along, serene though sad. Never had she looked more beautiful; the diamonds and velvet that she wore at court seemed to suit her less than the nun's dress. The most realistic imagination of an ardent Christian could not figure her in more becoming attire; nothing could be more touching than to see this transcendent beauty bend over the faces emaciated and disfigured by suffering, and this daughter of a king holding by the hand these unknown, dying soldiers.

Involuntarily Gabriel's thoughts flew back to Diana de Poitiers, who no doubt at that very moment was amusing herself with gay trifling and shameless love-making; and so, filled with wonder at the remarkable contrast between the two Dianas, he said to himself that God had no doubt filled the daughter with such excellent virtues in order to make good the crimes of the mother.

While Gabriel was thus losing himself, contrary to his usual custom, in dreamy comparisons, unheeding the minutes as they flew past, the confusion which reigned within the hospital began to cease. Already the evening was far advanced; the surgeons had made their last rounds, and the noise and confusion had ceased. Silence and rest were enjoined upon the sick men; and soothing medicines helped them easier to obey the command. Once in a while a low moan of pain could be heard, but the almost incessant, heartrending shrieks of pain had now ceased. Before fifteen minutes more had elapsed, everything became as quiet and noiseless as such suffering could be.

Diana had already said her last words of encouragement and comfort to her sick ones, and had left them after commending to them rest and patience. Her they did their best to obey, and it was an easier task to obey commands in such a sweet voice than those of the surgeons. At last, when she saw that the medicines which each was to have had arrived, and that her presence would be for some time unnecessary, she drew a deep breath as if to relieve herself from a burden whose oppressiveness she had not dared to confess even to herself; she took a few steps in the direction of the outer gallery, with the intention of getting a breath or two of fresh air after the stifling atmosphere of the hospital.

For a moment she leaned over the stone terrace, gazing up at the stars in the heavens above her; and so intent was she in looking at the sky that she did not hear the footfalls of Gabriel, who approached within a few feet of her, moved by a perfect ecstasy of joy at finding her. He seemed to be looking upon some apparition of heaven itself.

A nervous movement by Martin Guerre, who seemed in no way to share his master's feelings, brought Gabriel back again to the realities of life. Turning to his squire, he said in a low voice—

"You see, Martin, what a fortunate chance is here offered me. I cannot but take advantage of it and speak, who knows, perhaps for the last time, to Madame Diana. In the meantime, do you look out that we are interrupted by no one, and keep a strict watch a few paces from here, but do not go too far away to hear my voice. Now, go, my good fellow."

"But, sir," objected Martin, "do you not think that the superior—"

"Without doubt she is in another room," replied Gabriel. "Whether or no, I have no choice, for it may be that such a chance may never be mine again."

Martin appeared to acquiesce, and went away grumbling to himself.

Gabriel approached a little nearer to Diana; and in a voice so low as not to arouse the attention of any one else, he spoke her name—

"Diana! Diana!"

Diana trembled, for it was nearly dark, and she could not see him. "Who spoke?" said she.

"It is I."

"You, M. d'Exmès! is it really you? What do you

want of me at this hour, and in this place? If, as they told me, you brought me news of my father, you have been very tardy in delivering it."

"Diana, your cold words cut me to the heart; but I cannot call you, 'madame,' as you call me, 'monsieur.'"

"Call me neither madame nor Diana! it is Sister Bénie who is before you. Call me sister, and I will call you brother."

"I, call you sister!" cried Gabriel.

"It is the name that every one gives me now. There is nothing so dreadful in it, is there?"

"Oh, yes!—but no; it is a sweet name, and I will accustom myself to it—sister."

"Besides," said Diana, sadly, "if I am not yet a nun by vows, I am one in heart, and only await the permission of the king to become one. Do you bring it to me, Gabriel?"

"Oh!" said Gabriel, reproachfully.

"*Mon Dieu!*" said Diana, "it is not anger that makes me speak thus; it is grief. I have suffered so much among men that I seek a refuge with God."

"Listen," said Gabriel. "This cruel misunderstanding, which tears both our hearts, must cease. I can no longer bear the thought that you believe me cold and indifferent. But come a little way from here, I pray, lest we should be overheard or interrupted. It is necessary for my reason and tranquillity."

Diana did not hesitate, but placed her hand in his.

"Thanks," said he, "time is pressing; for the superior, who knows my love for you, would separate us if she saw us."

"That is the reason, then," said Diana, "why she has prevented me from going out for the last three days, and would have done so this evening but that I insisted on coming. Oh, Gabriel, it is not right to deceive this good friend."

"Alas!" said Gabriel, "I wish to speak to you only as

a brother. I must control my heart; and though I would die for you, my love must be silent."

"Speak, then, brother."

"Sister," said he, "I have two requests to make to you. You are good and generous, and will grant them to a friend who may never see you again, for a dangerous duty exposes him each hour to death."

"Oh, do not say so!" cried Diana.

"I do not speak thus to terrify you, sister, but that you may not refuse me a pardon and a grace—a pardon for all the grief I have caused you, and the terror with which I inspired you the last time I saw you in Paris. A horrible revelation—received only that day—had thrown me into despair, and almost maddened me. You remember, per- haps, that it was on quitting you that I was attacked by that illness which nearly cost me reason and life."

"Do I remember? Gabriel!"

"Do not call me Gabriel, for Heaven's sake! Call me brother; this name, which distressed me at first, I now wish to hear."

"As you please, my brother," said Diana, bewildered.

At this moment the sound of a body of troops marching was heard, and Diana exclaimed with fear, "Who comes here? *Mon Dieu!* they will see us."

"It is a patrol of our men."

"Oh, let me go. They will pass close by, and will rec- ognize me."

"No, it is too late; to fly now would be to show your- self. Rather come here with me." And followed by Diana, he hastily mounted a staircase hidden by a stone balustrade, which led to the ramparts. The patrol passed without seeing them.

"What a badly-protected point!" thought Gabriel; then turning to Diana, he said, "Be easy, now they have passed; but you have not yet told me that you have forgiven me."

"One does not forgive fever and despair; one pities and

consoles them. But I was never angry with you, I only wept; I was unhappy.''

"Ah, my dear sister, you should not feel resignation alone!'' exclaimed Gabriel; "you must dare to hope also, and that is why I wanted to see you. Remorse for the past you have taken from my heart, and for this I thank you; but the weight of suffering and anxiety for your future you have also to remove. I need not repeat to you that one of the objects for which alone I exist is you yourself; and I cannot be happy for one moment unless my mind is relieved in regard to you, so that I may hereafter pay my full attention to my duty and to the perils which surround me. I must have the hope that at the end of my arduous journey I shall find you awaiting me with a smile upon your lips— sad if I have failed, and full of joy if I have succeeded, but in any case with a smile of friendship. And on this account, let there be no misunderstanding between you and me. And in the meantime, dear sister, it is absolutely necessary for you to trust implicitly in my word, and have perfect confidence in me; for the secret which underlies my every action is not mine but another's, and I have taken an oath not to reveal it, for I have no right to demand that the promises made me should be kept if I do not in my turn keep those which I have made to another.''

"Explain yourself,'' said Diana.

"Oh,'' said Gabriel, "I hesitate, because I think of that dress you wear—of the name of 'sister' that I give to you, and I do not wish to pronounce even a word which may awaken memories too delightful; and yet I must tell you that your adored image has never been effaced or weakened in my soul, and that nothing, and no one, ever can weaken it.''

"My brother,'' interrupted Diana, confused and pleased.

"Oh, listen to me to the end, sister. I repeat to you, that nothing can alter the ardent devotion that I feel for you; and at least I may always be permitted to love you— only of what nature must that love be? God only knows now, alas! but, perhaps, we shall know one day. Confident in God and in your brother, you must let me act—hoping nothing, and yet not despairing; we must neither please ourselves with vain dreams, nor yet must we believe that all is over for us in this world. In a short time I will either come to you and say, 'Diana, I love you; remember our childhood and our vows, and be mine;' or else I shall say, 'My sister, an invincible obstacle opposes our love, and will not allow us to be happy. Nothing depends upon ourselves; the obstacle between us is placed by God himself. I give you back your promise—you are free. Give yourself to another, and I shall attach no blame to you; for dear and sacred as you must ever be to me, our lives can never mingle.' "

"What a strange and dreadful enigma!" said Diana.

"This enigma I shall then, doubtless, be able to explain to you; but until then you will vainly seek the key to it. Will you promise me to believe in my love, and to abandon all idea of a convent? Promise me to have faith and hope."

"Yes, faith in you and hope in God, I can promise. But why should I engage to return to the world, if it be not to walk then by your side? All would henceforth be darkness for me."

"Sister, I ask of you this promise to render me stronger for my work, and that I may find you free for our interview when I ask for it."

"Well, my brother, I will obey you."

"Oh, thanks, thanks! Will you give me your hand as a pledge of your promise, sister?"

"Here it is, brother."

"Oh, now I am certain to conquer!" cried the ardent young man. "I feel as if nothing can withstand me now."

But at this moment, as if to give a double contradiction to his words, they heard at the same time voices crying, "Sister Bénie, Sister Bénie!" and Gabriel thought he heard a noise from the moat.

"Oh, they call me," said Diana; "they are seeking me. *Mon Dieu!* if they found us together! Adieu, my brother; adieu, Gabriel."

"*Au revoir*, Diana. Go quickly; I will remain here."

Diana ran down and met a troop of people, headed by *La mère* Monique, in search of her. Gabriel, reassured by seeing her join them, was about to descend also when he saw a form behind him. One of the enemy, armed to the teeth, was climbing the wall. To run to this man, and push him backward, while he cried, "Alarm! alarm!" in a loud voice, was the work of a moment. It was evidently a nocturnal surprise, and he had been right in his fears. Before a second man had had time to follow the one already killed, our hero seized with iron hands the top of the ladder, and with a mighty push threw it with a crash to the ground, and with it the ten men who were upon it.

Gabriel's clarion shout "To arms!" was mingled with the agonized cries of the wretches as they struck the ground. But hardly twenty paces away a second ladder was already placed against the wall, at a point where it was impossible for Gabriel to get at it. Fortunately he saw in a shadow of the wall a large rock, and his strength increasing with his excitement, he was able to raise it upon the parapet, and to push it over so that it fell crash upon the second ladder, which at the blow snapped in twain; and the miserable wretches who were already swarming up were hurled into the moat wounded and dying, their heartrending shrieks filling the souls of their companions with terror.

In the meantime, Gabriel's shouts had given the alarm; it was taken up by the sentinels, and soon the drums were beating to arms, and the alarm-bell was ringing with loud clamor. In less than five minutes more, more than a hundred men stood beside the Viscount d'Exmès ready to assist him in hurling back any of the enemy who might still dare to show themselves. The poor wretches in the moat were soon killed by volleys from the arquebuses.

The bold attack of the Spaniards came to nothing. Its

first chance of success was, to be sure, in attacking a point which they believed to be undefended; but by mere chance Gabriel had happened to be there, and their plan failed. The Spaniards had no choice but to retreat—which they did in quick time, leaving behind their many dead, and carrying away a score of wounded.

Once more the city had been saved, and again by the hand of Gabriel. But there were four more long days during which the town must still hold out before the promise which he had made to King Henry would be fulfilled.

CHAPTER XXXIV

A GLORIOUS DEFEAT

FOR three days after, the enemy were quiet and made no further attempt, but contented themselves with playing their batteries and working their mines incessantly; and by these means the fortifications were gradually giving way, and the ditches were being filled up. On the fourth day they made another assault. It was the last day promised by Gabriel to the king, so if the enemy were repulsed this time his father was saved; if not, both he and Diana were lost, and all Gabriel's former efforts useless. Thus the courage and energy that he displayed it is impossible to describe. He fought as though he were invulnerable; he was wounded in two places, but without seeming to feel it. He appeared to be everywhere, and encouraging every one by his example and words. This lasted for six hours, and at seven o'clock the Spaniards beat a retreat. St. Quentin had withstood another day. When the last of the enemy had retired, Gabriel sank exhausted into the arms of those who surrounded him. They carried him home in triumph, and as his wounds were slight he soon recovered consciousness, and seeing Coligny standing by him, he said—

"It has been a dreadful assault, admiral, that we have repulsed to-day."

"Yes, friend; and chiefly thanks to you."

"And the eight days that the king asked for are passed, thank God!"

"And to fill your cup of happiness to the brim, my dear

friend," continued the admiral, "I am able to give you some glorious news. Relieved by our long defence of St. Quentin, the preparations for driving the enemy out of the whole kingdom seem to be perfect; one of my scouts, who after interviewing the constable has been able to get into the city during the assault to-day, assures me that we have every reason to hope. The Duke de Guise has arrived in Paris with the army from Italy, and in conjunction with the Cardinal of Lorraine is now enlisting new men and putting the cities in a condition to defend themselves. It is impossible that St. Quentin, in her dismantled and battered condition, could stand another assault; but her duty and ours is done, my friend, and we may say that France is saved. Back of our faithful walls everybody is arming; the nobility and the other orders have risen; voluntary enlistments abound; and even the clergy are sending free gifts for the war; two battalions of German mercenaries have been engaged. When the enemy shall have destroyed us, and I am sorry to say that that time is not far off, he will find other and just as brave opponents who dispute his way. Gabriel, France is saved!"

"Oh, monsieur, you do not know the good that your words do me. But permit me to ask you—and it is not from a feeling of vainglory that I speak, but from a serious and very grave motive—do you think that my presence here has aided to preserve St. Quentin?"

"It has done everything," replied the admiral, with generous frankness; "the day of your arrival you know that I was about to give way under my terrible responsibility, and to abandon the place to the Spaniards. The next day you brought into the city a reinforcement which, although small, sufficed to raise the spirit of our troops, and enabled us to resist. I do not allude to your excellent advice to the engineers, nor to the brilliant courage that you have displayed on every occasion; but to-day, with unexampled energy, you prolonged the defence, which, I confess, I had deemed hopeless. I tell you, Gabriel, with joy and profound gratitude, that you have saved this city, and consequently France.''

''Thanks, admiral, for your kind and generous words; but will you repeat this to his Majesty ?''

''It is not only my wish, but my duty to do so.''

''Oh, what an obligation shall I not be under to you! for the king has in his hands a recompense more wished for by me than all the honors and dignities in the kingdom. Yes, admiral, let him grant me this, and I shall be more than repaid.''

''It should, indeed, be a magnificent recompense; I only trust that the king's gratitude will not fail you. However, I will do all you wish.''

''It has been indeed a long and tedious time since I have felt such happiness and resignation in my heart as I do now. What a lovely thing it is to have faith and hope, even a little, for the future! And now I am off to the ramparts to fight with a light but stout heart, and a feeling that I must be invincible, with the feeling that iron and lead will never dare to touch a man in whose heart hope still reigns.''

''I would not put too much confidence in feelings of that kind,'' replied Coligny, with a smile. ''I am bound to say to you that you allow yourself to be deceived by your hopes of victory. Breaches have been made in every part of the walls, and a few well-aimed balls will soon level what there is left standing of our towers. And, worse than that, there is hardly an able-bodied man left to us; our soldiers who have hitherto made ramparts out of their own bodies have fallen one by one, and the next assault will undoubtedly leave the enemy masters of the city. So, you see, we must not allow ourselves to be deluded by false hopes.''

''But it is surely possible that Monsieur de Guise will send us reinforcements from Paris,'' said Gabriel.

''The Duke de Guise,'' replied Gaspard, ''will hardly risk his fresh and important squadron to go to the rescue of a city that is already three quarters in the hands of the enemy; and in this he will be quite right. It is better for him to keep his men in the centre of the country, where they will be most needed. St. Quentin is a sacrifice, an expiatory victim whose struggles have lasted a long time, thanks be to God! And but one duty remains to her—to succumb in a noble and dignified fashion; and to this we will do our best to assist her. We must make this victory of the Spaniard before St. Quentin dearer to him than a defeat, for it is no longer for our own safety that we fight, but purely for the sake of fighting."

"Yes, for the sport and the pleasure of it!" cried Gabriel, with joy—"a hero's pleasure, admiral, and a sport worthy of such heroes as you! Be it so, then; we will amuse ourselves by keeping the town a few days more from them. It will surely be rare sport to keep Philip II., Philibert Emmanuel, Spain, England, and Flanders all in check before a few crumbling towers, and it will be also a little more time for the Duke de Guise. What do you think?"

"I think, my friend, that your jest is noble and sublime, and that behind your pleasantry glory lurks."

The hope of the two was justified by the event. Philip II. and his commander, the Duke of Savoy, angered and furious at being kept back so long by one poor town, and having made in vain ten bloody assaults, came to the conclusion that they would not risk an eleventh without making sure of the outcome. On this account they waited three days, as they had done on previous occasions, and, instead of assaulting the walls, bombarded incessantly, since they had come to the conclusion that fortifications were easier to beat down and overcome than their defenders. The admiral and the Viscount d'Exmès spent the three days in repairing the damage done by the bombardment as well as they were able; but ammunition was getting low, and arms were scarce. By noon on the 26th of August not a single full section of the walls remained standing; houses were thus left defenceless as if no wall had ever protected them, and the soldiers were so few that not a single one of the principal positions could be adequately defended.

Even Gabriel himself was obliged to admit this; and before the signal for the assault was given by the Spanish commander St. Quentin was to all appearances already at the mercy of the assailants.

But anyhow it was not at the breach where Gabriel was posted that the Spaniards entered. With him were Du Breuil and Jean Peuquoy, and so desperately did they all fight that they three successive times hurled back their assailants. Gabriel especially went at his work with a zest; and so astonished was Jean Peuquoy at the terrible blows which he saw the young nobleman dealing right and left, that he came very near losing his own life as he stood there gazing in admiration at the young man, and twice Gabriel was obliged to ward off blows that would have brought death to the worthy weaver. On this account the good citizen swore eternal devotion and friendship for the viscount, and even averred in his enthusiasm that the friendship that he made in this last sad scene would act as a balm for his feelings, and that although he owed his life to St. Quentin he certainly owed the preservation of it to the Viscount d'Exmès!

However, in spite of the heroic efforts of Gabriel and his companions, it was impossible that the city could hold out longer. The fortifications were but a heap of smouldering ruins; and Gabriel and his friends were still fighting like lions, when they beheld behind them the streets filled with the enemy's soldiers, who had already taken possession of the town.

For seventeen days, however, had the gallant little place held out against the enemy, the Spaniards, and hurled back eleven assaults. Since Gabriel's arrival twelve days had passed, and he had thus more than fulfilled his promise to the king!

CHAPTER XXXV

ARNOLD DU THILL DOES A LITTLE BUSINESS

A T FIRST, rapine and carnage filled the city; but Philibert Emmanuel gave strict orders, and soon put an end to the confusion. Then sending for Coligny, he said to him—

"I cannot punish bravery; and St. Quentin shall not be more rigorously treated than if she had surrendered at once."

And the conqueror, equal in nobility to the conquered, invited the admiral to discuss with him the conditions of surrender.

Of course St. Quentin was declared a Spanish town; but those of the inhabitants who did not care to live under Spanish rule were allowed to leave the town—in which case, however, they were obliged to give up all claim to their houses. Furthermore, every soldier and citizen was released from captivity; and Philibert kept only fifty prisoners of both sexes and all conditions, who were selected by himself or his officers as hostages for the money which was demanded from the town. All property and persons were respected, and Philibert himself promised that there should be no disorder. As Admiral Coligny had lost all his personal fortune in carrying on the defence, no ransom was asked for him, but he would be allowed to start the next day for Paris to join his uncle the Constable de Montmorency, who had not found his captors so generous after the battle of St. Laurent, but had to pay a very large ransom, which would eventually have to come out of the royal coffers without doubt. Philibert Emmanuel, however, esteemed it an honor to make such a friend as Gaspard Coligny, and did not wish to put a price upon his freedom. His higher officers and the more wealthy among the citizens would be enough to cover the expenses of the siege.

Coligny accepted gladly these conditions, which were without doubt more favorable than he expected, and the citizens accepted them too with mingled joy and fear. The great question among them was, who would Philibert Emmanuel and his officers choose as his hostages? This would be decided the next day; and when the next day came, the proudest looked the most humble, and the wealthiest talked a great deal about their poverty.

Arnold du Thill thought a good deal about the situation far out through the night, and finally hit upon a plan which ought to turn out a very good thing for him. He dressed himself as elegantly as possible, and early in the morning walked with proud step through the streets, which were filled with the victorious mercenaries of all nations—German, English, Spaniards, Flemish, etc.

"A regular tower of Babel!" thought Arnold, hearing nothing but foreign languages. "Outside of a few English expressions, I do not see how I shall ever be able to bargain with any of these chaps. Some say, '*Carajo!*' others '*Goddam!*' and others, '*Tausend saperment!*' but not one—"

"*Tripes et boyaux!* Hold there, will you, you rascal?" called out a loud voice behind Arnold.

"What do you want?"

"I make you my prisoner," replied the man.

"Why so? Why me, more than another?"

"Because you are better dressed than most."

"Oh," cried Arnold, "by what right do you, a simple archer, arrest me?"

"I do not do it on my own account, but for my master, Lord Grey, to whom the duke has allotted three prisoners for his share—two nobles and a bourgeois—to draw from them what ransoms he can. My master has sent me to seek them, and as you are the richest-looking bourgeois I have seen, I take you."

"It is a great honor for a poor squire, but I hope your master will feed me well."

"Why? Do you think he will have you long?"

"Until it pleases him to set me free."

"Hum," murmured the archer, "can I have mistaken a poor devil for a rich bourgeois?"

"I fear so, M. Archer; and if Lord Grey has promised you a commission on the prisoners that you bring him, I assure you that you will get nothing out of me. However, you can try."

"You may be right, and I might lose the one per cent which Lord Grey has promised me off the ransoms."

"Well, friend, if I show you a rich prey—a prisoner who would be worth ten thousand livres, for instance—would you be grateful?"

"Ten thousand livres! there are not many prisoners worth so much; that would be one hundred livres for me."

"No, you must give fifty to me if I point him out to you."

"I agree, if you do it at once."

"We shall not have far to go to find him, only a few steps forward. Now, let me hide myself behind the angle of this wall. Do you see at the balcony of that house a gentleman talking with a bourgeois?"

"Yes; is that my man?"

"It is."

"He is called—"

"The Viscount d'Exmès."

"Ah, the Viscount d'Exmès! Is he as rich as he is brave?"

"That he is."

"Do you know him then?"

"*Pardieu!* I am his squire."

"Ah, Judas!" the archer could not help saying.

"No; for Judas hanged himself, and I certainly shall not."

"Perhaps some one may save you the trouble," said the Englishman.

"Tush!" said Arnold. "Does our bargain hold good?"

"Yes; I will take your master to Lord Grey, and afterward you shall show me a rich bourgeois, if you know one."

"Yes, I know one, at the same price—the half of your commission."

"You shall have it."

"Does your master pay ready money?"

"Yes, and in advance. You shall come with us under the pretext of accompanying your master. I shall get my money and will give you half; afterward you shall show me the others."

Then Arnold stepped forward to join his master, asking if he required him. While he was still speaking, the archer came up and said, bowing—

"Is it to M. le Vicomte d'Exmès that I have the honor of speaking?"

"I am he; but what do you want with me?"

"Your sword, monsieur."

"To you!" cried Gabriel, with a disdainful gesture.

"In the name of Lord Grey, my master. You are chosen for one of the fifty prisoners."

"Lord Grey might have come himself on this errand, I think, and it is only to him that I will give up my sword."

"As you please, monsieur."

"I suppose he will allow me ransom?"

"Certainly, monsieur."

"Then I follow you."

"But it is shameful," cried Jean Peuquoy. "You are wrong to yield thus, M. le Vicomte. You are not of St. Quentin; you do not belong to the city."

"M. Peuquoy is right," cried Arnold, making a sign to the archer; "and who should know better—he who knows all the city, a bourgeois for the last thirty years, and a syndic of the corporation? What do you say to that, archer?"

"I have to say," replied the Englishman, who understood him, "that if this be M. Peuquoy, I have orders to take him also."

"I?"

"Yourself, monsieur."

Jean looked at Gabriel. "Alas!" he said, "I fear that the best thing we can do after fulfilling our duty as soldiers is to accept quietly the conditions of the conqueror. Come then, knave," he continued, turning to the archer, "I am your prisoner, or your master's; and I promise him that he may keep me a long time, for he shall never see the color of my money, and he may feed me to my latest hour."

The archer looked frightened, but seeing that Gabriel and the squire both laughed at this, he took courage again.

Lord Grey was a phlegmatic soldier, for whom war was only a commerce, and who was much out of humor at being paid only by the ransom of three prisoners. He received Gabriel and Jean Peuquoy with cold dignity.

"So it is the Viscount d'Exmès whom I have the honor of holding prisoner," said he. "You have given us much trouble, monsieur, and if I demanded for ransom all that you have made Philip the Second lose, it would be the half of France."

"I have done my best," said Gabriel, simply.

"And it was much. But the chances of war have thrown you and your valiant sword into my hands. Oh, keep it, monsieur," said he, as Gabriel made a movement to give it up; "but to purchase the right of using it again, what will you sacrifice? Let us arrange that; I know that unfortunately bravery and riches do not always go together. What do you say to five thousand crowns? Is that a reasonable price?"

"No, my lord."

"No! you find that too much? Well, four thousand; that is not exorbitant."

"It is not enough, my lord."

"What! Monsieur?"

"You misunderstood me, my lord. You asked me if five thousand crowns was a reasonable price, and I said no, for in my opinion I am worth double that."

"Very good; and indeed your king may well pay that for you."

"I trust not to be compelled to have recourse to the king."

"So much the better. And when, may I ask, can you pay this?"

"You may imagine that I have not brought such a sum with me, but if you will give me time to send to Paris—"

"Very well; and until then will it suit you to remain at Calais, of which my brother-in-law Lord Wentworth is governor?"

"Yes," replied Gabriel, while a bitter smile passed over his pale face; "and if you will permit me, I will send my squire at once to Paris, that my captivity may be as short as possible."

"Certainly; and while awaiting his return, be assured that you will be treated with every consideration. You will have every possible liberty, and my brother-in-law will entertain you well, for he loves good living and de-bauchery—a little too well, perhaps. But that is his affair, and his wife—my sister—is dead." Gabriel bowed.

"Now for you, monsieur," said Lord Grey to Jean Peuquoy; "you are, I believe, the bourgeois who has been assigned to me."

"I am Jean Peuquoy, my lord."

"Well, Jean Peuquoy, what are you worth?"

"Not ten crowns, monseigneur."

"Nonsense! one hundred at least."

"Well, then, one hundred, since you value me so highly; but you do not want ready money, I hope?"

"What, have you not even this miserable sum at your disposal?"

"I had it, monseigneur, but I have given it all to the poor during the siege."

"You have at least relations—friends?"

"Friends? Oh, we must not think too much about them, my lord. As far as kinsmen are concerned, I have none. My wife died without children, and I never had a brother, only a cousin."

"Well, and this cousin?" asked the Englishman, on the verge of losing his patience.

"Without any doubt, my lord, this cousin, who lives in Calais, will pay the sum you ask."

"Indeed!" remarked Lord Grey, in a suspicious tone.

"*Mon Dieu!* yes," replied the weaver, with perfect sincerity. "His name is Pierre Peuquoy, and he has carried on the trade of gunsmith for over twenty years at the sign of the God Mars in the Rue du Martroi."

"Likes you, does he?" asked Lord Grey.

"I certainly believe so, my lord. Of my branch of the Peuquoys I am the last representative, on which account, of course, his affection for me is great. Over two hundred years ago a Peuquoy had two sons—one of whom was a weaver and settled in St. Quentin, while the other became an armorer and went to Calais to live. Ever since that time the Peuquoys of St. Quentin have been weavers, and those of Calais have continued to forge arms and armor; but although the two branches have lived apart, distance has never made them forget the brotherly affection which always existed between them, and whenever there was occasion they were always ready to help each other, as should be between those bound together by ties of blood and coming from the same ancestor. I have no doubt whatever that Pierre will lend me the money necessary to buy my freedom. At the same time, it is at least ten years since I have seen him, for you English have always been very careful how you granted the Frenchmen permission to visit your fortified towns."

"Yes," replied Lord Grey, in a more pleasant tone, "so

that for more than two hundred and ten years your Calais cousins have been Englishmen!''

"Oh," exclaimed Jean, with warmth, "the Peuquoys—" but suddenly he stopped.

"Well," said Lord Grey, "the Peuquoys—"

"The Peuquoys, my lord," continued Jean, fingering his cap in an embarrassed manner, "the Peuquoys have never concerned themselves very much with politics; that's what I was going to say. Whether they live under English or French rule, so long as they have an anvil in their possession by which they can earn their bread at Calais, and a shuttle here at St. Quentin, the Peuquoys ask nothing further."

"Who knows," replied Lord Grey, jokingly, "perhaps you may go to weaving at Calais and become a subject of our good Queen Mary, so that the Peuquoys will be again united after so many years!"

"Well," said Jean, innocently, "I don't know; that possibly could happen."

Gabriel was very much astonished to hear the honest weaver who had fought so hard in defence of his native town talk in this calm manner about becoming an Englishman. But a wink which Jean Peuquoy gave him, as Lord Grey happened to be looking the other way, reassured him as to his friend's heart, and showed him that there was some method in his joking.

Lord Grey then bade them both good-by.

"To-morrow, we will all start for Calais, and in the meantime you are quite at liberty to do what you like and to say good-by to your friends. I trust you the more easily on your word," he said, with his usual peculiar kind of delicacy, "because in any case you will be stopped at the gates, as no one is allowed to go out of the town without permission from the governor."

Without replying, Gabriel bowed to Lord Grey and left the house with Jean Peuquoy. He failed to notice that Martin Guerre, his squire, did not accompany him.

"What are your plans, my friend?" he asked Jean Peuquoy when they were again in the street. "It certainly is not possible that you haven't even a hundred crowns with you; why then do you wish to take this journey to Calais? Have you any cousin there? What peculiar object have you, anyhow?"

"Softly, sir," replied Peuquoy, mysteriously, "I hardly dare to speak a word here in this Spanish air. You have confidence in your servant Martin Guerre, I suppose?"

"Perfect," replied Gabriel. "His memory is sometimes at fault, but his heart is the most faithful in the world."

"Good!" said Peuquoy. "It would be better not to send him away from here in order to get the money for your ransom in Paris, but to take him along with us to Calais and let him go from there. We cannot have too many friends with us."

"But explain these precautions," said Gabriel. "I begin to understand—you have no relative at Calais, after all?"

"Oh, yes, I have," replied Peuquoy, with eagerness. "Pierre Peuquoy exists in reality, and has been brought up in the love and veneration of his old country France; and, furthermore, he lacks but the opportunity to strike a blow in her defence, if, while you are in that city, some plan for its deliverance should happen to occur to you."

"My good friend," replied Gabriel, shaking the weaver's hand, "I begin to understand you; but you place my talents altogether too high, and judge me by your own enthusiasm. You cannot understand how mixed with selfishness the feeling is which you call heroism, nor are you aware that in the future a duty, if possible, even more sacred than devotion to my country, will have the first and perhaps only claim upon my life."

"Well, sir," replied Jean Peuquoy, "all I have to say is that I have no doubt you will fulfil that duty as you have all your others; and among them," he added, in a low voice, "perhaps there will be one offered you at Calais to take your revenge for St. Quentin."

CHAPTER XXXVI

MORE OF THE HONORABLE NEGOTIATIONS OF ARNOLD DU THILL

WE WILL now take our leave, for the moment, of the young officer and the old citizen and their dreams of glory, and return to Lord Grey's house, where the false Martin Guerre and the archer were settling their accounts. When the two prisoners had gone, the archer asked of his master the commission which had been promised him, and received it immediately, Lord Grey being well satisfied with the selection which his servant had made. Arnold du Thill waited in his turn for his share of the booty—which we must say, in justice to the Englishman, was immediately brought to him. He found Arnold sitting in a corner, adding a few lines to his long account against the Constable de Montmorency, and talking to himself over a clever arrangement by means of which the Viscount d'Exmès was included in the prisoners of war, on which account monseigneur the constable was relieved of said viscount.

"What are you up to there, my friend?" asked the archer, putting his hand on his shoulder.

"What am I up to? Making up my accounts," replied the false Martin Guerre. "By the way, how does ours stand?"

"Here is what I promised you," replied the archer, giving Arnold the money, which he counted very carefully. "I have kept my promise, you see, and don't regret giving you the money; for you have put two very important prisoners into my hands, especially the viscount, who never demurred at the price, but on the contrary thought it was too low. The old chap made a good deal of trouble, to be sure; but that is to be expected from a citizen, and without your help, no doubt, it would have come off very much worse."

"No doubt about that," replied Arnold, as he pocketed the money.

"But," said the archer, "we have not finished yet. You see I pay well, and you must help me to find my third prize, the second noble, to whom my master has a right."

"By the mass!" exclaimed Arnold, "all you've got to do is to choose yourself."

"Quite so; but I want you to help in this task, for there are a great many men and women of noble birth in this good town."

"What! are women included?"

"Oh, yes. If you can find me one, young and pretty, that would do well. Lord Grey would sell her to his brother-in-law, Lord Wentworth, who likes female prisoners."

"Unluckily, I do not know one. Ah, yes—but it is impossible!"

"Why impossible? No one is exempt."

"No; but she of whom I speak must not be brought near to my master; and if they were both in the governor's house at Calais—"

"But Lord Wentworth would keep her to himself, you may be sure."

"Her father would pay well for her."

"What is her father—a duke?"

"A king."

"The daughter of a king here?"

"Yes; and a queen of beauty."

"Oh, for Heaven's sake, tell me her name!"

"On the same conditions—half of the money."

"Oh, yes."

"Well, it is Diana de Castro, commonly called here Sister Bénie."

"Where shall I find her?"

"At the convent of the Benedictines."

"I will run there," cried the archer, disappearing.

"Good!" said Arnold to himself. "I shall not charge that to the constable."

CHAPTER XXXVII

LORD WENTWORTH

THREE days afterward, Lord Wentworth, governor of Calais, after having taken his instructions from Lord Grey and seen him embark for England, remounted his horse and rode back to his house, where Gabriel, Jean Peuquoy, and Diana were detained prisoners—the latter, however, being unaware that her lover was so near her.

Lord Wentworth was a handsome man, and, although a few gray hairs were beginning to mingle with his dark curls, still young looking. He received his prisoners cordially.

"You are welcome to my house, M. d'Exmès," he said, "and I am much obliged to my brother-in-law for sending you here. Pardon me; but in this dull place society like yours is so rare that I cannot but hope that your ransom will be long in coming."

"Longer than I thought, my lord; for my squire, whom I was about to send to fetch it, got into a quarrel on the way here with one of the escort, and has received a wound on his head which will detain him in Calais longer than—I confess—I wished."

"So much the worse for him, but the better for me."

"You are too kind," said Gabriel, with a sad smile.

"The greatest kindness would be, no doubt, to send you to Paris on your parol; but I love your company too much, and then Lord Grey made me solemnly promise to keep you till I had the money. If you like, then, we will remain prisoners together, and do what we can to make our captivity as pleasant as possible."

Gabriel's only answer was a bow. It would have been much more agreeable if Lord Wentworth had allowed him to go on his parol, but, after all, as an absolute stranger he could hardly have asked for such a proof of confidence. The thought comforted him, however, that by that time Admiral Coligny had already seen the king. Gabriel had requested him to repeat to his Majesty what he had been able to contribute toward the defence of St. Quentin. It was not possible that Coligny could have failed to carry out this request; and King Henry, true to his royal word, was waiting, perhaps, only for the return of the son in order to make good what he had done to the father. It was not at all wonderful that Gabriel was not able to overcome his anxiety, for the reason that this was of a twofold character. Of another individual, still more dear to him, he had not succeeded in catching a glimpse before he left St. Quentin— on which account he cursed the misfortune that had happened to that drunkard Martin Guerre, and was very far from sharing Jean Peuquoy's easy mind on that point; for the worthy weaver was delighted in secret to find that his secret plans were forwarded by the very delay which was so unsatisfactory to Gabriel.

In the meantime Lord Wentworth, who did not choose to remark the melancholy distraction of his prisoner, continued—

"Furthermore, viscount, you may be sure not to find me a cruel jailer; and in order to prove to you immediately that what I do is not directed by any suspicion whatsoever, I will give you, with pleasure, permission to go in and out as you will, and in fact to go wherever and do whatever you like in the town, upon your mere word that you will not attempt to escape."

At these words Jean Peuquoy was not able to keep back a gesture of pleasure, and in order to communicate this to Gabriel he gave the young man's coat-tail a sharp pull, considerably to the latter's surprise.

"My lord, I gratefully accept your courteous offer," replied Gabriel, "and I give you my word of honor that I will not attempt to escape in any way."

"All of which is very satisfactory, monsieur," replied Lord Wentworth; "and if my hospitality, poor as it is, be tiresome to you, you need not accept it in the least, but you may take advantage of any more convenient quarters which you may be able to find."

"Oh, M. le Vicomte," cried Jean Peuquoy, "if you would deign to accept a room at my cousin's, you would render us both proud and happy, I assure you."

"Thanks, my friend; but I fear that to use Lord Wentworth's kind permission would be to abuse it."

"No; I assure you," replied Lord Wentworth, "you are perfectly free to accept M. Peuquoy's invitation. Pierre Peuquoy is a rich fellow; I know him well, and have often bought armor from him. He has a pretty sister, too, and I recommend you to go there."

Gabriel began to think, and rightly, that Lord Wentworth for some reason would prefer his absence; so he accepted Jean's invitation.

"I believe," continued Lord Wentworth, turning to Jean, "that it is from your cousin that your ransom is to come?"

"Yes, my lord; all that Pierre possesses belongs to Jean—it is always so between us. I was so sure of his hospitality that I have already sent M. d'Exmès' wounded squire there; and I am so sure of his purse that if you will send a servant with me, I promise you that he shall bring back the money."

"It is useless, M. Peuquoy. To-morrow I will come and choose instead one of those beautiful suits of armor which your cousin makes so well. And now, M. d'Exmès, I have only to add how welcome you will be whenever you please to pay me a visit, which perhaps you will better appreciate when you have experienced a little of the dulness of Calais. Your presence is a source of very great pleasure to me, I assure you; and if you remain away from me I shall not let

you alone, I warn you. Remember, too, that the liberty
which I have given you is but half a liberty, and that the
friend shall see that the prisoner is brought here often."

"I thank you, my lord," replied Gabriel; "I accept all
your kindnesses with gratitude. This may be my way of re·
venge," he continued with a smile; "for the fortune of war
is variable, you know, and the friend of to-day may become
the enemy of to-morrow."

"Quite true," said Lord Wentworth; "but I fancy I am
safe—alas! too safe—behind these terrible walls. If the fates
wished that the French should retake Calais, they would not
have waited two hundred years in order to do it. I am not
anxious about that; and as far as Paris is concerned, if it
ever falls to you to do me the honors of that city, it will not
be in time of war, I am inclined to think."

"All this, my lord, is in God's hands," replied Gabriel.
"My friend Admiral Coligny, who has just left us, was
accustomed to say that 'the course of the wise man was to
wait.'"

"Without doubt, and in the meantime to live as happily
and contentedly as possible. By the way, monsieur, it occurs to me that the state of your finances may not be a good
one, in which case I hope you will understand that my
purse is quite at your disposal."

"Again, I thank you, my lord; but my own purse, although not sufficiently well filled to pay for my ransom,
is still full enough to defray my expenses in Calais. My
only fear, Master Peuquoy, is that your cousin's house may
not conveniently be able to welcome three new guests; in
which case it would be better for me to look for other lodgings, where for a small sum of money—"

"You jest," interrupted Jean; "for, thank God! my
cousin Pierre's house is large enough for three families,
if necessary. They don't build houses so small and narrow
in the provinces as they do in Paris."

"Quite true," said Lord Wentworth; "and I assure you,
viscount, that the armorer's house is by no means unworthy

of an officer. A more numerous retinue than yours could easily find quarters there; and without any inconvenience two trades might easily be carried on under its roof. May I ask if it was not your purpose, Master Peuquoy, to live there yourself, and carry on your occupation of weaving? Lord Grey mentioned to me something of such a plan, which I should be very glad to see you carry out."

"And which very possibly will be carried out," replied Jean; "for if Calais and St. Quentin are both to become English, then I prefer to be in the city where the rest of my family is."

"Yes," replied Lord Wentworth, who misunderstood the clever weaver's meaning—"yes, without doubt St. Quentin will soon be an English town. But I am detaining you," he continued, "and you must really be in need of rest, viscount, after the fatigues of your long journey. Once more, then, you are both free. *Au revoir.* We shall meet again soon, shall we not?"

And accompanying the captain and the citizen to the door, he cordially shook the hand of the first, and nodded in a friendly manner to the other; after which he left them to proceed on their way to the Rue du Martroi, in which street our readers will remember lived Pierre Peuquoy, at the sign of the God Mars, and where in a short time, if God wills, we shall again find Gabriel and Jean Peuquoy.

"By my faith," said Lord Wentworth, when they had disappeared, "I believe that I was by no means stupid in thus getting the Viscount d'Exmès out of my house. He is a nobleman and has lived at court; and if he should ever catch sight of the beautiful prisoner who is in my power, it is not likely he would forget her. Ah, to be sure, for even I, although I have not yet conversed with her, was completely captivated by her beauty and grace as she merely passed by me. How lovely she is! I love her! I love her! Poor heart! so long still and dumb in this melancholy solitude, how you beat now! But this young man, courteous and brave as he is, might well be in my way, especially if he recognized the daughter of the king in the prisoner whom I intend to make my own. The presence of a countryman of hers, and possibly a friend, too, would no doubt have stood in the way of Madame de Castro's acquiescence, or encouraged her to refuse my hand. It is best to avoid having a third party in this affair at all; and although I have no intention whatever of employing means unworthy of myself, it would certainly be foolish to create additional obstacles.''

So saying, he struck a bell near him in a peculiar manner. In a moment a maid appeared.

"Jane," said he, "have you attended, as I ordered you, to the young lady?"

"Yes, my lord."

"How does she seem?"

"Sad, monsieur; but she is quite calm, and speaks gently but firmly."

"Has she dined?"

"She would take nothing, my lord."

"Well, go to her, and say that Lord Wentworth, to whom Lord Grey has assigned his rights over her, begs her to receive him."

In a few minutes Jane returned, saying that the lady was ready to see him.

"Go up, then, and say that I am coming." And Lord Wentworth followed with a beating heart; for Diana's transcendent beauty had made a deep impression on him.

CHAPTER XXXVIII

A JAILER IN LOVE

DIANA received Lord Wentworth with dignity, hiding all the inquietude which she could not but feel, under a calm exterior. Inwardly she trembled, as she acknowledged the salutation of the Englishman, and motioned him with dignity to be seated on the couch a short distance from her. She then made a sign to her two maid-servants, who were about to leave the room, to stay with her; and as Lord Wentworth seemed to be lost in admiration, she concluded that it was best herself to break the silence.

"You are Lord Wentworth, governor of Calais, I believe," she said.

"Yes, I am Lord Wentworth, your devoted servant, and I await your commands."

"My commands! You mock me. If they had listened, not to my commands, but to my prayers, I should not be here. You know who I am, my lord?"

"I know that you are Madame de Castro, the cherished daughter of Henry the Second."

"Why, then, am I a prisoner?"

"Precisely because you are the daughter of the king, and they thought your ransom would be a large one."

"But how did they know that I was at the convent? Only the superior and one other person knew my secret."

"That person must have betrayed you."

"Oh, no! I am sure not," cried Diana, with so much warmth that Lord Wentworth felt jealous without knowing why. "The day before St. Quentin was finally surrendered," she continued, "trembling and alarmed, I had taken refuge in the very inmost corner of my cell. Without, in the drawing-room, a voice asked for Sister Bénie, which, as you know, my lord, was my name as a novice. The voice was that of an English soldier, and without knowing why I instinctively dreaded some terrible information, some misfortune. Nevertheless, I went to the drawing-room under the influence of that terrible curiosity which even in suffering makes us anxious to find out the cause of our suffering. The English archer, whom I now saw for the first time, informed me that I was his prisoner. I resisted, of course, with indignation; but what could I avail against force? Three soldiers, my lord, were there, to arrest one poor weak woman. Pardon me if this story offends or hurts you, for I am only telling you the truth as it happened. These men laid hands upon me and compelled me to confess that I was Diana de Castro, daughter of King Henry. This I denied at first; but as they were dragging me off in spite of my words, I requested to be taken before Admiral Coligny, and as I knew that he did not know Sister Bénie I confessed that I was Diana. You will easily believe, my lord, that upon this avowal they would grant me my prayer to be taken before the admiral, who, of course, would have recognized me and procured my freedom. Not so; they simply boasted more of their capture, pulled me along roughly and more quickly, and threw me, in despair and tears, into a litter. Though half dead with fear and weeping, and quite overcome with grief, I still had strength enough to ask where I was to be taken. I was already outside the walls of St. Quentin and on the road to Calais. Lord Grey, who I was informed was in command of the force, refused to allow me an interview, and I learned from one of the soldiers that I was a prisoner and was being taken to Calais to await the payment to Lord Grey of my ransom. This is all I learned, my lord, until I came hither."

"I regret to say that I myself can tell you no more, madame," said Lord Wentworth, sorrowfully.

"Nothing, my lord," continued Diana; "you do not know why I am not allowed to see the superior of the Benedictines and Admiral Coligny, why I am detained here and not allowed to speak with those whom I might send to announce my captivity to the king, who would perhaps already have sent my ransom from Paris? I cannot understand these secret measures; why can I not even speak with Lord Grey, by whose order, I understand, all this is done?"

"But, madame, you did see Lord Grey not long ago, when you passed us; for it was he with whom I was talking, and who at the same time with me saluted you."

"Pardon, my lord, I did not know that it was he," said Diana; "but since you have seen Lord Grey, and since he is your kinsman, as this woman tells me, he must certainly have spoken to you of his intention in regard to me."

"Madame, his only object was to draw from you the largest sum of money possible. At first I laughingly reproved my greedy brother-in-law; but I saw you, and saw that if you were a king's daughter by birth, you were a queen by beauty. Then, I confess with shame that I changed my advice to him, and represented that in the present state of war between England and France the possession of you was important; that you might even, perhaps, at some time be worth a city for your ransom; and I advised him not to part with so rich a prize for a few francs."

"Oh, monsieur, how cruel! Why do you oppose my deliverance? You saw me but for a few minutes—why should you hate me?"

"Madame, I saw you but for a few minutes, and I loved you."

Diana recoiled in terror.

"Do not fear me, madame," said Lord Wentworth; "I am a gentleman, and it is I and not you who have reason to tremble. I love you, and could not help telling you so. Yes! when I saw you pass, looking like an angel, all my heart flew toward you. True, you are in my power here, but, alas! I am still more in yours; and of the two the true prisoner is not you. You are the queen, madame; order, and I will obey."

"Then, monseigneur, send me to Paris, from whence I will immediately forward whatever ransom you may fix."

"Anything but that, madame; such a sacrifice is beyond my strength when I tell you that a glance from you has chained my heart forever. Here, in this exile, I have never had before a worthy object of love. I have loved you but for two hours, it is true; but if you knew me, you would know that it is as if I had loved you all my life."

"But in Heaven's name, my lord, what do you want? What do you expect or hope for? What is your object?"

"I want to see you, madame, to enjoy your gracious presence; that is all. Once more, do not suppose I entertain any design unworthy of a gentleman. But I have the right, the blessed right, to stay near you, and that right I am resolved to defend."

"And do you believe, my lord, that such violence can force my love to yield to yours?"

"I do not believe so," said Lord Wentworth, gently. "But perhaps when you see me each day so resigned and respectful, coming only to ask how you are, with the sole aim of gazing upon you for a moment, you will—who knows?—be touched by the submission of him who has the power to coerce, and yet simply implores."

"And then," retorted Diana scornfully, "the vanquished daughter of France will become the mistress of Lord Wentworth?"

"And then," replied the governor, "Lord Wentworth, the last representative of one of the richest and most illustrious houses in England, will offer on his knees his name and life to Madame de Castro. You see my love is as honorable as it is sincere."

"Could he be ambitious?" thought Diana.

"Listen, my lord," she answered in a loud voice, trying to smile; "take my advice—give me my freedom, restore me to the king my father. I shall consider my ransom but a small part of my indebtedness to you. Peace is inevitable; and when it comes, rest assured that, though I may not give you myself, you will be the recipient of as many honors and dignities as if you were my husband. Be generous, my lord, and I will be grateful."

"I guess your thought, madame," said Wentworth, bitterly; "but I am at once more disinterested and more ambitious than you believe. Of all the treasures of the universe I wish only you."

"Then one last word, my lord," said Diana, with a mixture of confusion and pride. "My lord, another loves me."

"And you imagine I am going to deliver you to this rival by giving you your freedom!" exclaimed Wentworth, almost deranged. "No, he shall, at least, be as unhappy as I am! more so, madame, for he will not see you. From this day forward, only three events can deliver you: my death, and I am still young and vigorous; a peace with France, and you know the wars between France and England last a hundred years; finally, the capture of Calais, and Calais is impregnable. Putting aside these three almost desperate chances, you are likely to be my prisoner for a long time; for I have purchased all Lord Grey's rights over you, and I would not accept a ransom, though it were an empire! And as to flight, you will do as well not to think of it; for I guard you, and you will see what a watchful jailer is a man who loves."

Thereupon he bowed profoundly and retired, leaving Diana trembling and hopeless.

Still, she recovered her self-possession a little by thinking that death was a certain refuge—a refuge that was always left to the wretched when driven to the last extremity.

CHAPTER XXXIX

THE ARMORER'S HOUSE

THE house of Pierre Peuquoy formed the angle of the Rue du Martroi and the market-place. It was supported by wooden pillars on two sides, as is still the case in Paris with some of the houses in the Halles. It had two stories and an attic. On its front, there was a curious arrangement of wood, brick, and slate, producing a series of arabesques at once capricious and regular. Moreover, the supports of the casements and some other huge beams had queer, fantastic animals carved on them, framed in foliage equally fantastic; the whole was artless and rude, but not wanting in invention and life. The roof was high and broad, projecting far enough from the walls to shelter a railed exterior gallery which, as in the Swiss chalets, ran round the second story. Above the door of the shop swung the sign, a kind of wooden flag, on which a warrior, painted to inspire terror, was trying to represent the god Mars, and was no doubt aided in doing so by this inscription: *To the god Mars, Pierre Peuquoy, armorer.*

On the doorstep, a complete suit of armor, casque, cuirass, brassards, and cuissards, served as a speaking sign for those gentlemen who did not know how to read. Moreover, through the leaden-framed windows in the front of the shop could be distinguished, in spite of the obscurity, other panoplies and arms, defensive and offensive, of all sorts. The swords were especially notable for their number, variety, and richness.

Two apprentices, seated under the pillars, were appealing to the passers-by, inviting them with the most alluring persuasiveness to examine the merchandise inside.

As to the armorer Pierre Peuquoy, he usually stood majestically either in the rear of his shop looking on the yard, or in his forge placed under a shed at the back of the same yard. He came forward only when a buyer of distinction, attracted by the cries of the apprentices, or rather by the reputation of Peuquoy, asked for the master.

The rear of the shop, better lighted than the front, served both as parlor and dining-room. It was wainscoted everywhere in oak, and furnished with a square table having twisted legs, tapestried chairs, and a magnificent press, on which rested the masterpiece of Pierre Peuquoy, executed under the eyes of his father when he was received as master; it was a charming little suit of armor in miniature, all damascened in gold, and of the most finished and delicate workmanship. The patience and art needed to bring such a jewel to perfection cannot be even imagined.

Opposite the press was a niche in the wall, in which was a plaster cast of a statue of the Virgin surrounded with consecrated boxwood. Thus holy thoughts were always present in the family meeting-room.

From another part, a flight of wooden stairs, almost perpendicular, led to the two upper stories.

Pierre Peuquoy, enchanted at the idea of receiving Viscount d'Exmès and Jean Peuquoy in his house, insisted absolutely on surrendering the first story to Gabriel and his cousin. It was there, consequently, that the apartments of his two guests were placed. For himself, he lived in the second with his young sister Babette and her children. The wounded squire, Arnold du Thill, was also lodged in the second story. The apprentices slept in the attic. All the rooms were comfortable, and gave evidence, if not of wealth, at least of that ease and simple abundance which distinguished the old bourgeoisie at all times.

Gabriel and Jean Peuquoy were at table, where their worthy host had just done them the honors of a bounteous supper. Babette was serving the guests. The children held themselves respectfully apart at some distance.

" *Vive Dieu!* monseigneur, you are eating very little, if you will allow me to say so," said the armorer. "You are quite troubled, and Jean is quite pensive. Still, if the banquet is but middling, the heart that offers it is good. Take some of these grapes, then; they are rather rare in our country. I have it from my grandfather, who had it from his, that formerly, in the time of the French, the vine was generous in Calais and its clusters golden. But since Calais has become English, the grape thinks it is English, too, and grows in their island, where you know it never ripens."

Gabriel could not help laughing at these singular patriotic deductions of the good Pierre.

"Come," said he, "I drink to the ripening of the grapes of Calais."

Needless to say if the Peuquoys gave a heartfelt response to the toast. Then, supper over, Pierre said grace, which his guests listened to standing and uncovered. The children were sent to bed immediately after.

"You can now retire, Babette," said the armorer. "See that the apprentices don't make too much noise up yonder; and before returning to your room, do you and Gertrude go into that of the squire of M. le Comte, and find out if he needs anything."

Pretty Babette blushed, made a courtesy, and passed out.

"Now," said Pierre to Jean, "my dear gossip and cousin, we are quite alone, we three; and if you have any secret communication to make, I am ready to hear it."

Gabriel regarded Jean Peuquoy with astonishment; but the latter answered with his usual seriousness—

"Yes, Pierre, I told you I had to speak to you about important things."

"I will retire," said Gabriel.

"Excuse me, M. le Vicomte," said Jean; "but your

presence at our conversation is not only useful, but necessary; for, without your aid, the plans I am about to confide
to Pierre could not succeed."

"I will listen, then, my friend," said Gabriel, falling
back into his dreamy sadness.

"Yes, monseigneur; yes, listen," said the bourgeois.
"And after you have heard us, you will raise your head
hopefully, nay, even, perhaps joyfully."

Gabriel smiled sorrowfully, thinking that, as long as he
could not work for his father's freedom, as long as he was
kept away from Diana's love, joy would be for him an
absent friend.   Nevertheless, the courageous young man
turned to Jean Peuquoy, and made him a sign to begin.

Then addressing Pierre in a grave tone—

"Cousin," said Jean, "and more than cousin, brother, it
is for you to speak first, and show Viscount d'Exmès how
much can be based on your patriotism.   Tell us, therefore,
Pierre, in what sentiments you were trained by your father,
and he by his father before him.   Tell us whether, though
English by force for more than two hundred years, you have
ever become English in heart.   Tell us, in fine, whether,
if a crisis arose, you would believe your blood and your
support were due to the old land of your ancestors or to
the new country imposed on you?"

"Jean," replied the other bourgeois with as much solemnity as his cousin—"Jean, if my name and race were
English, I do not know what I should think or what I should
feel.   But I know well by experience that when a family has
been French, though it were only for a moment and that
moment was two centuries ago, all other foreign domination
is insupportable to the members of that family, and seems
to them hard as servitude and bitter as exile.   That ancestor of mine, Jean, who saw Calais fall into the power of the
enemy, never spoke before his son of France except with
tears, and of England except with hatred.   His son did the
same; and this twofold sentiment of regret and aversion
has been transmitted from generation to generation, with-

out weakening and without changing. It is preserved by
the atmosphere of our old bourgeois houses. The Pierre
Peuquoy of two centuries ago lives again in the Pierre Peuquoy of to-day; and, Jean, just as I have the same French
name, I have the same French heart. The affront is of yesterday, as well as the pain. Do not say, Jean, that I have
two countries; there is, there can never be, but one! And
if I had to make a choice between the country I have been
forced to belong to and the country God has given me,
I should not hesitate.''

"You understand, monseigneur?" said Jean Peuquoy,
turning to Viscount d'Exmès.

"Yes, my friend; yes, I understand, it is fine, it is
noble!" replied Gabriel, still a little absent-minded.

"But a word, Pierre," resumed Jean Peuquoy. "All
our old compatriots do not think as you do, unfortunately;
is not this the case? You are, no doubt, the only child of
France in Calais who, at the end of two hundred years, has
not become an ingrate to his mother.''

"You are mistaken, Jean," replied the armorer. "I
have by no means spoken for myself alone. I do not say
that all those who bear a French name like me have not
forgotten their origin; but many bourgeois families always
love and regret France, and it is from these families that
the Peuquoys select their wives. Nay, in the ranks of the
civic guard, to which I am compelled to belong, many a
citizen would break his halberd sooner than turn it against
a French soldier.''

"Good to know that!" murmured Jean Peuquoy, rubbing his hands. "And tell me, cousin, you have surely
some grade in that civic guard, have you not? Being so
loved and esteemed as you are, that is pretty certain.''

"No, Jean, I have refused every grade, in order to be
free of all responsibility.''

"So much the worse and so much the better then!
Is the service imposed upon you very laborious, Pierre?
Is it often renewed?''

"Why, yes," said Pierre, "it is frequent and rough enough, seeing that for a place like Calais the garrison is insufficient; and in my case, I have to enter on duty the fifth of each month."

"The fifth of each month regularly? These English have no prudence to fix thus in a certain manner the day of service of each."

"Oh!" replied the armorer, "there is no danger, after two centuries of possession. Besides, as they always have a little distrust of the civic guard, they confide to it only posts impregnable in themselves. I am always stationed as a sentinel on the platform of the Octagon tower, which is better defended by the sea than by me, and which the seamew alone can approach, I imagine."

"Ah! you are always stationed, the fifth of each month, on the platform of the Octagon tower?"

"Yes, from four till six in the morning. The district officer allows me to select that hour. I prefer it, because, during three-fourths of the year, I can see the reflection of the sunrise on the ocean, and even for a poor tradesman like me, that is a divine spectacle."

"A spectacle so divine indeed," replied Jean, lowering his voice, "that if, in spite of the impregnable situation, some bold adventurer should try to scale your Octagon tower on that side, I wager you would not see him, so deeply would you be absorbed in your meditations."

Pierre regarded his cousin with surprise.

"I would not see him, it is true," he replied, after a moment's hesitation; "for I should know that only a Frenchman could have any interest in penetrating into the city, and as I am forced, I am under no obligation to those who force me. Rather than repulse the assailant, I would, perhaps, aid him."

"Well said, Pierre!" exclaimed Jean Peuquoy. "You see, monseigneur, that Pierre is a devoted Frenchman," he added, addressing Gabriel.

"I see it," replied the latter, still inattentive, in spite

of himself, to a conversation that seemed to him useless. "I see it, but, alas! what is the good of this devotion?"

"What is the good? I am going. to tell you," replied Jean Peuquoy, "for it is now my turn to speak, I think. Well, then, if you wish it, M. le Vicomte, we can take our revenge for St. Quentin at Calais. The English, confident in their two hundred years' possession, have fallen asleep in deceptive security; this security ought to be their destruction. We have, monseigneur sees, auxiliaries ready in the place. Let us bring this idea to maturity, let your influence with those who have the power come to our help, and my reason, even more than my instinct, tells me that a bold *coup-de-main* will render us masters of the city. You understand me, do you not, monseigneur?"

"Yes, yes, certainly!" replied Gabriel, who in reality was no longer listening, but whom this direct appeal awaked from his revery. "Yes, your cousin wishes to return—does he not?—into our fair realm of France; to be transferred to some French city—Amiens, for example? Well, I will speak about it to Lord Wentworth and M. de Guise. The thing can be done; and my influence, which you claim, shall not be wanting. Go on, my friend; you may rely on me. Certainly I am listening to you."

And he became again lost in his thoughts.

For the voice he was listening to at that moment was not the voice of Jean Peuquoy; no, it was that of Henry the Second ordering the instant release of Count Montgommery, after hearing the narrative of the siege of St. Quentin drawn up by Coligny. Again it was the voice of his father attesting, still gloomy and jealous, that Diana was really the daughter of his crowned rival. In fine, it was the voice of Diana herself who, after so many trials, was at last able to utter these divine words, "I love you!"

It can be easily understood that, plunged in this sweet dream, he only half heard the hazardous and triumphant projects of worthy Jean Peuquoy.

But this grave citizen was naturally somewhat hurt at

the want of attention shown by Gabriel to an enterprise that was certainly not lacking in grandeur and courage, and it was with a little bitterness that he resumed:

"If monseigneur had deigned to pay a little more regard to our conversation, he would have discovered that the ideas of Pierre and of myself were neither so personal nor so unimportant as he supposes."

Gabriel did not answer.

"He does not hear you, Jean," said Pierre Peuquoy, pointing to their guest, who was again insensible to his surroundings; "he has perhaps also his plan, his passion."

"His is not more disinterested than ours," returned Jean, not without some severity. "I should say even that it is selfish, if I had not seen this gentleman brave danger with a sort of madness; and even expose his life to save mine. No matter! he ought to have heard me when I spoke for the welfare and glory of the country. But without him, in spite of all our zeal, we should be but useless instruments, Pierre. We have only the sentiment; we lack the wisdom and the power."

"For all that, the sentiment was good; for I have understood you, yes, I have understood you, my brother!" said the armorer.

And the two brothers solemnly clasped each other's hands.

"Meanwhile we must renounce our idea, or at least adjourn it for the present," said Jean Peuquoy; "for what can the arm do without the head? what can the people do without the nobles?"

This bourgeois of the olden time added with a singular smile:

"Until the day when the people is both arm and head."

CHAPTER XL

IN WHICH A VARIETY OF EVENTS ARE GROUPED TOGETHER WITH MUCH ART

THREE weeks slipped by; the last days of September were approaching, and, so far, no change of importance had been wrought in the situation of the different characters of our story.

Jean Peuquoy, as he was bound to do, paid the ransom, the amount of which he had succeeded in fixing himself, to Lord Wentworth. Moreover, he obtained permission to settle in Calais. We must say, however, he appeared in no hurry to establish a business and set to work. Indeed, he seemed to be of a very inquisitive, but of a very free and easy disposition, did our honest bourgeois. And he was seen from morning to night lounging on the ramparts and chatting with the soldiers of the garrison, from all appearance taking as little thought of his weaver's trade as if he had been an abbot or a monk.

Nevertheless, he had not cared, or else was unable, to make his cousin Pierre Peuquoy a partner in his idleness, and never had this skilled armorer turned out more arms or finer ones.

Gabriel was growing daily sadder and sadder. Only news of a general character reached him from Paris. France was beginning to breathe again. The Spaniards and English had lost time that could never be regained in taking a few miserable fortresses; the country knew where it stood once more, and Paris and the king were safe. This news, which the heroic defence of St. Quentin had not a little contributed to render so glorious, elated Gabriel, no doubt; but not a word of Henry the Second, of Coligny, not a word of his father or of Diana. These thoughts cast a gloom over his countenance and prevented him from responding to the friendly advances of Lord Wentworth as he might perhaps have done, were he circumstanced differently.

The affable and good-natured governor seemed, in fact, to be seized with the strongest friendship for his prisoner. Doubtless the fact that he was bored, added to a certain degree of melancholy caused by the events of the last couple of days, contributed not a little to this sympathy. The society of a clever young gentleman of the French court was a precious relief in this dull Calais. Consequently Lord Wentworth never let two days pass without visiting Viscount d'Exmès, and would have him dine with him at least three times a week. On the whole, this affection was rather troublesome; for the governor swore laughingly that he would release his captive only at the last extremity, would never accept his parole, and would never submit to the harsh necessity of separating from so dear a friend until the last crown of his ransom was duly paid.

As at bottom this might be only an elegant and lordly fashion of showing his distrust, Gabriel did not dare to insist, and from a feeling of delicacy made no complaint, but waited for the recovery of his squire, who, it will be remembered, was to have gone to Paris for the stipulated ransom that was to set Viscount d'Exmès at liberty.

But Martin Guerre, or rather his substitute, Arnold du Thill, was recovering only very slowly. At the end of a few days, however, the surgeon attending to the wound the rascal had received in a scuffle retired, declaring his task finished and his patient well. One or two days' rest and the good nursing of gentle Babette were all now needed to complete the cure.

On this assurance, Gabriel announced to his squire that he must start for Paris in two days. But on the morning of the day appointed, Martin Guerre complained of such faintness and dizziness that he could not take a step outside his room unless supported by Babette, and would be sure, he said, to encounter serious falls on the road. A new delay, asked and granted, of two days. At the end of that time, poor Arnold became the victim of general prostration; this lassitude, caused by his sufferings assuredly, could only be vanquished by means of baths and a severe regimen. But the regimen occasioned such weakness that another delay was judged indispensable to give the faithful squire time to renew his strength by nourishing food and a little generous wine. At least so affirmed the weeping Babette to Gabriel, swearing that if Martin Guerre set out at once, he would perish of inanition by the way.

This singular convalescence was thus prolonged for two weeks, in spite of the nursing. A calumniator might say because of the nursing of Babette, the entire illness having lasted a month since the arrival of Gabriel in Calais.

But this could not continue longer. Gabriel at last grew impatient, and Arnold du Thill himself, who at first was fertile in expedients, declared now with an authoritative and conquering air to the tearful Babette that he could not risk angering his master, and that by starting the quicker he should return the quicker; decidedly then, the best thing to do was to start. But the red eyes and downcast mien of poor Babette proved that she was anything but convinced by his logic.

On the eve of the day when Arnold du Thill, after this formal declaration, was to set out for Paris, Gabriel was at supper with Lord Wentworth. The governor seemed even more melancholy than ordinary; he tried to shake it off, but his forced gayety bordered on extravagance.

When he left Gabriel, after conducting him to the courtyard lighted at that hour by a lamp already growing dim, the young man, at the moment he was wrapping his cloak about him preparatory to the journey, saw one of the doors looking on the yard open, and a woman he recognized as one of the servants of the house stole up to him and, with a finger on her lips, slipped a paper into his hand.

"For the French gentleman whom Lord Wentworth receives," she said in a low voice as she was handing him the note.

And before the astonished Gabriel could question her, she had taken flight.

The young man, who was by nature rather inquisitive and possibly imprudent, had his curiosity very much aroused. It would take him a quarter of an hour to reach his room in the darkness, and read the letter at his ease; he thought it was quite too long to wait for the solution of an enigma that seemed to have some piquancy about it. He looked around him then, and, finding he was alone, approached the smoky lamp, unfolded the note, and read, not without emotion, what follows:

"Monsieur, I do not know and have never seen you; but one of the women who wait upon me says that you are a Frenchman, and, like me, a prisoner. This gives me courage to appeal to you in my distress. You are, no doubt, detained for ransom. You will probably soon return to Paris. You will be able to see my people, who are ignorant as to what has become of me. You could tell them where I am, that Lord Wentworth keeps me from communicating with a living soul, refusing to accept a ransom for my liberty, and that, abusing the cruel rights my position gives him, he dares to speak to me every day of a love which I repulse with horror, but which this very scorn and the certainty of impunity may push to crime. A gentleman and, above all, a fellow-countryman will surely help me in this terrible extremity; but I have decided to tell you who I am, in order that duty—"

Here the letter broke off without a signature. Some unexpected accident, some unforeseen obstacle, probably caused an interruption; and yet the writer determined to send it, though unfinished, so as not to lose any precious opportunity, and because, incomplete as it was, she nevertheless had said all that she wanted to say, except the name of the woman so unworthily kept under constraint.

Gabriel did not know this name; the hasty and trembling writing he could not know; and yet a strange trouble, an incredible presentiment, stole into his heart. And, pale with emotion, he was approaching the lamp again to read the letter more carefully, when another door opened and gave passage to Lord Wentworth himself, who, preceded by a little page, crossed the courtyard on his way to his bedroom.

Perceiving Gabriel, whom he had escorted to this very spot five minutes before, the governor paused in some astonishment.

"You still here, my friend?" going up to him with his usual affectionate interest. "What has detained you? Not an accident, an indisposition, at least I hope?"

The loyal young man, without replying, handed him the letter he had just received. The Englishman threw his eyes over it, and became paler than Gabriel; but he knew how to keep cool, and, while pretending to read, was arranging an answer in his own mind.

"The old idiot!" he said, crumpling the letter and flinging it from him with well-assumed contempt.

No words were fitter to disenchant Gabriel than these; only a short time ago he had been absorbed in thoughts bearing on his own fortunes, and his interest in the unknown lady soon grew cold. Still, he did not lose it all at once, and he said with some distrust—

"You do not say who is this prisoner detained by you in spite of herself, my lord?"

"In spite of herself; you never said a truer word!" replied Lord Wentworth, in a careless tone. "She is a relative of my wife, a crack-brained creature, if there ever was one. Her family was desirous of removing her from England, and I have been persuaded to become her guardian, very much against my will; but they thought this was a place where mad people, as well as other prisoners, could be easily watched. Since you have, my dear friend, penetrated a family secret, I think it better to explain the whole matter to you. The mania of Lady Howe, who has read too many romances of chivalry, is to believe herself, in spite of her fifty years and her gray hairs, an oppressed and persecuted damsel, and to interest in her story, more or less well-founded, every young and gallant knight who comes within her reach. And, by my faith, Gabriel, it looks as if the old lady's tale has touched you. Come now, confess her missive has somewhat disturbed you, my poor friend!"

"You must acknowledge yourself, my lord, that the story is somewhat strange," replied Gabriel, rather coldly; "and you have never mentioned, as far as I remember, this relation, have you?"

"No, indeed," answered Lord Wentworth. "As a rule, one does not care to introduce strangers into one's family secrets."

"But how comes it that this kinswoman of yours happens to be French?" said Gabriel.

"Oh, probably the better to arouse your interest," returned Wentworth, with a constrained smile.

"But what about this lover who persecutes her, my lord?"

"An old maid's illusions! she takes memories for hopes!" retorted Wentworth, who was beginning to show a little impatience.

"And it is to avoid ridicule, is it not, that you hide her away from all eyes, my lord?"

"Oh, we have had enough of questions!" exclaimed Lord Wentworth, frowning, but still controlling himself. "I did not imagine you were so exceedingly inquisitive, Gabriel. But it is now a quarter past nine, and you must return to your lodgings before the curfew has rung; for your parole is hardly so extensive as to allow a breach of the regulations for the security of Calais. If you are so much interested in Lady Howe, we can resume the conversation to-morrow. In the meantime, I must ask you to keep silence on this rather delicate family matter, and I wish you good-night, M. le Vicomte."

Thereupon the governor of Calais saluted and withdrew. He wished to retain his self-possession, and was afraid he might lose it if the conversation were prolonged.

After a moment's hesitation and reflection, Gabriel quitted the governor's residence and returned to the armorer's. But Lord Wentworth's self-control was not so strong as to efface all suspicion from the heart of Gabriel; and the doubts of the young man—doubts which a secret instinct encouraged—assailed him anew on the road.

He resolved henceforth to maintain silence on this point with Lord Wentworth, who would certainly give him no information, but to try to find out by observation and inquiry whether the unknown lady was a Frenchwoman and a prisoner or not.

"But, good heavens!" said Gabriel to himself, "even if I should prove the latter to be the case, what could I do? Am I not myself a prisoner? Are not my hands tied, and cannot Lord Wentworth demand again the sword I wear only by his sufferance? This must have an end, and I must get out of an equivocal position. Martin Guerre shall start to-morrow without any further delay. I will signify as much to him this evening."

As soon as an apprentice opened the door for him, Gabriel went up to the second story instead of remaining, according to custom, in his apartment on the first. The entire household was sleeping at this hour, and Martin Guerre doubtless slept like the others. But Gabriel was determined to awake him in order to intimate to him his exact will. He advanced noiselessly, however, to the room of his squire, in order not to disturb the sleep of anybody. The key was in the first door, and Gabriel opened it gently. But the second door was shut, and he could hear bursts of laughter and the clinking of glasses. He rapped with some violence, and mentioned his name in an imperious voice. There was silence on the instant, and as Gabriel raised his voice still louder, Arnold du Thill hastily unbolted the door. But he was just a little too hasty, and Gabriel as he entered was able to catch a glimpse of a woman's skirt disappearing through a side door.

The young man believed he had become cognizant of some amour with a servant of the house; and as he was not excessively prudish, he could not keep from laughing while he was rebuking his squire.

"Ah, ha! it seems you are better than you pretend to be, Martin; a table spread, three bottles, two covers. I fancy, too, I saw another guest on the run. No matter; the proofs of your cure are flagrant, and I can have no scruple in ordering you to set out to-morrow."

"It was, you know, my intention, monseigneur," said Arnold, in a penitent tone, "and I was, in fact, taking leave of—"

"One of your friends? You have a good heart," said Gabriel, "but friendship must not make you forget duty, and I require you to be on the road to Paris to-morrow before I rise. You have the governor's pass, your retinue is ready, your horse rested like yourself, your purse full, thanks to the confidence of our worthy host in us, whose only regret is, the excellent man, not to be able to pay my ransom in full. Nothing is lacking, Martin; and if you start early in the morning, you're sure to be in Paris in three days. Do you remember what you have to do when there?"

"Yes, monseigneur. I'm to go immediately to the hôtel in the Rue des Jardins St. Paul, and reassure your nurse as to your safety. I then ask her for ten thousand crowns for your ransom, and three thousand for your debts and other expenses here, and as a token, show her this note from you and your ring."

"Useless precautions, Martin, for my good nurse knows you well; but I have given way to your scruples. Only let this money be ready as soon as possible, you understand?"

"Do not be uneasy, monseigneur. And as soon as I

have the money, and have handed your letter to M. l'Amiral, I am to return here as speedily as possible."

"And no wretched quarrels on the road, especially."

"There is no danger, monseigneur."

"Good-by then, Martin, and good luck!"

"In ten days from now, you shall see me again, monseigneur, and to-morrow at sunrise I will be far from Calais."

This time Arnold du Thill kept his promise. He allowed Babette to accompany him the next morning, but only to the gate of the city. He kissed her for the last time, swearing that she should see him soon again. Then, giving his steed both spurs, he galloped off gayly, like the rogue he was, and disappeared at a turn of the road.

The poor girl hastened to reach the house before her terrible brother, Pierre Peuquoy, was risen; then she had to say she was unwell, in order to be able to weep at her ease in her bedchamber.

From that moment it would be difficult to tell whether she or Gabriel was most impatient for the return of the squire.

But both had to wait for that return a long time.

CHAPTER XLI

HOW ARNOLD DU THILL HAD ARNOLD DU THILL HANGED AT NOYON

ON THE first day, Arnold du Thill did not meet with any unpleasant adventure, and continued on his journey without encountering too many obstacles. From time to time, he came up with bands of the enemy— German deserters, disbanded Englishmen, and Spaniards made insolent by victory; for in this poor wasted France there were now more foreigners than Frenchmen. But to all inclined to be troublesome, Arnold proudly exhibited Lord Wentworth's pass, and all, though not without regrets and murmurs, respected the bearer of the governor's signature.

Nevertheless, on the second day, a Spanish detachment in the neighborhood of St. Quentin attempted to confiscate his horse; they employed an artful quibble for the attainment of their object, claiming that the horse was not included in the pass. But the false Martin Guerre displayed great firmness, demanding to be led at once to their commander, and horse and rider were quickly released.

Still, the adventure taught him a lesson, and he decided to avoid as much as possible any troops he might be likely to encounter. The thing was difficult. Although the enemy had not gained any decisive advantage since St. Quentin, they occupied the whole country. Le Catelet, Ham, Noyon, and Chauny belonged to them; and when Arnold came near Noyon on the evening of the second day, he resolved, in order to prevent further annoyance, to take a circuitous route and sleep at the next village.

But to do so, it was necessary to leave the highroad. Arnold knew the country badly; he went astray; and while searching for a path, he fell suddenly into the midst of a troop of reiters, who appeared to be searching also.

Now, Arnold's satisfaction may be imagined when he heard one of them, as soon as he perceived him, cry out—

"Ho there! have we really caught that rascal Arnold du Thill by chance?"

"What! Arnold du Thill on horseack?" said another reiter.

"Good God!" said the squire to himself. "It seems I am known here; and if I am known, I am lost."

But it was too late to fly; the reiters were flocking around him. Happily, the night was already rather dark.

"Who are you, and where are you going?" asked one of them.

"My name is Martin Guerre," replied the squire, turning pale. "I am the squire of Viscount d'Exmès, now a prisoner in Calais, and I am going to Paris for the money for his ransom. That is the pass from Lord Wentworth, governor of Calais."

The leader of the troop ordered one of the soldiers to bring a torch, and gravely set about verifying the pass.

"The seal is authentic and the pass genuine," said he. "You have told the truth, friend, and can continue your journey."

"Thanks!" said Arnold, beginning to breathe once more.

"One word more with you, however, my friend. Would you, by any chance, have met on your way a man evidently on the run, a rascal, a gallows-bird, answering to the name of Arnold du Thill?"

"I don't know any Arnold du Thill," Arnold du Thill hastened to say.

"You may not be acquainted with him, friend, but you might have happened to encounter him on some of these paths. He is your shape, and, as well as can be judged on a dark night, somewhat of your appearance. Only he is anything but as well dressed as you are. He wears a brown mantle, round hat, and gray hose, and must be hiding somewhere in the direction you came from, the brigand! Only let us get a grip of that imp of hell Arnold!"

"What has he done?" timidly inquired Arnold.

"What has he done? He has escaped us for the third time. He claims we make life too hard for him. I should think so! His first escapade was carrying off his master's mistress. That deserved punishment, I should say. And then he has not money enough to pay his ransom. He has been sold over and over again. He passes from hand to hand, and no one wants to have anything to do with him. It is right for him to afford us some amusement, as we can't get any profit by him. But, lo and behold you! he stands on his dignity; he refuses and escapes. Yes, escapes three times! But if we catch the scoundrel—"

"What will you do to him?" asked Arnold again.

"The first time we beat him, the second time we half killed him, the third time we intend to hang him."

"Hang him!" repeated Arnold, terrified.

"At once, my friend, and without further trial. It will divert us, and be a lesson to him. Look on your right, friend. You see yon gibbet? There's where we'll hang this devilish rascal, if we catch him."

"Ah, capital!" said Arnold, laughing, but his laughter was a little forced.

"We'll do as we say, my friend; so if you meet the rogue in your travels, bring him to us, and we won't prove ungrateful. And now a safe journey to you!"

They were riding off. Arnold felt he was out of danger and called them back—

"Excuse me, my masters, one good turn deserves another! I have gone astray, as you see, and I don't know where I am. Please then to put me on the right road."

"That's easy enough, friend," replied the reiter. "Do you see the postern and walls behind you? that's Noyon.

You are looking too much toward the right, in the direction of the gibbet. It is there on your left, where you see the pikes of our comrades; for our company is on guard at that postern to-night. Now, wheel round; Paris is before you, beyond that wood. Twenty yards from here, the road branches in two. You may take either right or left, as you please; the one road is as long as the other, and both unite again at the Oise ferry, a quarter of a league from here. After you cross the ferry, always keep to the right. The first village is Auvray, a league from the ferry. And now you know as much as myself. A good journey, friend!"

"Thank you, and good-night," said Arnold, putting his horse to a trot.

The information given him was correct. Twenty yards away, he found the spot where the road branched, and took the road to the left.

It was a dark night, and the forest was very thick. However, at the end of ten minutes, Arnold du Thill reached a clearing, and the moon shed a faint light on the path through pearly clouds.

Arnold du Thill was reflecting on his late terror, and on the singular adventure which tried all his coolness. He felt no dread as to the past, but he contemplated the future with anything but assurance.

"It can only be the real Martin Guerre they are pursuing under my name," he thought. "I know that impudence may save me, but it can also destroy me. Why should this rascal care to escape? He is, in truth, becoming very troublesome! and those brave enemies would be doing me a charity if they hanged him. The man is decidedly my evil genius."

Arnold was still indulging in this edifying monologue, when he perceived, or thought he perceived—he had keen and well-trained eyes—a man a hundred yards in front, or rather a shadow, quickly disappearing in a ditch, as he approached.

"Ha! another unpleasant encounter, an ambuscade of some sort," thought the prudent Arnold.

He tried to advance into the wood, but he found it impossible to clear the ditch. After waiting a few minutes, he ventured to look round. The phantom, which had risen for a moment, fell back into the ditch.

"What if he were as much afraid of me as I am of him?" said Arnold to himself. "Are we really trying to avoid each other? But I must come to some decision, for these infernal thickets will not allow me to reach the other road through the wood. Shall I turn back? It would be the most prudent thing to do. Shall I bravely dig the spurs into my horse, and pass on like a flash? It would be the shortest course. He is on foot, and unless a shot from an arquebuse— I have it! I shall not give him time."

His resolution was at once executed. He spurred his horse and passed the man, who was either in ambush or concealment, like lightning. The man did not budge.

This restored all Arnold's courage. He even turned back a few yards, and then a sudden idea seized him. He rode quietly to the edge of the ditch.

But at that very moment, and before he had time to say Jesus! the man leaped up, pulled Arnold's right leg from the stirrup, lifted it up, dragged the squire violently from the saddle, fell on top of him, and then placed his knee on his chest and his hand on his throat.

All this had not lasted twenty seconds.

"Who are you, and what do you want?" demanded the conqueror of his prostrate foe.

"For God's sake, release me!" said Arnold, in a strangled voice, for he knew he had met his master. "I am a Frenchman, and have a pass from Lord Wentworth, governor of Calais."

"If you are a Frenchman," said the man, "and indeed you haven't the accent of those damned foreigners, I don't need to see your pass. But why were you so inquisitive about me?"

"I thought I saw a man in the ditch," said Arnold, no longer under the stress of such vigorous pressure; "and I advanced to find out if he was wounded, and to bring him help, if there was occasion."

"The intention was good," said the man, withdrawing his hand and lifting his knee. "Come, get up, comrade," he added, offering a hand to Arnold, who was soon on his legs. "My reception has been just a little rough; excuse me. I don't want any one poking his nose into my affairs at present. But you are a fellow-countryman, and that makes a difference. Far from injuring, you can help me. We shall come to an understanding immediately. I am Martin Guerre; who are you?"

"I? I am—Bertrand," said Arnold, starting. For this man, whom he ordinarily got the better of by craft and knavery, became his superior by strength and courage, now that they were alone together in a forest by night.

Fortunately, the extreme darkness of the present night sheltered the incognito of Arnold, and he disguised his voice as best he could.

"Well, then, comrade Bertrand," resumed Martin Guerre, "learn that I am a fugitive prisoner, escaped for the second, some say for the third time, from those Spaniards, English, Germans, and Flemings; in short, from that swarm of enemies that has fallen on our poor country like a cloud of locusts. For may God confound me if France does not, at the present moment, resemble the Tower of Babel! For a month I have been the slave, such as you see me, of twenty jabberers of different nations, and every day I had to listen to some fresh gibberish more barbarous than that of the day before. I grew tired of being hawked from one village to another, the more so as they were apparently making sport of me, and finding a pleasure in tormenting me. They were always casting in my teeth that a pretty little piece of mischief named Gudule had fallen in love with me, and that I had carried her off."

"Ah, ah!" said Arnold.

"I tell you what they said. Well, their gibes made me tired; so one fine day—it was at Chauny—I showed them a clean pair of heels. As ill-luck would have it, I was taken and then cudgelled in such a fashion that I bewailed my condition, I can tell you. But what was the good? Still, though they swore they would hang me if I attempted such a thing again, I thought of nothing but attempting it; and this morning a lovely chance presented itself, and while they were fixing on their quarters at Noyon, I left my tyrants in the lurch nicely. God knows how eagerly they have searched for me: and to hang me! But I have a decided distaste for that sort of exercise, and so I perched, if you please, on a big tree in the forest waiting for nightfall. I could not help laughing, alarmed enough, when I saw them growling and swearing under my tree. When evening came I left my look-out. But in the first place, I went astray, having never been in these woods before; and in the second, I am dying of hunger, for I have not had a morsel between my teeth for the last twenty-four hours, except leaves and roots—not a very sumptuous feast. This is why I am so weak, as you can see for yourself."

"Tut!" said Arnold; "I haven't seen that at all, and a while ago you seemed to me rather vigorous, on the contrary."

"Ah, yes!" replied Martin, "because I handled you somewhat roughly. Don't feel any grudge on account of that. It was, in reality, the fever of hunger that gave me such energy. But, now, you are my providence; for since you are a countryman of mine, you won't let me fall into the hands of my enemies—isn't that so?"

"Certainly not, if I can prevent it," replied Arnold du Thill, who was slowly revolving the revelations of Martin.

He was beginning to see how he might recover the advantage for a moment endangered by the iron wrist of his Sosia.

"You can do a great deal for me," continued the innocent Martin. "Do you know the neighborhood around here well?"

"I belong to Auvray, a quarter of a league from here," said Arnold.

"You are going there?"

"No; I was coming from it," replied the astute knave, after a little hesitation.

"Is Auvray in that direction?" said Martin, pointing to the quarter in which Noyon was situated.

"Quite correct," answered Arnold; "it is the first village beyond Noyon on the Paris route."

"On the Paris route!" cried Martin. "Just see how a person can be lost in the woods. I thought I was turning my back on Noyon, and I was doing the exact opposite. I imagined I was going to Paris, and I was going away from it. Your confounded country, as I said, is perfectly unknown to me. I must then proceed in the direction you came from, if I'm not to make a bungle of it again."

"Just as you say, master. I am going to Noyon myself; but come with me for a short distance and we'll find, close to the Oise ferry, another road leading to Paris."

"A thousand thanks, friend Bertrand," said Martin. "I should like to meet as short a cut as possible, for I am very tired and very weak, being as starving a man as you could meet in a day's journey. You would not chance to have any provender about you, friend Bertrand? You would be twice my savior, if you had—once from the English and once from hunger, which is quite as horrible as the English."

"Alas!" replied Arnold, "I have not a crumb in my wallet. But if you would like to drink, I have plenty of wine."

In fact, Babette had been careful to fill a large vessel with Cyprus wine, a rather heady wine of the time, for her faithless lover, and Arnold had been wisely sparing of the bottle, so that he might retain full possession of his senses, which were easily upset, during the perils of the road.

"Drink? I should say so!" cried Martin, enthusiastically. "A little wine is never out of place."

"Drink, then, my worthy friend," said Arnold, tendering him the bottle.

"Thanks, and may God reward you!" returned Martin.

And he forthwith gulped down without any distrust this wine, which was as treacherous as the rascal who supplied it, and its fumes began to confuse his empty brain almost immediately.

"Ah!" said he, growing quite hilarious, "that claret of yours is rather fiery."

"Good gracious, no! it is very innocent," said Arnold; "and I drink two bottles of it at every meal. But stay, the evening is beautiful; let us sit down on the grass, and you can rest and drink at your ease. I have plenty of time; if I reach Noyon before ten, at which hour the gates are closed, I shall be all right. On the other hand, although Auvray still belongs to France, you will, if you follow the highroad so early, be likely to encounter troublesome patrolling parties; while, if you abandon it, you will go astray again. The best thing is for us to have a friendly conference on the subject. Where were you made prisoner?"

"I do not know exactly," said Martin Guerre; "for on that, as on every part of my poor life, there have been contradictory opinions—those I believe myself, and those I am told by others. I have been told I was taken and held for ransom at the battle of St. Quentin, while I fancy such was not the case, and that I fell into the hands of the enemy later on."

"What is your meaning?" asked Arnold du Thill, feigning surprise. "Have you, then, two histories? Your adventures seem to me to be very interesting and instructive, to say the least of them. Nothing in the world gives me such delight as narratives of that sort. Come now, have five or six good swallows to quicken your memory, and tell me something of your life. You are not from Picardy, are you?"

"No," replied Martin, after a pause spent in emptying three-fourths of the vessel; "no, I am from the south, from Artigues."

"A fine country, it is said. You have your family there?"

"Both wife and family, my dear friend," replied Martin Guerre, who had by this time become very confiding and very confidential, thanks to the light wine of Cyprus.

And excited partly by Arnold's questions, partly by his constantly renewed potations, he began to relate volubly his history in its most private details—his youth, his love, his marriage. His wife was charming, but had one little fault: her hand was at once too heavy and too light. In truth, a blow from a woman does not dishonor a man; but one grows tired of that sort of thing in the long run. This was why Martin Guerre left his too vivacious partner. The narrative was complicated by the causes, accidents, and consequences of this rupture. And yet, in the depths of his heart, he always loved that dear Bertrande. He still wore on his finger the iron ring of his marriage, and on his heart the two or three letters Bertrande had written to him at the time of their first separation. And thereupon worthy Martin wept, for this wine was capable of exciting the tenderest emotions. He wanted to recount next all that happened to him since he entered the service of Viscount d'Exmès—how a demon pursued him; how he, Martin Guerre, was double; and how, in one state of existence, he never knew what he might be doing in the other. But this part of his history did not appear to have much interest for Arnold du Thill, who always brought the narrator back to his childhood, his father's house, his friends and relatives in Artigues, the graces and blemishes in Bertrande.

In less than two hours, the treacherous Arnold du Thill knew all he wanted to know as to the old habits and most secret actions of poor Martin Guerre.

At the end of two hours, Martin Guerre, with head on fire, rose, or rather attempted to rise; for he stumbled as he did so, and fell back heavily on the grass.

"Well, well, what's the matter?" said he, laughing as if he would never stop. "This impudent wine of yours has floored me neatly, devil take me if it hasn't! Give me your hand, comrade, till I see if I can stand."

Arnold courageously uplifted him and planted him on his legs, but not in quite classical equilibrium.

"Ho there! look! what a number of lanterns!" cried Martin. "Well, I am an idiot. I took the stars for lanterns."

Then he began singing in a thundering voice—

> "I charge you send to hell's best inn
> Old Nick, that wanton wight of sin,
> And bid him from it hither bear
> The choicest wine to grace our fare."

"Silence!" said Arnold. "If some of the enemy were passing and heard you?"

"Bah! I don't care a fig for them," said Martin. "What could they do to me—hang me? Hanging wouldn't be so bad either. You have made me drink too much, comrade —I who am ordinarily as sober as a lamb—and I don't bear drunkenness well, and then I was fasting and hungry; now I am thirsty.

> "I charge you send to hell's—"

"Hush!" said Arnold. "Come, try to walk. Do you wish to sleep at Auvray?"

"Oh, yes—sleep," stammered Martin; "but—not at Auvray. Here, under God's lanterns, on the grass."

"Yes," retorted Arnold; "and to-morrow morning, a Spanish patrol will find you and send you to sleep with the devil."

" 'Old Nick, that wanton wight of sin?' " hummed Martin. "Well, I think I would sooner make an effort and drag myself to Auvray. It's that way, isn't it? I'm off."

But it was all very well trying to make an effort. He

described such extravagant zigzags that Arnold saw, if he did not support him, Martin would be lost again: that is to say, saved, for the time. Now this was not the rascal's cue at all.

"Come on," he said; "I have a charitable soul, and Auvray is not far. I will bring you there. Just let me untie my horse; I am going to lead him, and give you my arm."

"Faith, I am willing," said Martin. "There's no pride about me, and, between ourselves, I think I am a little under the weather. I hold to my first opinion—your claret is fiery."

"Let us be going then; it's getting late," returned Arnold du Thill, linking arms with his Sosia and starting on the road he came by, which led directly to the postern of Noyon. "But," he resumed, "why not shorten the road by telling me some good story of Artigues?"

"Shall I tell you the story of Papotte?" said Martin. "Ha, ha! poor Papotte!"

The story of Papotte was, however, of too involved a character to be related here. It was hardly finished when our two menechmi of the sixteenth century reached, not in the best condition, the postern of Noyon.

"There," said Arnold, "there is no need for me to go further. Do you see that gate? That's the gate of Auvray. The porter will open it for you. Mention my name, and he will direct you to my brother's house, a few yards from there, where you will find a good supper and a good bed. So good-by now, comrade. Your hand again, and God be with you."

"Good-by and thanks," answered Martin. "I am but a poor creature, and may never be able to make any return for all you have done for me. But rest easy; God, who is just, will know how to reward you. Adieu, my friend."

It is strange, these words, a drunkard's prediction, actually sent a shudder through Arnold, who was yet by no means superstitious; and for a moment he had the thought of recalling Martin. But the latter was already knocking loudly at the postern.

"Poor devil, he is knocking at his tomb," thought Arnold; "but, pshaw, away with such childishness!"

Martin, who had no suspicion that his companion was observing him from a distance, was meanwhile crying as if he would burst his throat—

"Ho there, porter! ho, Cerberus! are you going to open, clown? I come from Bertrand; honest Bertrand sent me here."

"Who's there?" asked the sentinel inside. "It's too late to open. Who are you that make such a racket?"

"Who am I? you idiot! I am Martin Guerre, or if you wish, Arnold du Thill, or if you wish, Bertrand's friend. I am several people together, particularly when I'm drunk. I am a score of lads, who will cudgel you within an inch of your life, if you don't let me in at once."

"Arnold du Thill. Are you Arnold du Thill?" inquired the sentinel.

"Yes, Arnold du Thill is one of us, twenty thousand cart-loads of devils," said Martin, beating the door with feet and hands.

There was a noise of soldiers behind the gate, who were running up in response to a call of the sentinel.

Then the door was opened by some one who held a lantern; and Arnold du Thill, from his hiding-place behind some trees, could hear several voices all crying together in amazement—

"It is himself. Devil take me if it isn't himself!"

But Martin Guerre, when he recognized his persecutors, uttered a cry of despair which smote Arnold in his place of concealment as a malediction.

After this Arnold judged by the tramping and outcries that poor Martin, seeing all was lost, had engaged in an impossible struggle. But what could two fists do against twenty swords? The noise diminished, then became more

remote, then ceased altogether. Martin was led away cursing and blaspheming.

"If he thinks to mend matters by curses and blows!"
said Arnold to himself, rubbing his hands.

When he no longer heard anything, he gave himself up
to his reflections for a quarter of an hour; for he was a very
thoughtful rascal, was Arnold du Thill. The result of his
meditations was that he plunged into the wood for three or
four hundred yards, tied his horse to a tree, laid the saddle
and horse-cloth on over a pile of withered leaves, wrapped
his cloak about him, and in a few moments was in one of
those dreamless slumbers which God gives oftener to the
hardened sinner than he does to the innocent saint.

He slept eight hours without a break.

Nevertheless, when he awoke it was still dark, and he
saw from the position of the stars it was about four o'clock
in the morning. He rose up, shook himself, and, without
untying his horse, advanced cautiously as far as the high-
way.

The body of poor Martin Guerre was swinging gently
from the gibbet he had been shown on the previous evening.

A hideous smile wandered over Arnold's lips.

He approached the body without trembling; but it hung
too high for him to reach it. Then he climbed along the
beam of the gallows, with his sword in his hand, and severed the rope.

The body fell to the earth.

Arnold descended, drew from the dead man's finger an
iron ring not worth the trouble of stealing, searched his
clothes, and found some papers which he carefully put
away. Then he muffled himself in his cloak and quietly
withdrew, without a look, without a prayer for the unfortunate being whom he had tormented during life and robbed
at death.

He found his horse in the thicket, saddled him, and rode
furiously toward Aulnay. He was contented, the wretch!
Martin would frighten him no more.

Half an hour after, when a feeble light began to dawn in the east, a wood-cutter, chancing to pass on the way, saw the rope of the gibbet cut and the hanged man lying on the ground. At once fearful and inquisitive, he approached the dead man, who lay with his clothes in disorder and the rope loose about his neck. He was in doubt whether the body had fallen from its own weight or had been cut down by some friend who came too late. He ventured to touch the victim, in order to make sure he was quite dead. Then, to his great terror, the hanged man moved his head and hands and rose on his knees. The frightened wood-cutter ran as if the devil was at his heels into the wood, making any number of signs of the cross and recommending his soul to God and the saints. ·

CHAPTER XLII

THE PASTORAL DREAMS OF ARNOLD DU THILL

CONSTABLE DE MONTMORENCY, who had returned to Paris the evening before after paying a royal ransom, had presented himself at the Louvre in order to find out at once how he stood in the king's favor. But Henry the Second received him with coldness and severity, at the same time praising the administration of the Duke de Guise, who, he told him, had so managed matters as to lessen, if he could not repair, the misfortunes of the realm.

The constable, pale with anger and envy, hoped to find a little consolation, at least, with Diana de Poitiers. But the favorite showed him as much coldness as the king; and when he complained of his reception and expressed a fear that in his absence, another, .more fortunate than he, had succeeded him in the good graces of the duchess, she retorted pertly—

"Doubtless you have heard the new saying of the people of Paris, constable?"

"I have just arrived, madame, and am ignorant—" stammered the constable.

"Well, our malicious Parisians say, 'It is to-day the day of St. Laurent; he who abandons a fortress surrenders it.'"

The constable became pallid, saluted the duchess, and left the Louvre stricken to the heart.

When he returned to his hotel and entered his chamber, he flung his hat violently on the ground. "Kings and women are alike!" he exclaimed—"ingrates all. They love only the successful."

"Monseigneur," said an attendant, "there is a man outside who wishes to speak with you."

"Send him to the devil!" returned the constable. "I am not well disposed to receive visitors at present. Send him to M. de Guise."

"Monseigneur, this man has asked me to mention his name; it is Arnold du Thill."

"Arnold du Thill!" cried the constable, now thoroughly interested. "That's different; let him enter."

The servant bowed and retired.

"This Arnold," thought the constable, "is clever, crafty, and greedy, utterly without scruples and without conscience. Oh, if he could help me to be revenged on all these people! To be revenged, hem! after all, what good will that do me? If he could help me to be restored to favor rather; he knows many things. I had already thought of utilizing this secret of Montgommery; but if Arnold can enable me to dispense with the necessity of having recourse to it, so much the better."

At this moment Arnold du Thill was introduced. The face of the rogue was beaming with joy and impudence. He bowed to the ground when he saluted the constable.

"I thought you were a prisoner," said Montmorency.

"I was so, monseigneur, like yourself."

"But you have got free, I see."

"Yes, monseigneur, I paid them in my own coin—monkey's coin. You used your money, I my wit, and so we are both free."

"Ah, sirrah! do you dare to be impertinent?" said the constable.

"No, monseigneur; it is humility, and all it means is that I need money."

"Hum!" returned Montmorency, grumbling; "what do you want with me?"

"Money, since I need it."

'And why should I give you money?"

"To pay me, monseigneur."

"Pay you for what?"

"The news I bring you."

"Let us see your news."

"Let us see the crowns."

"Rascal, I'll have you hanged."

"To make my tongue loll out of my mouth would be a detestable method of loosening it, monseigneur."

"He is so insolent," murmured Montmorency, "that he must know I cannot do without him."

"Well," said the constable aloud, "I consent to make you some advances."

"Monseigneur is very good," replied Arnold; "and I shall remind him of his generous words when he has settled his indebtedness to me in the past."

"What indebtedness?" asked the constable.

"Here is my note, monseigneur," said Arnold, presenting the famous document we have seen him add to so often.

Anne de Montmorency cast his eyes over it.

"Yes," said he, "you have noted some services that are perfectly illusory and chimerical, and others useful, perhaps, at the moment when they were rendered; but the recollection of them is only calculated to call up vain regrets now."

"Bah, monseigneur! perhaps you exaggerate your disgrace."

"What? do you and others know already that I am at present in disgrace?"

"I suspect it, monseigneur, and others also."

"Well then, Arnold," replied Montmorency, bitterly, "you should also suspect that it was useless to separate Diana de Castro and Viscount d'Exmès at St. Quentin, since in all probability the king and the grand séneschale will refuse their daughter to my son."

"Great heavens, monseigneur! I have an idea that the

king will very gladly give her to him, if you are able to re-store her to the king."

"What do you mean?"

"I mean, monseigneur, that Henry the Second, our Sire, must be very grieved at present, not only by the loss of St. Quentin and the battle of St. Laurent, but also by the loss of his very dear daughter, Diana de Castro, who disappeared from St. Quentin, without anybody since being able to find out what became of her; for twenty contradictory rumors have been current as to this disappearance. You were your-self, of course, ignorant of it, monseigneur, as you only re-turned yesterday. I knew of it myself only this morning."

"I have so many cares of other kinds," answered the constable; "and have naturally thought more of my present disgrace than of my past favor."

"It is natural, monseigneur. But would not that favor flourish again, if you could say to the king, for example, 'Sire, you weep for your daughter, you search and inquire for her in all directions; but I alone know where she is, sire'?"

"And do you really know, Arnold?" asked Mont-morency, quickly.

"To know is my trade," returned the spy. "I told you I had news to sell. You see my wares are not of bad qual-ity. Give the matter your best consideration, monseigneur; reflect upon it."

"I have reflected that kings remember the failures of their servants, but not their merits," said the constable. "When I restore Henry his daughter, he will be at first transported; all the gold and honors in the kingdom will not suffice to reward me. And then Diana will weep, Diana will say that she would rather die than marry any one but Viscount d'Exmès; and the king, entirely influenced by her and controlled by my enemies, will remember the battle I lost, and will not remember that I found his daughter. So the result of all efforts will be to make Viscount d'Exmès happy."

"It would, therefore, be necessary," returned Arnold, with his evil smile, "that when Madame de Castro reappears, Viscount d'Exmès should disappear. Ah, that would be a nice trick to play, eh?"

"Yes, but I have a dislike toward extreme measures," said the constable. "I know your hand is sure and your lips discreet. Still—"

"Ah! monseigneur misconceives my intentions," cried Arnold, putting on an air of virtuous indignation. "Monseigneur does not do me justice. Surely, monseigneur does not believe I would free him from this man by violence." (He made a gesture of protest.) "No, I have a better way than that, a hundred times better."

"What is it then?" the constable asked quickly.

"Let us first settle our little account, monseigneur," replied Arnold. "Then I will tell you the place where the wandering fair one has found a home, and during the time necessary for conclusion of the marriage with Monseigneur Francis, I insure the silence and absence of his dangerous rival. Are not these two useful services, monseigneur? And now what will you do for me on your part?"

"What do you ask?"

"You are reasonable; I will be the same. In the first place, you liquidate the little account of past debts which I have had the honor to present to you, and that without cutting down any of the items, do you not?"

"Granted," replied the constable.

"I knew we should have no difficulty as to this first point, monseigneur; the total is a mere trifle, and is not sufficient for my travelling expenses and the purchase of a few presents I reckon on buying in Paris. But gold is not everything."

"What!" cried the constable, astonished and almost dismayed, "is it Arnold du Thill that tells me gold is not everything?"

"Yes, Arnold du Thill himself, monseigneur; but not that needy and avaricious Arnold with whom you are ac-

quainted. No, another Arnold, content with the moderate
fortune he has acquired, and whose sole desire is to pass
the remainder of his life peacefully in the country of his
birth, under his father's roof-tree, amid his childhood's
friends and in the bosom of his family. Such has always
been the dream, monseigneur, such has been the calm and
delightful goal, of my agitated life."

"Yes, indeed," said Montmorency; "if one must pass
through the tempest to enjoy calm weather, you will be
happy, Arnold. But have you become rich?"

"Comfortable, monseigneur, comfortable. Ten thousand crowns for a poor devil like me is a fortune, especially in my humble village and in the bosom of my modest
family."

"Your family! your village!" exclaimed the constable;
"and I believed you to be without hearth or home, living
from hand to mouth, with a second-hand coat on your back
and a name that is not your own."

"Arnold du Thill is in fact an assumed name, monseigneur. My true name is Martin Guerre, and I was born
in Artigues, near Rieux, where I have left my wife and
children."

"Your wife!" repeated old Montmorency, more and more
astounded. "Your children!"

"Yes, monseigneur," returned Arnold, in the most
comically sentimental tone imaginable. "I have, therefore, to give you notice that henceforth you can no longer
reckon on my services, and that the two projects in which
I offer to co-operate with monseigneur will be the last with
which I shall be connected. I shall then retire from business, and try to live an honorable life ever after, surrounded
by the affection of my relatives and the esteem of my fellow-
citizens."

"All very fine. But if you have become so modest and
pastoral that you will not hear any mention of money, what
price do you ask for the secrets you say you possess?"

"I ask more and less than money," replied Arnold, this

time in a natural tone. "I ask honor, not honors; but understand, only a little honor, of which at the present moment I stand in great need."

"Explain," said Montmorency; "for truly you speak in riddles."

"Well, this is how the matter is, monseigneur. I have prepared a document which attests that I, Martin Guerre, have been in your service for so many years—as your squire (it is necessary to embroider a little); that during all that time I have been loyal, faithful, and devoted, and that you have acknowledged this devotion, monseigneur, by presenting me with a sum sufficiently large to shelter me from want during the remainder of my life. Place your seal and signature at the bottom of this document, and we are quits, monseigneur."

"Impossible," retorted the constable. "I should be a forger, and called a felon lord, if I were to sign such falsehoods."

"They are not falsehoods, monseigneur, for I have always served you faithfully, as far as my means allowed; and I solemnly declare that, if I had saved all the money I obtained from you up to now, I should be worth ten thousand crowns. You do not, therefore, expose yourself to any such accusation as you mention, while I have exposed myself to the most terrible dangers in order to bring about the happy results of which you will reap all the fruits."

"Wretch! this comparison—"

"Is just, monseigneur," rejoined Arnold. "We have need of each other, and equality is the daughter of necessity. The spy restores you your credit; do you restore his to the spy. Come, monseigneur, no one hears us. Away with false shame; clinch the bargain; it is a good one for me, a better one for you. One good turn deserves another. Sign, monseigneur."

"Not yet," returned Montmorency. "As you say, one good turn deserves another; I wish to be acquainted with your means of achieving the twofold result you promise.

I wish to know what has become of Diana de Castro, and what may become of Viscount d'Exmès."

"Well, monseigneur, except with a few reservations which I deem necessary, 1 am willing to satisfy you on these two points; and you will be forced to agree that chance and I have, between us, managed matters pretty well in your interest."

"I am listening," said the constable.

"In the first place, as to Madame de Castro," replied Arnold du Thill, "she has neither been killed nor carried off; she has only been made prisoner at St. Quentin, and included among the fifty persons of distinction who were held for ransom. Now, how comes it that the person into whose hands she has fallen has not mentioned her capture? Why has no news come from Madame de Castro herself? These are questions to which I can give no answer. To tell the truth, I believed her already free, and expected to find her in Paris on my arrival. It was only this morning the report became current that no one at court knew where the king's daughter was, and that this uncertainty was not the least of the anxieties of Henry the Second. Perhaps, in these troubled times, the letters of Madame Diana have been misdirected or gone astray; perhaps there is some other mystery hidden under this delay. But on this point I can dispel all doubts, and give positive information as to where and by whom Madame Diana is kept prisoner."

"Such information would, in truth, be valuable enough," said the constable; "where is the place, and who is her jailer?"

"Wait a moment, monseigneur," returned Arnold, "would you not be equally pleased to learn something of Viscount d'Exmès? For if it is well to know where are our friends, it is better to know where are our enemies."

"A truce to your maxims!" said Montmorency. "Where is this d'Exmès?"

"A prisoner also, monseigneur. Who has not been a prisoner now and then in these latter days? Why, it has been quite the fashion. Now, Viscount d'Exmès has conformed to the fashion, and he is a prisoner."

"Oh, he is certain to make his whereabout known, he must have friends and money; he will find what is needed for his ransom, no doubt, and on the first day of his release we may look out for squalls."

"You are perfectly correct, monseigneur. Yes, Viscount d'Exmès has money; yes, he is impatient to get free, and desires to pay his ransom as soon as possible. He has, in fact, already sent a messenger to Paris to procure money, with what speed he may, for this very purpose."

"What can we do to prevent that?" inquired the constable.

"Luckily for us and unluckily for him," continued Arnold, "I happen to be the messenger he has sent to Paris in such haste. I have served M. d'Exmès as squire, monseigneur, under my true name of Martin Guerre. You see, then, you will do nothing strange in making me a squire also."

"You have not fulfilled your mission, rascal, have you?" said the constable. "You have not collected the ransom of your so-called master?"

"I have, monseigneur, and that with great care; one doesn't leave such things lying around. Consider, moreover, that not to take this money was to excite suspicion. I have taken it conscientiously, for the good of our enterprise. Only, do not be uneasy! I shall not take it away from here under any pretext for quite a long time. These are the ten thousand crowns, monseigneur, that are going to enable me to lead a pious and honorable life for the rest of my days, and which I shall be considered to owe to your generosity, in virtue of the document you are about to sign."

"Sign it? never! you infamous wretch!" cried Montmorency. "I shall not knowingly make myself an accomplice in a theft."

"Oh, monseigneur, how can you give such a harsh name

to an action rendered necessary by my devotion to your service? What! I bid my conscience be still, prompted by this very devotion, and it is thus you reward me. Be it so. Let us send this sum of money to Viscount d'Exmès, and he will be here as soon as Madame Diana, if not sooner. While if he does not receive it—"

"If he does not receive it?" said the constable.

"We gain time, monseigneur. In the first place, M. d'Exmès will wait patiently for me for a fortnight. All that time is needed to collect the ten thousand crowns, and his nurse only counted them out to me this morning."

"And this poor woman trusted you?"

"Yes, monseigneur, she also trusted the ring and hand-writing of the viscount. And then she recognized me. Let us say, therefore, a fortnight of impatient expectation, a week of anxious expectation, another week of intolerable expectation, and there we are. Viscount d'Exmès will not send another messenger in search of the first for a month or a month and a half. But the first will not be found; and if it is hard enough to get ten thousand crowns together, it will be almost impossible to obtain a second ten thousand. You will have leisure enough to marry your son twenty times over, monseigneur; for Viscount d'Exmès vanishes, as if he was dead, for more than two months, and will return alive and furious only in the following year."

"Yes, but he will return!" said Montmorency; "and when he does, will he not make inquiries as to the fate of Martin Guerre?"

"Alas! monseigneur," replied Arnold, tearfully, "he will be told, it is with bitter grief I inform you of the fact, that the faithful Martin Guerre, when returning to his master with the ransom he had gone in search of, fell unfortunately into the hands of a party of Spaniards who, after having, in all probability, pillaged and stripped him, cruelly hanged him, to insure impunity, in front of the gates of Noyon."

"What! you have been hanged, Arnold?"

"Yes, monseigneur; you see how far my zeal extends. The only thing in doubt is the date of the hanging, the reports on this point being somewhat contradictory. But how can the thievish reiters be believed who have an interest in disguising the truth? Not likely. And now, monseigneur," went on the impudent Arnold, gayly and resolutely, "you see I have taken all my precautions skilfully, and that having a lad as wary as I am in his service, your Excellency stands in no danger of being compromised. If prudence were banished from the earth, it would take refuge in the heart of him who has been—hanged. Besides, I repeat, you only affirm the truth: I have been long your servant; a number of your people will say the same, and you have really given me ten thousand crowns, if all the items were summed up—you may rely on that. Would you wish me," continued the rascal with a lordly air, "to give you my receipt?"

The constable could not help smiling.

"Yes, yes," he said; "but if, knave, at the end of the account—"

Arnold du Thill interrupted him.

"Ah, monseigneur, you only hesitate as to the form; and what are forms for superior minds like ours? Sign without further ceremony."

He spread the paper, which only wanted this signature, on the table in front of Montmorency.

"But, first, the name of the city where Diana de Castro is a prisoner, and the name of the man who holds her?"

"Name for name, monseigneur, yours at the bottom of this paper, and you shall know the others."

"Here goes it, then!" said Montmorency.

And he traced the bold scrawl which served him for a signature.

"And the seal, monseigneur?"

"There it is. Are you satisfied?"

"Just as much as if monseigneur gave me ten thousand crowns."

"And now where is Diana?"

"In the hands of Lord Wentworth at Calais," said Arnold, trying to withdraw the parchment from the constable, who still retained it.

"Wait a moment," said he; "and Viscount d'Exmès?"

"At Calais, also in the hands of Lord Wentworth."

"Why, then, he and Diana see each other?"

"No, monseigneur; he lodges in the house of an armorer of the city named Pierre Peuquoy, and she lives in the governor's hôtel. Viscount d'Exmès knows no more than you do, I swear it, that his fair one is so near him."

"I'll run to the Louvre," said Montmorency, releasing the paper.

"And I to Artigues," cried Arnold, triumphantly. "Good luck, monseigneur! try and make them take your constableship seriously."

"Good luck, scamp; try and don't get hanged for good and all."

And each went his way.

CHAPTER XLIII

PIERRE PEUQUOY'S ARMS, JEAN PEUQUOY'S ROPES, AND BABETTE PEUQUOY'S TEARS

NEARLY a month slipped by at Calais without bringing, to their great regret, any change in the situation of the persons we left there. Pierre Peuquoy still turned out arms industriously. Jean Peuquoy had resumed his occupation as a weaver, and when not busy at his trade, was making ropes of a quite unconscionable length; Babette Peuquoy was weeping.

As for Gabriel, his suspense had gone through the various phases predicted by Arnold du Thill to the constable. He had borne up well enough for a fortnight; but since he had grown impatient indeed.

He now went only very seldom to Lord Wentworth's, and his visits were very short. There was a coolness between them ever since the day Gabriel had interfered with the so-called private affairs of the governor.

The latter, we have the satisfaction of telling, was becoming more melancholy every day. It was not, however, the three messengers sent to him since the departure of Arnold by the King of France, at short intervals, that troubled Lord Wentworth. All three, it may well be suspected, insisted on the same thing—the first politely, the second sharply, and the third menacingly; this was the release of Madame de Castro, such ransom being paid as the governor of Calais might fix himself. But to all three he made the same reply: he intended keeping Madame de Castro as a hostage, with the object of exchanging her for some important prisoner during the war, or restoring her to the king without ransom at its conclusion. He was exercising only his undoubted rights, and behind his strong walls he braved the anger of Henry the Second.

It was not then this anger that troubled him, although he often asked himself how did the king come to learn of the captivity of Diana. What troubled him was the increasing and contemptuous indifference of his fair prisoner. Neither submission nor respectful attention had been able to soften the proud and disdainful temper of Madame de Castro. She was always sad, calm, and dignified in presence of the impassioned governor, and, when he spoke of love, a look, at once sorrowful and haughty, pierced the heart and offended the self-esteem of poor Lord Wentworth. He did not dare to speak to Diana either of the letter written to Gabriel or of the attempts made by the king for her release, so much did he dread to hear a bitter word, an ironical reproach, from that charming and cruel mouth.

But as Diana no longer met the servant who had taken charge of her letter, she understood fully that this desperate chance had failed. Nevertheless, the pure-minded and noble girl did not lose courage. She wept and prayed. She trusted in God, and in death, if need be.

It was the last day in October, and Gabriel had determined he should not wait longer for Martin Guerre. He decided, therefore, to ask Lord Wentworth's permission to send a second messenger to Paris.

About two o'clock he left the house of the Peuquoys, in which Pierre was polishing a sword and Jean twisting one of his enormous ropes, and where poor Babette, her eyes red from weeping, had been hovering around him for several days, but had not courage to speak, and started directly for the governor's hotel.

Lord Wentworth was busy at the moment, and sent word to Gabriel to have the goodness to wait five minutes, when he should be at his service.

The hall in which Gabriel found himself looked on an

inner court. He approached the window to examine it, and began mechanically beating a tattoo on the glass. Suddenly certain characters traced with a ring on the pane, under his very hand, attracted his attention. He drew nearer to observe them more carefully, and saw these words: *Diana de Castro.*

It was the signature missing at the bottom of the mysterious letter he had received the month before.

A cloud passed across his eyes, and he was obliged to lean for support against the wall. His presentiments had not lied, then. Diana! Diana, his *fiancée* or his sister, was actually in the power of that debauched wretch Wentworth; to this pure and gentle creature the villain had dared to speak of his love.

With an involuntary gesture, Gabriel carried his hand to the hilt of his missing sword.

At this moment Lord Wentworth entered.

Without uttering a word, Gabriel led him to the window and showed him the accusing signature.

The governor at first turned pale, then at once recovering that self-possession which he possessed in an eminent degree—

"Well! what is the matter?" he asked.

"Is that the name of the mad relation you are guarding?" said Gabriel.

"Possibly; what follows?" retorted Lord Wentworth, with a haughty air.

"In that case, I happen to know this relation—a very distant one, no doubt, my lord. I have often seen her at the Louvre. I am devoted to her, as every French gentleman must be to a daughter of the house of France."

"And then?"

"And then, my lord, I will hold you to account for the manner in which you retain and treat a prisoner of this rank."

"And if I should refuse to render you any account, as I have already done in the case of the King of France?"

"Of the King of France?" repeated Gabriel, astounded.

"Undoubtedly, monsieur," returned Lord Wentworth, with unalterable coolness. "An Englishman is hardly bound, I should think, to answer for his actions to a foreign sovereign, particularly when his country is at war with that sovereign. Supposing, then, I should also refuse to render an account to you, M. d'Exmès?"

"I should ask you to give me satisfaction, my lord," cried Gabriel.

"Oh, you hope to kill me with the sword you wear by my permission, and which I can ask you to surrender at any moment?" retorted the governor.

"Ah, my lord, my lord!" said Gabriel, furiously, "you shall pay me for this!"

"Willingly," replied Lord Wentworth. "I will not deny my debt when you have acquitted yours."

"Powerless!" cried Gabriel, wringing his hands; "powerless, when I would have the strength of ten thousand men."

"It is, of course, annoying," retorted Lord Wentworth, "that your hands happen to be tied by law and propriety. It would be very convenient, would it not, if a prisoner of war and a debtor were able to get his quittance and his liberty by cutting the throat of his creditor and his enemy?"

"My lord," said Gabriel, recovering his calmness by an effort, "you are not ignorant that I sent my squire a month ago to Paris for the sum about which you seem so anxious. Has Martin Guerre been wounded or killed on the road in spite of your safe conduct? Or has he been robbed of the money on his return? These are questions to which I cannot give an answer. The fact remains that he does not return, and I come now to ask you to let me send another agent to Paris, since you do not trust the word of a gentleman, and have not suggested that I should go for the money myself. Now, my lord, you have no longer the right to refuse me this permission, or rather I have the right to say that you are afraid to give me my liberty, and that you dare not restore me my sword."

"And to whom would you say this, monsieur," replied Lord Wentworth, "in an English city placed under my immediate authority, and where you can be regarded only as a prisoner and an enemy?"

"I would say it aloud, my lord, to every man that feels and thinks; to every man that has a noble heart or a noble name; to your officers, who know what honor means; to your very workmen, whom instinct would instruct; and all would agree with me, my lord, that by refusing me the means of leaving this place, you show yourself unworthy to command gallant soldiers."

"But you do not think," coldly rejoined Lord Wentworth, "that before you could spread a spirit of mutiny among my people, I could have you, by a gesture, by a word, flung into a dungeon, where you could make your accusations to the walls at your leisure?"

"Ah, that is true; a thousand devils, it is true!" murmured Gabriel, with lips compressed and hands clinched.

The man of feeling and emotion felt himself impotent in presence of the impassiveness of the man of bronze and iron.

But a word changed the aspect of affairs and restored the balance between Lord Wentworth and Gabriel.

"Dear Diana! dear Diana!" repeated the young man, distractedly, "not to be able to aid you in your peril!"

"What is that you said?" asked Lord Wentworth, starting. "You said, I think, 'Dear Diana!' Did you say it or have I not heard aright? Do you also love Madame de Castro—you?"

"Yes, I love her!" cried Gabriel. "You love her too; but my love is as pure and devoted as yours is shameful and cruel. Yes, before God and His angels, I love her to adoration."

"And what was all this you were saying to me about the protection every gentleman owes to a persecuted daughter of France?" returned Lord Wentworth, losing all self-control. "Ah, you love her! and you are, no doubt, the one she loves, the one whose memory she invokes when she desires to torture me! You are the man for whose sake she despises me! The man except for whom she would, perhaps, have loved me! Are you, then, the man she loves?"

Lord Wentworth, lately so sarcastic and scornful, now regarded with a sort of reverential terror the man whom Diana loved; and Gabriel, as he heard the words of his rival, gradually raised his head, while joy and triumph lighted up every feature.

"And she loves me thus!" he exclaimed, "she thinks of me still! she summons me, you say? Well, I will go to her, will aid and rescue her. Yes, my lord, take my sword, gag me, bind me, imprison me. In spite of the universe and in spite of you, I shall aid and preserve her, since she still loves me, my saintly Diana. Since she still loves me, I brave and defy you; and with that love for my divine shield, though you be armed and I unarmed, I am sure to conquer you."

"It is true, it is true; I can have no doubt of it!" murmured Lord Wentworth, in a tone of despair.

"Therefore it would not be generous in me now to challenge you to a duel," continued Gabriel; "summon your guards and tell them to cast me into your dungeon. To be in prison near her and like her is a kind of happiness."

There was a long silence.

"Monsieur," answered Lord Wentworth, after some hesitation, "you came to ask me, I believe, for permission to send a second messenger to Paris for your ransom?"

"Yes, my lord," returned Gabriel, "such was my intention when I arrived here."

"And you have accused me, it seems, of not having had sufficient confidence in your word as a gentleman to allow you to go for your ransom yourself?"

"It is true, my lord."

"Well, monsieur, you can go to-day; your request is granted: the gates of Calais are opened to you."

"I understand," said Gabriel, bitterly. "You wish to separate me from her. And if I refused to leave Calais?"

"I am the master here," replied Wentworth; "and there is no question of acceptance or refusal, but of obedience."

"Be it so, then. I will go, but, rest assured, without feeling at all indebted to your generosity."

"I do not need your gratitude, monsieur."

"I shall go," continued Gabriel; "but be sure I shall not continue long your debtor, and will return to pay you all my debts together. And as I shall no longer be your prisoner then, and you will no longer be my creditor, there will be no further pretext to prevent the sword I shall then have the right of wearing from crossing yours."

"I might still refuse this combat, monsieur," said Lord Wentworth, moodily; "for the chances between us are not equal. If I kill you, she will hate me the more; if you kill me, she will love you the more. No matter; I must accept, and I accept. But do you not fear," he added gloomily, "to drive me to extremities? When all the advantages are on your side, might I not abuse those that are left to me?"

"God in the next world, and the nobility of all countries in this, will judge you, my lord, if you basely take your revenge on those who have conquered you by persecuting those who cannot defend themselves."

"However that may be, monsieur," replied Wentworth, "I refuse to accept you as one of my judges."

He added after a pause—

"It is three o'clock, monsieur: the inner gates are shut at seven; you have until then time to make your preparations for your departure from the city. I will give orders, so that you may be allowed to pass freely."

"At seven," answered Gabriel, "I shall no longer be in Calais."

"And rest assured you shall never return to it during your life; and though I be slain by you in this duel outside of our ramparts, my precautions will be so well taken that you shall never possess, nay, never even see, Madame de Castro again. You may rely on my jealousy making my words good!"

Gabriel had already turned to leave the room. He stopped at the threshold.

"What you say is impossible, my lord," he said. "I shall surely see Diana again some day or other."

"That shall not be, nevertheless, I swear to you," returned Lord Wentworth, "if the wishes of the governor of a fortress or the last orders of a dying man can prevent it."

"It shall be, my lord. I do not know how, but I am sure of it," retorted Gabriel.

"Then, monsieur, you are going to take Calais by storm," answered Lord Wentworth, disdainfully.

Gabriel reflected a minute.

"I will take Calais by storm," said he. "*Au revoir*, my lord."

He saluted and left, leaving Lord Wentworth petrified, and at a loss to know whether he should be alarmed or amused.

Gabriel returned at once to the home of the Peuquoys.

Pierre was still polishing his sword, Jean twisting his rope, and Babette sighing.

He told his friends of his late conversation with the governor, and announced his immediate departure.

He did not conceal even the rash words he had spoken just as he was leaving the governor.

Then he said—

"I am now going to my room, and I leave you, Pierre, to your sword; you, Jean, to your ropes; and you, Babette, to your sighs."

He ran upstairs at once to make his preparations for the journey. Now that he was free, he longed to be in Paris to save his father, and back again in Calais to save Diana..

When he left his room, half an hour later, Babette Peuquoy met him on the landing.

"You are leaving, then, monseigneur?" she said. "You do not ask me why I am in tears?"

"No, my child," he answered. "I hope, on my return, there will be no more tears."

"I hope so too, monseigneur," returned Babette. "So, in spite of the governor's threats, you expect to return?"

"There is not the slightest doubt of that, Babette."

"With your squire, Martin Guerre, I suppose?"

"Assuredly."

"So then you are sure of finding Martin Guerre in Paris, monseigneur?" said the young girl. "He is not a dishonest man, is he? He has not made away with your ransom, has he? He is incapable of—infidelity, is he not?"

"I can take my oath as to that," said Gabriel, passably astonished at these questions. "Martin has shown himself rather changeable in temper, particularly of late, and there would seem to be two men in him—one simple-minded and of a quiet disposition, the other cunning and quarrelsome. But, apart from these variations in temper, he is a loyal and faithful servant."

"And I have heard," continued Babette, "he would no more deceive a woman than he would his master; is that true?"

"Oh, I'm not so sure of that, and I could no longer answer for him in that respect, I confess."

"Then, monseigneur," said poor Babette, turning pale, "will you be kind enough to give him this ring? He will know where it comes from and what it means."

"I will do so, Babette," said Gabriel, surprised, recalling the eve of his squire's departure. "I will do so, but the person who sends it knows that Martin Guerre is—married, I presume."

"Married!" cried Babette. "Then, monseigneur, keep the ring or throw it away, but do not give it to him."

"But, Babette—"

"Thanks, monseigneur, and farewell," murmured the poor girl.

She fled to the second story, and had hardly entered her room when she fell on a chair fainting.

Gabriel, vexed and disturbed by the suspicion which for the first time entered his mind, pensively made his way down the wooden staircase of the old house of the Peuquoys. At the foot he met Jean, who was approaching him with an air of mystery.

"M. le Vicomte," said the weaver, in a low voice, "you have often asked me why I was fashioning ropes of such length. I cannot let you go, especially after the noble words in which you bade farewell to Wentworth, without solving the enigma. If you unite two long solid ropes, such as those I am making, by means of small ones placed cross-wise, M. le Vicomte, you have an immense ladder. This ladder can be transported in sections by a member of the city guard, such as Pierre has been for twenty years and I have been for three days, and placed under the sentry-box on the platform of the Octagon tower. Then on a dark morning of December or January, it will be possible for some person, moved by a spirit of curiosity, who happens to be sentinel at the time, to fasten the two ends to these pieces of iron driven into the battlement, and let the two other ends fall into the sea, three hundred feet below, where some daring boatsman might happen to find himself at the time."

"But, my brave fellow," interrupted Gabriel.

"Enough on this subject, M. le Vicomte," returned the weaver. "But, excuse me, I should wish before we separate to leave you a souvenir of your devoted servant Jean Peuquoy. Here is a plan, such as it is, of the walls and fortifications of Calais. I made it for my amusement, after those eternal promenades that used to excite your astonishment. Hide it under your doublet; and when you are in Paris, look at it occasionally, I beg you, through friendship for me."

Gabriel wanted to interrupt again, but Jean Peuquoy did not give him time; and, shaking the hand the viscount offered him, he bid him adieu with these words—

"*Au revoir*, M. d'Exmès. You will find Pierre at the door, where he will take leave of you. His adieus will supply what is wanting in mine."

In fact, Pierre was standing in front of the house, holding the reins of Gabriel's horse.

"Accept my thanks for your hospitality, master," said Gabriel. "I shall send you the money you have been kind enough to advance soon; perhaps I may even bring it myself. I should like to add to it, if you have no objection, a handsome gratuity for your people. In the meantime, be so good as to give this little diamond on my behalf to your dear sister."

"I accept it for her, M. le Vicomte," replied the armorer; "but on condition that you accept on your part something of my own making—this horn which I have hung to your saddle-bow. I have fashioned it myself, and I should recognize its sound through the roaring of the most tempestuous sea, say on the fifth of each month, on those nights when I perform sentry duty from four to six in the morning on the Octagon tower overlooking the waves."

"Thanks!" said Gabriel, pressing his hand to show him that he understood.

"As to those arms you were surprised at seeing me make in such quantities," returned Pierre, "I repent, in truth, of having so many of them in my shop; for, look you, if Calais were to be besieged some fine day, the party that still clings to France might get possession of these arms and make a dangerous diversion in the very heart of the city."

"It is true!" said Gabriel, with a stronger grasp of the brave citizen's hand.

"Thereupon I wish you a good journey and good luck," rejoined Pierre. "Adieu, and come again soon, M. d'Exmès."

"Soon," was Gabriel's answer.

He turned round and waved a final farewell to Pierre, who was standing on the threshold, to Jean, who was leaning out of the window of the first story, and to Babette, who was looking from behind a curtain on the second.

Then he gave the spur to his horse and galloped away.

The soldiers at the city gate had received their orders from Lord Wentworth, and no obstacle was placed in the way of the prisoner, who was soon on the highroad to Paris, alone with his hopes and his fears.

Could he deliver his father on his arrival at Paris? Could he deliver Diana on his return to Calais?

CHAPTER XLIV

CONTINUATION OF MARTIN GUERRE'S TRIBULATIONS

FRENCH roads were not safer for Gabriel de Mont-gommery than they had been for his squire, and he had to display all his intelligence and activity to avoid obstacles and mischances. Still, in spite of all his diligence, he did not reach Paris until the fourth day after leaving Calais.

But the perils of the way troubled Gabriel less, perhaps, than his anxiety as to the end to be attained. Although he was not of a nature to indulge much in day-dreams, his solitary journey almost forced him to speculate unceasingly on the captivity of his father and Diana, on the means of freeing these dear and sacred beings, on the promise of the king, on the plans it should be necessary to adopt if Henry the Second broke that promise. But no! Henry the Second was not the first gentleman of Christendom for nothing. The fulfilment of his oath was not agreeable to him, and he was doubtless waiting until Gabriel came to demand of him the pardon of the rebellious old count; but he would pardon him. And yet if he did not pardon him?

Gabriel, when this desperate thought pierced his soul, just as if a poniard had pierced his heart, dug the spurs into his horse's flanks and grasped the hilt of his sword.

Then the painful yet sweet remembrance of Diana de Castro would calm his agitated soul.

It was in the midst of such uncertainty and anguish that he reached Paris on the morning of the fourth day. He had travelled all the night, and the pale glimmer of the dawn was scarcely breaking through the darkness that overhung the city when he crossed the streets in the neighborhood of the Louvre.

He halted in front of the royal residence, still closed and showing that its inmates were asleep, and asked himself whether he should wait or ride on. But his impatience could not endure inaction. He resolved to go at once to his own quarters in the Rue des Jardins St. Paul; there he might learn something of what he feared or of what he wished.

His way led him before the sinister turrets of the Chatelet.

He drew rein in front of the fatal gate. A cold sweat bathed his temples. His past and his future were behind these humid walls. But Gabriel was not the man to give to emotion much of the time that should be consecrated to action. He shook off those sombre thoughts and rode on, saying to himself, "Forward!"

When he reached his hôtel, which he had not seen for so long, a light was shining in the windows of the lower hall. The vigilant Aloyse was already up.

Gabriel knocked and gave his name. Two minutes after he was in the arms of the good and worthy woman who had been to him a mother.

"Ah, it is you, then, monseigneur! it is you, then, my child!"

It was all she had strength to utter.

Gabriel, after embracing her tenderly, drew back a little and looked at her.

There was in that profound look a mute inquiry more eloquent than words could render it.

Aloyse understood it, and yet she bent her head and did not answer.

"No news from the court, then?" asked the viscount, as if he was not at all satisfied with the revelation contained in this silence.

"No news, monseigneur," replied the nurse.

"Ah! I suspected as much. If anything had happened, fortunate or unfortunate, I should have heard it from you at the first kiss. You know nothing, then?".

"Alas! nothing."

"Oh, I understand," rejoined the young man, bitterly. " I was a prisoner, dead, perhaps. Who acquits his debts to a prisoner, and, above all, to a dead man? But here I am alive and free, and I must be reckoned with; yes, yes, willingly or by force, I must be reckoned with."

"Oh, take care, monseigneur!" exclaimed Aloyse.

"Fear nothing, nurse. Is M. l'Amiral at Paris?"

"Yes, monseigneur, and he has sent here ten times to inquire as to your return."

"Good. And M. de Guise?"

"He is back also. The people are depending on him to repair the misfortunes of France and alleviate the general suffering."

"God grant he do not find these misfortunes too great to be repaired!"

"As to Madame de Castro, who was believed lost," continued Aloyse, eagerly, "M. le Connétable has discovered that she is a prisoner in Calais, and it is hoped she'll be soon liberated."

"I knew it, and I hope as they do," said Gabriel, in a singular tone. "But you do not speak of the cause that has made me so long a prisoner myself; you say nothing of Martin Guerre and why he has delayed returning. What has become of Martin?"

"He is here, monseigneur, the good-for-nothing, worthless idiot."

"What! here? But since when? What is he doing?"

"He is lying asleep up yonder," said Aloyse, who spoke of Martin with much bitterness. "He says he feels a little unwell, because, as he pretends, he has been hanged."

"Hanged!" cried Gabriel; "probably in order to rob him of the money for my ransom, was it?"

"The money for your ransom, monseigneur? Yes, talk to that threefold imbecile about the money for your ransom, and see what answer you'll get. He will not know what you mean. Just only fancy it, monseigneur, he comes here, quite in a hurry and full of zeal, and after I received your letter, I get ten thousand crowns together, and count them out to him without more ado. He is away again at full speed, not losing a minute. A few days after, whom do I behold with my very eyes? None other than Martin Guerre, with the most woebegone and hang-dog look imaginable. He pretends that he did not receive a red denier from me. Taken prisoner before the capture of St. Quentin, he says that he has not known what has become of you for the last three months. You did not charge him with any mission, and he has been beaten and hanged. He succeeded in escaping, and enters Paris now for the first time since the war. Such are the tales with which Martin Guerre dins our ears from morning to evening whenever any one speaks to him about your ransom."

"Explain yourself, nurse," said Gabriel. "Martin Guerre never appropriated this money, that I'll take my oath on. He is not a dishonest man, assuredly, and has always served me loyally."

"No, monseigneur, he is not dishonest; but he is mad, I fear—mad enough to lose thought and memory; in fact, only fit for a strait-jacket. Although not yet vicious, he is dangerous, to say the least. In fine, I am not the only one that saw him here; all your people bear overwhelming testimony to the fact. He has really received the ten thousand crowns. Master Elyot has, in fact, had a good deal of trouble in collecting them so rapidly."

"Well, Master Elyot will have to collect the same sum, and that as soon as possible; nay, even a larger sum. But we need not talk of that now. It is daylight, and I am going to the Louvre to speak to the king."

"What, monseigneur, without taking a moment's repose?" said Aloyse. "Besides, you do not consider that it is only a little after seven, and that the gates of the Louvre do not open until nine."

"You are right, Aloyse, still two hours of waiting. O God! grant me the patience to wait two hours, since I have already waited two months! But I shall at least," said Gabriel, "find M. de Coligny and M. de Guise."

"No; for they are probably at the Louvre," returned Aloyse. "The king does not receive before noon, and I fear you cannot see him sooner. You will have three hours, therefore, to devote to M. l'Amiral and M. le Lieutenant-Général. The latter is, you are aware, the new title the king has conferred on M. de Guise, in view of the grave circumstances in which we are placed. Meanwhile, monseigneur, you will not refuse to take some nourishment, and to receive your faithful old servitors, who have so long sighed for your return."

At the same moment, as if to occupy the young man's mind and distract him from his irksome waiting, Martin Guerre, who had no doubt been informed of his master's arrival, hurried into the room, paler from joy than from the consequences of his sufferings.

"What, it is you, monseigneur!" he cried; "you! oh, what happiness!"

But Gabriel received coldly enough the raptures of the poor squire.

"If I have fortunately arrived, Martin," he said, "you must confess it has not been your fault, and that you have done all in your power to keep me a prisoner forever."

"What! you too, monseigneur!" said Martin, with consternation. "You, too, instead of justifying at the first word, accuse me of having handled these ten thousand crowns. Who knows? Perhaps you will say that you commissioned me to receive them and bring them to you?"

"Undoubtedly," replied Gabriel, astounded.

"So," rejoined the poor squire, in a hoarse voice, "you judge me, Martin Guerre, capable of basely turning to my own use money that did not belong to me—money intended to procure the freedom of my master?"

"No, Martin," replied Gabriel, moved by the tone of his loyal servant; "my suspicions have never led me to doubt your honesty, and I was just saying so to Aloyse. But this sum might have been taken from you; you might have lost it on the way back to me."

"On the way back to you," repeated Martin. "Back where, monseigneur? Since we first left St. Quentin, may God strike me dead if I know where you have been! Where, then, could I go back to you?"

"At Calais, Martin. However harebrained you may be, you cannot have forgotten Calais?"

"How could I forget a place I have never known?" said Martin, calmly.

"Why, you unhappy being, can you forswear yourself to such a degree as this?" cried Gabriel.

He said some words in an undertone to the nurse, who retired. Then approaching Martin—

"And what of Babette, you ungrateful rascal?" said he.

"Babette! what Babette?" asked the squire, stupefied.

"The woman you seduced, you shameless fellow."

"Ah, that's good Gudule!" exclaimed Martin. "You are mistaken in the name. It was not Babette; it was Gudule, monseigneur. Ah, yes, the poor girl! But frankly I have not seduced her; she has seduced herself all alone, monseigneur, I swear it."

"What! another also!" replied Gabriel. "But I don't know her; and whoever she may be, she cannot be so unfortunate as Babette Peuquoy."

Martin Guerre did not dare to show impatience; but if he had been of the rank of the viscount, he would have done so surely.

"Stay, monseigneur, they all say here that I am mad, and, by St. Martin! from hearing them continually saying so, I believe I am in a fair way of becoming mad. However, I have still my reason and my memory, devil take me if I haven't! and, although I have had to undergo trials and misfortunes for the sake not only of one person, but of two, yet if you desire it, I will relate, point after point, all that happened to me during the three months since I left you. At least," he added, "all I can recall as falling to—my share."

"Indeed, I shall be glad to hear any explanation of your strange conduct."

"Well, monseigneur, when after you left St. Quentin to obtain the succors promised by M. de Vaulpergues, each of us, as you must remember, took his own way, what you had foreseen happened. I fell into the hands of the enemy. I tried, as you recommended, to brazen it out. But a strange thing happened: the enemy recognized me. I had been their prisoner before."

"Come now," interrupted Gabriel; "you begin to wander already."

"Oh, monseigneur, for God's sake!" appealed Martin, "let me tell what I know as I know it. I find it hard enough to recognize myself; you can criticise after. As soon as the enemy recognized me, monseigneur, I confess I felt resigned to everything. For I knew, and in your heart you know also, monseigneur, that I am two persons rolled into one, and that without giving me a hint of his intention, my other I often makes me do his will. Then *we* accepted our lot; for henceforth I intend speaking of myself, or rather, of ourselves, in the plural. Gudule, a pretty Fleming we had abducted, recognized us also, and this, by the way, procured us a hailstorm of blows. We were the only persons that did not recognize ourselves. To relate to you all the misery that ensued, and into the hands of how many different masters, all speaking a different gibberish, your unhappy squire fell, would take too long, monseigneur."

"Yes, cut short your lamentations," said Gabriel.

"I'll pass over them and over worse things still. My number two escaped once, and I was cudgelled within an inch of my life for his fault. My number one, the person of whom I am conscious and whose martyrdom I am narrating, succeeded in escaping anew, but had the folly to get caught again, and was almost beaten to death. No matter. I ran away a third time; and I was captured a third time by a double treason. The traitors were wine and a chance acquaintance. I was so beside myself that I laid about me with the fury of drunkenness and despair. And the end of it all was that my executioners, after scoffing at me and torturing me the whole night, hanged me early the next morning.''

"Hanged you!" cried Gabriel, judging that the monomania of his squire was returning. "Hanged you, Martin! What do you mean by that?''

"I mean, monseigneur, that they hoisted me up between heaven and earth by means of a stout hempen rope, fastened to a gibbet, otherwise called a gallows. And in all the tongues and dialects by which my ears have of late been scarified, that means being hanged, in the popular acceptation, monseigneur. Is not that plain?''

"Not quite, Martin; because really for a man hanged—''

"I seem in rather fair health, monseigneur—yes, that is a fact; but you have not heard the end of the story. My grief and rage were such when I saw myself hanging that I became unconscious. When I came to myself, I was lying on the fresh grass with a severed rope around my neck. Had some wayfarer, as he passed by, moved by compassion, attempted to pluck from the gibbet its human fruit? My present misanthropy forbids the idea. I am inclined to imagine rather that some thief wished to strip me, and cut the rope to rummage my pockets at his ease. The disappearance of my nuptial ring and of my papers authorizes me, I think, to affirm as much without excessively wronging the human race. The fact remains, however, that I had been cut down in time, and though my neck was somewhat dislocated, I was able to escape a fourth time through woods and fields, hiding during the day, advancing cautiously during the night, living on roots and wild herbs—a detestable aliment, by the way, to which the beasts must find great difficulty in becoming habituated. In fine, after going astray a hundred times, I was able to see Paris once more and this house, whither I came twelve days ago, and where I have been received more shabbily than I expected after so many trials. And now you have my story, monseigneur.''

"Well," said Gabriel, "with regard to this same story of yours, I could tell you another entirely different—a story in every incident of which you have been an actor under my own eyes.''

"The story of my number two, monseigneur," said Martin, composedly. "Faith, monseigneur, if I am not troublesome, and if you were kind enough to favor me with a little bit of it, I should like to know it.''

"Are you making sport of me, you rascal?" said Gabriel.

"Oh, monseigneur, you know the profound respect I have for you. But, strange to say, this other self of mine has been the occasion of many misfortunes to me, has he not? He has got me into many a cruel difficulty. And yet, in spite of all, I do not know but that I feel an interest in him. Upon my word of honor, I do not know but that I shall end by loving him, the rogue!''

"Rogue indeed!" said Gabriel.

He was about to enumerate, perhaps, some of the offences of Arnold du Thill; but he was interrupted by his nurse, who entered, followed by a man clad as a peasant.

"What does all this mean?" said Aloyse. "Here is a man who claims he was sent here to inform us of your death, Martin Guerre.''

CHAPTER XLV

WHEREIN THE CHARACTER OF MARTIN GUERRE BEGINS TO BE REHABILITATED

"MY DEATH?" cried Martin Guerre, turning pale at the terrible words of Dame Aloyse.

"Ah, Christ have mercy on us!" cried the peasant, in turn, as soon as he caught a glimpse of Martin Guerre.

"Oh, gracious heavens! can my other self be dead?" exclaimed Martin. "Shall this existence of mine be subject to continual change? Well, really, upon reflection, I am somewhat sorry. But yet, upon the whole, I am rather satisfied. Speak, friend, speak," he added, addressing the dumfounded peasant.

"Ah, master," answered the latter, "how is it I find you here before me? I swear to you I have made as much speed as man could to carry your message and earn your ten crowns; and unless you took a horse, it would be absolutely impossible, master, for you to have passed me on the road, where I should have seen you, in any case."

"All very fine, my good man; but I never saw you before in my life," said Martin Guerre, "and yet you speak as if you recognized me."

"Recognized you!" said the astounded peasant. "Perhaps you'll say, then, it wasn't you who sent me here to announce that Martin Guerre had been hanged."

"What! Martin Guerre? Why, I am Martin Guerre," said Martin Guerre.

"You? not likely. You couldn't announce your own hanging, could you now?" retorted the peasant.

"But why, where, and when have I announced to you any such atrocity?" demanded Martin.

"Is there any need to tell you of it now?" said the peasant.

"Yes, all the need in the world."

"In spite of the story you advised me to make up?"

"In spite of the story."

"Well, then, since you have such a bad memory, I'll tell all; so much the worse for you, if you force me to it. Six days ago, I was setting about hoeing my field in the morning—"

"In the first place, where is your field?" inquired Martin.

"Am I to answer the true truth, master?" said the peasant.

"Undoubtedly, you brute!"

"Well, my field is the other side of Montargis; there now! I was working; you were passing along the road with a travelling-bag on your back.

" 'Eh, friend, what are you doing there?' said you.

" 'I am hoeing, master,' said I.

" 'And how much does your hoeing fetch you?' said you.

" 'Taking the good years with the bad, four sols a day,' said I.

" 'Would you like to earn twenty crowns in two weeks?' said you.

" 'Wouldn't I?' said I.

" 'I ask a yes or a no,' said you.

" 'Yes, indeed,' said I.

" 'Well,' said you, 'you'll start at once for Paris. By walking fast, you ought to get there at the latest in five or six days; you will ask for the hôtel of Viscount d'Exmès in the Rue des Jardins St. Paul. It is to this hôtel I am sending you. The viscount will not be there; but you will find Dame Aloyse, his nurse, a good woman, and this is what you'll tell her. Listen attentively. You will say to her:

"I have come from Noyon"—do you understand?—not from Montargis, but from Noyon. "I have come from Noyon, where an acquaintance of mine was hanged a fortnight ago. His name is Martin Guerre." Keep a good grip of that name, Martin Guerre. "He was hanged by persons who robbed him of the money he had with him, and were afraid he might afterward accuse them of the crime. But before he was conducted to the gallows, he had time to ask me to inform you of his misfortune, in order that you might provide a new ransom for his master. He promised that you would pay me ten crowns for my trouble. I saw him hanged, and then came here."

" 'That is what you'll say to the good woman. Do you understand me?' said you.

" 'Yes, master,' said I; 'only you spoke of twenty crowns before, and you speak of ten now.'

" 'Idiot! here are ten in advance,' said you.

" 'That's the way to talk. But if good Aloyse should ask me what sort of a looking chap was this Martin Guerre, whom I have never seen and could have never seen, what then?' said I.

" 'Look at me,' said you.

" 'I'm looking at you,' said I.

" 'You'll paint Martin Guerre as if he' was the dead image of me,' said you."

"It is strange!" murmured Gabriel, who was listening to the peasant with extreme attention.

"And now I have come, master," resumed the latter, "ready to repeat my lesson by heart, just as you have taught it to me, and here I find you before me. True, I lagged by the way and made ducks and drakes of your ten crowns in the taverns on the road; but then I was careful to keep within the term you fixed. You gave me six days, and it is exactly six days since I left Montargis."

"Six days!" said Martin Guerre, sadly and musingly. "So I have been six days ago at Montargis, have I? I was on the way to the land of my birth six days ago? Your tale is truly probable and probably true, my friend, and I believe it true."

"Why, no," interrupted Aloyse, quickly. "This man is evidently a liar, on the contrary, since he claims he saw you at Montargis six days ago, and for twelve days you have not stirred from here."

"That's right enough," said Martin. "But then my number two."

"And besides," continued the nurse, "according to him you were hanged at Noyon less than a fortnight ago; while, according to your own showing, it was a month ago."

"You couldn't be more accurate if you tried," rejoined the squire. "Just what I thought when I awoke this morning—a month ago to the minute. But still my other self—"

"Oh, stuff!" cried the nurse.

"No," said Gabriel, interfering; "if I am not greatly mistaken, this man has put us in the way of finding out the truth."

"Oh, my good lord! you are not mistaken," said the peasant. "Shall I have the ten crowns?"

"Yes," said Gabriel; "but leave us your name and address. We may have need of your testimony some day. I am beginning to get a glimpse of many crimes, although my suspicions are not yet very precise."

"Still, monseigneur—" objected Martin.

"Enough on the subject," interrupted Gabriel, abruptly. "See, my good Aloyse, that this man goes away satisfied. The matter will be attended to in due time. But you know," he added in an undertone, "before I punish a betrayal of the squire, I may have to avenge a betrayal of the master."

"Alas!" murmured Aloyse.

"It is now eight," returned Gabriel. "I cannot see our people until after my return, for I wish to be at the gates of the Louvre as soon as they open. If I do not see the king until noon, I shall at least have some conversation with the admiral and M. de Guise."

"And after seeing the king you will return here immediately, will you not?" asked Aloyse.

"Immediately; and don't be alarmed, my good nurse. Something tells me I shall triumph over all the hidden obstacles which intrigue and audacity have heaped up around me."

"Yes, if God grant my ardent prayer, that will surely be," said Aloyse.

"I am going now. Remain here, Martin; I wish to be alone. Rest assured, my friend, you will be justified and delivered from your enemy; but there is another justification and another deliverance to be accomplished first of all. We shall soon meet again, Martin; *au revoir*, nurse."

Both kissed the hands tendered them by the young man. Then he went out, alone and on foot, wrapped in his great cloak, and gravely and proudly made his way to the Louvre.

"Alas!" thought the nurse, " 'twas thus I saw his father depart once, and he never returned again."

At the moment when Gabriel, after passing the Pont au Change, was crossing the Grève, he remarked in the distance a man also covered with a great cloak of coarser material, and arranged more carefully than his. This man, besides, was evidently trying to hide his features under the wide brim of his hat.

Although Gabriel had a vague impression that he could distinguish the features of a friend, he was, however, pursuing his course. But when the unknown perceived the face of Gabriel, he started, appeared to hesitate, then suddenly stopping, "Gabriel, my friend," he said, cautiously.

At the same time he half uncovered his face, and Gabriel saw he was not mistaken.

"M. de Coligny!" he said, but without raising his voice. "You in this place and at this hour!"

"Hush!" answered the admiral. "I confess to you I

should not like to be recognized, spied, and followed at present. But when I saw you, my friend, after so long a separation, and especially as I have been so anxious about you, I could not resist the temptation to address you and shake your hand. How long have you been at Paris ?"

"Only since this morning, and I was going to meet you at the Louvre."

"Well, if not in too great a hurry, walk along with me, and tell me what you have been doing during your absence."

"I intend telling you all I can tell you, for you have been the most devoted and faithful of friends," replied Gabriel. "Still, you must permit me, M. l'Amiral, to question you on a subject that to me is the most important in the world."

"I foresee what you would ask," said the admiral; "but ought you not also, my friend, to foresee my answer? You are going to ask me, are you not, whether I have kept my promise to you—whether I have told the king of the glorious and effectual part you took in the defence of St. Quentin?"

"No, M. l'Amiral, that, in truth, is not what I was about to ask you. For I know you, I have learned to trust your word; and I am quite sure your first care, on your return here, was to fulfil your promise, and declare to the king, and to the king alone, that I counted for something in the resistance offered by St. Quentin. I have no doubt either but that you gave an exaggerated account of my services to his Majesty. This I did not need to be told. But what I am ignorant of, and what it is of the utmost importance to me to know, is the reply of Henry the Second to your kind words."

"Alas! Gabriel," said the admiral. "Henry's sole reply was a question as to what had become of you. I felt some embarrassment in answering. The letter you left for me after your departure from St. Quentin was not very clear, and merely reminded me of my promise. I answered the king, however, that I was sure you were not dead, but in all probability a prisoner, which a feeling of delicacy had prevented you from mentioning to me."

"And the king?" asked Gabriel.

"The king, my friend, said, 'It is well!' and a smile of satisfaction flickered on his lips. Then when I was insisting on your services and great exploits, and on the obligations which the king and France had contracted in your regard, 'Enough on the subject,' replied Henry, and, imperiously changing the conversation, he forced me to speak of something else."

"Yes, it is what I anticipated," said Gabriel, with an ironical smile.

"Courage, my friend!" said the admiral. "You remember I told you at St. Quentin we should not reckon upon the gratitude of the great of this world."

"Oh," returned Gabriel, in a threatening tone, "the king may have been able to forget when he believed me dead or imprisoned; but now that I am about to remind him of my rights, face to face, he will have to remember."

"And should he persist in his forgetfulness?" asked Coligny.

"M. l'Amiral," said Gabriel, "when a man has been wronged, he appeals to the king, and the king does him justice. When the king himself is the wronger, his victim can only appeal to God, and His is the vengeance."

"And yet," rejoined the admiral, "I imagine you would not be unwilling to become the instrument of divine vengeance?"

"You are right, monsieur."

"Well, perhaps this is the place and the time," answered Coligny, "to remind you of a conversation we once had on the religion of the persecuted, in which I spoke to you of a sure method of punishing kings while serving the truth."

"Oh, yes! I recall that conversation," said Gabriel.

"I have not a poor memory by any means. I may have recourse to your method, if not against Henry the Second, at least against some of his successors, since this method of yours is efficacious against all kings."

"That being so," answered the admiral, "can you spare me an hour at present?"

"The king does not receive until noon; I am at your service till then."

"Come with me where I am going, then," said the admiral. "You are a gentleman, and I have been able to test your character; I do not, therefore, ask you to take an oath. Simply promise that you will observe absolute secrecy as to the persons you are about to see and the things you are about to hear."

"I promise to be as secret as you can wish," said Gabriel.

"Follow me, then," replied the admiral; "and should you be unjustly treated at the Louvre, you will at least have your revenge in your own hands in advance. Follow me."

Coligny and Gabriel crossed the Pont au Change and the Cité, and plunged into the tortuous lanes that then bordered on the Rue St. Jacques.

M

CHAPTER XLVI

COLIGNY halted where the Rue St. Jacques begins, in front of the low door of a house mean in appearance. He knocked. A wicket was opened first and then the door, as soon as an invisible porter had recognized the admiral.

Gabriel, following his noble guide, traversed a long dark alley, and mounted the three flights of a worm-eaten staircase. When they had reached the garret almost, Coligny knocked at the door of the most lofty and wretched room in the house three times, not with his hand, but with his foot. It was opened, and they entered.

The room they found themselves in was large, but melancholy and naked. Two narrow windows—the one looking on the Rue St. Jacques, the other on a backyard —admitted but a faint, sombre light. The sole furniture consisted of four stools and a table with twisted legs.

As soon as the admiral entered, two men, who seemed to be expecting him, advanced to meet him. A third remained discreetly apart, at the casement overlooking the street, and from there made only a profound inclination to Coligny.

"Theodore and you, captain," said the admiral to the two men who had received him, "I have brought a friend with me whom I wish to present to you—a friend, if not in the past or of the present, in the future; at least, so I believe."

The two unknown saluted the Viscount d'Exmès silently.

Then the youngest, who was called Theodore, spoke to Coligny in a low but very earnest tone. Gabriel stood aside to let them converse at their ease, and had an opportunity of studying those to whom he had just been presented, and with whose names he was unacquainted.

The captain had the strongly marked features and decided bearing of a man of resolution and action. He was tall, brown, and nervous. There was no need to be a student of human nature to read boldness in his forehead, ardor in his eyes, and energy in the lines of his closely compressed lips.

The companion of this haughty adventurer had more resemblance to a courtier. He was a graceful cavalier, with a round, merry face, a shrewd look, and easy, elegant gestures. His costume, made after the lastest fashion, formed a striking contrast to that of the captain, which was simple and almost austere.

As to the third individual, who was standing apart from the others, his powerful physiognomy, in spite of his reserved attitude, would have attracted attention anywhere. His broad forehead, his deep and penetrating eyes, betrayed to the least observant the man of thought—nay, more, the man of genius.

After exchanging a few words with his friend, Coligny approached Gabriel.

"I ask your pardon," he said; "but I am not the sole master here, and I had to consult my brethren before I could tell you where and in whose company you are."

"And may I know now?" asked Gabriel.

"You may, my friend."

"Where am I, then?"

"In the poor chamber where the son of the cooper of Noyon, where John Calvin held the first secret meetings of the Reformed, and from whence he was near having to march to the stake. But he is to-day triumphant and omnipotent at Geneva; the kings of this world have to reckon with him, and his mere memory serves to illuminate the

damp walls of this den better than would the golden arabesques of the Louvre.''

Gabriel, at the name of Calvin, already great, uncovered.
Although the fiery young man had up to this troubled himself little about religious matters, yet he would not have
been of his age if the austere and laborious life, the sublime
and terrible character, the bold and absolute doctrines of the
legislator of the Reformation, had not excited his curiosity
more than once.

Nevertheless, he inquired calmly enough—

''And who are those now present in the venerated chamber of the master?''

''His disciples,'' replied Coligny—''Theodore Beza, his
pen; La Renaudie, his sword.''

Gabriel saluted the elegant writer who was to be the
historian of the Reformed Churches, and the adventurous
captain who was to be the instigator of the Tumult of
Amboise.

Theodore Beza returned Gabriel's salutation with his
customary graceful ease, and said with a smile:

''M. le Vicomte d'Exmès, although you have been introduced among us with some precautions, do not, I beg of
you, look upon us as dark and dangerous conspirators.   I
hasten to inform you that if the chiefs of the religion meet
secretly in this house three times a week, it is only for the
purpose of exchanging religious intelligence and receiving
either such neophytes as, sharing our opinions, desire to
share our perils, or such as, on account of their personal
merits, we should like to gain to our cause.   We thank the
admiral for having brought you hither, M. le Vicomte, for
you certainly belong to the latter class.''

''And I to the former, gentlemen,'' said the unknown,
who had been standing apart from the others, speaking sim- .
ply and modestly.   ''I am one of those humble dreamers
whom the light of your ideas attracts from the darkness,
and who would like to draw nearer to it.''

''But you shall be soon reckoned among the most illustrious of our brethren, Ambroise," said La Renaudie. "Yes, gentlemen," he said, addressing Coligny and Beza, "the man whom I present to you is a surgeon who has not yet attained fame, and he is still young, as you see; but he will be, I answer for it, one of the glories of the religion, for he works hard and thinks deeply; and since he comes to us of his own accord, we ought to rejoice, for we shall soon proudly boast that we number among us Ambroise Paré."

"Oh, M. le Capitaine!" protested Ambroise.

"By whom has Master Ambroise Paré been instructed?" asked Beza.

"By the minister Chaudieu, who has introduced me to M. de La Renaudie," replied Ambroise.

"And have you already solemnly abjured?"

"Not yet," replied the surgeon. "I wish to be sincere and not take any engagement unless I am perfectly convinced. I have still, I confess, some doubts; and certain points are too obscure for me to unite with you beyond recall and without reservation. To clear up these difficulties, I have sought the acquaintance of the chiefs of the Reformed, and would, if necessary, go to Calvin himself; for truth and liberty are my passions."

"Well said!" cried the admiral; "and you may be assured, master, none of us would care to interfere with the rare and lofty spirit of independence you possess."

"What did I tell you?" exclaimed La Renaudie, triumphantly. "Will not this be a precious conquest for our faith? I have seen Ambroise Paré in his library, and I have seen him by the pillow of the sick; I have seen him even on the field of battle; and always in presence of the errors and prejudices of men, as well as in presence of their wounds and diseases, he has always been the same—calm, cool, and superior, master of others and of himself."

Gabriel, quite moved by what he saw and heard, here asked leave to make a few remarks.

"May I be permitted to say a word?" he said. "I know

now where I am, and why my generous friend, M. de Coligny, has led me hither, where those whom King Henry the Second calls heretics, and looks upon as his deadly enemies, assemble. But I have certainly more need of being instructed than Master Ambroise Paré. Like him, I have been a man of action, perhaps; but, unlike him, I have, alas! not been a man of reflection; and he would render a service to one who has had these novel ideas but recently brought to his attention, if he should inform me of the reasons or the interests that have led a man of his noble understanding to embrace the party of reform."

"Not interests," replied Ambroise Paré; "for, in order to succeed in my profession as surgeon, my interests would attach me to the belief of the court and princes. It is not then interest, but certain reasons, M. le Vicomte, as indeed you said; and if the eminent persons in whose presence I am speaking authorize me, you shall hear those reasons in a few words."

"Speak! speak!" cried Coligny, La Renaudie, and Theodore Beza together.

"I will be brief," replied Ambroise; "my time is not my own. In the first place, I should wish you to know that my idea of reform has no connection with any theory or any formula. All this brushwood having been removed out of the way, these are the principles that appeared to my view—principles for which I would assuredly endure every kind of persecution."

Gabriel listened with an admiration he did not try to conceal to this disinterested confessor of the truth.

Ambroise Paré continued:

"The religious and political powers, the Church and the State, have up to this substituted their law for the will and reason of the individual. The priest says to every man, 'Believe this'; and the prince says to every man, 'Do this.' Now, things have been able to go on in this way as long as the minds of men were the minds of children and needed the support of such discipline in order to be able to walk along the pathway of life. But now we feel that we are strong; therefore we are strong. And yet prince and priest, church and king, refuse to abandon the authority that has become habitual with them. It is against this iniquitous anachronism that the Reformation, in my opinion, *protests.* That every soul should henceforth examine its belief, and reason out its submission, ought, it seems to me, to be the tendency of the renovation to which we are devoting all our efforts. Am I mistaken, gentlemen?''

''No, but you are going too far and too fast,'' said Theodore Beza; ''and your audacity in mingling religious matters with political matters—''

''Ah, that audacity is the very thing that pleases me,'' interrupted Gabriel.

''No, it is not audacity, but logic!'' retorted Ambroise Paré. ''Why should not that which is equitable in the Church be equitable in the State? How can you repulse as a guide to action what you receive as a guide to thinking?''

''There are many incentives to revolt in the daring words you have spoken, master,'' exclaimed Coligny.

''Revolt?'' replied Ambroise, quietly. ''Oh, what I had in my mind was revolution.''

The three reformers regarded one another with surprise.

''This man is even stronger than we imagined,'' their looks seemed to signify.

As to Gabriel, he did not abandon for a moment the eternal preoccupation of his life; but he connected it with what he had just heard, and he fell into a revery.

Theodore Beza said earnestly to the audacious surgeon—

''You must belong to us. What do you ask?''

''Only the favor of conversing with you occasionally, and submitting to your intelligence the difficulties that still hold me back.''

''You shall have more: you shall correspond directly with Calvin.''

"Such an honor for me!" cried Ambroise Paré, flushing with joy.

"Yes, you should know him, and he should know you," said the admiral. "A disciple such as you requires a master such as he. Give your letters to your friend La Renaudie, and we promise to have them sent safely to Geneva. You will receive the answers from us also. Nor will there be much delay. You have heard of the prodigious activity of Calvin; you will be satisfied."

"Ah!" said Ambroise Paré, "you reward me before I have done anything. How have I deserved such a favor?"

"Because you are what you are, my friend," said La Renaudie. "I knew well they were yours as soon as they saw you."

"Oh, thanks a thousand times!" replied Ambroise. "But unfortunately," he added, "I must leave you; there are so many sufferings that call me."

"Go, go!" said Theodore Beza; "your motives are too serious for us to try to retain you. Be your actions instinct with goodness as your thoughts are instinct with truth."

"But while leaving us," said Coligny, "remember you are leaving friends, or rather, as we term those belonging to our religion, brothers."

They took a cordial leave of him, and Gabriel, warmly pressing his hand, united his sentiment to theirs.

Ambroise Paré departed with joy and pride in his heart.

"A rare soul indeed!" cried Theodore Beza.

"What hatred for the commonplace!" added La Renaudie.

"And what uncalculating and unselfish devotion to the cause of humanity!" said Coligny.

"Alas, how paltry must my egotism appear to you when contrasted with such abnegation, M. l'Amiral!" exclaimed Gabriel. "I do not, like Ambroise Paré, subordinate facts and persons to ideas and principles. The reform, as you know too well, would be for me not an end, but a means.

In your great disinterested struggle, I would fight on my own account. I feel that my motives are too personal for me to dare defend so sacred a cause, and you will do well to reject me now from your ranks as one unworthy.''

"Surely you calumniate yourself, M. d'Exmès,'' said Theodore Beza. "Though you may be prompted by views less elevated than those of Ambroise Paré, the ways of God are different, and truth is not found on one road alone.''

"Yes,'' said La Renaudie, "we very rarely obtain such professions of faith as that you have just heard when we address this question, 'What do you ask?' to those who wish to be enrolled in our party.''

"Well,'' replied Gabriel, with a melancholy smile, "to this question Ambroise Paré has answered, 'I ask if justice and right be really on your side?' Do you know what I should ask?''

"No,'' replied Theodore Beza; "but we are ready to satisfy you on all points.''

"I ask, then, are you sure you have material power enough, I do not say to conquer, but to struggle?''

The three reformers looked at one another again with astonishment. But this astonishment had not the same significance as on the first occasion.

Gabriel gazed upon them in gloomy silence. After a pause Theodore Beza resumed:

"Whatever be the feeling that dictated your question, M. d'Exmès, I promised in advance to answer you on every point, and I keep to my promise. We have not only reason on our side, but also force, thanks be to God! The progress of the religion is rapid and indisputable. Since three years a Reformed church has been established at Paris; and the great cities of the kingdom—Blois, Tours, Poitiers, Marseilles, and Rouen—have maintained theirs. You can see yourself, M. d'Exmès, the prodigious crowds that attend our assemblies at the Pré-aux-Clercs. The people, nobles and courtiers abandon their amusements to come and sing with us the French psalms of Clement Marot. We reckon, next year, to give an idea of our number by a public procession; but at present I am inclined to think we have a fifth of the population on our side. We can, therefore, I may say without presumption, call ourselves a party, and inspire, I fancy, our friends with confidence and our enemies with terror."

"That being so," said Gabriel, coldly, "I may in a short time be in the number of the first, and aid you in fighting the second."

"But if we had been weaker?" asked La Renaudie.

"I would have sought other allies," replied Gabriel, tranquilly.

La Renaudie and Theodore Beza could not repress a gesture of astonishment.

"Ah, my friends!" cried Coligny, "do not judge him too hastily and severely. I saw him at St. Quentin, and the man who risks his life as he has risked it has no vulgar soul; but I know he has a sacred and terrible duty to fulfil that does not leave him the right to give to any other object even a part of his devotion."

"And, in default of this devotion, I can at least offer you my sincerity," said Gabriel. "If events should determine me to belong to you, M. l'Amiral can attest that I offer you a heart and an arm that may be relied on. But, in truth, I cannot give myself to you entirely or without calculation; for I am engaged in a necessary and formidable work which the wrath of God and the wickedness of man have imposed upon me, and as long as this work be not finished you must pardon me—I am not the master of my destiny. The destiny of another takes precedence of mine at all hours and in all places."

"There may be devotion to a man as well as devotion to an idea," said Theodore Beza.

"And in that case," replied Coligny, "we shall be happy to serve you, my friend, just as we should be proud if you should serve us."

"Our good wishes follow you and our aid, if necessary," continued La Renaudie.

"Ah, you are heroes and saints!" cried Gabriel.

"But take care, young man, take care!" said La Re-naudie, in his familiar and austere language; "take care. When once we have called you our brother, you must remain worthy of the title. We can admit into our ranks one devoted to some particular object; but the heart is sometimes deceived. Are you quite sure, young man, that when you believe yourself solely consecrated to the welfare of another, no thought of your own personal welfare mingles with your actions? Are you really and personally disin-terested in the end you pursue? Does no passion, though that passion be the most generous in the world, instigate you?"

"Yes," said Theodore Beza, "we have not asked your secrets; but descend into your heart, tell us whether, if you had the right to reveal your feelings and designs, you would not experience embarrassment at any moment, and we will believe your word."

"If they speak thus to you, my friend," said the ad-miral, in turn, "it is, in truth, because a pure cause must be defended by pure hands. If it were not so, misfortune would fall on the cause and on the individual concerned as well."

Gabriel heard and gazed upon these three men, as severe toward others as toward themselves, who, standing around him, were with serious, penetrating eyes questioning him as friends and judges at the same time.

Gabriel at their words turned alternately pale and red.

He was himself interrogating his conscience. As a man of action and movement, he was undoubtedly too little accustomed to reflection and self-examination. At this mo-ment he was asking himself with terror whether his love for Madame Diana was not the preponderating motive in his filial affection; whether he was not as anxious to learn the secret of Madame de Castro's birth as he was to deliver his father; finally, whether in this question of life or death he showed all the disinterestedness necessary, according to Coligny, to merit the kingdom of God.

Frightful thought! if through some selfish mental reservation he was compromising the safety of his father before God.

He shuddered, overwhelmed by a crowd of restless thoughts. A circumstance, apparently insignificant, recalled him to himself and to action.

The clock of St. Séverin's church struck eleven.

In an hour he would be in the presence of the king.

Then in a voice that had almost recovered its firmness, Gabriel said to the reformers:

"You are men of the golden age; and those who believe themselves irreproachable, when measured by your ideal, feel troubled and saddened by their unworthiness. Yet it is impossible that all belonging to your party are like you. That you, who are the head and heart of the Reformation, should watch severely over your intentions and your acts, is useful and necessary; but if I devote myself to your cause, it will be as soldier, not as leader. Now, the stains on the soul are alone indelible; those on the hand may be washed. I will be your hand—that is all. That hand, I venture to say, is courageous and bold; have you the right to refuse it?"

"No," said Coligny; "and we accept it now, my friend."

"And I pledge myself," said Theodore Beza, "that when it grasps the hilt of the sword, that grasp will be as pure as it is valiant."

"We may take," said La Renaudie, "as sufficient guarantee, the very hesitation produced in your scrupulous mind by our perhaps too rough and exacting words. We know how to judge men."

"Thanks, gentlemen," replied Gabriel. "Thanks, because you do not wish to weaken the self-confidence I need so much in the hard task I am about to accomplish. Thanks to you especially, M. l'Amiral, who have, according to your promise, furnished me with the means of punishing a breach of faith, even when committed by a crowned head. I must leave you now, gentlemen, and I do not say farewell, but *au revoir*. Although I am one of those influenced by events more than by abstract ideas, I think that which you have sown will germinate later on."

"We wish it, on our part," said Theodore Beza.

"Wish it not on mine," replied Gabriel; "for I have already confessed it—misfortune alone will render me an adherent of your cause. Once more, adieu, gentlemen. It is now the hour for me to enter the Louvre."

"And I accompany you thither," said Coligny. "I intend to repeat in your presence before the king what I have already said in your absence. The memory of kings is short; but he can neither forget nor deny. I am going with you."

"I should not have ventured to ask you for such a favor, M. l'Amiral," said Gabriel; "but I accept your offer gratefully.

"Let us start, then," said Coligny.

When they were gone, Theodore Beza took his tablets and wrote thereon two names:

Ambroise Paré.

Gabriel, Viscount d'Exmès.

"But," said La Renaudie to him, "you seem to me in rather too great a hurry to inscribe these two names. They are by no means pledged."

"These two men are ours," replied Beza; "the one seeks truth, and the other flees injustice. I tell you they are ours, and I shall write to Calvin that such is the case."

"This will be a fine day for the religion, then," returned La Renaudie.

"Certainly," replied Theodore. "We gain a profound philosopher and a valiant soldier, a powerful brain and a strong arm, a winner of battles and a sower of ideas. You are right, La Renaudie; this has been a fine day indeed."

CHAPTER XLVII

THE LOVELINESS OF MARY STUART IS AS FLEETING IN THIS ROMANCE AS IT IS IN THE HISTORY OF FRANCE

WHEN Gabriel arrived at the gates of the Louvre in company with Coligny, he was dismayed at the first word he heard.

The king did not receive that day.

The admiral, admiral though he was and nephew of Montmorency to boot, was too deeply stained with heresy to have much influence at court. As to the captain of the guards, Gabriel d'Exmès, the royal apartments had had time enough to forget all about him. The two friends had even some trouble in passing beyond the outer doors.

It was worse when they were inside. They lost over an hour in parleying, bribing, and threatening. When they raised one halberd, another barred their passage. All those dragons, more or less invincible, who guard kings, seemed to multiply as they advanced.

But when they reached the grand gallery, after struggling in every way possible, which led to the king's, they could not go further. The countersign was too strict. The king, who was with the constable and Madame de Poitiers, had given the strictest orders that he should not be disturbed under any pretext.

Gabriel had to wait until evening for an audience.

To wait and wait, when he had, he thought, attained the goal of so many struggles and so many sorrows! The few hours he had to pass through seemed to Gabriel more formidable and deadly than all the dangers he had up to then braved and vanquished.

Without listening to the kind words with which the admiral tried to console him and render him patient, he looked sadly through the window at the rain, which was beginning to fall from a clouded sky, and, seized with wrath and anguish, was handling feverishly the hilt of his sword.

How to get the better of the stupid guards and pass them by—those guards who prevented him from reaching the king's chamber, and obtaining, perhaps, the liberty of his father?

Suddenly the hangings of the royal antechamber were raised, and a white and radiant form appeared, in the eyes of the young man, to illuminate the gray and rainy atmosphere.

The little queen-dauphine, Mary Stuart, was crossing the gallery.

Gabriel, as if instinctively, uttered a cry, and stretched his arms to her.

"Oh, madame!" he exclaimed, unconscious of his actions.

Mary Stuart turned round, recognized the admiral and Gabriel, and came to them, smiling.

"So you are back again, M. d'Exmès?" she said. "I am glad to see you; I have heard a good deal about you of late. But what are you doing at the Louvre so early, and what do you want?"

"To speak to the king, madame; to speak to the king!" answered Gabriel, hoarsely.

"M. d'Exmès," said the admiral, "is most anxious to speak to the king. It is a serious matter, and concerns not only M. d'Exmès, but the king himself; and all those guards have forbidden him to approach his Majesty, saying he must wait until evening."

"As if I could wait until evening!" cried Gabriel.

"His Majesty," said Mary Stuart, "is at this moment giving important orders—I think so, at least. M. le Connétable de Montmorency is with him, and I am really afraid—"

A suppliant look from Gabriel prevented Mary from finishing the sentence.

"Well, we'll see; so much the worse! I'll risk it," she said.

She made a sign with her little hand. The guards stood respectfully aside. Gabriel and the admiral were allowed to pass.

"Oh, thanks, madame!" said the ardent young man. "Thanks to you, who, angel-like in everything, always appear to console or help me in my sorrows."

"The road is now free," returned Mary, smiling. "If his Majesty is very angry, do not betray the angel, except at the last extremity, I beseech you."

And, gracefully saluting Gabriel and his companion, she disappeared.

Gabriel was already at the door of the king's antechamber. An usher made some difficulty about allowing them to enter. But at that very instant the door opened, and Henry the Second appeared on the threshold, giving some final instructions to the constable.

Resolution was not the king's special virtue. At the sudden view of Viscount d'Exmès, he started back and even forgot to be irritated.

Firmness was Gabriel's special virtue. The first thing he did was to make a profound inclination to the king.

"Sire," said he, "deign to accept the expression of my respectful homage."

Then turning to Coligny, who was behind him, and for whom he wished to avoid the embarrassment of speaking first—

"M. l'Amiral," said he, "will you, in accordance with the kind promise you have made me, remind his Majesty of the part I have taken in the defence of St. Quentin?"

"What is the meaning of this, monsieur?" cried Henry, beginning to recover his coolness. "Why do you trespass thus on my privacy uninvited and unannounced? How dare you question M. l'Amiral in my presence?"

Gabriel, as daring in a decisive juncture as in the face of the enemy, and understanding that the present occasion above all others was not the one on which he should allow himself to be intimidated, answered respectfully, but firmly:

"I thought, sire, your Majesty was always ready to render justice to the humblest of your subjects?"

He had taken advantage of the backward movement of the king to enter boldly the royal cabinet, where Diana de Poitiers, with pale cheeks and looking as if she would start from her easy-chair of carved oak, looked on in astonishment and fury at the daring young man, powerless to hinder what he said or what he did by a single word.

Coligny had entered after his impetuous friend, and Montmorency, as astounded as the others, did the same.

There was a moment's silence. Henry had turned toward his mistress, and was questioning her with his eyes. But before he had taken, or she had dictated a resolution, Gabriel, who knew this was the decisive moment, again appealed to Coligny in a tone at once beseeching and dignified.

"I entreat you to speak, M. l'Amiral."

Montmorency made a quick sign to his nephew not to do so, but the brave Gaspard paid no attention to it.

"I will speak," said he, "according to my promise and according to my duty.

"Sire," he continued, addressing the king, "I shall repeat briefly in presence of M. le Vicomte d'Exmès what I have considered it my duty to give your Majesty a full account of before his return. It is to him, and to him alone, we owe the fact that St. Quentin held out longer than the term your Majesty had yourself fixed."

The constable made a significant movement, but Coligny looked at him firmly and continued:

"Yes, sire, three times, nay more, did M. d'Exmès save the city; and but for his courage and energy, France would not have now entered on that path of safety on which it is to be hoped she may henceforth hold her own."

"Come, come, nephew, you are either too modest or too complaisant!" cried Montmorency, no longer able to restrain his impatience.

"No, monsieur," said Coligny. "I am just and truthful, that is all. I have done my share, and that with all my strength, in defending the city confided to my charge. But M. d'Exmès revived the courage of the inhabitants, which I regarded as extinguished. Viscount d'Exmès introduced reinforcements I did not know were at hand. Viscount d'Exmès, in fine, rendered unavailing a surprise of the enemy which I had not foreseen. I do not speak of the manner in which he comported himself in the different conflicts; there we all did our best. But what he did alone, the immeasurable glory he then acquired, ought, I declare firmly, to diminish mine or even render it illusory."

And turning to Gabriel, the brave admiral added:

"Have I spoken as you wished, my friend? Have I kept my word, and are you satisfied with me?"

"Oh, I thank and bless you, M. l'Amiral, for such loyalty and goodness," said Gabriel, grasping the hands of Coligny with emotion. "I expected no less from you. But regard me, I beg you, as one who is eternally your debtor. Yes, from this hour your creditor has become your debtor, and he will remember his debt, I swear it you."

During all this time the king, with frowning face and downcast eyes, was impatiently tapping the floor with his foot and looked deeply annoyed.

The constable approached Madame Diana, and exchanged some words with her in a low voice.

They seemed to have arrived at a resolution, for Diana

smiled; and that feminine and diabolical smile made Gabriel shudder, who had his eyes, at the moment, fixed on the fair duchess.

But he found strength to add:

"I will not detain you longer, M. l'Amiral. You have done for me more than your duty, and if his Majesty should now deign to grant me a private interview for just a moment, as my first reward—"

"Later on, monsieur, I may consent," said Henry, quickly; "but it is impossible at present."

"Impossible!" cried Gabriel, sadly.

"And why impossible, sire?" interrupted Diana, to the surprise of Gabriel and even of the king himself.

"What! you think, madame—" stammered Henry.

"I think, sire, the most pressing of all duties for a king is to render each of his subjects what is due to him. Now your debt toward the Viscount d'Exmès is, it seems to me, a debt of the most sacred and legitimate character."

"Undoubtedly, undoubtedly," said Henry, regarding his mistress with an inquiring look, "and I wish—"

"To hear M. d'Exmès on the spot, sire," replied Diana, "it is right, it is but just, sire."

"But his Majesty knows," said Gabriel, more and more astounded, "that I require to speak with him alone."

"M. de Montmorency was about to withdraw as you entered, monsieur,". returned Diana; "M. l'Amiral was told by you that you would detain him no longer. As for myself, who have been a witness of the engagement contracted toward you by the king, and could recall even the precise terms to his Majesty, if necessary, you will, perhaps, permit me to remain?"

"Most assuredly, madame; I even pray you to do so," murmured Gabriel.

"My nephew and I will, therefore, take leave of your Majesty and of you, madame," said Montmorency.

When saluting Diana, he gave her a sign of encouragement, of which she apparently stood in no need.

On the other side Coligny shook Gabriel's hand warmly, and then followed his uncle.

The king and the favorite remained alone with Gabriel, who was terribly alarmed by the mysterious protection which the mother of Diana de Castro was at present granting him.

CHAPTER XLVIII

THE OTHER DIANA

DESPITE his rugged self-possession, Gabriel could not help the paleness that covered his face, or the emotion that shook his voice, when, after a pause, he said to the king:

"Sire, it is with some timidity, and yet with perfect confidence in your royal promise, that I, who escaped but yesterday from captivity, venture to recall to your Majesty the solemn engagement by which you deigned to pledge yourself to me. Count de Montgommery still lives, sire. Were it not so, you would long since have arrested my words."

He paused for a while, oppressed by emotion. The king remained impassive and mute. Gabriel resumed:

"Well, sire, since Count de Montgommery is still living, and since, according to the solemn testimony of M. l'Amiral, I have delayed the surrender of St. Quentin beyond the appointed term, I have, sire, more than fulfilled my promise; now keep yours. Give me back my father, sire."

"Monsieur—" said Henry, hesitating.

He looked at Diana de Poitiers, whose calmness and assurance seemed undisturbed.

The situation was difficult, however. Henry had accustomed himself to regard Gabriel as dead or in prison, and had not a reply ready for this terrible demand.

In presence of this hesitation, the agony of Gabriel was fearful.

"Sire," he resumed, in a sort of desperation, "your Majesty cannot have forgotten! Your Majesty surely re-

calls that solemn conversation. You recall the pledge
I took in the name of the prisoner, and your pledge
toward me?"

The king, in spite of himself, was affected by the
young man's grief and dismay; his better instincts were
aroused.

"I remember everything," he said to Gabriel.

"Ah, sire, thanks!" cried Gabriel, his face shining
with joy.

But at this moment, Madame de Poitiers quietly interposed.

"Without doubt the king remembers everything, M.
d'Exmès; it is you who appear to have forgotten."

A thunderbolt falling at his feet on some bright day in
June could not have appalled Gabriel more.

"What?" he murmured—"what have I forgotten, madame, pray?"

"The half of your task, monsieur," said Diana. "You
said, in fact, to his Majesty these words—if they are not
your own words exactly, they at least convey your meaning
—you said: 'Sire, to redeem Count de Montgommery I will
check the triumphant march of the enemy into the centre
of France.'"

"And have I not done so, madame?" asked Gabriel,
disconcerted.

"Yes, but you added: 'If it is necessary, I will assume
the offensive, instead of merely resisting attack, and will
seize one of the fortresses at present in the enemy's power.'
That is what you said, monsieur. Now, you have, as far as
I can see, only accomplished half of what you said. What
is your answer? You held St. Quentin during a certain
number of days. That was very well indeed, and I should
be the last to deny it. We have the city defended, but
where is the city taken?"

"My God! my God!" was all that Gabriel was able
to say.

"You see," continued Diana, with the same coldness,

"that I have a better and readier memory than you. Still you remember also, I hope, do you not?"

"Yes, you are right, I remember now!" cried Gabriel, bitterly. "But when I said that I only meant that, at need, I would do impossibilities. For is it possible, at the present moment, to take a city from the English or Spaniards? I ask, sire, whether your Majesty, when you allowed me to go, did not tacitly accept the first of my offers, and did not leave me under the impression that, after my heroic efforts and long captivity, I should not be called upon to execute the second? Sire, it is to you I address myself, is not a city sufficient return for a man's freedom? Does not the ransom content you? Do you insist, because of a mere word spoken in my excitement, on imposing upon me, a poor human Hercules, a labor a hundred times more rugged than the first; nay, sire, as you well understand, a labor incapable of realization?"

The king made a motion as if to speak, but the grande sénéschale hastened to anticipate him.

"Is the liberation then," said she, "any easier, or attended with less danger and folly, to set free a formidable prisoner guilty of high treason? To obtain the impossible, you have offered the impossible, M. d'Exmès. You have no right to require the fulfilment of the king's promise, when you have not kept yours. The duties of a sovereign are not less grave than those of a son. Only immense and superhuman services rendered to the state could excuse his Majesty for disregarding the laws of the state. It may be your duty to save your father, granted; but it is the duty of the king to guard France."

And with an expressive look that illustrated her words, Diana recalled to Henry the peril of allowing the Count de Montgommery and his secret to issue from the tomb.

Gabriel made a final effort, and, with outstretched arms, cried to the king:

"Sire, it is to your equity, nay to your clemency, that I appeal. Sire, at some future time, aided by time and circumstances, I pledge myself to restore to my country that city, or to die in the attempt. But meanwhile, sire, be merciful, let me see my father.''

But Henry, counselled by the steady gaze and the whole attitude of Diana, replied in a voice he tried to render firm:

"Keep your promise to the end, monsieur, and I swear before God that then, but only then, will I fulfil mine. My word is only as good as yours.''

"And this is your final decision, sire?'' said Gabriel.

"It is my final decision.''

Gabriel bent his head for a moment, crushed, con-quered, every nerve quivering in consequence of this terrible defeat.

In a minute a whole world of thoughts crowded on his mind.

He would be avenged upon this ungrateful king and upon this perfidious woman; he would fling himself into the ranks of the reformers; he would fulfil the destiny of the Montgommerys; he would strike Henry mortally, as the old count had been stricken; he would drive Diana de Poitiers from court, shamed and dishonored. Such would henceforth be the only aim of his will and his life; and this aim, remote though it was, and unlikely to be accomplished by a private gentleman, he would at last attain.

But then!—his father during that time would have died twenty times. To avenge him was well; to save him was better. In his situation, to take a city was not more diffi-cult, perhaps, than to punish a king. Only, the first object was holy and glorious; the second, criminal and impious.

With the attainment of the latter, he lost Diana de Cas-tro forever; with the attainment of the former, he might win her.

All the events brought to pass since the capture of St. Quentin flashed before his eyes.

In far less time than it takes us to write it, the valiant

and watchful soul of the young man recovered its tone. He had adopted a resolution, conceived a plan, caught a glimpse of an issue.

The king and his mistress saw, with astonishment, almost with dismay, that pale but tranquil face uplifted once more.

"Be it so!" was all he said.

"Are you resigned?" asked Henry.

"I am resolved," replied Gabriel.

"What? explain yourself!" said the king.

"Listen, sire. An enterprise involving the capture of a city in retaliation for the one taken from you by the Spaniards, seems to you desperate, impossible, insensate, does it not? Be sincere with me, sire, and you too, madame; is it not thus you regard it?"

"It is true," answered Henry.

"I fear it is," added Diana.

"In all probability such an attempt," continued Gabriel, "would cost me my life, and its sole result would be to make me pass for a ridiculous madman."

"It was not I who proposed it," said the king.

"And you will do well to renounce it," pursued Diana.

"And yet I am resolved to accomplish it," said Gabriel.

Neither Henry nor Diana could restrain a movement of admiration.

"Oh, take care!" cried the king.

"Care of what? my life?" returned Gabriel, with a laugh. "I made the sacrifice of it long ago. But, sire, no misconception, no evasion this time. The terms of the bargain we conclude before God and man are now clear and precise. I, Gabriel, Viscount d'Exmès, Viscount de Montgommery, will so manage that a town actually in possession of the English or Spaniards shall become yours. This city shall be no mere collection of huts, no mere village, but a fortified town as important as you yourself can desire. That is not ambiguous, I imagine!"

"No, indeed!" said the king, with some agitation.

"But you also," resumed Gabriel; "you, Henry the Second, King of France, solemnly engage on your part to throw open the dungeon of my father on my first demand, and to give me back the Count de Montgommery. Do you pledge yourself to this? Does what I have said stand?"

The king saw the incredulous smile on Diana's lips and answered:

"I pledge myself."

"Thanks, your Majesty. But this is not all: you must grant a further guarantee to this madman who flings himself with open eyes into the abyss. It is necessary to be indulgent to those about to die. I ask not your signature to a document. It might compromise you, and you would doubtless refuse. But yonder is a Bible; sire, lay your royal hand upon it, and swear this oath: 'In exchange for a city of the first rank, for which I shall be indebted to Gabriel de Montgommery alone, I pledge myself, upon the Sacred Scriptures, to release the father of Viscount d'Exmès, and I declare in advance that, should I violate this oath, the said viscount no longer owes any allegiance to me or mine. I further declare that all he does to punish the perjury is well done, and I absolve him for it before God and man, though it were a crime committed upon my person.' Swear that oath, sire."

"By what right do you ask me to do so?" demanded Henry.

"I have told you, sire; the right of one about to die."

The king still hesitated. But the duchess, with a scornful smile, made him a sign that he could do so without any fear.

In fact, she was thinking that, for the time at least, Gabriel had quite lost his reason, and she shrugged her shoulders compassionately.

"Be it so, I consent," said Henry, hurried away by some fatal influence.

And, with his hand on the Gospels, he repeated the oath dictated by Gabriel.

"At least," said the young man, when the king had finished, "that will be enough to spare me all remorse. The witness of our new bargain is not only you, madame, but God. I have now no time to lose. Farewell, sire. In two months I shall be dead, or I shall embrace my father."

He bowed to the king and duchess, and rushed out of the chamber.

Henry, in spite of himself, was for some moments serious and pensive; but Diana burst out laughing.

"What! you do not laugh, sire?" said she. "You see clearly that the man is mad, and his father will die in prison. Surely you ought to laugh, sire."

"Well, I am laughing," said the king; and he laughed.

CHAPTER XLIX

A GREAT IDEA FOR A GREAT MAN

THE Duke de Guise, ever since he was appointed lieutenant-general of the kingdom, occupied a suite of apartments in the Louvre. It was, therefore, in the chateau of the kings of France that the ambitious chief of the house of Lorraine now slept, or rather watched, every night.

What waking dreams did he not have under that roof peopled with chimeras! Did not these dreams reach much further at present than when he confided to Gabriel, in his tent at Civitella, his plans for acquiring the throne of Naples? Would that content him now? Was not the guest of the royal palace saying to himself that he might soon become its master? Did he not already feel around his temples the contact of a royal crown; and did he not regard with a complacent smile that goodly sword of his which, more potent than magician's wand, could transform his hopes into realities?

It is not unlikely that, even at this period, Francis de Lorraine nourished such thoughts! Just consider! Did not the king himself, by appealing to him for help in his distress, give a sanction to his wildest ambitious hopes? To confide the safety of France to him in that desperate crisis was to acknowledge him the first captain of the time! Francis the First would not have displayed such modesty; no, he would have grasped the sword of Marignano. But Henry the Second, though personally brave, lacked the will to command and the force to execute.

The Duke de Guise told himself all this; but he told himself also that it was not enough to justify these daring aspirations in his own eyes; they had to be justified in the eyes of France; they had to be justified by brilliant services and signal successes: thus only could he acquire rights and become the master of his destiny.

The fortunate general whose happy fate it was to check the second invasion of Charles the Fifth at Metz, felt he had not yet done enough to dare everything. Though he should now drive back the English and Spaniards to the frontiers, it was not yet enough. If France gave herself to him, or allowed him to take her, he must not only repair her defeats, he must gain for her fresh victories.

Such were the reflections that ordinarily engrossed the great mind of the Duke de Guise since his return from Italy.

He was rehearsing them over again upon the very day that Gabriel de Montgommery concluded his sublime and insensate pact with Henry the Second.

Standing alone by the window in his chamber, Francis de Guise was looking into the court, but taking no note of what he saw, and was drumming mechanically on the pane with his fingers.

One of his attendants scratched the door discreetly, and, receiving permission to enter, announced the Viscount d'Exmès.

"Viscount d'Exmès!" exclaimed the duke, who had the memory of Cæsar, and had, besides, good reasons for recalling Gabriel. "Viscount d'Exmès, my young comrade of Metz, Renty, and Valenza! Let him enter, Thibault! let him enter at once!"

The servant inclined, and left to introduce Gabriel.

Our hero (we have every right to give him that name) had not hesitated a moment. With that instinct which illuminates the soul at critical moments, and which, if it flashes across the whole ordinary course of existence, is called genius, Gabriel, when he quitted the king, as if he had foreseen the secret thoughts in which the Duke de Guise was then taking delight, proceeded straight to the apartments of the lieutenant-general of the realm.

He was, perhaps, the only living man who could understand and help him.

Gabriel had every reason to be pleased with his reception by his old general.

The Duke de Guise met him on the threshold, and pressed him to his heart.

"Ah, you have arrived at last, my gallant friend!" he said eagerly. "Where have you come from? What has become of you since St. Quentin? How often have I thought and spoken of you, Gabriel?"

"Indeed, monseigneur? Then I have had some place in your memory?"

"*Pardieu!* what a question for you to ask!" cried the duke. "You have your methods, have you not, of preventing people from forgetting you? Coligny, who is worth all the Montmorencys put together, has related to me (though his words were rather mysterious, I don't know why) a part of your exploits yonder at St. Quentin; and yet he was silent, so he said himself, about the best half of them."

"I did too little, nevertheless," said Gabriel, with a sad smile.

"Ambitious?" returned the duke.

"Oh, yes, very," answered Gabriel, with a melancholy shake of the head.

"Well, at all events, thank God, you are back, and we are together again, my friend! You know all the plans we discussed together in Italy. Ah, my poor Gabriel, France needs your valor now more than ever! To what straits they have brought the country!"

"All that I have, and all that I am, are consecrated to its defence, and I only await your signal, monseigneur."

"Thanks, my friend," replied the duke. "I will take advantage of your offer, rely upon it, and you will not have to wait long for my signal either."

"Then it will be my turn to thank you, monseigneur!" cried Gabriel.

"Nevertheless, to tell the truth, the more I look around me, the more embarrassing and serious I find the situation. I had first to run to the most critical point, organize resistance around Paris, offer a formidable line of defence to the enemy, and, in fine, arrest his progress. But that was nothing. He has St. Quentin! he has the north! I must and will act. But how?"

He paused as if to consult Gabriel. He knew the high mental capacity of the young man, and had often found occasion to adopt his opinion; but now the Viscount d'Exmès was silent, studying the duke, and determined to let him advance to the subject himself, so to say.

Francis de Lorraine continued therefore:

"Do not accuse me of being slow, my friend; I am not, as you know, one of those who hesitate, but I am one of those who reflect. You will not blame me, for you are a little like me, at once resolute and prudent. And," added the duke, "the thoughtfulness stamped on your youthful forehead seems to me to be even of a sterner cast than of yore. I do not dare to question you upon yourself. You had, I remember, grave duties to fulfil and dangerous enemies to discover. Have you other misfortunes to deplore besides those of your country? I am afraid so; for when I left you you were grave; now you are sad."

"Pray, monseigneur, let us not speak of myself," said Gabriel. "Let us speak of France. To do so will still be to speak of me."

"Just as you wish," answered the Duke de Guise. "I desire then to lay all my thoughts and anxieties before you. It seems to me that the thing absolutely necessary at the present time is to elevate the tone of our people by some dashing exploit, and at the same time renew our old military reputation; we must resume the offensive, and not confine ourselves to the task of repairing our reverses, but make up for those reverses by some brilliant success."

"That view is mine also, monseigneur!" cried Gabriel, surprised and delighted by a coincidence so favorable to his own plans.

"That is your view then, is it?" returned the duke; "and you have doubtless more than once meditated on the perils of our country, and the means of rescuing her from them?"

"I have indeed often meditated on the subject," said Gabriel.

"Well," rejoined Francis, "are you further advanced on the subject than I am? Have you contemplated the difficulty seriously? Where, when, and how is this exploit to be attempted which you judge to be as necessary as I do?"

"Monseigneur, I believe I know."

"Is it possible?" cried the duke. "Oh, speak, speak, my friend!"

"*Mon Dieu!* I have, perhaps, already spoken too early. The proposal I am about to make should, no doubt, not be approached without long preparations. You are very great, monseigneur; but, for all that, what I have to say to you may appear to you utterly extravagant."

"I am not easily made dizzy," said Francis, smiling.

"No matter, monseigneur, at first sight my project is going to appear to you strange, insensate, impracticable even. And yet it is only difficult and perilous."

"Why, that but makes it the more attractive!" said Francis de Lorraine.

"It is agreed then, monseigneur, that you are not going to be frightened when you first hear it. There will, I repeat, be great risks to be run. But the means of success are within my reach, and when I unfold them you will acknowledge so yourself."

"If that is the case, go on, Gabriel," said the duke. "But," he added impatiently, "some one is apparently coming to interrupt us. Is that you knocking, Thibault?"

"Yes, monseigneur," said the servant, entering. "You

have ordered me, monseigneur, to inform you when the hour for the meeting of the council arrived. It has just struck two, and M. de Saint-Rémy, with some other gentlemen, has come for you.''

"True, true," replied Francis, "there is a council now, and an important council. It is absolutely necessary for me to attend it. All right, Thibault, leave us. Show those gentlemen in when they arrive. You see, Gabriel, my duty calls me near the king. You can in the evening fully develop your plan at your leisure; it must be noble, since it is yours. But in the meantime, Gabriel, satisfy my impatience and curiosity, I entreat you, and that briefly. In short, what do you intend to do?" .

"In short, *to take Calais*, monseigneur," answered Gabriel, quietly.

"To take Calais!" cried the duke, starting back in his surprise.

"You forget, monseigneur," returned Gabriel, in the same quiet tone, "that you promised not to let your first impressions frighten you."

"But have you given the subject serious reflection?" said the duke. "Calais defended by a formidable garrison, impregnable ramparts and the sea! Calais in the power of England for more than two centuries! Calais guarded as only the keys of France are guarded by those who hold them. I love hardihood, but is not this rashness?"

"Yes, monseigneur, so rash that no one can even conceive the possibility of such an enterprise being undertaken; that is why it has the best chances of success."

"That is likely enough," said the duke, thoughtfully.

"When you have heard me, monseigneur, you will say: 'That is certain!' The policy to be observed by us is traced out in advance: absolute secrecy, deceiving the enemy by some false manœuvre, and arriving unexpectedly before the city. In a fortnight Calais will be ours."

"But," returned the duke, quickly, "these general indications are not enough. Your plan, Gabriel; you have a plan?''

"Yes, monseigneur, a simple and sure one—''

Gabriel could not finish. At that moment the door opened, and Count de Saint-Rémy entered, followed by a number of gentlemen attached to the fortunes of the Guises.

"His Majesty is waiting for the Lieutenant-General of the realm in the council chamber,'' said Saint-Rémy.

"I am yours, gentlemen,'' answered Francis de Guise, as he saluted the new-comers.

Then going up quickly to Gabriel, he said, in a low voice:

"You see, it is necessary to leave you, my friend. But this magnificent scheme of yours, a scheme surpassing belief, will not quit me to-day. You have, as it were, flung it into my brain, and it will stay there, I stake my soul upon it! Can you return at eight this evening? We shall have the whole night, and we are sure of not being interrupted.''

"At eight then; I will be punctual, and will make good use of my time in the meanwhile.''

"Permit me to observe, monseigneur,'' said Saint-Rémy, "that it is now after two.''

"I am ready, quite ready!'' replied the duke. He started for the door, then turned round to gaze upon Gabriel again, and approaching him, as if to make sure once more that he had heard correctly: "To take Calais?'' he whispered in a questioning tone.

Gabriel bowed in sign of assent, and answered with his calm and gentle smile:

"To take Calais.''

The Duke de Guise hastened out of the room, and Gabriel, following in his footsteps, soon left the Louvre behind him.

CHAPTER L

A SIDE VIEW OF CERTAIN WARRIORS

ALOYSE was suffering tortures as she watched for the return of Gabriel from one of the lower windows of the hotel. When she at last perceived him, she raised her eyes full of tears to heaven—tears, this time, of gratitude and happiness.

Then she ran and opened the door for her beloved master.

"God be praised! I see you again, monseigneur," she cried. "You come from the Louvre? Have you seen the king?"

"I have seen him," answered Gabriel.

"Well?"

"Well, my good nurse, I must wait longer."

"Wait longer!" exclaimed Aloyse, clasping her hands. "Holy Virgin! it is very sad and very hard to have to wait longer."

"It would be impossible," said Gabriel, "if I had to wait in inaction. But, thank God! I will act, and without ever turning my eyes aside from the end of the journey, I shall be able to occupy my mind on the way."

He entered the hall and flung his cloak on the back of an easy-chair.

He did not see Martin Guerre, who was sunk in deep reflection, seated in a corner.

"Very nice of you, Martin, isn't it?" cried Dame Aloyse. "You lazy fellow, you don't even help monseigneur to get rid of his cloak."

"Oh, forgive me, monseigneur!" said Martin, awaking from his revery and rising hastily.

"Don't disturb yourself, Martin," said Gabriel. "Aloyse, you must not torment my poor Martin; his zeal and devotion are now more necessary to me than ever, and I have matters of serious import to discuss with him at present."

A wish expressed by Gabriel was sacred for Aloyse. Now that the squire was restored to favor, she smiled on him in the most amiable fashion, and then discreetly retired, so that her master might be more at his ease in his conference with his follower.

"Now for it, Martin," said Gabriel, when they were alone. "What were you doing there in that corner? what subject were you meditating upon so seriously?"

"Monseigneur," replied Martin Guerre, "I have been delving in my brain, trying to make something out of the riddle of the man of this morning."

"Well, have you succeeded?" asked Gabriel, smiling.

"Not much, monseigneur, alas! It's all very well for me to open my eyes until they can widen no further; I can see nothing but darkness, I must confess."

"But I told you, Martin, didn't I, that I saw something else?"

"You did, monseigneur. But what is it? I'm killing myself trying to find out."

"The time has not yet come for telling you," said Gabriel. "Listen, you are devoted to me, Martin?"

"Is that a question you are putting, monseigneur?"

"No, it is your praises I am sounding. I now invoke this devotion of which I have spoken. You must for a time forget yourself; you must forget the shadow that has crossed your life, soon to be dissipated, I promise you. But at present I have need of you, Martin."

"Ah, so much the better, so much the better!" cried Martin Guerre.

"But let us understand each other clearly. I have need

of you all, entire, of your life and your courage. Will you trust me, put off for a time your personal troubles, and consecrate yourself exclusively to my fortunes?"

"Will I!" cried Martin. "Why, monseigneur, that is my duty, and, what is more, my pleasure. By St. Martin, it's only too long I've been separated from you! and, thunder and lightning, don't I wish to make up for all the days lost! Though there be legions of Martin Guerres tugging at my breeches, don't be uneasy, monseigneur, I won't care a fig for them. As long as you are before me, I see only you in the world."

"Noble heart!" exclaimed Gabriel. "Reflect, however, Martin, that the enterprise in which I am asking you to engage is full of perils and pitfalls."

"Not worth mentioning! We'll jump over them!" said Martin, cracking his fingers.

"We shall stake our lives a hundred times, Martin."

"The higher the stake, the better the game, monseigneur."

"But this game once entered upon, my friend, it will be impossible to rise from it until the end."

"Oh, a man is a good player, or he is not," returned the squire, proudly.

"No matter!" said Gabriel, "in spite of all your resolution, you have no idea of the formidable and unusual risks connected with the superhuman struggle to which I would conduct you; all these efforts, think well on it, may go unrewarded. Martin, consider this: when I am brought face to face with the project I am bound to undertake, it appalls even myself."

"Good! danger and I are old acquaintances," said Martin, with a consequential air, "and when a man has had the honor of being hanged—"

"Martin," continued Gabriel, "we must brave the elements, rejoice in the tempest, laugh at the impossible—"

"Well, then, we'll laugh," said Martin Guerre. "To tell the truth, monseigneur, ever since I was hanged, I have looked upon my days as days of grace; and I am not going to quarrel with the good God on account of the surplusage He deigns to grant me. It is not necessary to reckon up what the merchant gives you over and above the bargain; the man who does so is either ungrateful or foolish.''

"It's settled then, Martin, you will follow and share my fortunes.''

"To hell, monseigneur, provided, however, that I have not to have any trouble with Satan; for a Catholic is a Catholic, monseigneur, and I hope I'm a good one.''

"Have no fear upon that point,'' said Gabriel. "You may, perhaps, endanger your safety in this world in my company, but certainly not in the next.''

"That's all that's necessary,'' returned Martin. "But is my life all that monseigneur demands of me?''

"No, I have still another service to ask of you,'' replied Gabriel, smiling at the heroic simplicity of the question.

"What is it, monseigneur?''

"You must search out and find me as speedily as possible, to-day if you can, a dozen lads of your own mettle —brave, strong, and bold, fearing neither fire nor sword; laughing at hunger and thirst, heat and cold; obedient as angels, and able to fight like devils. Can you do this?''

"That's according to circumstances. Are they to be well paid?''

"A piece of gold for every drop of blood. My fortune gives me little concern, alas! in the pious but rude task I must now go on with to the end.''

"At that figure, monseigneur, I can pick up in two hours a band of stout knaves not given—I can answer for them on that point—to lamenting over their wounds. In France, and especially in Paris, such rascals are as plenty as blackberries. But who are they to serve?''

"Myself. It is not as captain of the guards, but as a volunteer that I am going to enter upon this campaign. They must belong to myself personally.''

"In that case, monseigneur, I can lay my hands in a jiffy on five or six of our old companions in the Lorraine campaign who will be ready to come at a whistle. They have had the jaundice, poor devils, ever since you disbanded them. Won't they be glad to be under fire again with you! Oh, if it's for you I am going to recruit, you'll have the full number this very evening."

"Good! There is one condition they must subscribe to if they are enlisted; they must consent to quit Paris at any hour, and follow me anywhere, without question or comment, without even looking to see if we go north or south."

"These fellows will march toward glory or money with eyes bandaged, monseigneur."

"I count on them and you then, Martin. As for your share—"

"Please don't speak of it, monseigneur," interrupted Martin.

"I must speak of it, on the contrary. If we survive the conflict, I solemnly pledge myself, my faithful follower, to do all for you that you have done for me, and to aid you in my turn against your enemies. Have no doubt upon that point. Meanwhile, your hand, my trusty friend."

"Oh, monseigneur!" said Martin Guerre, respectfully kissing the hand that was tendered him.

"Now, Martin, set about your search at once," continued the viscount. "Discretion and courage. Go, I wish to be alone."

"Excuse me, monseigneur, do you intend staying at your hotel?"

"Yes, until seven. I do not go to the Louvre before eight."

"In that case, monseigneur, I hope to be able to present you with some samples at least of the personnel of your troop."

He bowed and withdrew, quite proud of his mission, which engrossed all his thoughts already.

Gabriel spent the rest of the day by himself, in studying the plan given him by Jean, making notes, and striding up and down his chamber in meditation.

It was necessary that he should be prepared in the evening to meet every possible objection of the Duke de Guise.

He only interrupted his meditations from time to time by repeating, with firm voice and ardent heart:

"I will save thee, my father! And thee, too, my own Diana!"

Toward six he was forced by the persevering entreaties of Aloyse to eat a little, and while so engaged, Martin Guerre entered with a grave and composed air.

"Monseigneur," said he, "will you be pleased to receive six or seven of those who aspire to serve you under the orders of France and the king?"

"What! six or seven already!" exclaimed Gabriel.

"Six or seven strangers, monseigneur. Our old comrades of Metz will complete the dozen. They are all enchanted at the thought of risking their skins for such a master as you, and accept all your conditions."

"Faith, you haven't lost time," said Viscount d'Exmès. "Well, then, bring in your men."

"One after the other, isn't it? You'll be a better judge of them so."

"One after the other, if you like."

"One word more," said the squire. "I have no need to tell you, M. le Vicomte, that all these men are known to me either personally or by information on which I can rely. Their characters are different and their instincts varied; but the distinguishing feature common to all is a valor that has been tested. I can be their guarantee in this respect, if monseigneur will deal lightly with a few peccadilloes of little importance."

After this prelude, Martin Guerre went out for a few moments, and returned almost immediately, followed by a tall fellow with a swarthy complexion, brisk appearance, and a careless, sprightly expression.

"Ambrosio," said Martin Guerre, presenting him.

"Ambrosio. A foreign name that. Is he not a Frenchman?" asked Gabriel.

"Who can tell?" said Ambrosio. "I was found in the Pyrenees when a baby, and have lived there as a man, with one foot in France and the other in Spain; and faith, I have gayly turned my double bastardy to account, without complaining of God or my mother."

"And how have you lived?" demanded Gabriel.

"Oh, as for that," said Ambrosio, "as I was equally attached to both my countries, I endeavored to do away with the barriers between them, as far as my humble means permitted; to extend to each the advantages of the other, and, like a pious son, to contribute to their mutual prosperity by doing all in my power for the free exchange of those gifts they held separately from Providence."

"In a word," said Martin Guerre, "Ambrosio was a smuggler."

"But," continued Ambrosio, "as soon as I was brought to the notice of the Spanish authorities, as well as of the French authorities, I was misunderstood and persecuted by my ungrateful fellow-countrymen on both slopes of the Pyrenees. So I determined to give way and come to Paris, a city where a brave man can always find resources."

"Where Ambrosio would be happy," added Martin, "to place his bravery, his skill and long experience in endurance and danger, at the disposal of Viscount d'Exmès."

"Ambrosio the smuggler is accepted," said Gabriel. "Another."

Ambrosio left the room delighted, and gave way to an ascetic and circumspect-looking personage, wrapped in a long brown cloak, and with a chaplet of large beads hanging from his neck.

Martin Guerre announced him under the name of Lactance.

"Lactance," he added, "has served under M. de Coligny, who still regrets him, and will bear testimony to his merits.

But Lactance is a zealous Catholic, and did not like serving under a leader suspected of heresy."

Lactance silently signified by head and hands his approval of the words of Martin, who continued:

"This pious soldier will do all he can, as is his duty, to satisfy M. d'Exmès. But he requires to be allowed every facility and liberty for the rigorous fulfilment of the religious duties that are necessary for his salvation. Compelled by the profession of arms which he has embraced, and by his natural calling, to fight against his brothers in Jesus Christ, and kill as many of them as he can, Lactance wisely deems that it is, at least, needful to atone for these cruel exigencies by austerities. The more furious Lactance is in battle, the more ardent is he at mass; and he has given up in despair reckoning the fasts and penitences he has imposed upon himself on account of the dead and wounded he has sent, ere their time, to the footstool of the throne of the Lord."

"The devout Lactance is accepted," said Gabriel, smiling.

Lactance remained silent, and, after a profound inclination, passed out muttering a thankful prayer to the Most High for having granted him the favor of being accepted by so valiant a captain.

After Lactance, Martin showed in a young man of middle height, elegant and distinguished appearance, and with small, carefully-kept hands. From his ruffles to his boots, his dress was not only stylish but showy. He saluted Gabriel with the most graceful bow imaginable and stood before him in an attitude as easy as it was respectful, lightly shaking off from his right sleeve a few grains of dust that had found a lodgment there.

"You have now before you, monseigneur, the most resolute man of the whole of them," said Martin Guerre. "Yvonnet is a lion in battle whom nothing can stop. When thrusting or striking he is a sort of madman. But it is above all in an assault that he shines. He must be the first to plant his foot on the first ladder, and also plant the first French standard on the enemy's walls."

"Why then he must be a real hero?" said Gabriel.

"I merely do my best," answered Yvonnet, modestly, "and M. Martin Guerre estimates, no doubt, my poor efforts beyond their value."

"No, I only do you justice," said Martin, "and the proof of it is that, after calling attention to your virtues, I am about to speak of your faults. It is only on the field of battle, monseigneur, that Yvonnet is the fearless demon I have depicted. He requires as accompaniments of his valor the beat of drum, the whiz of arrow, and the roar of cannon. Away from these surroundings, Yvonnet is as timid, impressionable, and nervous as a young girl. His sensitiveness has to be managed with the greatest care. He does not like to be in the dark by himself. He has a great horror of spiders and mice, and faints if you only scratch him. He recovers his warlike ardor only when intoxicated by the smell of powder and the sight of blood."

"No matter," said Gabriel, "as we are leading him to fields of carnage and not to a ball, the susceptible Yvonnet is accepted."

Yvonnet saluted the Viscount d'Exmès in the form demanded by the laws of etiquette, and withdrew smiling, twisting his black, silky mustache with his white fingers.

He was succeeded by two blond colossuses, rigid and calm. One seemed to be about forty; the other could not have been over twenty-five.

"Heinrich Scharfenstein and Franz Scharfenstein, his nephew," announced Martin Guerre.

"Who the deuce are those fellows?" said Gabriel, astounded. "Who are you, my brave fellows?"

"*Wir verstehen nur ein wenig das Französich,*" said the elder of the giants.

"What does he mean?" asked Gabriel.

"We do not understand French well," replied the younger giant.

"They are German *reîtres*," said Martin Guerre. "In Italian, *condottieri*; in French, *soldats*. They sell their arms to the highest bidder, and estimate their valor at its just price. They have already labored for the Spaniards and English. But the Spaniards pay badly, and the English chaffer in too niggardly a fashion. Buy them, monseigneur, and you'll find you have a first-class bargain. They never discuss an order, and march to the cannon's mouth with unchanging coolness. With them courage is a matter of honesty; and, provided they are paid regularly, they will submit uncomplainingly to all the perilous or even dangerous vicissitudes of their commercial situation."

"Well, I retain these toiling hinds of glory," said Gabriel, "and for greater security I pay them a month in advance. But time presses, show in the others."

The two Teutonic Goliaths raised their hands mechanically to their caps in military fashion, and retired together, both keeping the step with soldierlike precision.

"The next is named Pilletrousse. Here he is."

A kind of robber, with ferocious mien and torn clothes, made his entrance, moving his body right and left, and looking upon Gabriel as he might have looked upon his judge.

"Why do you look ashamed, Pilletrousse?" asked Martin, benignly. "Monseigneur, whom you see before you, has asked me for men with stout hearts. You are a little more—pronounced than the others, but, on the whole, you have no reason to blush."

He continued gravely, addressing his master:

"Pilletrousse, monseigneur, is what is called a highwayman. During the general war between us and the Spaniards and English, he has until now made war on his own account. Pilletrousse roams along the highways, at this moment filled with foreign pillagers, and Pilletrousse pills the pillagers. As for his countrymen, he not only respects, but protects them. Pilletrousse then does not steal, he conquers. Pilletrousse lives by booty, not by theft. Nevertheless, he feels it is time to adjust his professional methods to legal requirements, and to be less—arbitrary in assailing the enemies of France. So he has eagerly accepted the chance of enrolling himself under the banner of Viscount d'Exmès."

"And I," said Gabriel, "accept your guarantee, Martin Guerre, and receive him on condition that he no longer makes roads and highways the theatre of his exploits, but strong cities and fields of battle."

"Thank monseigneur, you rogue, you are one of us now," said Martin to the highwayman, for whom, indeed, the said Martin seemed to have a weakness.

"Oh, yes, thanks, monseigneur!" said Pilletrousse, effusively. "I promise henceforth never to be satisfied unless I meet ten in battle instead of two or three."

"That's satisfactory, surely," said Gabriel.

The man who followed Pilletrousse was a pale, melancholy, and even anxious-looking individual who seemed to regard the universe with discouragement and sadness.

Martin Guerre presented this fellow, the seventh and last of his recruits, under the funereal appellation of Malemort.

"M. le Vicomte would be really culpable," said he, "if he refused poor Malemort. He is the victim of a passion, a passion deep and sincere, for Bellona, to speak mythologically. But this passion has so far been unfortunate. The hapless man has a pronounced and absorbing taste for war; he is never happy but amid some glorious carnage, never delighted but amid combats. And this delight, and this happiness, he has never tasted fully, only sipped. He rushes so blindly and furiously into the conflict that he always receives, at the very beginning, some wound that lays him prostrate, and sends him to the ambulance, where he lies during the remainder of the battle groaning, not because of his wound, but his absence. Indeed, his entire body is one wound. But he is robust, thank God! he recovers quickly. But he is compelled to wait for another opportunity. This long unsatiated desire undermines him more than all the blood he so gloriously lost. Monseigneur must see, therefore, that it would be a real hardship to deprive this melancholy warrior of the delight he can now bestow upon him, and which the latter can also reciprocate.''

"I accept Malemort enthusiastically, my dear Martin," said Gabriel.

A smile of satisfaction flickered across the pale face of Malemort. Hope sparkled in his sunken eyes, and he started to rejoin his comrades with a lighter step than when he entered.

"Are these all you have to present me?" asked Gabriel of his squire.

"Yes, monseigneur, all for the present. I hardly ventured to hope, monseigneur, that you would accept them all."

"I should be hard to please, Martin," said Gabriel; "your taste is sound and sure. Accept my congratulations on your happy selection."

"Yes, monseigneur," said Martin, modestly. "I really do like to think in my heart that Malemort, Pilletrousse, the two Scharfensteins, Lactance, Yvonnet, and Ambrosio are not exactly the sort of people to be disdained."

"Faith, I believe you," said Gabriel. "What a vigorous set of rufflers they are!"

"If," continued Martin, "you consented, monseigneur, to add Landry, Chesnel, Aubriot, Contamine, and Balu, our veterans of the Lorraine war, to their number, I fancy, with you at our head, and four or five people from here to serve us, we should have a troop fit to show to our friends, and, still better, to our enemies."

"Yes, assuredly," said Gabriel, "sinews of steel and heads of iron. Arm and equip this dozen of brave men as speedily as may be, Martin; but you must rest for to-day. You have spent your day well, and I thank you; mine, although full of activity and pain, is not yet finished."

"Where are you going then this evening, monseigneur?"

"To visit M. de Guise at the Louvre," said Gabriel; "he expects me at eight. Thanks to your promptitude and zeal, Martin, I hope that some of the difficulties that were likely to occur in our conversation have now disappeared in advance."

"Oh! I am very glad of that, monseigneur."

"And I, too, Martin. You have no idea how essential it is for me to succeed. But I will succeed!"

And the noble young man, as he was crossing the threshold on his way to the Louvre, repeated these words in his heart:

"Yes, I will save thee, my father! My own Diana, I will save thee!"

CHAPTER LI

NOT SUCH A FOOL AS HE LOOKED

LET us imagine that we have taken a leap over sixty
leagues and two weeks, and are back again in Calais
toward the end of the month of November, 1557.

Twenty-five days had not elapsed since the departure
of Viscount d'Exmès, when a messenger, despatched by
Gabriel, presented himself at the gates of the English
city.

He demanded to be led to Lord Wentworth, to whom
he was to make over the ransom of his late prisoner.

He seemed to be singularly clumsy and unwise, did this
same messenger. For it was in vain he had his way pointed
out to him. He passed the grand gate twenty times without
entering, although those he met almost killed themselves
in their efforts to show him where he was to go. Instead
of following their directions, the fellow was knocking stu-
pidly at every disused gate and postern, until the simpleton
had actually almost made the circuit of the exterior boulevards of the fortress.

At last, the information given him was so very precise,
and so minutely accurate, that he could not help finding
the right road; and such, even in that remote epoch, the
magic power of these words: "I am bringing ten thousand
crowns to the governor!" that when the usual rigorous
precautions were taken, when he was searched and Lord
Wentworth's orders in his regard received, the bearer of
so respectable a sum was willingly admitted into Calais.

• Decidedly, the Age of Gold is the only age that has not been an age of money.

Gabriel's unintelligent envoy missed his way more than once in the streets of Calais before finding the hôtel of the governor, to which kindly souls directed him at every hundred steps. Whenever he saw a soldier of the guard, he appeared to believe it his duty to ask him where he should find Lord Wentworth, and ran up to him accordingly.

After spending an hour on a journey that ought not to have taken ten minutes, he reached the governor's hotel at last.

He was shown in almost immediately, and Lord Wentworth received him with his usual gravity—a gravity that on this day had deepened to gloomy sadness.

When he had explained the object of his visit, and laid upon the table a bag bursting with gold pieces, the Englishman asked:

"Did Viscount d'Exmès merely charge you to deliver this money, without directing you to make any communication to me?"

Pierre, as the envoy was called, regarded Lord Wentworth with a stupid amazement that did little honor to his natural intelligence, if he had any.

"My lord," he said at last, "all I have to do with you is to hand over the ransom. My master gave me no other orders, and I don't understand—"

"Well and good!" interrupted Lord Wentworth, with a scornful smile. "M. d'Exmès has become more reasonable yonder, it appears. I congratulate him. The air of the French court is favorable to forgetfulness. So much the better for those who breathe it."

He murmured in a low voice, as if speaking to himself: "Forgetfulness is often the half of happiness."

"Have you any message, my lord, to send my master on your own account?" asked the messenger, who seemed to listen with a very heedless and idiotic air to the melancholy asides of the Englishman.

"I have nothing to say to M. d'Exmès, since he has nothing to say to me," he answered dryly. "However, stay— You can inform him, if you wish, that during another month, until the 1st of January, I shall wait for him, and be at his orders, both as a gentleman and as governor of Calais. He will understand."

"Until the 1st of January, my lord?" repeated Pierre; "I'll tell him so."

"Good. Here is your receipt, my friend, as well as something to compensate you for the inconvenience of your long journey. Pray, take it."

The man, who at first seemed disposed to refuse the gift of Lord Wentworth, apparently changed his mind and accepted it.

"Thank you, my lord," said he. "Will your lordship do me another favor?"

"What is it?" asked the governor.

"Besides the debt I have just settled with your lordship," continued the messenger, "M. d'Exmès contracted another while he was staying here, toward an inhabitant of the city, a man named—named— How was he called? Oh, yes! a man named Pierre Peuquoy, with whom he lodged."

"Well?" said Lord Wentworth.

"Well, my lord, will you permit me to go to Pierre Peuquoy's, and pay him the amount he has advanced?"

"Undoubtedly," said the governor. "Some one shall show you the house. Here is a pass enabling you to leave Calais. I should like to let you stay a few days in the city, for you have need, perhaps, of resting a while after your journey; but the regulations of the place forbid me to allow a stranger to remain, especially if he is a Frenchman. Good-by then, my friend, and I hope you'll have a pleasant journey."

"Good-by and good luck to you, my lord, with many thanks besides."

When the messenger quitted the governor's hotel, he made at least ten blunders before he found his way. At last he reached the Rue de Martroi, where, our readers will remember, the armorer Pierre Peuquoy dwelt.

The messenger of Gabriel found Pierre Peuquoy more depressed in his shop than even Lord Wentworth had been in his palace. The armorer, who at first had taken him for a customer, received him with marked indifference.

Nevertheless when the stranger announced that he came on behalf of Viscount d'Exmès, the face of the worthy citizen suddenly cleared.

"On behalf of Viscount d'Exmès!" said he.

Then addressing an apprentice who was arranging articles in the shop, and was within hearing distance:

"Quentin," said he, carelessly, "leave us, and inform my brother at once that a messenger has arrived from Viscount d'Exmès."

The 'prentice, disappointed, passed out.

"Speak now, my friend," said Pierre Peuquoy, eagerly. "Oh, we well knew that this excellent lord would not forget us! Speak quick! What do you bring us on his behalf?"

"His compliments and cordial thanks, this purse of gold, and these words: *Remember the 5th*, words he said you would understand."

"Is that all?" asked Pierre Peuquoy.

"Absolutely all, master. Well, upon my word, if they are not hard to please in these quarters!" thought the messenger. "It would seem they make light of crowns; but they have mysteries which the devil himself would not comprehend."

"But," returned the armorer, "there are three of us in this house: myself, my cousin Jean, and my sister Babette. You have fulfilled your commission as far as I am concerned; but have you nothing to say to Jean and Babette?"

Jean Peuquoy was entering just as Gabriel's messenger answered:

"I have no message for anybody except you, Master Pierre Peuquoy; and I have told you all I had to tell."

"Well, you see, brother," said Pierre, turning to Jean— "you see M. d'Exmès thanks us; M. d'Exmès sends us our money with all speed; M. d'Exmès transmits to us the word: 'Remember!' But he does not remember."

"Alas!" said a weak and sorrowful voice behind the door.

It was that of poor Babette, who had heard everything.

"Wait a moment," interposed Jean Peuquoy, who was still hopeful. "My friend," he continued, addressing the envoy, "if you belong to the household of M. d'Exmès, you must be acquainted with one of his servants and your companions named Martin Guerre."

"Martin Guerre? Ah, yes, Martin Guerre, the squire? Yes, master, I do know him."

"He is still in the service of M. d'Exmès?"

"Undoubtedly."

"But did he know you were coming to Calais?"

"Yes, he did," replied the messenger. "He was, I remember, in the hotel of M. d'Exmès when I quitted it. Indeed, his master, or rather our master, accompanied me to the door, and saw me start on my journey."

"And he has said nothing for me or for any one in this house?"

"Nothing at all, I assure you."

"Wait, Pierre, do not be impatient yet," persisted Jean. "Perhaps, my friend, Martin Guerre has been advised to give his message secretly? Well, you may understand that such a precaution has become useless. We know the truth now. The misfortune of—the person to whom Martin Guerre owes reparation has left us in ignorance of nothing. You may, therefore, speak freely in our presence. Moreover, if you have any scruples on the subject, we will withdraw, and the person to whom I allude, and whom Martin Guerre must have spoken to you about, will be here immediately, and converse with you on the matter."

"I swear to you upon my soul that I don't comprehend

one word of what you're talking about,'' replied the messenger.

"Enough, Jean, you must have had enough of this yourself!" cried Pierre Peuquoy, his eyes red with anger. "By the memory of my father, I cannot see what pleasure you can take, Jean, in dwelling upon the shame to which we have been subjected!"

Jean bent his head sorrowfully and silently. He saw that his cousin was speaking only too truly.

"Please count the money, master," said the messenger, rather embarrassed by the part he was playing.

"It isn't worth while," said Jean, who was calmer, if not less sad, than his cousin. "Take this for your trouble; I will see that you have something to eat and drink as well.''

"Thank you for the money," said the envoy, who, however, seemed rather unwilling to accept it. "As to eating and drinking, I am neither hungry nor thirsty, having breakfasted a short time ago at Nieullay. I have to set out at once; for your governor has forbidden me to remain any time in your city.''

"We do not wish to detain you, my friend," returned Jean Peuquoy. "Farewell. Say to Martin Guerre— But no, we have nothing to say to him. Only say to M. d'Ex-mès that we thank him, and that we remember the 5th. But we hope that he, too, will remember.''

"Stay a moment and hear me," added Pierre Peuquoy, forgetting his sombre preoccupations for the time. "Tell your master we intend waiting for him an entire month. In a month you can be in Paris, and he can send some one here. But if we do not receive any news of him at the end of the present year, we shall believe that his heart has no memory, and shall be as sorry for him as for ourselves. For indeed, his honor as a gentleman, which remembers so well the money he borrowed, might surely have urged him to remember still better the secrets that were confided to him. And now, adieu, my friend.''

"God keep you!" said the messenger, rising to leave. "All your questions and all your messages shall be faithfully reported to my master."

Jean Peuquoy attended the man to the door of the house. Pierre remained in a corner, utterly hopeless.

Our somewhat dilatory messenger, after many mistakes and many unnecessary detours in this intricate town of Calais, which he seemed to find so much difficulty in threading, reached the principal gate at last, where he showed his pass, was carefully searched, and then allowed to depart.

He walked three-quarters of an hour with a light step and without stopping. He did not slacken his gait until he was about three miles from the city.

Then he rested, sat down upon the turf, and seemed to be reflecting. A smile of satisfaction lighted up his eyes and his lips.

"Really," he said to himself, "for some reason or other, with which I am unacquainted, those folks in Calais would seem to be competing as to which should look the saddest and most mysterious. Lord Wentworth apparently has an account to settle with M. d'Exmès, and the Peuquoys have evidently a grievance against Martin Guerre. But, bah! what have I to do with all that? I have certainly no cause for sadness. I have got what I wanted, and what was necessary. Not a stroke of pen or bit of paper, it is true; but I have it all here in my head; and, aided by the plan of M. d'Exmès, I could easily reconstruct in my mind this fortress which renders those dwelling in it so gloomy, but the recollection of which gives me the liveliest pleasure."

He travelled rapidly again in imagination over the streets and boulevards and by the fortified posts his pretended stupidity had made him so thoroughly acquainted with.

"That's it," said he to himself. "Everything is as plain and clear as if I were looking at it still. The Duke de

Guise will be satisfied. Thanks to this journey, and to the valuable hints of his Majesty's captain of the guards, we shall be able to conduct our dear Viscount d'Exmès, and his squire along with him, to that meeting which both Lord Wentworth and Pierre Peuquoy refuse to put off beyond a month. In six months, if God and circumstances favor us, we shall be masters of Calais, or I will lose my name there.''

And when our readers learn that this name belonged to Marshal Pietro Strozzi, one of the most illustrious and skilful engineers of the sixteenth century, they will surely think to lose it would be a pity.

After resting a few minutes, Pietro Strozzi continued his journey, walking so fast that it was evident he was in a hurry to get back to Paris. He was thinking a good deal about Calais, but very little about its inhabitants.

CHAPTER LII

THE 31ST OF DECEMBER, 1557

IT WILL be guessed why Pietro Strozzi found Lord Wentworth so bitter and annoyed, and why the governor of Calais still spoke of Viscount d'Exmès with such haughtiness and animosity. It was because Madame de Castro appeared to hate him more than ever.

When he asked permission to visit her, she was always ready with pretexts to excuse herself for not receiving him. If, nevertheless, she had to submit to his presence, her icy and formal reception left no doubt as to the feeling with which she regarded him; and he left her with keener despair in his heart every time.

And still his love for her was not yet exhausted. Although he did not hope, he was far from despairing. He was anxious that he should at least be regarded by Diana in the same light in which he had been regarded at the court of Mary: a perfect gentleman whose reputation for exquisite courtesy was unequalled. He literally overwhelmed his prisoner with his attentions. She was surrounded with pomp and luxury of the most princely kind. She had a French page, and one of those Italian musicians who were the delight of the Renaissance was at her service. Diana sometimes found in her chamber robes and jewels of the highest value. Lord Wentworth had sent specially for them to London on her account; but she did not even look at them.

Once he gave a grand entertainment in her honor, to which the most illustrious Englishmen in Calais and France

were invited; his invitations even crossed the Channel.
Madame de Castro obstinately refused to be present.

Confronted by such coldness and disdain, Lord Wentworth was constantly repeating to himself that it would
assuredly be better for his repose to accept the royal ransom offered by Henry the Second, and restore Diana to
liberty.

But this would be restoring her to the successful love
of Gabriel d'Exmès, and the Englishman had neither the
strength nor courage to effect so rough a sacrifice.

"No, no," he said to himself, "if I do not have her, no
one else shall."

Days, weeks, and months slipped by amid such waver-
ing purposes and agonizing tortures.

On the 31st of December, 1557, Lord Wentworth succeeded in obtaining admission to the apartment of Madame
de Castro. As we have already said, he could breathe no-
where else, although he always left it more downcast and
smitten than ever. But to see Diana, even when she was
coldest, to listen to her words even when they were most
ironical, had become for him an imperious necessity.

They were conversing, she seated before the high fire-
place, he standing.

They were conversing on the one heartrending subject
that at once united and separated them.

"What, madame," said the amorous governor, "if, provoked by your cruelty and exasperated by your disdain,
I should, after all, forget that I am a gentleman and your
host?"

"You would dishonor yourself, my lord; you would not
dishonor me," replied Diana, firmly.

"We should be dishonored together," retorted Lord
Wentworth. "You are in my power. Where could you
find a refuge?"

"In death, my lord," she answered quietly.

Lord Wentworth turned pale and shuddered. He to
cause the death of Diana!

"Such obstinacy is not natural," he said, shaking his head. "At bottom, madame, you would fear to drive me to extremities, did you not indulge in some insensate expectation. You are always trusting to some impossible chance or other, then? Come, now, tell me from whom can you expect aid at present?"

"From God, from the king—" returned Diana.

There was a hesitation in her language, a reticence in her thoughts, which Lord Wentworth understood only too well.

"Ah, she is, beyond doubt, dreaming of that Gabriel d'Exmès!" he said to himself.

But it was dangerous to awaken such reflections. He contented himself, therefore, with this bitter rejoinder:

"Yes, count on the king! count on God! But if God had cared to help you, He would have done so on the first day, it seems to me; and now the year has passed, yet has He not apparently shown any design of protecting you."

"But I hope that during the year which begins tomorrow—" replied Diana, raising her eyes to heaven, as if to implore the divine aid.

"As to the king of France, your father," continued Lord Wentworth, "the affairs he has on his hands at present are sufficient to absorb all his energies and all his thoughts. The peril of France is even more urgent than that of his daughter."

"So you say," returned Diana, in a tone expressing doubt.

"Lord Wentworth does not lie, madame. Do you know how matters stand with your august father?"

"What can I learn in this prison?" retorted Diana, who, however, could not restrain a movement of interest.

"You have only to question me," returned Lord Wentworth, happy to be listened to for a moment even as a teller of evil tidings. "Well, then, the situation of France has not been improved in the least by the return of the Duke de Guise to Paris. Some troops have been reorganized, some garrisons have been reinforced, nothing more. At present the French are in a state of doubt; they really do not know what to do. Their forces on the northern frontiers may have arrested the triumphant march of the Spaniards; but they are undertaking nothing on their own account. Will they attack Luxembourg? or march on Picardy? Nobody can tell. Will they try to take St. Quentin or Ham—''

"Or Calais?" interrupted Diana, quickly, raising her eyes to his face in order to judge of the effect of this random shot.

But Lord Wentworth was not in the least affected, and replied with a scornful smile:

"Oh, madame, really you must permit me to put that question aside. A person with the slightest knowledge of war will not give a moment's attention to such a silly supposition; and the Duke de Guise is too experienced to expose himself to the laughter of Europe by attempting such an impossibility."

At the same instant there was a noise at the door, and an archer entered hurriedly.

Lord Wentworth rose impatiently, and went to meet him.

"What has happened, then, that you should dare to disturb me thus?" he asked angrily.

"I beg your pardon, my lord," replied the archer. "But Lord Derby ordered me to see you as soon as I could."

"And why this hurry? Explain yourself."

"Lord Derby has just been informed that a vanguard of two thousand French arquebusiers was seen within ten leagues of Calais yesterday; and Lord Derby sent me at once to inform your lordship."

"Ah!" cried Diana, who made no effort to dissemble her joy.

But Lord Wentworth coldly addressed the archer:

"And this is why you have had the audacity to even follow me here, rascal?"

"My lord," said the poor fellow, utterly bewildered, "Lord Derby—"

"Lord Derby," interrupted the governor, "is a little near-sighted, and takes mole-hills for mountains. You may go and tell him I said so."

"Then, my lord, the posts at which Lord Derby wished to double the guards as speedily as—"

"Let them remain as they are; and let me not be bothered again with these ridiculous panics."

The archer inclined respectfully and passed out.

"I am compelled to undeceive you on this matter now more than ever, madame," said Lord Wentworth, with his imperturbable assurance. "I can explain to you in two words the false alarm which has, to my astonishment, apparently deceived Lord Derby."

"Let us have your explanation then," said Diana, eager for information on a point on which her very life was concentrated.

"Well, then, madame, one of two things has happened: Either Messieurs de Guise and de Nevers, who are, I admit, prudent and skilful captains, want to revictual Ardres and Boulogne, and are in command of the troops that have been noticed; or they are making a feigned march on Calais to throw St. Quentin and Ham off their guard, then, abruptly returning the road they came, they intend surprising one of those cities."

"And how do you know, my lord," retorted Diana, imprudently, "that their feigned march is not on St. Quentin or Ham, in order to surprise Calais more surely?"

Happily, she had to do with a conviction firmly anchored on individual as well as national pride.

"I have had the honor already to inform you, madame," said Lord Wentworth, disdainfully, "that Calais is one of those cities that can neither be surprised nor taken. Before it could be approached even, both Fort St. Agatha and Fort de Nieullay would have to be carried. The enemy would have to be victorious at all points during a struggle lasting a fortnight, and England would be able, during every day of this fortnight, to bring all her power to the aid of a city she regarded as her most precious possession. Take Calais! Ha, ha! I cannot help laughing when I think of it.''

Madame de Castro was hurt, and retorted with some bitterness:

''My sorrow is your joy. How is it likely we should ever come to an understanding?''

''Ah, madame!'' replied Lord Wentworth, turning pale, ''my object is only to dispel the illusions that separate us. I only wish to show you that you are the victim of a self-deception, and that the mere conception of the idea you entertain by the court of France would prove it a prey to madness.''

''There is a madness that is heroic, my lord,'' said Diana, proudly, ''and, in fact, I know of certain great madmen who would not recoil before this sublime extravagance, moved by love of glory, or simply by devotion.''

''Yes, M. d'Exmès, for example!'' cried Lord Wentworth, carried away by a jealous feeling he found himself incapable of controlling.

''Who has mentioned that name to you?'' cried Diana, astounded.

''That name you must confess that you have had on your lips ever since the beginning of our conversation, madame,'' rejoined Lord Wentworth; ''and that you have been invoking in your heart a third liberator besides God and your father.''

''Am I obliged to render you an account of my feelings, my lord?'' asked Diana.

''You need not render me an account of anything, for I know everything,'' retorted the governor. ''I know that of which you know nothing, madame; and what it has pleased me to tell you to-day, I tell you in order to show you how little basis there is for your amorous romances. I know especially that Viscount d'Exmès, made a prisoner at the same time as yourself at St. Quentin, has also been brought at the same time here to Calais.''

"Can it be!" exclaimed Diana, astonished to the very highest degree.

"Oh, but he is no longer here, madame; otherwise I should not have told you. M. d'Exmès has been free for the last two months.''

"And I was ignorant that a friend was suffering like myself, and so near me.''

"Yes, you were ignorant of it; but he was not. I must confess that when he was aware of the fact, his threats were really formidable. Not only did he challenge me to a duel, but, as you have foreseen, pushing love to insanity, he did actually declare to my face that he would take Calais.''

"My hopes are now stronger than ever!" exclaimed Diana.

"Do not be too sanguine, madame," said Lord Wentworth. "Two months have passed since M. d'Exmès bade me that alarming farewell of his. True, I have had tidings of my antagonist during these two months. Toward the close of November, he sent me the amount of his ransom with scrupulous exactness. But of his proud defiance I have not heard a word.''

"Have a little patience, my lord; rest assured M. d'Exmès will pay all his debts.''

"I doubt it, madame, for the days of grace will soon be passed.''

"What do you mean?"

"I have informed M. d'Exmès, through the man he sent me, that I should await the result of his double challenge until the 1st of January, 1558. We are now at the 31st of December—''

"Well," interrupted Diana, "he has twelve hours before him still.''

"Quite right, madame; but if I receive no news from him at the exact hour—''

He did not finish. At this moment Lord Derby rushed, quite scared, into the room.

"My lord!" he cried, "I was not mistaken. They were Frenchmen, and they are threatening Calais!"

"Oh, nonsense!" retorted Lord Wentworth, who changed countenance in spite of his assumed confidence, "the thing is impossible. What proof have you? All mere rumor and gossip and chimerical terrors."

"Alas! no, facts, unfortunately," replied Lord Derby.

"Lower, then, speak lower," said the governor, drawing near him; "show a little self-control. What do you mean by your facts?"

Lord Derby replied in an undertone, in obedience to the command of his superior, who did not care to show any weakness before Diana.

"The French have unexpectedly attacked Fort St. Agatha. There was no preparation for their reception, either in the way of walls or men; and I am much afraid that at the present moment they are masters of the first bulwark of Calais."

"Even so, they would be still far away from us," rejoined Lord Wentworth, quickly.

"Yes," returned Lord Derby; "but in such a case there is no obstacle to hinder them carrying Fort de Nieullay, and the bridge of Nieullay is only two miles from here."

"Have you sent reinforcements to the different points, Derby?"

"Yes, my lord; although, forgive me, without your orders, and in spite of your orders."

"You have done well," said Lord Wentworth.

"But these succors will arrive too late," returned the lieutenant.

"Who knows? Let us not be alarmed; come with me at once to Nieullay. We'll make these audacious fellows pay dearly for their imprudence. And, if they have St. Agatha, all we have to do is to hunt them out of it."

"God grant it! But the beginning of their enterprise has been only too successful."

"We'll have our revenge. By the way, who commands them?"

"No one knows. Guise probably, or Nevers at least. All the ensign who returned at full speed with this incredible news could tell me was that he recognized your former prisoner, M. d'Exmès—"

"Damnation!" cried the governor; "come, Derby, come quick!"

Madame de Castro, with that keenness of perception often found in great circumstances, had heard almost every word of Lord Derby's report, although uttered in a low voice.

When Lord Wentworth took leave of her, saying:

"Excuse me, madame, I must quit you. Affairs of importance—"

She interrupted him, not without some feminine malice:

"Go, my lord, go and try to recover the advantages you have allowed to be so cruelly compromised. But, in the meantime, you had better learn two things: first, that the strongest illusions are precisely the illusions that never have any doubt of succeeding; and, secondly, that we should always reckon on a French gentleman keeping his word. It is not yet the 1st of January, my lord."

Lord Wentworth did not answer, and left the room furious.

CHAPTER LIII

DURING THE CANNONADE

LORD DERBY did not make much mistake in his conjectures. This is what had happened.

The troops of Nevers, having formed a junction rapidly during the night with those of Guise, and by a forced march reached Fort St. Agatha unperceived, three thousand arquebusiers, supported by twenty or thirty horse soldiers, carried the place in less than an hour.

When Lord Wentworth and Lord Derby arrived at Fort de Nieullay, they saw their own men flying across the bridge to shelter themselves within this second and better rampart of Calais.

But, the first moment of bewilderment past, it must be admitted that Lord Wentworth recovered all his valor. His soul was after all of a noble type; and, besides, that arrogance which is a distinctive characteristic of his race gave him immense energy.

"These Frenchmen must be really mad," he said with the utmost sincerity to Lord Derby. "But they shall pay dearly for their folly. Two centuries ago Calais held out for a year against the English; in the hands of the English it would hold out ten. We will not, however, have any such trouble now as then. Before the end of the week, Derby, you will see the enemy beat a shameful retreat. He has won all that could be won by a surprise. But we are now on our guard. There is nothing then to alarm any one; and we'll all have a good laugh at the *fiasco* of the Duke de Guise."

"Will you send for reinforcements to England?"

"What's the use?" was the governor's haughty reply. "Should these light-headed persons persist in their impru- dence, the English and Spanish troops in France will come to our aid during the three days that Fort de Nieullay holds them in check. If the haughty conquerors are still quite obstinate, a despatch to Dover will bring us ten thousand men immediately. But until then we must not do them too much honor by too much apprehension on our part. Our nine hundred soldiers and our good walls will give them a tough job. They can never go further than Nieullay."

On the next day—the 1st of January, 1558—the French were already at the bridge which Lord Wentworth had marked out for them as the limit beyond which they could not go. They had opened a trench, and, at noon, their cannon began to make a breach in Fort de Nieullay.

Meanwhile, a sad and solemn scene in a domestic tragedy was being enacted in the home of the Peuquoys, to which the terrible and regular thundering of the artillery of two nations served as an accompaniment.

The pressing questions addressed by Pierre Peuquoy to Gabriel's messenger have already doubtless taught the reader that Babette could not have been long able to hide her tears, and the cause of her tears, from her brother and cousin.

The wretchedness of the poor girl had so far only been half complete. Now, the reparation due from the so-called Martin Guerre was needed not only for herself but for her child also.

Babette Peuquoy was about to become a mother.

Nevertheless, while confessing her frailty and its harsh consequences, she had not dared to disclose the fact to Jean and Pierre that her future was hopeless, that Martin Guerre was married.

She did not acknowledge it to her own heart; she said to herself it was impossible, M. d'Exmès must be mistaken. God, who is good, does not crush so utterly a poor creature whose sole crime was love. She repeated to herself this childish reasoning daily in her artless fashion, and she hoped. She hoped in Martin Guerre, she hoped in the Viscount d'Exmès. Hoped what? she did not know; but still she hoped.

Nevertheless the silence kept during these two eternal months, by master and servant, had dealt her a terrible blow.

She was waiting, with mingled impatience and dismay, for that 1st of January which Pierre Peuquoy had ventured to fix as the last limit for the Viscount d'Exmès himself.

So the report, a report still vague and uncertain, current on the 31st of December, that the French were marching on Calais caused her an emotion of ineffable joy.

She heard her brother and cousin say that the Viscount d'Exmès was surely among the assailants; then Martin Guerre must be among them also. Then Babette had reason to hope.

Still it was with a sort of heartache she heard the invitation of Pierre Peuquoy, on the 1st of January, to meet himself and Jean in the lower hall and listen to a discussion on what was to be done under existing circumstances.

She appeared, pale and trembling, before this domestic tribunal—a tribunal nevertheless composed of the two beings she knew bore her an almost paternal affection.

"Cousin, brother," said she, in a trembling voice, "I am at your orders."

"Be seated, Babette," said Pierre, motioning to a chair prepared for her.

Then he continued gently, but gravely:

"When first, Babette, you confided to us the sad truth, being forced to do so by our pressing entreaties and our alarm, I could not, I remember regretfully, refrain from an instinctive impulse of anger and sorrow. I insulted, even threatened you; but Jean, happily, interfered between us."

"May God bless him for his generosity and indulgence!" said Babette, turning her tearful face to her cousin.

"Do not speak of that, Babette," returned Jean, more moved than he wished to appear. "What I did was very natural; and, after all, to inflict new sorrows on you would hardly be a remedy for the old ones."

"I understood that afterward," said Pierre. "Besides, Babette, your repentance and your tears have touched me. My fury changed to pity, my pity to tenderness, and I have pardoned you the stain you have brought on our heretofore stainless name."

"Jesus will be as merciful to you as you have been to me, brother."

"And moreover," continued Pierre, "Jean has led me to understand that the agent of your fault will consider it a duty as well as a legal obligation to free you from its consequences."

Babette grew red, and bent her head lower. When another than herself appeared to believe in this reparation, she believed in it no longer.

Pierre went on:

"In spite of this hope, which I received with transport, of seeing your honor and ours rehabilitated, there was no word from Martin Guerre; and the messenger sent by M. d'Exmès to Calais a month ago did not even bring us any news of him. But the French are now before our walls; and the Viscount d'Exmès with his squire are among them, I presume."

"You may be quite certain of it, Pierre," interrupted Jean.

"Certainly I am the last to contradict you, Jean, on that point. Let us admit then that M. d'Exmès and his squire are separated from us only by the moats and walls that guard us, or rather guard the English. In that case, should we receive them as friends or enemies, if we see them again? What do you think, Babette?"

"Whatever you do, brother, will be well done," said Babette, frightened at the turn the conversation was taking.

"But, Babette, have you no idea as to their intentions?"

"None, *mon Dieu!* I wait, that is all."

"But do you not know whether they come to save or abandon you; whether the cannon whose thunders serve as an accompaniment to my words is to us the herald of our liberators whom we ought to bless, or of wretches whom we ought to punish? Have you no answer to this, Babette?"

"Alas!" exclaimed Babette. "Why ask me, a poor girl without thought of aught except prayer and resignation?"

"Why ask you, Babette? Listen. You remember the principles in which our father trained us with regard to France and the French. For us the English have never been fellow-countrymen, but oppressors; and, three months ago, no music could have been so pleasant to my ears as that I am listening to now."

"For me," cried Jean, "that music is the voice of my country calling me!"

"Jean," returned Pierre, "the country is simply the home expanded; it is the family multiplied; it is fraternity widened. But are we bound to sacrifice to it the other fraternity, the other home, the other family?"

"Good heavens! what is the meaning of your words, Pierre?" inquired Babette.

"This," replied Pierre; "in the rough, plebeian, laborious hands of your brother, Babette, rests, at this very moment, perhaps, the fate of Calais. Yes, these poor hands, blackened by daily toil, can give the key of France to its king."

"And these hands hesitate!" cried Babette, who had truly sucked in at the breast hatred of the foreign yoke.

"Ah, noble girl!" exclaimed Jean; "yes, you are indeed worthy of our confidence."

"Neither my hands nor my heart would hesitate," replied Pierre, coolly, "if it were in my power to restore his fair city to Henry the Second, or to his representative the Duke de Guise. But circumstances are such that we shall be forced to make use of the intervention of M. d'Exmès.''

"Well?'' asked Babette, surprised at this reservation.

"Well,'' replied Pierre, "I should be as proud and happy to associate with me in this great enterprise the man who was our guest, and whose squire ought to be my brother, as I should be humiliated and ashamed at the notion of doing so great an honor to a gentleman void of all feeling, who has helped to sully our honor.''

"M. d'Exmès, a gentleman so loyal and kind-hearted!'' cried Babette.

"It is not the less true, Babette, that M. d'Exmès has learned your misfortune from yourself, and Martin Guerre knows it from his conscience, yet both are silent.''

"But what could M. d'Exmès say or do?'' inquired Babette.

"He could, since his return to Paris, have summoned Martin Guerre and compelled him to give you his name. He could have sent Martin Guerre here, instead of that stranger, and thus acquitted at the same time the debt due from his purse, and the debt due by his heart.''

"No, he could not,'' said the candid Babette, with a melancholy shake of her head.

"What! he was not free to give an order to his servant?''

"What would be the use of such an order?'' returned Babette.

"What would be the use?'' cried Pierre Peuquoy. "What would be the use of repairing a crime? of saving a reputation? Are you mad, Babette?''

"Alas, no, to my grief!'' said the poor girl; "the mad forget.''

"Then,'' continued Pierre, "how can you say, if you are in your senses, that M. d'Exmès has acted rightly in not using his authority as a master to force your seducer to marry you?"

"Marry me! marry me! ah, but then was it in his power?" said Babette, heartbroken.

"Who could hinder him?" cried Jean and Pierre, at the same time.

Both rose, moved by the same irresistible impulse.

Babette fell on her knees.

"Ah!" she cried in despair, "pardon me once more, my brother, I wished to hide it from you—I was hiding it from myself. And now that you are talking of our tarnished honor, France, that infamous Martin Guerre, M. d'Exmès, of—oh, what do I know? My head is turning round. You were asking if I was becoming mad? Yes, yes, I feel that I must be. Do you, who are calmer, tell me whether I am mistaken. Have I dreamed, or can what M. d'Exmès told me be true?"

"What M. d'Exmès told you!" repeated Pierre, seized with terror.

"Yes, in my room the day he left, when I begged him to hand Martin Guerre this ring. I did not dare to confess my fault to him, a stranger. And yet he must have under-stood me. And if he understood me, how could he have told me?"

"What? what has he told you? Finish!" shouted Pierre.

"Alas, that Martin Guerre was married already," said Babette.

"Wretch!" cried Pierre Peuquoy, beside himself with rage, rushing upon his sister and raising his hand to strike her.

"Ah, it is true then!" said the unhappy child, in a dying voice. "I feel that it is true now."

And she fell fainting on the floor.

Jean had just time to seize Pierre and hurl him back.

"What are you doing, Pierre?" he said severely. "It is not the unfortunate who should suffer but the guilty."

"You are right," replied Pierre, ashamed of his blind rage.

He drew aside, still fierce and gloomy, while Jean, bending over Babette, was trying to recall her to life.   There was a long silence.

Outside, the artillery continued to thunder, with almost regular intervals between the discharges.

At last Babette opened her eyes, and was evidently trying to remember.

"What has happened?" she asked.

She looked up vaguely at the face of Jean Peuquoy bent above her.

Strange to say, the face she beheld was not too melancholy. It was imprinted with profound tenderness through which shone a certain secret contentment.

"My good cousin!" said Babette, offering her hand.

The first words of Jean Peuquoy to the dear mourner were:

"Hope, Babette, hope."

But at that moment the eyes of Babette rested upon the gloomy and despairing countenance of her brother, and she started, for then everything flashed on her memory.

"Oh, Pierre, pardon! pardon!" she cried.

Moved by an affecting gesture of Jean Peuquoy, exhorting him to have mercy, Pierre advanced toward his sister, raised her and placed her upon a chair.

"Reassure yourself," he said, "it is not with you I am angry.   You must have suffered too much.   Reassure yourself, I will repeat after Jean: Hope!"

"Ah, what can I hope for now?" she said.

"Not for reparation, it is true, but at least for vengeance," replied Pierre, frowningly.

"And I," whispered Jean, in her ear, "I promise vengeance and reparation at the same time."

She looked at him in surprise.   But before she could question him, Pierre resumed:

"Once more, my poor sister, I pardon you.   On the

whole, your fault is no greater because a vile scoundrel has deceived you twice. I love you, Babette, because I have always loved you."

Babette, happy in spite of all her sorrow, threw herself into her brother's arms.

"But," continued Pierre, "my anger is not extinguished, it is only transferred. The object it shall reach now is that infamous traitor, that abominable perjurer, Martin Guerre!"

"Brother!" interrupted Babette, pleadingly.

"No pity for him!" cried the relentless citizen. "But to his master, M. d'Exmès, I owe a reparation which my loyalty shall find no difficulty in making."

"I told you how it was," said Jean.

"Yes, Jean, you were right, as you always are; and I have done wrong to this worthy lord. Henceforth, all is explained. His very silence was the result of delicacy. Why should he cruelly recall to us an irreparable misfortune? I was wrong! And when I think that through an irreparable mistake I was perhaps about to prove false to the convictions and instincts of my whole life, and make France, the object of my dearest affections, pay the penalty of a crime that does not exist—"

"From what trivial causes do the great events of this world often spring!" replied Jean Peuquoy, philosophically; "but, luckily," he added, "nothing is yet lost; and, thanks to the confession of Babette, we know now that M. d'Exmès is not undeserving of our friendship. Oh, I knew his noble heart; for except that he showed some hesitation when I first laid before him my plan for avenging the capture of St. Quentin, he has never given me cause for anything except admiration. But sure I am he is, at this very moment, making brilliant atonement for that hesitation."

And the brave weaver made a sign to them to listen to the roar of the cannon, now seeming to approach nearer.

"Jean," said Pierre, "do you know what this cannonade is saying to us?"

"It says that M. d'Exmès is there," replied Jean.

"Yes, brother; but," added Pierre, in the ear of his cousin, "it is also saying, 'Remember the 5th!' "

"And we intend remembering, do we not?"

These whispered confidences alarmed Babette, who, ab-sorbed by one fixed idea, murmured:

"What are they plotting? Jesus! If M. d'Exmès is there, God grant that at least Martin Guerre be not with him!"

"Martin Guerre?" returned Jean Peuquoy, who heard her. "Oh, M. d'Exmès has surely scourged that vile ser-vant from his presence. He will have acted well in doing so, even in the traitor's own interest; for no sooner would he have set his foot in Calais than we should have chal-lenged and killed him; is it not so, Pierre?"

"In any case," replied Pierre, inflexibly, "if not in Calais, in Paris; wherever he be, I will kill him."

"Oh!" cried Babette, "these reprisals are just the thing I dread, not for him, for I no longer love him, but for you, Pierre, for you, Jean, who have both shown me such brotherly love and devotion."

"So," said Jean, much affected, "in a combat between him and me, it is for my success, and not his, you would pray?"

"Ah!" returned Babette, "that question is the most cruel punishment you could inflict upon me for my fault. Between you so good and merciful, and him so vile and treacherous, how could I hesitate to-day?"

"Thanks!" cried Jean. "What you have just said fills me with pleasure, Babette; and, believe me, God will re-ward you."

"I am sure at least," said Pierre, "that God will punish the base scoundrel. But let us not think of him, Jean; we have now other things to do, and only three days in which to make our preparations. We must go out, see our friends, reckon up our arms—"

He repeated in a low voice:

"Jean, let us remember the 5th!"

A quarter of an hour after, while Babette, who had retired into her chamber in calmer mood, was thanking God, she scarcely knew for what, the armorer and weaver were hurrying through the city, quite engrossed by the enterprise they were about to undertake.

They no longer seemed to be thinking of Martin Guerre, who, by the way, for his part had little suspicion of the reception intended for him in a city where he had never set his foot.

Meanwhile, the cannon continued to thunder, and, as Rabutin says, "were charging and discharging with amazing fury their tempest of artillery."

CHAPTER LIV

UNDER THE TENT

ON THE evening of the 4th of January, three days after the scene described, the French, in spite of the predictions of Lord Wentworth, had made some way.

They had not only passed beyond the bridge, but had gained possession of Fort de Nieullay in the morning, and were now masters of all the arms and munitions it contained.

From this position they could close up every passage by which the Spaniards or English might attempt to relieve the city from the land side.

Such a result was surely well worth the furious and murderous struggle which it cost.

"Am I the sport of a dream!" exclaimed Lord Wentworth, when he saw his troops flying in great disorder toward the city, despite all his efforts to hold them at their post.

And, to complete his humiliation, he had to follow them. His duty was to be the last to die.

"Fortunately," said Lord Derby to him, when they had reached a place of safety, "Calais and the Vieux-Chateau, notwithstanding the few troops that are left us, can hold out for two or three days longer. The Risbank fort and the entrance by sea remain free, and England is not far off!"

And in fact the council of Lord Wentworth was no sooner assembled than it declared with confidence that their salvation must come from there. The time for pride was past. A despatch must be sent to Dover at once. The day after, at the latest, reinforcements would arrive, and Calais would be saved.

Lord Wentworth adopted this plan with resignation. A ship sailed for Dover immediately, with an urgent message to the governor.

Then the English took measures for concentrating all their energies on the defence of the Vieux-Chateau.

It was the vulnerable side of Calais. On the other hand, Fort Risbank was sufficiently protected by the sea, the dunes, and a handful of the urban militia.

While the besieged are organizing in Calais resistance at all the points liable to attack, let us turn our attention for a while to what the besiegers are doing outside the city, and notably to what Viscount d'Exmès, Martin Guerre, and their gallant recruits are doing on this same evening of the 4th.

The soldier's task and not the sapper's was theirs, and as their place was not in the trenches or in the labors of the siege, but in the brunt of the battle and the assault, they must be taking their rest at the hour we are about to view them. We have only in fact to lift the canvas at a corner of the tent, pitched somewhat apart from the right of the French camp, to find Gabriel and his little band of volunteers again.

The tableau presented to our gaze is at once picturesque and varied.

Gabriel, with his head bent, seated in a corner on the only stool the tent contained, appears absorbed in deep meditation.

At his feet, Martin Guerre was fixing the buckle of a sword-belt. He raised his eyes anxiously to his master from time to time; but he respected the silent meditation in which he saw him plunged.

Not far from them, on a kind of bed made up of cloaks, lay and groaned a wounded man. Alas! this wounded man was no other than the unlucky Malemort.

At the other end of the tent, the pious Lactance was telling his beads on his knees with activity and fervor. Lactance had the misfortune, at the taking of Fort de Nieullay in the morning, to knock on the head three of his brethren in Christ Jesus. He owed, therefore, to his conscience three hundred *Paters* and the same number of *Aves*. It was the ordinary penance laid upon him by his confessor for those he killed. The reparation in the case of those he wounded required only half the amount.

Near by Yvonnet, after carefully cleaning his boots and brushing the mud and dust from his clothes, was looking round him for some spot where the dampness was not too excessive to hinder him from stretching his limbs and snatching a little repose, the prolonged watching and exhausting labor being quite out of harmony with the constitution of that delicate person.

Two yards from Yvonnet, Scharfenstein uncle and Scharfenstein nephew were making complicated calculations on their enormous fingers. They were trying to estimate what the morning's booty should bring them. Scharfenstein nephew had had the ability to lay his hands on a coat of mail of price, and the two worthy Teutons with radiant faces were dividing in advance the money they reckoned on getting for their rich prey.

As for the rest of our paladins, they were grouped around the centre of the tent, playing at dice; and gamblers and bettors were following eagerly the varied chances of the game.

A big smoky candle, fixed in the ground, lighted up their faces—some joyous, some disappointed, and cast a few flickering gleams on the other countenances whose decidedly different expressions we have endeavored to disclose and sketch in the partial shadow.

A groan from Malemort, more doleful than usual, compelled Gabriel to raise his head, and he said to his squire:

"Martin Guerre, do you know what time it is?"

"Monseigneur, not very well. This rainy night has quenched all the stars. But I fancy it is not very far from six; for it has been dark for more than an hour."

"And this surgeon promised you that he would surely come at six?"

"At six exactly, monseigneur; and here he is," said Martin, as the hangings were lifted.

The Viscount d'Exmès cast a single glance upon the newcomer, and although he had only seen him once before, recognized him. But the face of the surgeon was one of those which, once seen, are never forgotten.

"Master Ambroise Paré!" cried Gabriel, rising.

"M. le Vicomte d'Exmès!" said Paré, with a profound inclination.

"Ah, master! I did not know you were in the camp, and so near us," returned Gabriel.

"I always try to be where I can do most good," was Paré's answer.

"There I recognize that generous heart; and I am doubly grateful to you to-day, for I am about to have recourse to your science and ability."

"Not for yourself, I trust. What is the matter?"

"It concerns one of my followers, who, while rushing on the enemy with a kind of madness, received a lance-thrust in the shoulder."

"In the shoulder? That cannot be very serious."

"I fear it may be," said Gabriel, lowering his voice; "for one of the comrades of the wounded man, named Scharfenstein, that is he yonder, tried to pull out the lance-head in such a rough and awkward fashion that the iron remained behind."

Ambroise Paré showed by his face that he augured badly for the result.

"Well, let us look at it," he said with his usual calmness.

He was conducted to the couch of the patient. All the adventurers had risen, and now gathered about the surgeon

—some abandoning their game, others their calculations, and one his attempt to render his costume spick and span. Lactance alone went on with his penance; for it was his custom never to omit this atonement for his valiant feats, except to engage in others.

Ambroise Paré removed the linen wrappings of Malemort's shoulder and examined the wound attentively. He shook his head doubtfully; but he said aloud:

"It will be nothing."

"Ugh!" growled Malemort, "if it is nothing, then I can return to fight to-morrow?"

"I don't think so," replied Paré, who was probing the wound.

"Ah, do you know you are hurting me a little?" returned Malemort.

"I can well believe that," said the surgeon; "courage, my friend!"

"Oh, I have courage enough!" growled Malemort; "and what I have suffered so far has not been too hard to bear. But won't it be harder when you come to pulling out this damned iron?"

"No, for here it is," replied Paré, triumphantly, raising the lance-head he had just extracted, and showing it to Malemort.

"I am very much obliged to you, Master Surgeon," said Malemort, politely.

A murmur of admiration and astonishment greeted this masterstroke of Master Ambroise Paré.

"What, all over?" cried Gabriel. "Why, it is a miracle!"

"It must also be acknowledged," answered Paré, smiling, "that our patient is anything but chicken-hearted."

"Nor the operator a bungler, by the mass!" cried a new arrival, who had entered unperceived on account of the general anxiety.

But at this well-known voice all stood aside.

"M. le Duc de Guise!" said Paré, recognizing the commander-in-chief.

"Yes, master, M. de Guise, who is astounded at your coolness and skill. By St. Francis, my patron, I have seen some stupid donkeys of doctors just now at the ambulance yonder, and I swear they were doing more harm to our soldiers with their instruments than the English with their weapons. But you have plucked out that stake with as much ease as if it were a white hair. And I did not know you! What is your name, master?"

"Ambroise Paré, monseigneur."

"Well, Master Ambroise Paré, I guarantee you that your fortune is made; but on one condition."

"And may I know it, monseigneur?"

"It is that should I receive a wound or a bruise—and either is very possible, more so at present than ever—you take charge of me, and treat me with as little ceremony as that poor devil there."

"Monseigneur, I will do so," said Ambroise Paré, bowing. "When men suffer they are equal."

"Hum!" rejoined Francis de Guise; "try then to prove, in the case referred to, that a similar equality marks the mode of curing them."

"Will monseigneur now permit me to close and bandage this man's wound? There are other sufferers to be attended to to-day."

"Of course, Master Ambroise Paré. Don't pay any attention to me. I am in a hurry myself to send you to the rescue of our poor fellows from the hands of those confounded followers of Æsculapius. Besides, I want to confer with M. d'Exmès."

Ambroise Paré at once returned to his task of dressing Malemort's wound.

"Master Surgeon, I beg to thank you again," said the wounded man. "But may I ask you to render me another service?"

"And what is it, my brave fellow?" asked Paré.

"It is this, monsieur. Now that I no longer feel the presence of that horrible fragment in my flesh it looks, does it not, as if I am very nearly cured?"

"Yes, very nearly," replied Ambroise, tying the ligatures.

"Well, then," returned Malemort, in a simple and free-and-easy tone, "would you have the goodness to tell my master, M. d'Exmès, that if there is to be any fighting to-morrow, I am perfectly fit to be in it."

"You fight to-morrow!" exclaimed Ambroise. "Oh, indeed! Well, you may as well get that idea out of your head."

"Ah, but I cannot!" replied Malemort, dolefully.

"But, you unreasonable man, I must prescribe absolute rest for a full week, confinement to your bed, and a very light diet."

"Oh! as much abstinence from food as you wish; but not from battle, doctor, I humbly beg."

"You are mad!" continued Paré. "Why, if you were to rise, you would have an attack of fever, and all would be up with you. I have said a week, and I shall not bate an hour of it."

"Ugh!" yelled Malemort, "in a week, good-by to the siege. Am I never to have my fill of fighting then?"

"A tough customer that!" said the Duke de Guise, who had been listening to this singular dialogue.

"That is Malemort's way," returned Gabriel, smiling, "and I beg you, monseigneur, to have him removed to the ambulance, and watched while he is there. For, if he hears the slightest sound of battle, he is capable of trying to rise in spite of everything."

"Well, nothing more simple," replied the Duke de Guise. "Order your people to remove him there."

"But, monseigneur," replied Gabriel, with some embarrassment, "I shall have need of my, men to-night, perhaps."

"Indeed!" said Francis de Guise, regarding Gabriel with surprise.

"If M. d'Exmès wishes," said Ambroise Paré, who approached them after dressing the wound, "I can have our doughty champion removed on a litter by two of my assistants."

"I accept your offer with thanks," returned Gabriel, "and I know it is needless to ask your utmost vigilance in his regard."

"Ugh!" howled Malemort, again in utter despair.

Ambroise Paré passed out, after taking leave of the Duke de Guise. The followers of M. d'Exmès, on a sign from Martin Guerre, all withdrew to the end of the tent, and Gabriel was to some degree alone with the commander-in-chief of the expedition.

CHAPTER LV

LITTLE BOATS SAVE BIG SHIPS

A S SOON as Viscount d'Exmès found himself alone, or almost alone, with the Duke de Guise, he began by saying:

"Well, are you satisfied, monseigneur?"

"Yes, my friend, satisfied with what we have gained; but, I confess, anxious as to the prospect of gaining more. This anxiety has made me leave my tent, wander through the camp, and come to you for encouragement and counsel."

"But has anything fresh happened?" returned Gabriel. "The result has, as it seems to me, exceeded all your expectations. You have become master in four days of the two bucklers of Calais. The defenders of the city and of the Vieux-Chateau cannot now hold out more than forty-eight hours."

"True," replied the duke, "but they may hold out for forty hours, and, by doing so, ruin us and save themselves."

"Oh! monseigneur, you must really allow me to doubt that," said Gabriel.

"No, my friend," returned the duke, "my old experience does not deceive me; unless there happen some stroke of fortune or some opportunity unforeseen by human calculation, our enterprise has failed. You may believe what I say."

"And why so?" asked Gabriel, with a smile that was singularly out of keeping with the painful intelligence he was hearing.

"I can easily show you, basing my conclusions on your own plan. Follow me closely."

"I am all attention, monseigneur."

"The strange and hazardous adventure into which my wary ambition has been hurried by your youthful ardor could only succeed when aided by the astonishment and isolation of the English garrison. Calais could not be taken, but might be surprised. Was it not on this basis we reasoned out our mad undertaking?"

"And, so far, facts have not proved our reasoning was wrong."

"No, undoubtedly," said the Duke de Guise, "and you have proved, Gabriel, that you were as capable of judging men as of observing things, that you had studied the heart of the governor of Calais as skilfully as the interior of his city. Lord Wentworth has not belied any of your conjectures. He believed his nine hundred men and his formidable outposts would suffice to make us repent of our audacious raid. He set too little value on us to be alarmed, and did not summon a single company to his aid either from the Continent or from England."

"Yes, I think I formed a correct notion as to how his disdainful pride would affect his action under the circumstance."

"So, thanks to his overweening arrogance, we have taken the fort of St. Agatha without firing a shot, and that of Nieullay after a successful encounter of three days."

"And the result now is," said Gabriel, joyously, "that should the English or Spaniards attempt to bring any help to their countrymen or their allies from the land side, they would be crushed by the batteries of the Duke de Guise, not supported by the cannon of Lord Wentworth."

"They will be on their guard and will not come too close to us," returned Francis de Guise, smiling, who was allowing himself to be won over by the hopeful cheerfulness of the young man.

"Well, is not that an important point gained?" returned Gabriel.

"Undoubtedly," said the duke. "It is not the only point, however, nor the most important one. We have shut one of the gates by which a relieving force could enter Calais, but another is left open."

"What one, monseigneur?" said Gabriel, who feigned to be puzzled.

"Cast your eyes upon this map drawn by Marshal Strozzi according to the plan supplied by you. Calais may be suc-cored from two quarters, from Fort de Nieullay, which de-fends the roads, and approaches by land."

"But which defend them for us at present," interrupted Gabriel.

"Perfectly correct," said the duke. "But look seaward and what do you observe? Fort Risbank, protected by the ocean, the dunes, and the marshes—Fort Risbank, or, if you prefer to call it so, the Octagon tower, which com-mands the entire harbor and opens or closes it to ships. Only let a hint of what has happened reach Dover, and, in a few hours, English vessels will bring reinforcements and provisions enough to render the place safe for years. Thus, Fort Risbank guards the city and the sea guards Fort Ris-bank. Now, do you know, Gabriel, what Lord Wentworth is doing this very hour to repair his late misfortune?"

"Certainly," replied the Viscount d'Exmès calmly, "Lord Wentworth, guided by the unanimous opinion of his council, is sending to Dover the information he had delayed too long, and counts on receiving to-morrow, at a fixed hour, the reinforcements which he has at last acknowl-edged to be necessary."

"And what follows? You have not finished surely?" asked M. de Guise.

"I confess, monseigneur, that I do not see much fur-ther," answered Gabriel. "I have not the prescience of God."

"The foresight of man is all that is required here, and

since yours stops half way, I shall finish the journey for it."

"Have the goodness, then, to tell me, monseigneur, what is likely to happen," said Gabriel, bowing.

"The matter is very simple," returned the duke. "The besieged, having all England to call upon if necessary, will be able, from to-morrow, to meet us at the Vieux-Chateau with superior, nay, invincible forces. If, nevertheless, we hold our ground, all the English and Spaniards in Ardres, Ham, and St. Quentin will gather together and fall like an avalanche upon the suburbs of Calais. Then, when they judge themselves sufficiently numerous, they will besiege us in their turn. I admit they will not take Nieullay all at once, but they will recover St. Agatha easily, and then we shall be between two fires."

"Such a catastrophe would, indeed, be frightful," said Gabriel, quietly.

"And yet it is only too probable," returned the Duke de Guise, with a gesture of discouragement.

"But, monseigneur, you must have thought of some way to prevent such a terrible catastrophe?"

"I have thought of nothing else," replied the duke.

"And the result?" asked Gabriel, carelessly.

"Well, our only chance, a chance precarious at the best, alas! is to make a desperate attack upon the Vieux-Chateau. We cannot, of course, make proper preparations, but we must push on the works to-night with all possible activity. I see no other plan, and this is less mad than to wait until the English reinforcements arrive. The *furia francesa*, as they say in Italy, may by its marvellous impetuosity carry these inaccessible walls."

"No, it would dash itself to pieces against them," rejoined Gabriel, coldly. "Pardon me, monseigneur; but the French army seems to me neither strong enough nor weak enough at present to venture on the impossible. A terrible responsibility weighs upon you, monseigneur. It is probable that, after losing half of our men, we should be finally repulsed.   What will the Duke de Guise do then ?''

"Not expose himself at least to total destruction or to a complete check," said Francis de Lorraine, dejectedly; "but rather withdraw his troops from those accursed walls —at least, such as are left—and preserve them until better days for king and country."

"The conqueror of Metz and Renty think of retreating!" cried Gabriel.

"That is better than continuing a useless struggle, as the constable did at the battle of St. Laurent," said the Duke de Guise.

"No matter; it would be a disastrous blow both to the glory of France and your own fame, monseigneur," replied Gabriel.

"Who knows that better than I?" cried the duke. "Such is success and fortune! If I had succeeded, I should have been a hero, a great genius, a demigod. I fail, and I shall be but a vainglorious dreamer who well deserves his shame and his fall. The same enterprise which, if it had prospered, would have been styled noble and astonishing, now that it has failed will render me the laughingstock of Europe, and adjourn or even destroy in their germ all my projects and all my hopes. See on what paltry incidents the wretched ambitions of this world turn!"

The duke stopped speaking, apparently having become utterly hopeless. There was a long silence, which Gabriel was careful not to interrupt.

He was determined to let the trained eyes of his commander measure all the terrible difficulties of the situation. Then, when he concluded the duke had thoroughly sounded them, he said—

"I see, monseigneur, that you are at present a prey to that uncertainty which, in the very middle of the greatest deeds, often seizes on those who do them. Allow me a word, however. Surely a captain of such surpassing genius as the one whom I have the honor to address would never have engaged in so serious an enterprise as this from motives of little weight. The slightest details, the remotest eventualities, were foreseen before you left the Louvre. You must have found solutions in advance for all perplexities and remedies for all evils. How comes it, then, that you hesitate and seem puzzled now?"

"Good heavens!" said the Duke de Guise, "your youthful enthusiasm and assurance fascinated and blinded me, Gabriel!"

"Monseigneur!" replied Viscount d'Exmès, reproachfully.

"Oh! do not be annoyed; I am not angry with you; I admired your idea, which was grand and patriotic. But reality is the death of fine dreams. Still, I recall the fact that I did offer certain objections which had reference to the very condition we find ourselves in, and you removed these objections."

"How, if you please, monseigneur?" asked Gabriel.

"You promised," said the duke, "that if we took St. Agatha and Nieullay in a few days, you would, by means of the understanding you had with certain parties in the city, place Fort Risbank in our hands; and then Calais could not be relieved either by sea or land. Yes, Gabriel, I remember, and you must remember, too, that you promised this."

"Well—" said Viscount d'Exmès, without appearing in the slightest degree disturbed.

"Well!" retorted the duke, "your hopes have deceived you, have they not? Your friends in Calais have not kept their word, naturally. They are not yet certain of our victory; they are afraid, and will only show themselves when their aid is no longer needed."

"Excuse me, monseigneur, who told you so?"

"Why, your own silence, my friend. The moment has come when your auxiliaries should serve you, and might save us. They do not stir, and you are silent. I conclude you no longer count upon them, and we may give up hopes of aid from that quarter."

"If you knew me better, monseigneur, you would have learned that I care little about speaking when I can act."

"What! you have still hopes?"

"Yes, monseigneur, for I am still alive," said Gabriel, with a melancholy and grave expression.

"Then Fort Risbank—"

"Will be yours, if I am not dead, at the appointed time."

"But, Gabriel, that is to-morrow, to-morrow morning."

"We shall have it, then, to-morrow morning," replied Gabriel, calmly; "that is, I repeat, if I am not dead, and, in that case, you cannot reproach me with a breach of my word, for I shall have given my life to keep my promise."

"Gabriel," said the duke, "what are you about to do— to brave some mortal peril, to run some insensate risk? I will not have it! France has too much need of men such as you."

"Do not be alarmed, monseigneur," rejoined Gabriel. "If the peril is great, the aim is great also, and the game is well worth the risk connected with it. Do you think only of profiting by the results, and leave me to think of the means. I am responsible only for myself, you are responsible for all."

"What can I do to aid you, at least? What part do you allot me in your plan?"

"Monseigneur, if you had not done me the favor to come to my tent, I should have entered yours with a request—"

"Speak! speak at once!" interrupted Francis de Guise, quickly.

"On to-morrow, the 5th of January, at daybreak, that is to say, at eight o'clock, for the nights are long in January, have the kindness to station a trustworthy man on that promontory yonder from which Fort Risbank can be seen. If the English flag continues to float there, attempt the desperate assault you had resolved on; for I shall have failed, in other words, I shall be dead."

"Dead! cried the duke. "Gabriel, you confess yourself that you are about to destroy yourself!"

"In that case, lose no time in regretting me, monseigneur. Only let everything be ready for your last effort, and I pray that God may give you success. Courage, monseigneur! Let every man march to the assault! The English succors cannot arrive before noon; you will have four hours of heroism to prove before retreating that the French are as intrepid as they are prudent."

"But yourself, Gabriel, yourself; tell me, at least, that you have some chances of success."

"Reassure yourself, monseigneur, I have. Be calm and patient, therefore, like the strong man you are. Let not your assault be too precipitate. Until necessity constrain you, do not venture on this hazardous extremity. Finally, you will only have to let Marshal Strozzi and his sappers quietly continue the works on the siege lines, and your soldiers and gunners seize the favorable moment for an assault, if, at eight o'clock, you are told the standard of France floats over Fort Risbank."

"The standard of France over Fort Risbank!" cried Francis de Lorraine.

"Where the sight of it, I fancy, will be sufficient warning to the ships coming from England that they had better return thither."

"I think as you do," said M. de Guise. "But, my friend, how do you intend—"

"Let me keep my secret, I beg you, monseigneur," said Gabriel. "My plan is so strange that perhaps you would try to turn me from it if you knew it. There is now no more time for doubt or reflection. Besides, in all I compromise neither the army nor you. The men who are there, the only ones I shall employ, are all my own volunteers, and you have engaged to let me deal with them as I like. I desire to accomplish my task unaided or to die."

"And why this pride?" asked the Duke de Guise.

"It is not pride, monseigneur, but I wish to repay you

for the priceless favor you were good enough to promise to do for me in Paris, and which, I hope, you remember.''

"What priceless favor do you speak of, Gabriel? I pass for having a good memory, especially regarding my friends. But I confess, to my shame, I cannot recall—''

"Alas, monseigneur, the thing is, nevertheless, so important for me! This is what I solicited from your kindness: If you were assured in your own mind that not only the idea of the capture of Calais, but the execution of that idea was due to me, I asked you, not to give me the honor of it publicly, for such honor belonged to you as the chief of the enterprise, but only to declare to King Henry the Second the part I had taken in this conquest under your orders. Now, you were kind enough to let me hope that this reward should be granted to me.''

"What! so that was the unheard-of favor to which you alluded, Gabriel? Why, hang me! if I ever suspected it! My friend, that is no reward, it is simply justice; and in secret or in public, according to your wish, I shall be always ready, as is my duty, to acknowledge and attest your merits and services.''

"My ambition does not go further. Let the king be informed of my services. He has a prize in his hands which to me is worth all the honor and all the good fortune in the world.''

"The king shall know all you have done for him, Gabriel. But can I do nothing for you further?''

"Yes, monseigneur, I have a few other services to ask of your good will.''

"Name them,'' said the duke.

"First, I require the countersign, so that I and my people can leave the camp at any hour to-night we wish.''

"You have but to say, *Calais and Charles*, and the sentinels will let you pass.''

"Then, monseigneur, if I fall and if you succeed, I venture to remind you that Madame de Castro, the king's daughter, is Lord Wentworth's prisoner, and has the most legitimate right to your courteous protection.''

"I will remember my duties as a man and a gentleman.. What next?''

"In fine, monseigneur, I am about to contract a considerable debt to-night to a fisherman of the coast named Anselme. I have written to Master Elyot, the steward of my domains, to provide for the support and comfort of his family, in case he fall with me. But I should wish you to see to the execution of my orders, for greater security.''

"It shall be so. Is that all?''

"That is all, monseigneur. Only if you do not see me again, think of me sometimes, I beg of you, and with some regret, and speak of me with some esteem, either to the king, who will certainly be satisfied with my death, or to Madame de Castro, who will, perhaps, be sorry for it. And now I shall not detain you any longer, but bid you adieu, monseigneur.''

The Duke de Guise rose.

"Banish these gloomy ideas of yours, my friend,'' he said. "I shall now leave you alone with your mysterious project, but I assure you my anxiety will let me sleep but little until eight o'clock to-morrow morning, especially on account of the obscurity that, as far as I am concerned, rests upon all you are about to do. Something tells me I shall see you again, and so I do not say adieu.''

"Thanks for the augury, monseigneur! for, if you see me again, it will be in the French city of Calais.''

"In that case,'' replied the duke, "you can boast of having rescued both the honor of France and my own from great peril.''

"Little boats, monseigneur, sometimes save big ships,'' said Gabriel, inclining.

The Duke de Guise pressed Gabriel's hand warmly for the last time, on the threshold of the tent, and returned in deep reflection to his quarters.

CHAPTER LVI

OBSCURI SOLA SUB NOCTE

WHEN Gabriel returned to his seat, after conducting M. de Guise to the door, he made a sign to Martin Guerre, who rose immediately and passed out without seeming to need any other explanation.

The squire entered again, a quarter of an hour after, accompanied by a miserable-looking creature miserably clad.

Martin approached his master, who was again absorbed in his meditations. As to the others, they were gambling or sleeping, according to their several idiosyncrasies.

"Monseigneur," said Martin, "this is our man."

"Ah! good!" said Gabriel. "You are the fisherman Anselme of whom Martin Guerre has spoken to me?" he added, addressing the newcomer.

"Yes, I am he, monseigneur," said the man.

"And you know," resumed Viscount d'Exmès, "the service expected of you?"

"Your squire has mentioned it, monseigneur, and I am ready."

"Martin Guerre must also have mentioned," continued Gabriel, "that in this expedition, you, as well as ourselves, risk your life."

"Oh!" returned the fisherman, "he had no need to tell me that. I knew it as well as or even better than he."

"And yet you have come?" said Gabriel.

"Yes, I am at your orders," replied Anselme.

"Good! My friend, you must have a stout heart."

"Or a miserable livelihood," answered the fisherman.

"Why so?" asked Gabriel. "What do you mean?"

"What do I mean!" cried Anselme. "By our Lady of Grace! I brave death every day to catch a single fish, and very often don't catch one at all. There isn't much merit, then, in risking this tanned hide of mine for you to-day, seeing you pledge yourselves, whether I live or die, to secure the welfare of my wife and three children."

"Yes," said Gabriel, "but the perils you meet daily are hidden or dubious. You never embark in a storm. This time the peril is visible and certain."

"Ah! yes, surely," returned the fisherman, "one must surely be a madman or a saint to venture out to sea on such a night as this. But that is your affair, and doesn't concern me. It is your idea. You have paid in advance for my boat and my body. But you will owe a fine candle to the Blessed Virgin, I can tell you, if you reach land safe and sound."

"And once we are there," said Gabriel, "your task is not over. After rowing, you must fight, if called on, and do the work of a soldier after doing that of a sailor."

"All right," said Anselme; "don't discourage me too much. You shall be obeyed. You guarantee me the lives of those dear to me. I give you mine. The bargain has been struck. No need talking about it."

"You are a brave man," returned Viscount d'Exmès. "Have no anxiety as to your wife and children. They shall be taken care of. I have written to my intendant Elyot my orders on the subject, and besides, M. le Duc de Guise will see to the matter."

"It is more than is necessary, monseigneur, and you are more generous than a king," said the fisherman. "Though you had only given me the sum which has saved us from misery in these hard times, I should never have asked for more. I hope you may be as satisfied with me as I am with you."

"Now let us see," resumed Gabriel. "Can your boat hold fourteen?"

"She has held twenty, monseigneur."

"You'll need some help in rowing, won't you?"

"Well! I should think so!" said Anselme. "I'll have enough to do with the helm and sail, that is, if she can carry sail."

"We have," said Martin Guerre, "Ambrosio, Pille-trousse, and Landry, who can row as well as if they never did anything else in their lives. And as for myself, I can swim as well with the oars as with my arms."

"That's first-rate!" rejoined Anselme, gayly. "I shall look like some brisk skipper, I hope, with such a fine crew serving under me. Master Martin has now left me in ignorance of one thing—the exact point where we are to land."

"The Risbank fort," replied Viscount d'Exmès.

"Risbank fort! Did you say Risbank fort?" cried Anselme, astounded.

"Yes, undoubtedly," said Gabriel. "Have you any objection?"

"None," returned the fisherman, "except that there is scarcely any place where you can land, and, for my part, I have never cast anchor there. It is all rock."

"Do you refuse to carry us?" asked Gabriel.

"No, by my soul, and, although I don't know much about those quarters, I'll do my best. My father, who, like myself, was by birth a fisherman, used to say: 'Don't attempt to domineer over fish or customers.' I'll lead you to Risbank fort, if I can. A nice time of it we'll have when we get there."

"At what hour are we to be ready?" asked Gabriel.

"You wished to be there at four, I think?" said Anselme.

"Between four and five, not earlier."

"Well! it will take us about two hours to get there from the place where we start if we do not wish to be seen or excite suspicion. The important point is not to tire ourselves out uselessly in the water. Then, we must reckon on our journey from here to the creek costing us an hour."

"We should quit the camp an hour after midnight then?" said Gabriel.

"Yes, about that time," replied Anselme.

"I shall now warn my men to be ready," returned Viscount d'Exmès.

"Do so, monseigneur," said the fisherman. "I will only ask your permission to sleep till one o'clock with them. I have taken leave of my family; the boat is waiting for us, carefully concealed and safely moored; there is nothing at present to call me outside."

"You are right, Anselme, take what rest you can," answered Gabriel; "you will have fatigue enough to stand to-night. Martin, warn your comrades."

"Halloo! you gamblers and sleepers!" shouted Martin Guerre.

"What? What's up? What's the matter?" they cried, rising and approaching.

"Monseigneur's private expedition will begin in an hour," said Martin.

"Good! capital! perfect!" was the unanimous response of the fire-eaters.

Malemort contributed a hurrah to these unequivocal signs of satisfaction.

But at this very moment entered the four assistants of Ambroise Paré with the announcement that they were about to take the wounded man to the ambulance.

Malemort uttered loud cries.

In spite of his protest and resistance, however, he was placed on the litter. In vain did he address the harshest reproaches to his comrades, calling them deserters, traitors, and cowards, to go away to fight without him. No attention was paid to his insults, and he was carried off, howling and cursing.

"We must now," said Martin Guerre, "make all our arrangements and assign to each his rank and his part."

"What sort of a job is it to be?" asked Pilletrousse.

"Some kind of assault," answered Martin.

"Then of course I am to be the first to mount!" cried Yvonnet.

"I have no objection," said Martin.

"No! that's not fair!" protested Ambrosio. "Yvonnet always monopolizes the post of danger. One would think it was made for him specially, upon my word!"

"Let him alone," said Viscount d'Exmès, interfering. "In the perilous ascent we are about to attempt he who mounts first will be, I think, the least exposed. The proof of this is that I shall be the last to mount myself."

"Then Yvonnet is nicely tricked!" said Ambrosio, laughing.

Martin Guerre assigned to each his number for the order of march, for the boat, and for the assault. Ambrosio, Pilletrousse, and Landry were told off for rowing. In fact, every precaution that could be taken was taken, so as to avoid, as far as possible, misunderstandings and confusion.

Lactance took Martin aside for a moment. "Excuse me," he said, "but is there going to be any killing?"

"I don't know for certain, but it is very possible," answered Martin.

"Thanks," said Lactance, "in that case, I shall say in advance my prayers for three dead and as many wounded."

When everything was settled, Gabriel advised his followers to take a few hours' rest. He undertook to awaken them himself when it was necessary.

"Yes, I shall be very glad to sleep for a while," said Yvonnet, "for my poor nerves are in a horrible flutter this evening, and, when I fight, I need to be self-possessed and fresh!"

After a few minutes, nothing was heard in the tent but the regular snoring of the veterans and the monotonous paternosters of Lactance. The last also soon died away; Lactance grew drowsy, and was at last vanquished by sleep.

Gabriel alone watched and thought. Toward one o'clock, he awoke his men one after another. All rose and armed themselves in silence. Then they softly passed out of the tent and camp.

At the words *Calais and Charles*, uttered in a low voice by Gabriel, the sentinels let them pass without difficulty.

The little troop, guided by Anselme the fisher, advanced then across the country and along the coast. No one spoke a word. The only sounds heard were the wailing of the winds and the roaring of the sea in the distance.

The night was dark and foggy. Our adventurers encountered no one on their way. Had they done so, though, they could not have been seen, or, if seen, they would have been taken for phantoms.

In the interior of the city, there was also a man who was still awake.

It was Lord Wentworth, the governor. And yet, counting on the arrival of the succors he had summoned from Dover, Lord Wentworth had returned to his apartments to get a few moments' repose.

He had not slept, in fact, for three days, had exposed himself, it must be admitted, at every endangered point with a courage that never weakened, and had multiplied himself, as it were, at all the points where his presence was necessary.

On the evening of the 4th of January, he had himself visited the breach in the Vieux-Chateau, stationed the sentinels, and reviewed the urban militia charged with the easy task of defending Fort Risbank.

But in spite of his weariness, and although all was safe and quiet, he could not sleep.

A vague, absurd, yet incessant fear kept him awake on his couch.

All his precautions were, however, well taken. The enemy could not attempt a nocturnal assault through a breach so slight as that of the Vieux-Chateau. As to the other points, they were guarded by the marshes and the ocean.

Lord Wentworth repeated all this to himself a thousand times, and yet he could not sleep.

He had an unaccountable sensation that a formidable peril, an invisible enemy, was prowling around the city in the night.

His imagination did not present this enemy in the form of Marshal Strozzi or the Duke de Nevers, or even the great Francis de Guise.

What! could it be his late prisoner whom his hatred had several times recognized in the distance from the top of the ramparts? Was it truly that madman, that Viscount d'Exmès, the lover of Madame de Castro?

A laughable adversary this for a governor of Calais in a city still so formidably guarded!

Yet Lord Wentworth, with all his efforts, could not master his instinctive dismay, nor account for it.

But he felt it, and he did not sleep.

CHAPTER LVII

BETWEEN TWO ABYSSES

FORT RISBANK—called also, on account of its eight sides, the Octagon tower—was built, as we have stated, at the entrance of the port of Calais, fronting the dunes. Its black and formidable mass of granite rested on a mass of rock .quite as gloomy and enormous.

The sea, when it was high, dashed its waves against this rock, but never reached the lowest blocks of stone in the fort.

Now, the sea was very strong and very menacing on the night of the 4th and 5th of January, 1558, toward four in the morning. Its loud and mournful lamentations made it resemble a soul that is always in pain and always in despair.

At a certain moment, a little after the sentinel, stationed on the platform of the tower from two to four, was replaced by the sentinel stationed there from four to six, a sort of human cry, uttered as it were by a throat lined with copper, was heard distinctly through the tempest, blended with the eternal moan of the ocean.

Thereupon, the new sentry might have been seen to start, listen eagerly, and place his arbalete against the wall, after he had recognized the nature of the strange sound. Next, when he had proved to himself that no eye could observe him, he raised up the sentry-box with his powerful arms, and drew from under it a pile of ropes forming a long ladder, which he fastened firmly to certain iron bolts in the battlements of the fort.

Finally, the man attached the different fragments of rope

to one another solidly, let them down over the battlements, and two leaden balls caused them to descend rapidly to the rock upon which the fort was seated.

The ladder measured two hundred and twelve feet in length and the Risbank fort two hundred and fifteen.

Hardly had the sentinel completed his mysterious operation when a roundsman appeared at the top of the stone staircase leading to the platform.

But the roundsman found the sentry standing near his sentry-box, received the countersign, and went off without seeing anything.

He recovered his tranquillity and waited. It was already a quarter past four.

On the sea, after superhuman struggle and effort, a boat, manned by fourteen men, at last succeeded in reaching Fort Risbank. A wooden ladder was planted against the rock. It reached an excavation of stone where five or six men could manage to stand.

Silently, one by one, the hardy adventurers climbed this ladder, and without stopping at the excavation, clambered still, using only their hands and feet, taking advantage of all the peculiarities of the rock.

Their aim was certainly to reach the foot of the tower.

But the night was dark, the rock was slippery. Their nails were torn off, their fingers were cut by the sharp stones. One of them missed his footing, could not hold on, and fell into the sea.

Fortunately, the last of the fourteen men was still in the boat, which he was vainly trying to moor before ascending the ladder.

The man who had fallen, and who, when falling, had the courage to repress a single cry, swam vigorously to the boat, and the other had the satisfaction of pulling him in, although the pitchings of the little craft under him rendered the task difficult.

"What! it's you, Martin Guerre!" cried the boatman, thinking he recognized him in the darkness.

"It is myself, I acknowledge, monseigneur," replied the squire.

"How did you manage to slip, you awkward fellow?"

"Better that this should happen to me than to another."

"Why?"

"Another might have cried."

"All right; since you are here, help me to pass this rope round yon big root. I sent Anselme with the others, and I was wrong."

"The root won't hold, monseigneur. A shock would break it, the boat be destroyed, and we should be destroyed with it."

"But we can't do anything better; so no more talk, but to work."

When they had fastened the boat as well as they could—

"Mount," said Gabriel to his squire.

"After you, monseigneur. Who would hold the ladder for you, if I did?"

"Mount, I say!" cried Gabriel, stamping his foot impatiently.

It was not a time for discussion and ceremony. Martin Guerre clambered up to the excavation, and from there held the uprights of the ladder while Gabriel mounted in his turn.

He had his foot upon the last rung when a violent wave shook the boat, broke the cable, and carried boat and cable away into the open sea.

Gabriel would have been lost, if Martin, at the risk of his own life, had not leaned over the chasm, and, with a movement quicker than thought, seized the collar of his master's doublet. Then, with all the energy of despair, the brave squire pulled Gabriel, uninjured like himself, up on the rock.

"You have saved me in your turn, my brave Martin," said Gabriel.

"Yes, but the boat has vanished!" replied the squire.

"Bah! it's paid for, as Anselme would say," returned Gabriel, in a light tone meant to hide his real anxiety.

"All the same," said the prudent Martin, shaking his head, "if your man isn't doing sentry duty yonder, if the ladder does not hang from the tower or breaks under our weight, if the platform is occupied by a superior force, all chance of retreat, all hope of safety, is lost with that confounded boat."

"Well, so much the better!" answered Gabriel; "we must now succeed or die."

"Very true," said Martin, with his artless and unconscious heroism.

"To work!" cried Gabriel. "Your companions must be at the foot of the tower, for I no longer hear any noise. We must join them. See that you keep a resolute grip this time, Martin, and don't loose one hand until the other is firmly fixed."

"Do not be uneasy," said Martin, "I'll try."

They began their perilous ascent, and, at the end of ten minutes, after having vanquished dangers and difficulties innumerable, they joined their twelve comrades, who were waiting for them, full of anxiety, grouped on the rock at the bottom of the Risbank fort.

It was now less than a quarter to five.

Gabriel perceived with unspeakable joy the ladder of ropes hanging along the rock.

"You see, my friends," he said in a low voice, "we are expected yonder. Thank God for it, because we cannot turn back: the sea has carried off our boat. Forward, then! and God protect us!"

"Amen!" said Lactance.

Gabriel's followers must have been determined men indeed! The enterprise, which at any time was a rash one, became now almost insensate. And yet, at the news that all retreat was cut off, not one of them stirred.

Gabriel, by the aid of the dull glimmer that falls from

the murkiest sky, examined their manly faces attentively: they were all equally impassive.

They all cried after him: "Forward!"

"You remember the order agreed upon?" said Gabriel. "You pass first, Yvonnet, then Martin Guerre, then each in the order arranged. I go last. I hope the ropes and knots of the ladder are firm?"

"Firm as iron, monseigneur," said Ambrosio. "We have tested it. It would bear thirty as easily as fourteen."

"Forward then! my brave Yvonnet," returned the Viscount d'Exmès. "Your share in the enterprise is not the least dangerous. Forward, and courage!"

"As for courage, I don't think I lack it, monseigneur, particularly when drums beat and cannon roar. But I confess I am as much a stranger to silent assaults as to swaying cordage. So I am very glad to be the first to mount and have the others behind me."

"A modest pretext to insure for yourself the post of honor!" said Gabriel, who did not care to enter upon a dangerous discussion. "Come! a truce to phrases. Although the wind and the sea drown your words, we must act and not talk. Up! Yvonnet, and remember you must not rest until you reach the hundred and fiftieth round. You are ready? You have your musket on your back and your sword between your teeth?—Look up and not down, and think of God and not of the danger. Forward!"

Yvonnet placed his foot upon the first rung.

It had just struck five; a second night patrol passed before the sentinel of the platform.

Then, slowly and silently, these fourteen fearless men ventured, one after another, on that frail ladder moving backward and forward in the wind.

It was nothing as long as Gabriel, who was the last to mount, remained within a few feet of the ground. But as they advanced, and as this living cluster swayed more and more, the peril assumed incredible proportions.

It would have been a superb and terrible. spectacle for any one who saw it—these fourteen demons, amid storm and darkness, scaling the black wall, at the top of which death was possible, at the bottom of which death was certain.

At the one hundred and fiftieth rung, Yvonnet stopped. All did the same.

It was agreed that they should rest there, while they recited two *Paters* and two *Aves*.

When Martin Guerre had finished his prayers, he saw with astonishment that Yvonnet did not stir. He had made a mistake as to the number of *Paters* and *Aves* he said, and began them again conscientiously.

But Yvonnet still never stirred.

Then, although they were not more than a hundred feet from the platform, and it was dangerous to speak, Martin Guerre struck Yvonnet on the leg and said:

"Go on!"

"No, I cannot," said Yvonnet, in a stifled voice.

"You cannot, wretch, and why?" asked Martin, with a shudder.

"I'm dizzy," said Yvonnet.

A cold sweat bedewed the face of Martin.

For a moment he did not know what to do. If Yvonnet became a prey to vertigo and fell, all fell with him. To descend was quite as hazardous. Martin felt himself unequal to the task of accepting any responsibility whatever in this terrible crisis. He contented himself with saying to Anselme, who was next to him—

"Yvonnet has the vertigo."

Anselme shuddered as Martin had shuddered, and said to his neighbor Scharfenstein—

"Yvonnet has the vertigo."

And each of them, taking his poniard for a moment from between his teeth, said—

"Yvonnet has the vertigo, Yvonnet has the vertigo."

Until at last the news reached Gabriel, who turned pale and trembled in his turn on hearing it.

CHAPTER LVIII

ARNOLD DU THILL WORKS MORE EVIL TO POOR MARTIN
GUERRE WHEN ABSENT THAN WHEN PRESENT

IT WAS an agonizing moment, and a supremely critical one as well.

Gabriel saw himself face to face with three dangers: beneath him a howling sea that seemed to be calling for its prey with its awful voice, before him twelve frightened, motionless men who could neither retreat nor advance, and who barred the way to the third peril—the English pikes and arquebuses perhaps awaiting them yonder.

Terror and death were present at every point of this swaying ladder.

Happily, Gabriel was not a man to hesitate long amid dangers, however menacing, and he came to a resolution in a minute.

He did not stop to ask himself if he should lose his hold or dash his brains against the rock below. He raised himself up, grasping the rope at his side, by the mere strength of his wrists, and passed in succession the twelve men before him.

Thanks to his marvellous vigor of soul and body, he reached Yvonnet without accident, and could place his feet beside those of Martin Guerre's.

"Will you go on?" said he to Yvonnet, in a sharp, imperious voice.

"I have—the vertigo," replied the unfortunate adventurer, his teeth chattering and his hair standing on end.

"Will you go on?" repeated Viscount d'Exmès.

"Im—possible—I feel—that if I—once move, I shall—fall," said Yvonnet.

"We shall see!" said Gabriel.

He lifted himself up as far as the waist of Yvonnet and pricked him with his poniard.

"Do you feel the point of my poniard?" he asked.

"Yes, monseigneur. Mercy! mercy! I am afraid!"

"It is sharp and keen," continued Gabriel, with marvellous coolness. "The slightest exertion will plunge it into your body. Listen attentively, Yvonnet. Martin Guerre will pass in front of you, and I shall remain behind. If you do not follow Martin, if you even seem to shrink, I swear by God you shall not fall or cause others to fall. I will nail you with my poniard to the wall, so that all may pass over your corpse."

"Mercy, monseigneur, I will obey," said Yvonnet, cured of one fear by another still stronger.

"Martin," said Gabriel, "you have heard me. Pass forward."

Martin Guerre executed the same movement he had seen his master perform, and took the first place.

"Forward!" said Gabriel.

Martin began to climb up bravely, and Yvonnet, whom Gabriel, using only his left hand and his feet, continued to menace with the poniard, forgot his dizziness and followed the squire.

So the last one hundred and fifty rungs were cleared.

"*Parbleu!*" thought Martin, "*parbleu!* my master has discovered a sovereign remedy against the vertigo!" For Martin's gayety returned as soon as he saw the distance which separated him from the tower diminish.

He had finished making this pleasant reflection when his head had reached the level of the edge of the platform.

"Is that you?" cried an unknown voice.

"Faith, yes!" answered Martin in a free-and-easy tone.

"It was time," returned the voice. "In five minutes the patrol would have been round again."

"Well, we'll receive him this time," said Martin Guerre. And he planted one knee triumphantly upon the ledge of stone.

"Ah!" suddenly cried his interlocutor, trying to examine his features in the darkness, "what is your name?"

"Martin Guerre, to be sure."

He had scarcely finished when Pierre Peuquoy, for such was the speaker, without giving him time to raise the other knee, pushed him furiously with both hands, and hurled him over the precipice.

"Jesus!" was all that poor Martin Guerre said.

And he fell, but without uttering a cry, turning aside from the ladder by a last, supreme effort so as not to endanger his comrades and his master.

Yvonnet, who followed him, and who, as soon as he felt himself on firm ground, had recovered his daring and audacity, leaped on the platform, then Gabriel and the others.

Pierre Peuquoy made no further resistance. He remained standing, apparently insensible, and like a man turned to stone.

"Unfortunate man!" said Viscount d'Exmès, seizing him by the arm and shaking him. "What insensate fury has taken possession of you? What has Martin Guerre done to you?"

"To me? nothing," replied the armorer, in a dull voice. "But to Babette! to my sister!"

"Ah! I had forgotten!" cried Gabriel, suddenly recalling what had occurred. "Poor Martin!—But he was not the man!—Can nothing be done to save him?"

"Save him after falling more than two hundred and fifty feet!" said Pierre Peuquoy, with a strident laugh. "Come, come, M. le Vicomte, you will do better by thinking of saving yourself and your companions at present."

"My companions and my father and Diana!" said the young man to himself, recalled by these words to the duties and perils of the situation. "I am sorry for poor Martin all the same!" he said aloud.

"This is not the time to shed tears over a guilty wretch," interrupted Pierre Peuquoy.

"Guilty! he was innocent, I tell you! I can prove it. But you are right, now is not the time. You are still disposed to serve us?" asked Gabriel of the armorer, with some abruptness.

"I am devoted to France and to you," replied Pierre Peuquoy.

"Well!" said Gabriel, "what have we to do next?"

"A night patrol," replied the armorer, "consisting of four men, is about to make the rounds; they must be gagged and bound. But," he added, "the time for taking them unawares is past. Here they are!"

While Pierre Peuquoy was speaking, the urban patrol filed out on the platform by an inner staircase. If it gave the alarm, all was, perhaps, lost.

Happily, the two Scharfensteins, uncle and nephew, very curious and inquisitive people they were by nature, happened to be rambling in that very direction. The roundsmen had not time to utter a cry. A big hand from behind closed each of their mouths and hurled them violently on their backs also. Pilletrousse and two others ran up, and it was an easy task to gag and disarm the four stupefied militiamen.

"Well begun!" said Pierre Peuquoy. "Now, monseigneur, we must make sure of the other sentinels and then boldly attack the guards. We have two posts to carry. But do not be afraid of being outnumbered. More than half of the urban militia have been gained by Jean and myself; they are devoted to France, and only wait for an opportunity to serve her. I shall now go and inform these allies of your success. Meanwhile do you attend to the sentries. When I return, my words shall have effected three-fourths of the business!"

"Ah! I should be grateful, but for that death of Martin Guerre," said Gabriel. "And yet, in your eyes, the crime was justice!"

"Monseigneur, I must again ask you to let me leave that affair to God and my conscience," gravely answered the stern burgher. "I quit you for a time. Do you do your duty, while I am doing mine."

Everything happened as Pierre Peuquoy had foreseen. The sentinels, for the most part, were on the French side. One of them, who attempted resistance, was soon bound and rendered harmless. When the armorer came back to the platform, accompanied by Jean Peuquoy and some trusty friends, the entire summit of Fort Risbank was already in the power of the Viscount d'Exmès.

The task to be accomplished now was the capture of the guardhouse. With the reinforcement brought by the two Peuquoys, Gabriel did not hesitate to descend thither at once.

There was skilful advantage taken of the first moments of surprise and indecision.

At this early hour, most of those who held for the English by birth or self-interest were sleeping upon their camp beds. Before they were awake, they were, so to speak, seized by the throat.

The tumult, for it was not a battle, lasted only some minutes. The friends of Peuquoy cried "*Vive Henri II.! Vive la France!*" The neutral and indifferent ranged themselves, as is their habit, on the side of success. Such as offered resistance had to yield to numbers. There were in all but two killed and five wounded, and only three shots were fired. The pious Lactance had the pain of being responsible for one of the dead and two of the wounded. Fortunately, he had left himself a margin!

Before it struck six, all Fort Risbank was in the hands of the French.

Those who showed themselves unfriendly or were suspected were secured, and all the rest of the urban guard hailed Gabriel as their deliverer.

And so, almost without firing a shot, in less than an hour, by an effort strange and superhuman, was carried

that fort which the English did not even dream of fortify-
ing, so potent a defender did it appear to have in the sea!
that fort which was the key of the port of Calais, nay, even
the key of Calais itself!

The affair was so well and promptly conducted that the
Viscount d'Exmes had placed new sentinels with a new
countersign before anything was known in the city.

"But as long as Calais is not also surrendered," said
Pierre Peuquoy to Gabriel, "I do not regard our work as
accomplished. Consequently, M. le Vicomte, it is my opinion that you should keep Jean and half our men to hold
the fort, and let me return to the city with the other half.
We could do more service to the French there than here
by some useful diversion. After the ropes of Jean, it is as
well to utilize the weapons provided by Pierre."

"Are you not afraid Lord Wentworth in his fury may
do you an injury?" said Gabriel.

"Do not be alarmed," returned Pierre Peuquoy, "I will
employ cunning: a legitimate weapon against our oppressors
for two centuries. If necessary, I intend accusing Jean of
having betrayed us. We were surprised by superior numbers, and, in spite of a vigorous resistance, forced to surrender at discretion. Such of us as refused to accept the
new state of things were turned out of the fort. Lord
Wentworth's affairs are at too low an ebb for him not to
thank us, and at least pretend to believe us."

"Agreed! return then to Calais," answered Gabriel.
"You are, I see, as dexterous as you are brave. And I
am certain you will be a great help to me, if I attempt
a sortie."

"Oh! don't attempt any such risk, I entreat you!" said
Pierre Peuquoy. "You are now intrenched in an impregnable fortress. Stay in it. If you assumed the offensive,
Lord Wentworth might easily recover the fort. It would
be a pity if, after doing so much, all our trouble went for
nothing."

"But," cried Gabriel, "do you expect me to stand idle.

with my sword in the scabbard, while the Duke de Guise and his men are fighting and staking their lives?"

"Their lives are their own, monseigneur, and Fort Risbank is the king's," replied the prudent burgher. "Listen, however. When I judge the moment favorable for striking a last decisive blow for the rescue of Calais from the English, I will call upon all those who share my opinions to rise. Then, when everything is ripe for victory, you can give us a hand, make a sortie, and open the city for the Duke de Guise."

"But who will warn me of the proper time to act?" asked Viscount d'Exmès.

"Be kind enough to give me that horn which I presented you with," said Pierre Peuquoy, "by the sound of which I knew you were at hand. When you hear it a second time, make your sortie fearlessly, and you will again share in the triumph you have so well prepared."

Gabriel cordially thanked Pierre Peuquoy, aided him in choosing the men who were to return to the city and help the French at need, and graciously escorted them to the gates of the very fort from which they were supposed to have been shamefully expelled.

When this was over, it was half-past seven, and the light of day was beginning to whiten the sky.

Gabriel wished to see for himself that the standards of France, which were to tranquillize the Duke de Guise and strike terror into the English fleet, should float over Fort Risbank. He mounted that platform, therefore, which had witnessed the events of this terrible and glorious night.

He turned pale as he approached the place where the ladder was fastened, the place from which poor Martin Guerre, the victim of the most fatal mistake, had been hurled.

Shuddering, he leaned over the precipice, expecting to see on the rock the mutilated body of his faithful squire.

At first he did not perceive him, and gazed in every direction with a surprise not unmingled with hope.

In fact, a leaden spout, which carried off the rain-water from the tower, had intercepted the body half way in its terrible fall, and Gabriel beheld it suspended there, bent in two, motionless.

At first sight, he believed it lifeless. But he was at least determined to render it the last pious offices.

Pilletrousse, who was weeping beside him and whom Martin Guerre had always loved, seconded by his devotion the pious resolution of his master. He had himself firmly attached to the ladder of ropes and ventured down the chasm.

When he had, with considerable difficulty, climbed up again with the body, it was perceived that Martin still breathed. A surgeon who was summoned also declared there was life in him, and, in fact, the brave squire recovered consciousness after a while.

But it was for greater suffering. Martin Guerre was in a cruel state. An arm was out of joint and a thigh shattered.

The surgeon thought he could manage the arm, but he judged the amputation of the leg necessary, and yet did not like to take upon himself the responsibility of so difficult an operation.

Gabriel was more annoyed than ever at the idea of being shut up, although he was a conqueror, in Fort Risbank. The delay, painful enough in the beginning, soon became unbearable.

If he could only communicate with Ambroise Paré, that skilfulest of all adepts would, perhaps, save Martin Guerre.

CHAPTER LIX

LORD WENTWORTH AT BAY

THE Duke de Guise, although on reflection he had begun to despair of the success of this rash enterprise, resolved, however, to ascertain if Viscount d'Exmès had succeeded or not. When people are reduced to such a pass as he was, they hope even for the impossible.

Before eight, he arrived with a numerous suite at the cliff which Gabriel had pointed out to him, and from which Fort Risbank could, in fact, be perceived with a telescope.

At the first look in that direction, the duke uttered a cry of triumph.

He could not be mistaken! he recognized clearly the standard and colors of France. Those around him affirmed it was no illusion, and shared his joy.

"My brave Gabriel!" he exclaimed; "he has really achieved this miracle. Is he not superior to me who doubted of it? We can now, thanks to him, make our preparations for the capture of Calais at our leisure. Should England try to relieve it, Gabriel will know how to meet her!"

"Monseigneur, it would seem as if you had called her," said one of the duke's attendants, who, at this moment, was pointing the telescope seaward. "Look, monseigneur, are not those English vessels on the horizon?"

"If so, they have certainly shown due activity," returned the duke.

He took the glass, and looked in his turn.

"Our English friends undoubtedly!" said he. "By my faith, they haven't lost time, and I did not expect them so soon! Do you know that if we had happened to be attacking the Vieux-Chateau at the present moment, the sudden arrival of these reinforcements would have played us an ugly trick? So, we ought to be doubly grateful to M. d'Exmès. He not only gives us victory, but saves us from the shame of defeat. But since we are no longer in a hurry, let us see what the new-comers will do, and how the young governor of Fort Risbank will conduct himself in their regard."

It was full daylight when the English vessels arrived in sight of the fort.

The French flag appeared to them, in the first flush of the morning, like some menacing spectre.

And as if to confirm this portentous apparition, Gabriel saluted them with three or four cannon shots.

There was no longer any doubt! It was really the standard of France that fluttered in the breeze above the English tower. The city, as well as the tower, must, therefore, be in the hands of the besiegers. With all their hurry, the reinforcements had arrived too late.

After a few minutes of surprise and irresolution, the English ships gradually stood off, and returned to Dover.

They had brought forces enough to relieve Calais but not to recover it.

"*Vive Dieu!*" cried M. de Guise. "Did any one ever know the like! This Gabriel of ours is as well able to keep as to conquer! He has Calais in his hands, and when we grasp them, we, too, have the fair city."

And, mounting his horse, he returned joyously to the camp to press on the works of the siege.

Human events have always two faces, and when they make some laugh, they make others weep.

While the Duke de Guise was rubbing his hands, Lord Wentworth was tearing his hair.

After a night agitated, as we have seen, by sinister presentiments, Lord Wentworth fell asleep toward morning, and only left his chamber when the pretended prisoners of Fort Risbank, Pierre Peuquoy at their head, brought the fatal news into the city.

The governor was nearly the last to learn it.

In his grief and anger he could not believe his ears. He ordered the leader of these fugitives to be led before him.

Pierre Peuquoy was soon in his presence; he looked utterly depressed, having carefully composed his countenance for the occasion.

The artful burgher related, as well as his terror allowed him, the night surprise, and described the *three hundred* fierce adventurers who had suddenly scaled Fort Risbank, aided undoubtedly by treachery, which, however, he, Peuquoy, had not had time to get to the bottom of.

"Who commanded these three hundred men?" asked Lord Wentworth.

"Why, none else than your late prisoner, M. d'Exmès," replied the armorer, frankly.

"Ah! my dreams have been realized!" exclaimed the governor.

Then, with bent brows, struck by an inevitable recollection—

"Ah! but M. d'Exmès, during his stay here, was your guest, if I am not mistaken," said he to Pierre Peuquoy.

"Yes, monseigneur," replied Pierre, unmoved, "and I have every reason to believe—why should I hide it from you?—that my cousin Jean, the weaver, has had more to do with this plot than I should like to think of."

Lord Wentworth regarded the burgher sternly, and the burgher returned the look intrepidly.

As Pierre in his daring soul had conjectured, the governor felt himself too weak and knew the armorer's power in the city too well to show his suspicions.

After asking a few final questions, he dismissed him with sad but friendly words.

When he was alone, Lord Wentworth fell into a state of hopeless dejection.

Had he not reason! The city, reduced to its feeble garrison, deprived henceforth of all aid from land or sea, shut in between Fort Nieullay and Fort Risbank, both of them a menace instead of a defence—the city could hold out only for a few days, perhaps for a few hours.

A horrible state of things for the arrogant pride of Lord Wentworth.

"No matter!" he whispered to himself, pale with astonishment and rage, "no matter! Their victory shall cost them dear! Calais is now theirs, that is only too certain! But I will hold out to the bitter end, and they shall pay for this invaluable conquest of theirs with as many dead bodies as I can find among them. And as to the lover of the beautiful Diana de Castro—"

He stopped; a devilish thought lighted up his sombre visage with a hellish glare.

"As to the beautiful Diana de Castro," he resumed with a sort of complacency, "if I bury myself, as is my duty and my wish, under the ruins of Calais, I will at least give him cause for not rejoicing too much at my death. Let him beware! his tortured and vanquished rival has a frightful surprise in store for him!"

Thereupon, he rushed out of his hotel to reanimate the courage of his soldiers and give orders.

Reinvigorated and calmed by some sinister design or other, he displayed such cool courage that his very despair restored hope to more than one despairing soul.

It does not enter into the plan of this work to enter into all the details of the siege of Calais. Francis de Rabutin, in his "Guerres de Belgique," will give them to you in all their prolixity.

The 5th and 6th of January were consumed in efforts equally energetic on the part of besiegers and besieged. Workmen and soldiers on both sides acted with the same courage and the same heroic. obstinacy.

But the splendid resistance of Lord Wentworth was paralyzed by superior force. Marshal Strozzi, who conducted the works of the siege, seemed to divine all the means of defence and all the movements of the English, as if the ramparts of Calais had been transparent.

The enemy must evidently have had a plan of the city!

We know who had furnished this plan to the Duke de Guise.

Consequently, Viscount d'Exmès, though idle and inactive, was still useful to his fellow-soldiers, and, as M. de Guise remarked in his grateful feeling of justice, though at a distance, the salutary influence of Gabriel made itself felt.

Still, the impotence to which he was reduced weighed heavily on the impetuous young man. Imprisoned as it were in his conquest, he was obliged to employ his activity in watching, and this was both too easy and engrossed too little of his time. When he had made his rounds with that scrupulous vigilance he learned at St. Quentin, he generally returned and sat down by the bedside of Martin Guerre to console and encourage him.

The brave squire endured his sufferings with admirable patience and serenity. But what astonished and pained him beyond measure was the wicked manner in which Pierre Peuquoy had behaved toward him.

His artless vexation and surprise, when he was questioned upon this dark subject, would have dissipated the last suspicions of Gabriel, if he still had any as to the good faith of Martin.

The young man decided, therefore, to recount to Martin Martin's own history—at least, what he surmised his history to be from conjectures and appearances. It was now clear that a scoundrel had profited by the marvellous resemblance between himself and Martin to commit, under the name of the latter, all kinds of blamable and villanous actions, the responsibility for which he was careful to decline, while he was equally careful to monopolize all the benefits and advantages that were the rightful dues of his Sosia.

Gabriel determined to make this revelation in the presence of Jean Peuquoy. Jean was both afflicted and frightened, in his conscience as an honest man, by the results of the fatal mistake. But he was particularly anxious about the person who had abused them all. Who was this wretch? was he married also? where did he hide himself?

Martin, on his side, was dismayd at the idea of such astounding perversity. While rejoicing that his conscience was relieved of a heap of misdeeds which had been so long a reproach to it, he was driven wild by the thought that his name had been borne and his reputation compromised by such a scoundrel. And who knew what excesses the rascal would indulge in, under the shelter of his pseudonym, at the very hour Martin was lying on his bed of pain!

What specially filled the heart of the good squire with sadness was the episode of Babette Peuquoy. Oh! he now excused the brutality of Pierre. Not only did he pardon, but he approved. He had certainly done well to thus avenge his outraged honor! It was now Martin Guerre who consoled and reassured the affrighted Jean Peuquoy.

But our excellent Martin, in commending the brother of Babette, forgot only one thing; it was that he suffered in place of the true culprit.

When Gabriel smilingly called his attention to this:

"Well, no matter!" said Martin Guerre, "for all that, I bless my accident! At least, if I survive, the lameness, or still better, the absence of my leg, will serve to distinguish me from that impostor and traitor."

But, alas! even this mediocre consolation which Martin hoped for was still very doubtful: for would he survive? The surgeon of the city guard would not answer for it. The prompt aid of a first-class surgeon was indispensable, and two days had nearly slipped by without other relief for the alarming state of Martin than a few insufficient dressings.

This was not one of the least reasons for Gabriel's impatience, and very often, during the night as well as during the day, he stood up and listened for the blast on the horn that was to rescue him from his enforced idleness. But no noise of the kind came to vary the distant, monotonous rumble of the two artilleries of France and England.

Only on the evening of the 6th of January, Gabriel, who had now for thirty-six hours been in possession of Fort Risbank, thought he could distinguish a greater uproar than usual from the direction of the city and unusual cries of triumph or distress.

The French were entering the Vieux-Chateau triumphantly, after a furious struggle.

Calais could now not hold out longer than twenty-four hours.

Nevertheless, the whole of the 7th was passed in incredible efforts on the part of the English to recover so important a position and retain all the points they still possessed.

But M. de Guise, far from letting the enemy recover an inch of ground, was gaining upon them gradually, and it was becoming more and more plain that the morrow would be the last day of English domination.

It was three in the afternoon. Lord Wentworth, who had not spared himself for the last seven days and had been seen constantly in the first rank, dealing death and braving it, deemed that there were only two hours of physical force and moral energy left to his men.

Then he summoned Lord Derby.

"How long," he asked, "do you think we can hold out?"

"Not more than three hours, I fear," sadly answered Lord Derby.

"Would you answer for two hours?"

"Yes, except something unexpected happen," said Lord Derby, calculating the distance the French had still to make.

"Well, my friend," continued Lord Wentworth, "I intrust the command to you and retire. If in two hours— two hours, not before, you understand!—the chances do not turn in our favor, and there is little sign of it, I permit, nay, order you, to relieve you from all responsibility, to sound the retreat and demand a capitulation."

"In two hours, that is sufficient, my lord," said Lord Derby.

Lord Wentworth then imparted to his lieutenant the conditions he should ask and would no doubt obtain from the Duke de Guise.

"But, my lord, you make no mention of yourself in these conditions. Shall I not also ask the Duke de Guise to receive you into ransom?"

A sombre light shone in the gloomy eyes of Lord Wentworth.

"No, no, take no thought of me, my friend," he rejoined, with a singular smile. "I have arranged everything in my own case that is necessary, everything I wish."

"Still—" objected Lord Derby.

"Enough!" said the governor, authoritatively. "Do what I tell you, nothing more. Adieu. Bear witness in England that I did what was humanly possible to defend my city, and have only yielded to fatality. As for yourself, struggle up to the last moment, but be sparing of English honor and English blood, Derby. That is my last word. Adieu."

And, without wishing to say or hear more, Lord Wentworth shook Lord Derby's hand, quitted the field of battle, and retired to his deserted hotel alone, forbidding any one, under the severest penalties, to follow him.

He was sure of having at least two hours before him.

CHAPTER LX

LOVE DISDAINED

LORD WENTWORTH believed himself certain of two things: first, he had two full hours before the surrender of the city, and Lord Derby would assuredly demand a delay of five hours before capitulating; then, he should find his hotel entirely empty, for he had taken the precaution to send all his people to the breach in the morning. André, Madame de Castro's French page, had also been confined by his orders. Diana must be alone with one or two of her women.

Every place along the route of Lord Wentworth was, in fact, abandoned, and gave Calais the aspect of a dead city; for, like unto a body from which life is slowly retiring, she had concentrated all her energies on the spot where the last struggle was made.

Lord Wentworth, gloomy, savage, and in some sort drunk with despair, went straight to the apartments occupied by Madame de Castro.

He did not cause himself to be announced, as was his custom, but entered abruptly as a master into the room where she sat with one of the attendants he had given her.

Without saluting the astonished Diana, he said imperiously to the attendant—

"Leave the room at once! The French may enter the city this evening, and I have neither the means nor the desire to protect you. Go and find your father. Your place is by his side. Go immediately, and tell the two or three women who are here that I order them to do the same."

"But, my lord—" objected the attendant.

"Ah!" retorted the governor, stamping on the floor in his rage, "have you not heard then what I said to you? obey!"

"Still, my lord—" Diana was beginning in her turn.

"I have said to her: obey! madame," rejoined Lord Wentworth, with an inflexible gesture.

The attendant passed out in a state of terror.

"In truth, I do not recognize you, my lord," returned Diana after a silence full of anguish.

"Because you have not seen me conquered until now, madame," answered Lord Wentworth, with a bitter smile. "For you have been an excellent prophetess of woe and malediction in my case, and I was indeed a fool not to have believed you. I am conquered, quite conquered, conquered without hope or resources. Rejoice!"

"Is the success of the French really so fully assured?" said Diana, who had some trouble to hide her delight.

"Why not, madame? Fort Nieullay, Fort Risbank, the Vieux-Chateau are in their power. The city is exposed to three fires. Yes, Calais is assuredly theirs. Rejoice!"

"Oh!" returned Diana, "with such a man as you, my lord, for an adversary, one ought never to be certain of victory, and, in spite of myself, yes, I acknowledge it, in spite of myself, I still doubt."

"What!" cried Lord Wentworth, "do you not see, madame, that I have given up the game? After having been present at every battle, do you not see that I did not wish to be present at a defeat, and that therefore I am here? Lord Derby will surrender in an hour and a half. In an nour and a half, madame, the French will enter triumphantly into Calais, and Viscount d'Exmès with them. Rejoice!"

"My lord, you say all this in such a tone that I do not know whether I ought to believe you or not," said Diana, who, however, was beginning to hope, her eyes and smile becoming radiant at the thought of freedom.

"Then, in order to persuade you, madame," returned Lord Wentworth, "for I wish to persuade you, I will take another course, and I will say to you: Madame, in an hour and a half the French will enter here in triumph, and Viscount d'Exmès with them. Tremble!"

"What do you mean?" cried Diana, turning pale.

"What! Am I not sufficiently clear?" said Lord Wentworth, approaching Diana with a menacing laugh. "I say to you: In an hour and a half, madame, our parts will be changed. You will be free, and I a prisoner. Viscount d'Exmès will come and restore you to liberty, love, and happiness; me he will fling into some dungeon cell. Tremble!"

"But why should I tremble?" answered Diana, recoiling under the sombre and burning gaze of this man.

"Great heavens! it is very easy to understand," said Lord Wentworth. "At this moment, I am the master; in an hour and a half I shall be the slave, or rather in an hour and a quarter, for the minutes are passing. In an hour and a quarter, I shall be in your power; now you are in mine. In an hour and a quarter, Viscount d'Exmès will be here; now I am here. Therefore, rejoice and tremble, madame!"

"My lord! my lord!" cried Diana, whose heart was palpitating as she repulsed Lord Wentworth, "what do you want with me?"

"What do I want with you? with you!" repeated the governor, in a hoarse voice.

"Do not approach me! or I will cry out, call for help, and dishonor you, wretch!" exclaimed Diana, now a prey to mortal terror.

"Cry, call for help; it is all the same to me," said Lord Wentworth, with sinister tranquillity. "The hotel is deserted; the streets are deserted. No one will hear your cries, at least for another hour. Look: I have not even taken the trouble of shutting the doors and windows, so sure am I that none will come here before an hour."

"But in an hour they will surely come, and then I will accuse you, denounce you, and they will kill you."

"No," said Lord Wentworth, coolly; "I will kill myself. Do you believe I could survive the capture of Calais? In an hour I shall kill myself, upon that I am resolved. But before that, I will take you from your lover, and, by giving free course to one last and terrible tide of voluptuousness, satisfy both my honor and my love. Come, my beauty, your refusals and disdains are no longer in season. I no longer beg; I order! I no longer implore; I command!"

"And I die!" cried Diana, drawing a knife from her bosom.

But before she had time to strike, Lord Wentworth rushed upon her, seized her little weak hands in his vigorous grasp, tore the knife from her, and flung it aside.

"Not yet!" cried Lord Wentworth, with a frightful smile. "I do not wish you to die yet, madame. Afterward, you can do what you like; and if you prefer death with me to life with him, you shall certainly be free to do so. But this last hour of your existence, for now there is only an hour, belongs to me. I have but this hour to compensate me for an eternity of hell. Think you, then, I am going to renounce it?"

He wished to seize her. Fainting, and feeling her strength escaping, she fell at his feet.

"Mercy, my lord!" she cried, "mercy! I ask for mercy and pardon on my knees! In the name of your mother, remember that you are a gentleman."

"A gentleman!" retorted Lord Wentworth, shaking his head, "yes, I was a gentleman and comported myself as one as long as I triumphed, hoped, and lived. But now I am no longer a gentleman; I am simply a man—a man who will avenge himself and die."

He raised Madame de Castro, who lay at his feet, and held her in a frenzied embrace. Her lovely body was bruised by the leather of his belt. She tried to entreat, to cry out, but she could not.

At this moment there was a great uproar in the streets.

"Ah!" cried Diana, the fading light of her eyes again kindling under the influence of hope.

"Good!" said Wentworth, with an infernal laugh; "it seems the people are amusing themselves by pillaging each other before the arrival of the enemy. They are quite right, and their governor is about to set them an example."

He lifted Diana as he would a child, and laid her, breathless and exhausted, on a sofa.

"Mercy!" she succeeded in saying once more.

"No, no," returned Lord Wentworth; "you are too beautiful."

She fainted.

But the governor had not had time to kiss the colorless lips of Diana when the tumult drew nearer and the door was violently burst open.

The Viscount d'Exmès, the two Peuquoys, and three or four French archers appeared upon the threshold. Gabriel leaped upon Lord Wentworth, sword in hand, and with a terrible cry. "Scoundrel!"

Lord Wentworth, with teeth clinched, grasped his sword, which lay upon a chair.

"Back!" cried Gabriel to his people, who were inclined to interfere, "I will chastise this wretch myself."

Without a word, the two antagonists crossed swords furiously.

The Peuquoys and their companions drew back to give them room—mute but not indifferent witnesses of this deadly combat.

Diana still lay unconscious.

The reader must have guessed how this providential help had come to the defenceless prisoner sooner than Lord Wentworth expected.

Pierre Peuquoy, during the two preceding days, had, in accordance with his promise to Gabriel, aroused all those who sympathized with himself and France. Now, as the victory was no longer doubtful, the latter had naturally become rather numerous. They were, for the most part, prudent, cautious burghers, who all agreed in thinking that, since there was no longer any means of resisting, the best course was to capitulate under the most favorable terms possible.

The armorer, who wished to strike the decisive blow safely, waited till his band was strong enough and the siege advanced enough to avoid all risk of uselessly endangering the lives of those who confided in him. As soon as the Vieux-Chateau was taken he resolved to act. But it took some time to bring the conspirators together. It was only when Lord Wentworth abandoned the breach that the movement inside Calais gave evidence of its existence.

The more slowly, however, the movement had been prepared, the more it was irresistible.

But at the first resounding blast of Pierre Peuquoy's horn, which acted like magic, d'Exmès, Jean Peuquoy, and half their men rushed out of Fort Risbank, promptly disarmed the feeble detachment that guarded the city on that side, and opened the gate to the French.

Then all the adherents of the Peuquoys, increased by this reinforcement and emboldened by the first easy success, hurried to the breach, where Lord Derby was trying to fall as honorably as he could.

But when this kind of revolt caused the lieutenant of Lord Wentworth to be hemmed in between two fires, what was left for him to do? The French flag had already entered Calais with Viscount d'Exmès. The insurgent urban militia was threatening to open the gates to the besiegers. Lord Derby preferred to surrender immediately. This would be only to advance a little the execution of the governor's orders, and an hour and a half's useless resistance, even if such resistance had not become impossible, would not lessen the defeat, and might render the reprisals more severe.

Lord Derby sent a flag of truce to the Duke de Guise.

This was just what Gabriel and the Peuquoys wanted. The absence of Lord Wentworth disturbed them. They therefore left the breach, where a few scattered shots still resounded, and, urged by a secret presentiment, made for the governor's hotel with two or three soldiers.

All the doors were open, and they had no difficulty in reaching the apartment of Madame de Castro, whither Gabriel was leading them.

It was time; and the sword of Diana's lover was brandished above her at the right moment to protect her from the foulest of outrages.

The combat of the governor and Gabriel was long. The two antagonists seemed equally skilled in fencing. They showed the same coolness and the same fury. Their swords entwined like two serpents, and crossed like two flashes of lightning.

However, at the end of two minutes, Lord Wentworth's sword escaped from his hand, struck by a vigorous counter of Exmès.

Lord Wentworth, in trying to avoid the stroke, slipped on the floor and fell.

Anger, contempt, hatred—all the violent feelings fermenting in the heart of Gabriel left no room there for generosity. A foe like this deserved no courtesy. He was on him in a moment, with his sword raised to slay him.

Not one of those present, moved with indignation at what they had just seen, would have stayed his avenging arm.

But Diana de Castro had recovered consciousness during the combat.

Opening her heavy eyelids, she saw, she understood, and darted between Gabriel and Wentworth.

By a sublime coincidence, the last cry she uttered when fainting was the first she spoke when restored to life—

"Mercy!"

She entreated for him by whom her entreaties had been spurned.

Gabriel, at the sight of his beloved Diana, at the sound of her all-powerful voice, felt only the promptings of his tenderness and love. Clemency took the place of rage in his soul.

"Do you wish him to live?" he asked.

"I beg his life of you, Gabriel," said Diana. "Ought he not to have time to repent?"

"Be it so!" replied Gabriel. "Let the angel save the demon; it is her office."

And all the time holding under his knee Lord Wentworth, who was furious and bellowing with rage—

"Do you," he said to his companions, "approach and tie this man while I hold him. Then you will fling him into the prison of his own hotel, until M. le Duc de Guise decides on his fate."

"No! kill me! kill me!" cried Lord Wentworth, struggling.

"Do what I say," replied Gabriel, keeping his hold. "I am beginning to believe that life will punish him better than death."

The viscount was obeyed; and although Lord Wentworth struggled, foamed at the mouth, and hurled insults at his assailants, he was securely tied and gagged. Then two or three men carried off, without ceremony, the late governor of Calais.

Gabriel next addressed Jean Peuquoy in presence of his cousin.

"My friend," said he, "I have related in your presence Martin Guerre's singular history, and you now possess the proofs of his innocence. You have deplored the cruel mistake which struck the innocent instead of the guilty; and all you ask, I know, is to relieve the terrible sufferings he endures for the crimes of another as speedily as possible. Will you render me a service?"

"I guess what it is," interrupted Jean Peuquoy. "I am to go for Master Ambroise Paré, am I not? I will do so at once; and to insure the greatest care for Martin, I'll have him transported to our house, if it can be managed without danger."

Pierre Peuquoy, stupefied, regarded and heard his cousin and Gabriel as if he were in a dream.

"Come, Pierre," said Jean, "you must help me in this. Ah, yes, you are astonished; you do not comprehend. I will explain this on the road, and will convince you so thoroughly that you will share my conviction without any difficulty. You will then be the first, as I know, to repair the evil you have involuntarily committed."

Thereupon, Jean, after saluting Diana and Gabriel, passed out in company with Pierre, who was already beginning to question him.

When Madame de Castro remained alone with Gabriel, she fell on her knees, from an impulse of piety and gratitude, and, raising her eyes and hands toward Heaven, said—

"Blessed be Thy name, O God, twice blessed, because Thou hast saved me, and saved me by him!"

BND OF PART ONE OF "THE TWO DIANAS"